Thomas Rowan

Thomas Rowan is a father of three, Air Force veteran, and lives in Wisconsin. Apart from reading and writing, Thomas spends most of his free time on various hobbies including painting, fitness, and martial arts.

Maximum Gold

Maximum Gold is a social media personality and a multi-business owner who currently lives in Wisconsin. Apart from creative writing, content creation, and business, Max has a passion for music and fitness.

Oscar Johnson

Oscar Johnson currently resides in a small town in Wisconsin. Apart from writing, Oscar shares a passion for history, and spending time with friends and family.

Thomas Rowan and Maximum Gold and Oscar Johnson

Kralavia

Book 1

The Reckoning

AUSTIN MACAULEY PUBLISHERS®
LONDON • CAMBRIDGE • NEW YORK • SHARJAH

This is a work of fiction. Names, characters, businesses, places, events, locales, and incidents are either the products of the author's imagination or used in a fictitious manner. Any resemblance to actual persons, living or dead, or actual events is purely coincidental.

Ordering Information
Quantity sales: Special discounts are available on quantity purchases by corporations, associations, and others. For details, contact the publisher at the address below.

Publisher's Cataloging-in-Publication data
Rowan, Thomas; Gold, Maximum and Johnson, Oscar
Kralavia – Book 1

ISBN 9798891555631 (Paperback)
ISBN 9798891555648 (ePub e-book)

Library of Congress Control Number: 2024914844

www.austinmacauley.com/us

First Published 2024
Austin Macauley Publishers LLC
40 Wall Street, 33rd Floor, Suite 3302
New York, NY 10005
USA

mail-usa@austinmacauley.com
+1 (646) 5125767

Special thanks to my father, Shane Rowan, who encouraged the explorations of worlds beyond within the pages of a book.

Table of Contents

Prologue 12
Chapter 1: Invasion 15
Chapter 2: Special Guests 20
Chapter 3: We Stand, We Fight 29
Chapter 4: Grave News 36
Chapter 5: Family Tensions 39
Chapter 6: It Was a Good Plan 44
Chapter 7: Reinforcements 50
Chapter 8: The King's Stag 57
Chapter 9: Family Secrets 63
Chapter 10: Forbidden Love 67
Chapter 11: The Wedding 72
Chapter 12: The Reception 78
Chapter 13: The King's Orders 88
Chapter 14: Unknown Horizons 93
Chapter 15: Visions 100
Chapter 16: Valkos 106
Chapter 17: The Remnant 111
Chapter 18: Deep Thoughts and Near Death 114
Chapter 19: Hard Words and Soft Lessons 125
Chapter 20: Unusual Happenings 135
Chapter 21: Over My Dead Body 141
Chapter 22: Alkeroth 146
Chapter 23: The Raid 156
Chapter 24: Deeper Truths 162
Chapter 25: War Has Begun 172
Chapter 26: Fort Elias 178
Chapter 27: Ghosts of The Past 182
Chapter 28: Not a King Yet 189
Chapter 29: Aid in The Darkness 195
Chapter 30: The Field of Denesious 200

Chapter 31: Over Life and Death — 206
Chapter 32: At What Cost? — 216
Chapter 33: Hidden Secrets — 225
Chapter 34: The Shadow of Greed — 233
Chapter 35: Secrets and Surprises — 238
Chapter 36: Decisions in the Dark — 248
Chapter 37: What No One Saw Coming — 255
Chapter 38: Suspicions — 259
Chapter 39: The Funeral — 262
Chapter 40: Absolute Power… — 269
Chapter 41: Tensions Rising — 272
Chapter 42: Corrupts Absolutely — 277
Chapter 43: Rematch — 283
Chapter 44: Regret — 290
Chapter 45: The King's Command — 294
Chapter 46: The Choices We Make — 300
Chapter 47: Calm Before the Storm — 303
Chapter 48: Last Chance — 310
Chapter 49: To Fight Another Day — 317
Epilogue — 320
Prologue Kralavia Book 2: The Spark of Rebellion — 325
Index — 327

Uncharted Region
Telmond
Heaven's Peak
Kralavia
Zyka
Tanrean
Halika
Alwirya
Althalos
Yasalia
The Great River
Dead Lands
Carnheller
Valkos
Stelmond.
Oxrion

Lexon
Alnirya
Taureau
Yar
Dead Lands
Halika
Éstalion
Althalos
Stalbak
Purple Mountains
Vasalia
Arkeanos
Stelbeck Keep
Alkeroth
Arkenot
The Great River
Frosbike
Carnheller
Daymar
Crysanta
Terrowin
Emerald Lake
Valkos
Germond
Haywood
Stelmond
Gordost
Kamdon
Aetos
Onrion
Field of Denesious
Handon

Prologue

A long time ago, across the Western Sea, there was a void. In the beginning, before time had meaning, Athalon, the greatest of all the gods, golden in color with white hair and bright eyes, beheld this space and touched it. Immediately the world shook, mountains pushed up from beneath the surface, and the seas roared with a mighty force. It was then that time took shape, setting in motion the stars and the sun.

When Athalon stood and saw his creation, he was pleased and called others to his side to enjoy the splendor of his efforts. These eight mighty gods of their own are so named: Denesious, Obar, Dolos, Valenear, Renibaun, Alynia, Kilith, and Broden. Together these gods were known as the Unatari or The Creators.

These gods began time and collectively worked to create a place where all their creations could thrive. The sisters, Valenear and Alynia, began to sing, and this song brought forth the trees of old forests and the rivers that water them. Renibaun withdrew to the mountains and made the world echo his music of the rock, which rang loud but beautiful sounds that brought forth the deep treasures that are hidden within. Dolos, speaking to the air, gave breath to the creatures of flight. Denesious and Kilith both spoke to the ground. And out of the words of Denesious came forth beasts of the earth; Kilith brought plants for food, color, and shelter alike.

Broden brought forth the animals of the sea, quick as he moved and spoke only in a whisper; still, the waters obeyed. Obar sat on the new earth and brought forth from his thought's small creatures and insects, keepers of the ground and the balance to the rest of nature.

Finally, when the other gods filled the earth, Athalon touched the ground once more. He spoke no words and sang no songs; still, the ground brought forth his greatest creation, humanity. Awakened from a dark and dreamless sleep beneath the surface of the earth, they arose, clawing their way into existence.

Together in unity, the nine gods ruled and reigned in this land. As it was settled and humanity expanded, the gods decided to call this land, Kralavia. The gods ruled, and the humans grew in understanding and innovation, building great cities and kingdoms for themselves.

For two and half thousand years, this world remained as it was.

As a tribute to the Unatari, the humans built each for them a kingdom as they spread out and settled in Kralavia and named each one in their honor. In the northwest, Alnirya is for the goddess Alynia. Then, moving east across the Great Mountain Ridge, Taureau for Broden and Halika for Obar. To the southwest, Ornion, named for Kilith, then Valkos for Denesious. In the deep south came the wooded mountain region of Stelmond, which was the home of Valenear. In the far east grew the island nation of Carnheller, to whom Dolos belonged. West of Carnheller on the mainland was Vasalia, made in honor of Renibaun and the very mountains he filled.

In the center of the other kingdoms that filled the corner of the continent, the humans established the kingdom of Althalos. In honor of Athalon, the greatest of all the gods. For it was here in the center of Althalos that Athalon touched the ground and brought the humans out of their slumber.

It was during this first age of time when man and god lived in harmony. Then, strange beasts and creatures of terror roamed the earth in dark places. Dolos, not content with his position, was known to push the limits of his power with the others from time to time and saw the humans as less than the gods. He experimented with the dark things and created the foul beasts of the deep places. Some crawled on the ground; others, winged beasts with great power, took to the skies. It was not enough that the gods were honored; Dolos wanted more; he did not want to live with the humans; he wanted to control them. Though the terrifying creatures of the night and dragons were attributed to mutation and happenchance to the human population, Athalon knew that Dolos was flexing his might.

Athalon may have been the greatest of all the gods, but he could not stand against one of his own. Another could not directly challenge their power as it was written in the stars before them. Still, Athalon knew he needed to withstand the evil brooding within his brother. So, at the start of the Second Age, three thousand years after the beginning. Athalon drew up to the stars and pulled out the written magic of the heart of the first star.

There he created nine weapons, one for each god. Once wielded by one of the gods, these weapons would give them great power and ability; however, each would lose their immortality. Each god would remain eternal, not grow old or weak, but if the humans so chose, they could fight and possibly even kill any of them. A price that Athalon was willing to make to allow for some balance in his creation. Each weapon was made from the core of the star and is known in Kralavia as Althinian. A magic metal that would take the shape and appearance of anything the original god wished, but it would be more robust than anything that could ever be made in any age to come.

To himself, Athalon brought forth a golden sword, powerful and elegant. For Denesious, a spear is simple and true. Valenear brought forth a dagger, cunning and secret as she. Renibaun pulled out a mighty hammer, strong and fierce. Alynia withdrew a bow, tactical and calculated. Obar, a battle-ax, was his choice, though gentle in nature, deadly if needed. Broden, a bo staff, wooden in appearance and fast as lightning. Kilith brought out a short sword, deadly on his mighty stead. Dolos brought forth a massive Guan Dao, the weapon of death.

Unknown to the others, Athalon had the gods wield these weapons and use them to manage each other, not knowing their lives could now be taken. Before long, whispers of evil within the Unatari grew among the humans, and with that, so did the understanding of their mortality.

Sometime after, during the end of the Second Age, the revolt and the Great War started. All the records of those sixty years went missing during that time. All we know is that the Unatari…lost. Some say they were all defeated and are no more. Others say that a few gods survived and went into hiding. Or that they left the nine kingdoms to other parts of Kralavia and settled in the land in the west, past the Great Desert, also known as the Dead Lands.

Only Athalon's sword was found or taken (depending on the storyteller). Either way, it was King Ventril who used it first. Ventril was the grandfather of Althalos's current ruler, King Ivan, and was there when the Great War was started—or rumored to have started it himself. But Ivan's father, Animas, ended the war when he inherited the Golden Sword after Ventril died suddenly. Sometime after the war ended, Animas also died, leaving Ivan to bring peace to the territories in the aftermath.

In the end, the nine realms remained as such, and the humans, building off the foundations of the gods, built for themselves great kingdoms within these countries. Time continued, The Third Age began, and the territories remained relatively peaceful, other than minor conflicts between the kings and lords.

Until now…

Chapter 1
Invasion

The Third Age—6070 A.C.
Stelbeck Keep, the Coastal Outpost of Althalos, in Vasalia.

The cool night air felt good after the heat of the sun they had just experienced; it had been sweltering for this time of year. The assignment to the Stelbeck Keep wasn't one that most soldiers complained about, though it wasn't one to write home about either. The guard shifted uncomfortably in his armor as he stood on his part of the wall keeping watch. Lightning flashed sporadically in the distance, which he hadn't thought much about until the thunder suddenly burst. The sudden noise echoed against the stone walls and added to the rhythmic sounds of waves crashing against the bottom of the cliffside and beach below.

Stelbeck Keep was a fort just outside the city of Alkeroth, in Vasalia, as the detachment of the country of Althalos. The two countries had excellent relations, and as part of a trade agreement with the lands across the sea to the east, Vasalia agreed to host a detachment of troops from Althalos here on the coast, so long as they paid for their own upkeep. Vasalia was allowed a percentage of the trade specific to Althalos as payment.

These were more than agreeable terms for Althalos since they did more than double that cost in the ocean trade alone. So, the two country's leaders signed an accord, and since then, every soldier has had to do his turn and be stationed here while serving in the army of Althalos.

The fort was nestled on the cliff side near the eastern shore that overlooked a small beach near the exit point of the Great River. Its northern wall, tightly built into the small mountain there, provided some much-needed cover should the need arise. To the west was the main gate that led to Alkeroth, while the southern gate opened up to the woods and a main road to the beach and the small harbor at the river's mouth. The Great River and Vasalia's location allowed the country to be a focal point in trade throughout the continent, controlling and using the river's connection to the sea to send goods further inwards and the exports of various inland countries.

"I don't like this," one guard said as he approached another guard nearby. He had been at Alkeroth for a few months, most of which was spent on the night watch with no trouble. Still, something stirred in the air tonight that he couldn't shake off.

The other guard shrugged casually, "A little thunder never hurt anybody." He then took a swig of his bottle before offering it to the other. The first guard shook his head and resumed his gaze out to the sea.

As the first guard watched the water, he glanced at the flags on the nearby pole mounted on the wall. *No wind*, he thought to himself. Curious now, the guard turned his attention back to the horizon. The moon shone over the castle, but the storm kept everything dark in the distance.

"Did you see that?"

"See what?" the other questioned annoyedly.

The first guard didn't respond immediately but kept staring into the distance. The clouds continued to roll in, pressing closer. More thunder, and then, he saw it again. Or at least, he thought he did.

"There was something on the water."

The other guard stood up and followed his gaze out at the ocean. "I don't see anything…"

"Wait." The first hissed through his teeth. The lightning cracked again, much more intently this time, causing the whole cloud line to be illuminated. There was no denying it now; something was in the water and headed toward them. The first guard glanced back at the flags; *still nothing*. Another flash came with thunder pounding as both guards remained locked with their eyes on the water. Two dozen large dark objects could be seen on the water, "What the hell is that?"

"There's no wind," said the first guard, ignoring the question.

The second guard looked at the other, "What do you mean?"

He gestured to the flag mounts, "The flags haven't moved since that storm appeared on the horizon."

"And?"

"With a storm that size coming this way. We'd be feeling something."

The second guard stepped closer, "What exactly are you suggesting?"

"That's not a natural storm."

A low scoff came from the second guard as he grabbed his optical scope and scanned the water again, waiting for the next lightning strike. A flash of light lit the area. Then the fear took over, though you couldn't see it. The guard slowly handed the scope to the other, who followed suit. As the lightning cracked, he saw it as well. The dark clusters were Corsair ships heavily armed with mounted catapults and full of soldiers ready for battle.

"Shit," the first guard muttered as he dropped the scope and looked out with his eyes. Thunder boomed again, this time much more intently and closer than before.

"We need to sound the alarm," said the other. But the first was already headed toward the tower to do so.

Leaning over the wall, the second guard cupped his hands around his mouth and shouted, "Sound the alarm! Sound the alarm!"

Running along the wall, he continued to call, "To arms! To arms!" A muster of groans and metal began to fill the area as the men rose from their slumber.

Suddenly the clang of a heavy bell echoed in the castle; realizing the other guard had gotten to the warning bell, the second guard ran down to the barracks to ensure everyone was getting ready.

It only took a few moments to reach the barracks at the base of the wall. The guard ran through roughly, waking the sleeping group and shoving several out of bed as he continued calling about the impending attack. "Get up now! All of you!"

Meanwhile, the first guard had held his post at the bell keeping his eyes fixed on the distant scene. The storm had gotten increasingly close now. Frantically the guard continued to ring the alarm, shouting in-between the tones, "We're under attack!"

He glanced at the second guard who had begun his descent to the barrack below, then he looked back at the flags in the distance, dimly lit now that the moon was almost completely covered. *Still no wind*, he thought to himself. His eyes grew wide as he considered the options, which made him ring the bell all the harder.

Down below, the men bustled along in a hurry to their posts. Metal rattled loudly as the armor was adorned, and each man reached his post. After the second guard cleared the barracks, he raced to the commander's quarters. He banged on the door quickly, "Sir! To arms! To arms!" There was no immediate response, so the guard pounded the door again. "Commander Gregson!"

The door finally opened, and a groggy Commander Gregson stepped out into the light, "Yes, yes, what is it?" The guard took a few deep breaths. "Well, out with it? What's all the fuss?"

Before the guard could respond, another man approached, "Sir!"

"Captain Wilkins," the commander addressed. "What the hell is going on here?"

"Invasion fleet," said the guard, taking the words from the captain, who nodded in affirmation.

"We're under attack, sir," Wilkins concurred. He gestured to the guard beside him. "They spotted the fleet moments ago."

Suddenly a shower of fire came down from the sky as flaming boulders were seen coming over the wall. "Incoming!" a voice rang out above the rest. But it was too late; Captain Wilkins and the other guard were thrown back as the ball of fire directly hit the commander's quarters. Commander Gregson's body took a direct impact which caused parts of his body to be thrown everywhere. Wilkins quickly recovered and scanned the wreckage looking for any sign of Gregson. The captain stopped short when he saw the commander, well, what was left of him.

At this time, the other guard had reached the captain, almost gagging when he saw the scene. Captain Wilkins turned to the guard, "No time to mourn now. To your post, man!" he stated firmly.

Wilkins ran across the courtyard as more fiery boulders rained down on the fort. The screams of the men being crushed by them filled the entire area. Wilkins glanced up at the defensive positions on the wall as he ran. The men had been attempting to return fire with their own catapults. But for each one of their shots came dozens more in return.

Crash! Wilkins stopped short as another boulder took out the catapult directly in front of him and the men around it. By this time, others had been called out and were attempting to give medical aid to those wounded by the fire and stone. Water was brought to help douse the flames and ease the suffering of the men, but the damage was happening faster than they could keep up.

Screams and cries echoed loudly through the courtyard. Wilkins watched helplessly as another boulder struck a group of men on the wall; the boulder shattered, sending flaming hot shrapnel into the soldiers nearby. It tore through their armor like a sword through cotton. *What evil is this?* Wilkins thought quickly as he ran up to the man nearest him.

The captain franticly attempted to help the soldier, only to quickly realize that his attempts were futile. The soldier's skin was melting from the heat; the damage was already done. Blood oozed from the wounds where the shrapnel had penetrated. Wilkins dropped his head and exhaled heavily.

The screams and destruction echoed in the background as he looked the soldier in the eye, "Hang in there, son. You're going to be alright."

The soldier could only whimper in response, "Tell...tell my wife..." He coughed hard.

Captain Wilkins leaned closer without breaking eye contact, "You're going to be fine." He sat up, holding the soldier in his lap, and pulled out his dagger. He pried out some of the debris, making the soldier start to flail in pain, crying out for relief.

"Tell…tell my wi…" The soldier stopped as he passed out from the pain.

Wilkins bowed his head and stopped, "I will." A tear in his eye ran down his face, and he pressed the dagger deep into the soldier's heart.

A loud crash broke Wilkins out of his pitiful state. Glancing across the wall, he watched in horror as the bell tower, which had been ringing the alarm, was now falling. The ringing sound of the bell echoed loudly as it hit the ground. But not nearly as loudly as the screams of his men, crushed by it before being instantly silenced.

"Soldier!" Wilkins cried out as he made his way to what was left of the eastern wall. The soldier he addressed was helping carry another wounded man to safety. "We need to call for aid," he said quickly.

"A boulder took out the call birds cage, sir," the soldier replied. "We don't have any to send."

"Then find some riders!"

"Some?" The soldier questioned. "How many do you need?"

"At least three," Wilkins answered as he continued on, leaving the soldier to his tasks.

Fires burned brightly. Wilkins left the soldier to his task as he headed to the only vantage point on the wall near him. As he reached it, he glanced up and saw the storm overhead. *No rain?* He thought to himself as he brought his eyes out over the water. Then his jaw dropped in awe and horror as he finally had a full view of what awaited them outside the castle walls.

At least fifty fully armed ships lined the coast. Further down, he could see the longboats approaching the shore. Wilkins had to duck and cover briefly as the other ships continued their barrage of the boulders of fire, one almost finding its target. Glancing around as he pulled himself up from the cover of the wall, Wilkins realized that he was hopelessly outnumbered. As screams of pain filled the air, Wilkins's gaze slowed as he observed the destruction around him. Body parts and dead soldiers were all over. The wall was barely holding at this side of the castle. Who knew what the army would do once they reached the mainland.

It was going to be a long night.

Chapter 2
Special Guests

Stalbak, the Capital City of Althalos

In the center of the continent of Kralavia stood the country of Althalos. Centrally located within the country sat the great capital city of Stalbak, once a wonderful holy city of the gods that ruled Kralavia in times past. Now, less so, though the local leaders would not have you believe that.

By all accounts, it was a great city that was well-placed and designed. Its central castle stood on top of a hill. From the top of each of the shear smooth stone walls, you could see as far as the eye could see in every direction. The city spread several leagues down the slope and across the flat lands. The country itself was not the largest by any means, but because of its location, wealth, and access to lavianite, a rare and precious metal, it was known as the Heart of Kralavia.

The capital city had two major social classes housed in two separate, distinct areas of the city, separated by a thick wall. The upper-class society had the privilege of living closer to the castle walls within the innermost parts of the town, keeping them safe from any invasion and free from witnessing the lesser and more impoverished life on the outskirts.

Apart from their location inside the city, the upper class could be distinctly known among the lower class if you ever saw them together. The quality of the clothing of the upper class and the decorative pieces they adorned themselves with were among the few items that set them apart. The housing was also very different, with elaborate structures having exquisite designs and architecture.

The lower class lived outside this inner wall and usually provided most of the daily essentials to the upper class and the castle staff. Their houses and clothing were much more worn and poorer in appearance, with far fewer fancy jewels and accessories. The rough and bumpy cobblestone roads that served the lower-class district were passable for what they were. Still, they paled compared to the flat slate used in the upper-class community and throughout the castle, giving these traveling areas a much smoother surface.

Despite being the lower class, these people were still protected well, as the outermost wall was the true defense of Stalbak. The outer wall was several feet thick and towered over the cityscape in its height. Along the top were ballistae and archers' stations, with round-the-clock troops on the watch.

King Ivan stood on top of the wall near the main gate. Usually, he would never dare to wander about this far out, not when he could see everything from his castle tower. However, today was different. Today, it was more important to greet his coming guests than to worry about his ego.

While he waited, King Ivan turned and gazed over his city. He took an unusual joy in watching his people scurry about in their daily lives. The streets were busy and packed full as they usually were this time of day. But there was some commotion among the people busy buying and selling things today. *Excitement*, Ivan thought to himself. And why shouldn't they be? Tomorrow was a special day. A wedding, but not just any wedding. The wedding.

Ivan felt a wet drip from his nose running down his mouth; he leaned forward and caught the mysterious liquid with a rag from his tunic. Blood, he realized. As a horn sounded from above the keep, Ivan turned to look and saw the oncoming caravan coming into view. He quickly cleaned off his face and regained his composure.

"Open the gates!" A voice called from the watch tower nearby.

Ivan headed down to greet his guests as they arrived in the keep of the outer wall. As he reached the entrance, King Ivan nodded to his three generals. Oswald Cromwell, one of the longest standing generals in Ivan's army. Having made his way up the ranks of the infantry during the aftermath of the Great War, Oswald was one of Ivan's most trusted generals. The next was Isaac Ulrich, who had almost as much time in as Oswald. However, while Ulrich was great on the battlefield, he lacked humility. He was always eager to control more. Ivan knew this and kept Ulrich busy with training the new recruits as they came in an effort to try and help him remember his place.

The last general was Segarus Rollins. As the youngest and newest general of the army, Rollins said very little. Partly due to his reserved nature, but also in part for the respect of the knowledge of the other leaders. Rollins was the last to nod to Ivan from his horse as the king strode past.

Ivan took his position next to Bronwyn Duma, the Captain of the King's Guard, who quickly straightened up and shouted orders to their men to get in position. *First impressions are always the most important, Ivan thought as he adjusted his belt.*

After a few moments, King Haldair Ventril of Valkos and his entourage entered the gates into the city keep. Ivan stood firmly but warmly with his men in their formation behind him. The sun shone brightly and glistened off their armor's well-polished steel and the woven lavianite throughout.

Ivan raised his hand, and his son, Prince Aldrich, dismounted and stepped forward.

Prince Aldrich was a slender lad wearing a similar outfit to his father's. Dark pants and boots, with a blue and white tunic and his decorative sword at his side. Across his shoulders was a short auditory-style cape that bore the blue and white colors of the realm with a golden crown in the center. The underside of the mantle was a rich black to offset the colors in his shirt. His crown was a gold band; though it was simple in design, it still sparkled in the sunlight.

The king of Althalos was not a high king overall, but they attempted to get the people to think he was so. Ivan wore something similar to his son, but his cape was full length, fastened to his shoulders by golden decorative clasps and gently blowing in the wind, which fit his tall, muscular figure well. He wore a thick crown with nine different gems that dazzled as the sun hit them, one for each kingdom of Kralavia.

King Haldair's caravan stopped once they were inside the city walls; the carriage carrying Haldair rocked roughly as his plump figure stepped out to greet his hosts. "Brother! Ha-ha!" Haldair's arms opened wide as he stepped up to greet them.

Ivan smiled and chuckled in return as he moved in to meet Haldair, "Look at you!" The two men embraced a moment, then Ivan stepped back to get a better look at Haldair, "I didn't think you'd survive the journey, you old dog. You're beginning to look as old as me, brother." He chided.

Haldair laughed, slapping Ivan on the shoulder, "Old in looks, but twice the wisdom to go with it." Haldair then turned his attention to Aldrich, "Well, if it isn't my favorite nephew."

Aldrich stepped up, and Haldair gave him a more formal and respectful embrace than he had given his brother. "It's good to see you, Uncle. But last I checked; I was your only nephew."

Haldair stepped back in silence for a moment. A smile grew across his face, "Well then, lucky for you; the competition isn't too fierce." Aldrich smiled in return before Haldair's complexion sobered as he looked past Ivan to his generals behind him. Haldair stepped forward and offered a firm handshake, "Oswald Cromwell, in the flesh once more. Always a pleasure. It looks like nothing will ever take you out. Though I thought for sure in that skirmish with Halika might have done it, had I not saved you."

"Not quite how I remember it," Oswald laughed. He returned the firm grip and straightened up on his steed, "The pleasure is all mine, I assure you."

Haldair nodded softly in response.

After the two exchanged greetings, Haldair looked back at Aldrich, "Well, there will be plenty of time for further pleasantries during the celebration," he said casually. "But as of right now, there are matters that your father and I must attend to before your bride arrives."

Aldrich smiled to hide his skepticism and nodded, "Of course."

"Come, brother," Haldair gestured to Ivan to join him in the carriage. "We must talk."

Ivan bowed slightly and took Haldair's invitation to join him in the carriage. As the driver pulled away, Ivan looked out and saw that Bronwyn was dismissing the troops, and Aldrich had already mounted his steed and joined the entourage behind Haldair's lead carriage.

The trip through the city was pleasant, even for the lower-class portion. Despite being the lower class, all the citizens respected Ivan and the royal family. Stalbak sat on a rich mineral mine that was used in crafting architecture and was a big part of the trade of that area. This, in turn, meant that the poor and impoverished of Stalbak were still better off than most other regions' lower-class societies.

It would be a while before they reached the castle walls, yet the two men sat silently for the first part of the ride. "So, when is the wedding party arriving?" Ivan asked, breaking the long silence.

"Later today," Haldair replied. "My guess would be after dark tonight." He was looking out the window as they approached the inner wall entering the upper-class portion of the city. "Still as beautiful as I remember."

The shimmering stones and jewels from the local mineral ore used in the city's construction were seen all around. Every house and structure glistened in the sun like diamonds and glass. Lavianite was a hard, crystal-like mineral that could be ground into and mixed with clay for stability and strength. Or cut and used as decorative pieces for roads and buildings. Ivan's family was the first to utilize this mineral in their armor and weapons, making them more resistant to damage in battle.

At the back of the entourage, Oswald rode next to the prince, followed by Ulrich and Rollins with Bronwyn and the King's Guard picking up the train's rear. "So?"

Aldrich snapped out of his thoughts, "What?"

"Save all the sweat for the bedsheets," Oswald said jokingly. "She hasn't even arrived yet, and you look like you're going to drown yourself in anxiety and sweat."

Aldrich laughed gently, "I'm fine."

Oswald laughed harder this time, "No, no, no. You can't lie to me. I see it in those eyes." Aldrich began to roll his eyes. "What's wrong? You need me to walk you through the deed?" Oswald asked. "I recommend pulling one of her…"

"It's not that," Aldrich cut in sharply. "If you must know. I'm nervous about her brother."

"Who? Merrek? He's harmless."

Aldrich sighed, "Merrek is responsible for over a hundred victories for Haldair." He began. "He's also delivered the heads and fingers of slain generals on platters, and that's not through orders. No, that's by his own will. He's psychotic, is what he is."

Oswald's demeanor dimmed slightly, "Where did you hear this?"

"I, ah… I don't know," Aldrich stammered. "I read it somewhere."

"Huh."

"What?"

"I didn't realize you could read," Oswald said sarcastically.

Aldrich chuckled, "General, you realize I can have you executed, right?"

Oswald shook his head gently, "I don't know if you want to be making such threats, young prince. I happen to know and be close friends with your soon-to-be brother-in-law."

Aldrich's face went pale at this idea until Oswald could no longer hold his complexion and began laughing. "Come on," Oswald said as he caught his breath. "Come on. Let's find Thomas, have some laughs, and get drunk. It's a wedding, after all."

"I should probably keep it to a minimum tonight since I am the one who's getting married tomorrow," Aldrich said.

Oswald drew his horse closer to Aldrich's, leaned over, and lowered his voice, "If not now, then when, my friend?" Aldrich shot Oswald a playful grin. "Then it's settled," he said, resuming his original position in the formation. "Prince Aldrich's last night of freedom. Tomorrow will be a day that you will never forget."

Aldrich nodded, still smiling.

"Though for the sake of our dignity and reputations, let us make this a night we shall never remember, huh?" Oswald chided. As the two continued to ride through the city, a chorus of cheers could be heard randomly throughout the trip as some citizens shouted praise and admiration for their king and prince.

It was early afternoon when Haldair and Ivan arrived at the castle. Haldair made a point to mention the beauty of the stonework as he stepped out of the carriage. Ivan followed his gaze up the side of the looming towers. Perhaps he was more accustomed to it, so he didn't feel as phased by the beauty of it. Maybe, he didn't feel like he deserved the splendor of Stalbak as his own, so he chose not to see it.

Whatever the reason, Ivan simply smiled and agreed with Haldair as they entered the castle's main hall together. Ivan directed his people to attend to the rest of the entourage and the horses. Aldrich and Oswald took care of themselves before heading to the castle courtyard.

As Ivan and Haldair entered the study, Ivan directed that they be brought food and wine. Haldair withdrew a document from his carrying bag and set it on the main table in the center of the room. Moments later, the servant set down a platter of wine and fruit.

Ivan's study was yet another piece of the grandeur that was Castle Stalbak. Across from the doorway sat a large fireplace that nearly took the total span of the wall. The room itself was large enough to host a few dozen men comfortably, perhaps a few more if some of the furniture was to be removed. If the walls were not covered in shelves of books from across the continent, they were decoratively covered in wood carvings lined with the same mineral as the streets and castle, which reflected off the light shining in from the large stained-glass window that overlooked the main desk that Ivan used.

On the mantel above the fireplace, displayed with a brilliant hue, was the large Golden Sword. It sat as an heirloom to Ivan. The blade of Athalon was used by his grandfather after the god disappeared before the Great War against the other gods. Images flashed in Ivan's mind of when he wielded that sword. It's power and strength; none could match.

On the center table were maps of the continent from different times. The footnotes showed who ruled what kingdom and for how long. Haldair gently slid these parchments to the side as he rolled out his scroll for Ivan to read.

Haldair explained that this was the marriage contract for his son Aldrich who was to be married to one of Haldair's baronesses. The deal was that through the legality of the marriage, Ivan would pay a large sum of money to Valkos that would absolve the bride and her family of any debts owed by them.

As Ivan read the document, he hesitated. There was nothing new in this agreement that Ivan hadn't already discussed with Haldair before this meeting. But this time, there was something. Ivan glanced up at the sword on the mantle before gazing at Haldair. "You sure this is the right course of action?"

"There is no reason for doubt, brother," Haldair began. "Even the rest of the Five Crown Alliance agrees. Once you sign, your son will have his beautiful bride in a day. At last, her family's debts will be paid off, and one of the finest soldiers this land has ever known may finally have his lands returned to him in full."

Ivan set the paper down, signed it, and stamped it with his seal next to Haldair's. His brother smiled as he picked it up to see the signature. "Very good. Now, how about a drink?"

Ivan gestured to the platter of food and wine the servants had dropped off upon arrival. "To marriage and peace," Ivan said as he poured the goblets.

Haldair smiled again and raised his cup, "To celebrate the furthering of the greatest union Kralavia has ever seen." Ivan raised his glass to meet Haldair's. "And the union of a fine woman and a man I trust will be a king as honorable as his father."

The glasses clink, Ivan's face grows sad after they drink, and the reality of Haldair's words sinks in. Looking back at the sword on the mantel, Ivan recalled the horrors he's done as king. The fear of his legacy extending to his sons and having them drenched in bloodshed also bothered Ivan. His people loved him, and his kingdom thrived, but at what cost?

"Therein lies the problem, brother," he finally said after his moment of silence.

"What do you mean?" Haldair asked.

Ivan didn't respond right away. He kept his gaze fixed on the sword, "Never mind," he said quickly, shaking off his thoughts. "It's nothing."

Meanwhile
Arkeanos, Capital City of Vasalia

Though it was far less in decorative flare than that of Althalos or most of the kingdoms of Kralavia, it was no less regal. Vasalia was a rugged region that sat comfortably with the Purple Mountains on its western border, which wrapped up around the northern boundary a great distance, and the coastline along its eastern shore. To the south, the Great River came from the continent's northwest and ran into the sea to the east.

The land within was rocky soil, which meant the country didn't do well for farmland or cattle. However, this was never a concern for King Leoxtra or his people. They used the control of the seaport to build wealth through trade. Vasalia was also home to some of the largest iron reserves within the mountains surrounding it.

Arkeanos, the capital city, sat to the north. Built into the foothills of the mountains there and giving it direct access to the sea. Because of this,

Vasalia held one of the largest naval fleets on the continent and often patrolled the coastline, protecting the trade routes from the eastern lands.

Though rich in prospects and trade, because of the terrain, Vasalia's cities and structures were more modest than some of its partners. Simple stone buildings and wooden roofs were typical when touring the countryside. The castle in Arkeanos was no different, sitting on the northern side of the city. The castle was almost built into the mountain entirely; what was exposed was the same simple stone that everything was made of.

Within the castle, large banners and tapestries were hung throughout. The throne room was the central room in the palace; it had large stone pillars that lined the inside, leading up to the decorative stone steps that led up to the throne at the rear. By itself, the throne room could host several hundred people in this room alone.

It was early morning, and King Leoxtra was seated on his throne speaking to his advisor and his general when the large wooden doors at the entrance to the room burst open, "My lord!" cried the man as he hurriedly entered and approached the throne. He wore the colors of Althalos, though severely worn through and torn in several places.

"Easy, lad," said the advisor firmly. "What business is this that you would bother the king unannounced?"

The messenger reached the steps that led up to the throne and fell to his knees in exhaustion, "We're under attack…" He took a few deep breaths. "Stelbeck Keep, in Alkeroth, is falling."

The advisor looked at the king curiously and then at the general, "Who and how?"

"No one could've gotten through our borders unknown to us," General Thaddeus cut in, doubting the report.

"No, my lords," said the messenger, who had now regained his composure. "Not by land. The attack has come from the sea."

This information sat uneasily with the advisor, who immediately addressed the king to his plan of action, "Sire?"

King Leoxtra looks at his general on his left, "If we are to protect the city of Alkeroth, we must reinforce Stelbeck Keep."

"I agree," Thaddeus acknowledged. Then turning to the messenger, "What else can you tell me?"

"Fifty ships or more, sir. A full invasion fleet," he replied earnestly. "We don't have the means at Stelbeck to defend against that. The coastal defense will fall."

"Which banner are they flying?"

"We could not tell, sir," the messenger replied. "Darkness followed them as they approached, and combined with the night, we could not see."

The general rubbed his goatee and considered the best possible action plan. "How many men are stationed at Stelbeck now?"

"Less than three hundred, but that was before the attack. I'm unaware of the current number," the messenger answered.

A grim expression grew across Thaddeus' face. "Sire," he said, turning to the king. "Some of our fleet is out on regular patrols and training, but Admiral Huxton should have enough ships in the harbor to provide a small counterattack. I can take my men on horseback; we'd be there by midday."

"I agree," said the king. "If they sent fifty ships, then I'll send a hundred! Send word to Admiral Huxton to take all his ships and head south to deal with the invasion fleet. And send birds to our closest ships to return home and prepare for a fight. Then take a cavalry battalion of your men to the fort to provide aid. And ready, my horse, I will ride with you."

General Thaddeus bowed low, "Yes, sir." Then he turned and left the room.

Then King Leoxtra addressed the messenger, "Did you send out other riders?"

"Yes. Two others, your Excellency. One went to Althalos and King Ivan as we are his citizens." The king nodded as the messenger continued, "The final rider went through the city of Alkeroth and into the countryside to muster any other aid we could."

The king seemed pleased by this. "Did Commander Gregson send you?"

"Commander Gregson died early, as the fight began. Captain Wilkins has taken command and given me my orders."

"Very well," the king said solemnly. "Go, freshen up, and be ready to ride with my men back to the fort." The messenger bowed again and followed the general's path out of the room. Turning to his advisor, King Leoxtra said, "Send a bird to Althalos; hopefully, it'll quicken their response. That rider won't reach them until tomorrow evening at best."

"It may interrupt the wedding."

"I don't care what it interrupts!" King Leoxtra snapped. "What good is this Five Crown Alliance if nothing happens when a real threat is shown? Our land hasn't experienced a full invasion since the time of the old gods, and I'm not about to lose our foothold now. Our connection with Althalos is strong, and it's not one I'm willing to break."

The advisor bowed his head, "Yes, Sire."

Chapter 3
We Stand, We Fight

Stelbeck Keep, the Coastal Outpost of Althalos, in Vasalia.

Daylight had come, though it was still dark across the area. The thick clouds overhead and the smoke around them kept most of the sunlight from reaching through. Wilkins walked through the rubble; the damage was immeasurable. The more critically injured men were laid out on tables in a makeshift triage center against the western wall so their wounds could be attended to by the surgeons as soon as possible. At the same time, some others who, at the very least, could walk were slumped up against the walls, taking their first rest since the attack began.

The naval bombardment continued on and off throughout the night. Only now, after the morning had finally come, did it end. The once-strongly-built coastal fortress was in shambles. The eastern wall was all but completely gone. The northern corner held firm as it was tucked into the side of the small cliff the keep was nestled against. There, Captain Wilkins observed the flag of Althalos, the blue and white checkered background with a golden crown in the center, tattered but still flying.

As the captain walked around the keep accessing the destruction, he entered the triage area and paused as the wails of pain from a nearby soldier echoed. Wilkins quickly rushed over to assist, holding the man down as the aid attempted to remove several large splinters.

"Easy soldier," Wilkins said empathetically. "You're doing great." The soldier only grunted in response as another shard was taken out of his leg.

"Hold him tight, captain," the surgeon said as he grabbed the hot iron.

"Could I… Could I?" the weak voice of the wounded soldier broke clear as he pointed to the bottle of liquor on the ground by the surgeon. Wilkins nodded and proceeded to help the soldier get a short drink.

Tearing off a piece of his tunic, Wilkins wadded up the cloth and stuffed it in the man's mouth, "Bite on this."

The surgeon placed the hot iron on the wound when the rag was secure in the soldier's mouth. The smell of burnt flesh quickly filled the nostrils of the men there, and Wilkins and his lieutenant firmly held the soldier down as the muffled screams of pain were forced out. The man managed not to pass out during the final cauterizing. He could hold in the pain a bit, only letting out a deep grunt from behind his clenched teeth. Wilkins grabbed the soldier's hand and rested the other hand on his shoulder.

"Captain! Captain!" a voice rang out above the rest of the moans and screams that lingered throughout the fort.

Wilkins turned to address the source of the voice as another soldier reached him. "Yes?"

"Sir," he said quickly. "We've identified them."

Wilkins nodded to the surgeon, putting a soothing ointment on the wounded soldier and bandaging the leg. Then, he followed after the soldier to see what brand of evil had just torn this fort apart.

"Show me," Wilkins said, exiting the triage. As they quickly walked to the southeast corner of the wall where they still had some visual vantage point, Wilkins called for his lieutenant, attending to another injured soldier nearby. "Get me a full damage assessment while we still have time."

"Yes, sir."

"And find out where the troops of Alkeroth are; they should be here by now," Wilkins shouted as he continued on. The lieutenant acknowledged the orders and turned on his heels to follow through with them. It took a few minutes, but Wilkins finally reached one of the few high points on what remained of the wall facing the coastline. "Report," he said firmly as he got the two men stationed there as lookouts.

"It's Carnheller, sir," the lookout replied as he handed Wilkins the spotting scope. "We couldn't make out their sigil at night, but now it's clear, despite the cloud cover."

Wilkins grabbed the scope and looked through in disbelief, "Since when does the island nation have a war fleet? And why would King Valtor break the treaty of the Five Crown Alliance?"

"There's no mistaking it, sir," one of the lookouts confirmed.

Wilkins scanned the fleet with the scope; the lookout was indeed correct. There was no mistaking it; this was a fleet from Carnheller. Their black banner with a red scorpion in its center was very distinct. Wilkins continued looking across the ships; he remembered the boats that made landfall at night.

As he moved his gaze down, he asked, "What of the men that reached the shore?"

"No movement, Captain," the lookout replied. "They were probably told to secure the beach and wait."

"Possibly."

Wilkins dropped the scope and stared out with his own eyes. Carnheller, an island nation, excelled at naval warfare, but their small size prevented them from obtaining a massive fleet. Most of their needs were met through trade since few resources were available. However, as Captain Wilkins knew, the true might of the Carnheller army was in their berserker units, highly trained men that wore little to no armor.

Before an attack, their torsos were wrapped in a tight ceremonial cloth to reduce blood flow, and they breathed in the fumes of a drug native to their island. This drug increased adrenaline and reduced feelings of pain or morality, allowing them to move faster and cut through their enemies without hesitation, even if the man was mortally wounded. They would land on smaller boats after the foe was weakened, move in fast, and slaughter the survivors. It was an effective strategy that had served Carnheller well in its past skirmishes with the nations to the east across the sea.

"Sir," the lookout said, breaking Wilkins's thoughts. "Is there any aid coming?"

"We sent out riders as soon as possible," he replied. "One was sent to Arkeanos and King Leoxtra," he paused and glanced back out to sea. "Hopefully, his fleet can muster in time."

"And the others?"

Wilkins turned back to face the lookout, "Another was sent to our capital Althalos and King Ivan…"

"That's a two-day ride, sir," the lookout interjected. "They won't get here in time."

Wilkins didn't respond immediately. He understood the concern and the risk that his men were facing. After what happened last night, hope was starting to fade. "I sent another to Alkeroth and the countryside of Vasalia; hopefully, a nearby lord can muster his men here as well." As he finished, he scanned the fleet again with the scope. Only a couple of the attacking ships had taken damage in the onslaught.

Wilkins carefully looked over each ship. "What are you looking for?" asked the lookout.

"The lead ship," Wilkins replied without taking his eyes off the water. "Found it," he said as he paused and focused more. "Well, well, if it isn't Admiral Mortem." Wilkins dropped the scope and continued to look out at the fleet. Longboats began to enter the water, and a tinge of fear came through Wilkins. "Time to muster the men."

Wilkins handed the scope to the now confused lookout as he carefully but quickly climbed down the remnants of the wall and called out for his lieutenant.

"Captain," the lieutenant said as he approached.

"What are we looking at?" Wilkins asked.

"We have a hundred and twenty men strong and ready," the lieutenant began. "About fifty more are wounded but able to fight."

"What's the loss, lieutenant?" Wilkins snapped, knowing they didn't have time for sentiments just yet.

"Current count is one hundred and four, sir," the lieutenant finally said. "Several still unaccounted for, presumed dead."

"What of the assistance troops from Alkeroth?" Wilkins asked.

"The messenger returned only moments ago; one hundred city guards are ready with two hundred more in reserve coming."

Wilkins exhaled a small sigh of relief at the news, "Direct them to rally in with our men. We must limit our direct attacking with what's coming ashore."

"Sir?"

Captain Wilkins didn't respond immediately, "I want every able-bodied man armed and ready," he said firmly, breaking his silence. "Have the men ready to fight in the courtyard by the southern gate. That one has the most straightforward access; that's the one they'll use."

"Are you sure?"

"Yes," Wilkins said as he looked around, trying to think of an appropriate battle plan. "The coastal access road leads there, and they can't climb the cliff side to get through the eastern wall that they so utterly demolished." Wilkins paused as he thought about what was coming.

"Sir?" The lieutenant asked skeptically, "Is that all?"

Wilkins examined the southern wall, "We need to corner them. Tell Lieutenant Collins to get his archers along the southern and western walls with as many of the city's guards as possible. The berserkers won't attack the city until the fort is taken, so if we can lock them in here, it should keep the town safe." Wilkins directed his gaze at the lieutenant as he continued, "Tell the reserve unit of the city's guard to hold within the city until the enemy is at the fort; once they break through, we'll have them come in from behind, and we can corner them in the fort and hopefully…" he paused as he looked around at his broken men. "Hold them and destroy them."

The lieutenant nodded and headed off to organize the men. Wilkins watched as the archers began to line up above the causeway. Thankfully most of the woods had been cleared away as the trade grew at the riverbank. *If the doors to the fort hold long enough,* Wilkins thought to himself. *We might just last out the morning.*

Admiral Mortem stood in the bow of his flagship, which sat in the second row of the fleet of the Corsair ships that he brought. As he stood there, Mortem looked through his telescope and saw that the Althalos flag, though torn and tattered, still flew from the top of the last standing tower in the northern corner.

As he scanned the area further to the south, Mortem saw two men posted looking out into the water in his direction. Admiral Mortem focused on the two. The first man he didn't recognize, but the other he did. Captain Wilkins, he thought, *as a member of the King's Guard, what has brought you so far from home?* The admiral lowered his telescope with a slight smirk as one of the other crew members approached.

"Captain," he greeted, still looking at the fort in the distance.

"Admiral. The shoreline is still secure, and the vessels await your next orders." The captain said, standing at attention.

"I truly admire an enemy too naive to surrender," Mortem said, seemingly ignoring the request. Then turning to the sailor, "It makes this so much more enjoyable."

"Sir?"

"Captain," Mortem said. "Let us begin our push into the mainland. Drop the longboats and send in the berserker units. We have a schedule to keep here."

The captain gave a quick salute with his right arm in a single pound against his chest, bowed slightly, and stepped away smiling. "Send in the berserker units!" echoes of joyous shouts rang across the fleet.

As the shouts of eagerness continued, several longboats were dropped into the water, and dozens of lightly armored men climbed out from below deck. As the men lined up on the edge of the deck, the captain wrapped his face with a rag and opened a small wooden box; the other men stepped back to avoid breathing in the aroma by mistake, and each ship in the fleet followed suit.

The captain walked along the berserker formation, pausing long enough for each man to inhale deeply. Almost instantaneously, each man beat his chest, and their eyes reddened as bright as the scorpion displayed on their breastplates; then, the men quickly climbed into the landing boats. The drug only lasted a few hours, so time was crucial for utilizing these men in this way.

Once the drug wore off, it made the men crash with exhaustion, and any pain inflicted during the drug use would come back stronger, creating nothing more than a worthless soldier. Each man within the berserker units was armed with a small shield and short sword, allowing quick yet strong movements. Failure, for them, was not an option.

As the berserker units approached the shoreline, the captain had each ship ready with their light infantry units for a follow-up. Usually only needed in an extreme case, these infantrymen wore light armor and chainmail and usually swept in after the berserkers did their job to clean up whatever was left.

Admiral Mortem watched in pleasure as his berserkers reached the shoreline and headed up the coastal road to the fort. As he scanned the rubble of the fort, he noticed the archers getting in place among the stones in what was left of the walls. He scoffed, "They think they actually have a chance."

There is a new bustle within the fort as Wilkins had every man set his station. The clouds remained thick and heavy in the sky above them. There had still been no rain or wind, which had Wilkins concerned, but he could not overthink that. Wounded or not, the soldiers still could walk and carry a weapon, rushed to gather swords, spears, axes, and shields.

"Lieutenant Collins," Wilkins called out as he walked to the southern gate.

"Here, sir," Collins said as he broke away from a nearby group of men. As he left, the group left quickly and headed up to the wall with their bows in hand.

"Lieutenant," Wilkins said. "How goes the archer placement?"

"Well," Collins replied sheepishly. "We are making do with what is left of the vantage points. With the city guards' help, I think it'll hold."

"Hey," Wilkins said softly as he stepped closer. "More help will come; we only need to hold them off. Use the rubble to your advantage. All they've done is give us more of a fighting chance. Keep your eyes focused on the road outside. Stay low, and don't do anything until I make a move. Do you understand me? We should be able to pick them off before they even breach the gate."

Captain Wilkins saw the lookout running for him, then turned to Collins, "Go." Collins nodded in understanding and quickly left, barking orders to his men.

"Captain!" cried the lookout breaking through the noise.

Wilkins ran to meet him, "What is it?"

"The boats…" he paused as he tried to breathe.

"Spit it out, man!"

The lookout took a deep breath, "Sir. I count almost one hundred boats that made it ashore. Roughly a dozen men in each."

Wilkins's face went white. They didn't have the strength to fight off a thousand men. "We need to buy more time."

"How can we stand against that?" the lookout exclaimed. "These are not mere men; these are monsters. With red eyes and frothing mouths."

Wilkins puts a hand up to silence the lad, "Soldier."

"Yes, sir," the lookout said.

"Get up to that tower," Wilkins said, pointing to the northeast corner. "Do not let that flag fall."

"Yes, sir!"

Wilkins got his bow and arrows from the armory and stepped out into the destroyed courtyard, making his way toward the eastern wall. He stopped to glance out into the water. He didn't need a telescope to see what was coming. His gaze slowly moved across the beach to the road that led up to the fort and the rows of Admiral Mortem's berserker units that were quickly moving up the road.

Looking across the fort, he saw Lieutenant Collins' archers getting in a position where they could. Wilkins looked to the west; he could make out bits of the horizon over the cityscape. The purple mountains looked almost gray in the light. Wilkins took one final look out to sea and looked for any sign of help. Nothing.

As he returned to the courtyard, Captain Wilkins was greeted by the sad faces of the men that believed—by every right—that they would die soon. As he scanned their faces, Wilkins mustered his courage, "Men! We are the first line of defense for Althalos and all of Kralavia! We were not trained to cower in fear from the sight of our enemies or retreat from our post at the sight of its destruction!" He exclaimed as he strode through the ranks. "We were trained to die for it. Hell, we were *built* to die for it. And die we may!" He continued as he reached the front line by the barricaded gate. "But if we go down. If we crumble and burn, countless more of these bastards are coming with us! We will fight to the last man. Look not for hope. Look for honor and find it within yourselves. You do not know pain; you do not know fear. Show them no mercy! You are soldiers of Althalos!"

Shouts and cheers echoed loudly from the men, "Do not waste your arrows!" Wilkins called Collins. "Wait until they are in range and make them climb over themselves to get to us!"

Chapter 4
Grave News

Amias started to feel numb from the ride, but he needed to move as fast as possible, minimizing his stops. The sun was setting beyond the Purple Mountains before him; darkness was setting on the horizon. He felt tired, catching himself nodding off as the horse's speed steadied. After several attempts to stay awake, Amias put a stiff heel on the horse, and she burst out in a sprint. "Not much farther now, girl," he said to the horse as she picked up her pace into a full gallop. He felt terrible; they hadn't stopped for several hours after their last water break.

His first goal was to get to the small town of Arkeanot, a mostly farm and trading town. But it had a unique location along the main road that led across the country of Vasalia through the Purple Mountains and into Althalos. Amias hoped he could garner a fresh steed to make it the rest of the way to Castle Stalbak. Behind him to the east, the dark clouds in the distance made it seem darker across the land. By now, surely Stelbeck Keep was either victorious or overrun. Either way, Amias must complete his mission and warn King Ivan. *Hopefully,* he thought as he pressed on, *the victory was already won, and Ivan would have little to worry about.*

It was after dark when Amias finally arrived in Arkeanot. He had barely enough time to slow the horse down properly before he quickly dismounted and ran up to the first house he came across. "Help! Help!" Amias cried as he loudly banged on the door. "Open up in the name of the King!"

Barely a moment went by, and the door to the farmhouse opened quickly. An elderly man with a long beard answered the door, "Yes, yes, what is it?" he said in a sleepy voice.

Typically, Amias would've exchanged more courtesy at this moment; however, the urgency of his mission prevented any such pleasantries.

"Quickly, sir," Amias said, catching his breath slightly. "I am on an urgent errand of the King." This caused the attitude of the elderly man to soften a little against the abrupt intrusion. "I have news from Alkeroth."

The elderly man paused momentarily. "Aye," he finally said. "What be your need?"

"A fresh horse. I must reach Stalbak tomorrow."

"Stalbak?" the elderly host questioned. "You'll have to ride hard all night to reach Stalbak by tomorrow," he continued as he stroked his beard. "Evening at the earliest, I reckon."

The update didn't faze Amias; he knew how long it took to reach Castle Stalbak. "Sir," he pleaded. "If you cannot help me, where might I find someone who can? She'll surely fall by morning if I press on with my current steed."

The elderly farmer eyed Amias' horse, "Aye, you be right about that, son." He glanced back into his house as if getting approval from the dark space behind him. "Tell ya what," he said, turning back to Amias. "You leave your horse with me, and I'll see her fed and rested. Take my horse in her stead; he's young and a bit rough around the edges yet, but you find no better horse to run the mountain pass this side of 'em."

Amias bowed quickly, "Thank you." As the old man gathered his horse, Amias stripped his of the saddle and gear. "Get some rest, Delilah," he told the horse, patting her neck. "You did great." Once the farmer's steed was brought out front, he helped Amias get his things strapped in.

"Is there anything else you need, lad?"

Amias paused as he mounted his ride, "If you can, get word to the neighboring towns and city's guards. Stelbeck Keep is under attack and possibly already fallen."

The man's face sobered as the news sunk in, "Aye," he said. "I'll get some warnings out and muster what I can find." Amias nodded, and he was off into the darkness with a sharp heel to the horse.

The sun had begun to break through the horizon behind him. The air around him had started to reflect a purplish hue. The road through the Purple Mountains was easy to traverse even at night, thanks to the faint glow of the mineral ore that gave them their purplish hue. It also offered several beautiful places that gave travelers a magnificent countryside view. As he reached a minor summit near the top of the mountain pass, Amias decided he could afford a short break and dismounted, leading his horse to the nearby stream.

The water came from deep within the mountains and broke through in several places, giving rest points on the journey for anyone traveling the mountains and a marker to account for how much was left to travel. Though the mountain pass was easily followed, in the shadow of the mountains, it was easy for anyone to get a false sense of time and become disoriented should they take one of the smaller hunting trails by mistake.

Unfortunately, Amias didn't have the luxury of enjoying the sightseeing opportunities. The sky above him lightened before the sunlight broke through the mountain peaks. Amias knelt to wash the sleep off his face; he must stay awake. Hopefully, it would get easier once the sun was higher. He stared at his reflection for a moment; the purple tint to the rock made the water reflect traces of faint purple colors as it moved gently along the shoulder of the road. Amias sighed as he stood, he knew the importance of his mission, but the knowledge of what he carried made him no less feel almost like he had abandoned the others.

Amias shook this feeling and quickly mounted the horse and, with a sharp heel, continued galloping on through the mountains. He was thankful that though it had some dangerous spots, the road through the mountains was wide and easy to traverse. Built during the Great War, it was designed to allow for faster troop movements since the only other road from Althalos to Vasalia was to go to the south around the mountains.

A couple of hours later, Amias reached the top. Here, the mountain pass leveled off for a few miles before taking the winding trail back down into the country of Althalos. He glanced back to the east; the sun had risen well above the horizon. Amias wondered how the fort was holding and if the other riders had enough reinforcements to help. Storm clouds began to form overhead. *Strange,* he thought. Though the Purple Mountains were tall and broad, the weather was always mild on the summit.

Turning back to the west, Amias gazed over the road to come. Stalbak could be seen as a faint speck in the distance, only spotted by the reflecting light off the castle's peaks. The dark green landscape contrasted the blue sky well, with the Purple Mountains adding to the majesty of the overall view. Mustering his resolve, he rode on; he would arrive in Stalbak at evening at best, provided the road was smooth traveling and the horse held up.

Chapter 5
Family Tensions

The Southern Forests of Althalos

The carriage rattled along roughly as the caravan headed through the woods. The sun shone brightly, though the tree line overhead mostly concealed it. Despite the gloominess of the area, it gave the riders a reprieve from the sun's heat, which had beaten on them for most of this journey north. Unlike most of the royal caravans, this one was far less pronounced. Despite the armed escort of the primary two carriages, which totaled about two dozen armed troops on horseback, the appearance and nature of the rest of the procession were very modest by comparison.

"You can stop your sulking, Merrek," the feminine voice said, breaking his silent thoughts. Merrek quickly shot a look of question at his sister, Laura, who sat across from him in the main carriage. She looked casually out the carriage window and did not engage Merrek further.

Merrek's features softened as he watched his sister. She had long brown hair and sharp facial features. For most of her life, many a man sought her for marriage, which was no surprise to Merrek, as even he had to acknowledge his sister's beauty. Merrek was older than Laura by a couple of years, but apart from his black hair and a few days' beard growth on his face, one would think that these siblings were twins.

"I'm sorry, Laura," said Merrek solemnly. "Just a lot on my mind." Merrek and Laura were the Baron and Baroness of Frosbike, a regional territory within Valkos that neighbored the kingdom of Althalos on its southern border. In comparison, most of the countries of Kralavia held similar stations within their borders. But Valkos, the largest country in land mass and population, effectively utilized this form of political structure.

Laura pulled her gaze away from the sunbeams dancing in the trees to look at Merrek directly, "It'll be okay; this is a good thing."

Merrek said nothing.

"We already owe everything to Haldair, and if King Ivan pays off our family debts as part of the marriage union, you can finally relax and stop trying to find a way just to get by." She gestured to the rough and plain interior of their carriage.

"Is this really what you want?"

"It's not about what I want," Laura said. "It's about what we need."

Merrek sighed and softly nodded his head in agreement. Laura was right, of course, As much as Merrek admired her ability to think with calculations instead of emotions. Merrek often felt that if Laura showed some emotion in her choices, she wouldn't go through with some of them. She's too kind, he thought.

The two sat silently for some time, and Merrek stared down at his sword. Unlike all of his other possessions, this sword had been well taken care of, and the only possession he still had that was not in some way owned or borrowed from King Haldair. The hilt of this sword was brushed bronze in the shape of the falcon, which was the coat of arms for Valkos, whose wings spread out on the cross-guard with the head of a falcon encroaching on the blade faced forward with purpose. In the talons, the bottom of the hilt held a single red gem. This sword was the one thing that Haldair could never take from him.

Over the years, Merrek's family had made several bad investments and chances that the king then had to correct. These choices meant that Merrek's parents' actual property and possessions and, by default, then Merrek and Laura's, had significantly diminished as time went on. Merrek and Laura were royalty by title only; they had nothing of their own, and the Baron and Baroness of Frosbike had become little more than a public formality.

Merrek's thoughts broke as an approaching horse echoed within the carriage. As he looked out, he relaxed and realized it was the captain of his guard and dear friend, Wully. "General," Wully's voice was strong and clear.

Merrek grinned slightly and rolled his eyes as he set his sword to the side. "Wully, it's just Baron now. You don't need that battlefield courtesy here." Wully smiled and nodded. Merrek smiled, knowing that Wully would always refer to him as 'General' after their last war together. Merrek never pressed too much since most of the respect and bond these two shared was because of their time in battle together.

"Permission to ride ahead, sir?" Wully asked plainly. "This road is a common target for bandits and the like. I want to ensure it's safe as we approach the final stretch of our journey."

"As you wish, Captain," Merrek replied. "Take a few men with you and report back quickly."

"Yes, sir," Wully replied as he began to pull ahead.

"Oh, and Wully," Merrek called out, causing his captain to hold fast. "Be careful. We don't need any trouble if we can help it."

Wully chuckled and nodded again, "Sir." Then turning to Laura, he paused, "Milady."

Laura nodded quickly but returned her gaze immediately to Wully's eyes. The two locked together until, finally, Wully gave a short heel to his horse and rode up ahead. Laura watched as best she could as the captain ordered three men of his to join him.

"Mmmhhmm," Merrek hummed through his smile.

Laura snapped out of her trance and looked at her brother, "What?"

"How long will you fail at hiding it before you just come forward and tell me the truth?" Laura said nothing. Instead, she continued to look out the window at the passing trees.

"You think I haven't suspected?" Merrek finally interjects, leaning forward in his seat, "I see how you two look at each other." Laura didn't move.

"I'm not angry, Laura," he continued. "He is an honorable man. Far more honorable and more worthy of my sister's hand in marriage than Ivan's entitled prick of a son."

Laura sighs as she brings her gaze from the window to her brother. "I know he's not your first choice. But I have spent time with him. It'll be fi…"

"One evening!" Merrek interrupted. "If you can even count that. Since, from what I've heard, it was only one dance. And now you expect me to hand you over forever?" As he finished, Merrek sat back in his seat and crossed his arms.

"What's really going on?" Laura asked softly.

Merrek shook his head, "I just… I feel like this wedding only makes me look like I sold my sister."

"Hey," Laura said as she leaned in. "This is also my choice. Besides," she leaned back in her seat. "Father left us with very little, and Mother left us with nothing but each other. Something needed to be done, and this is our last chance."

"But this isn't fair to you. It's not right. You should be free to marry whomever you choose, not be pawned to the highest bidder," Merrek said. "Just because Ivan agreed to pay our debts doesn't mean you should feel obligated to marry this man. We can manage without; we've been doing it this long and can continue to."

"Merrek, you know we can't manage without. We never have. We've tried and failed for so many years." Laura's voice almost cracked as she spoke. "Our family's house, lands, livestock, everything has been taken."

"But I can."

"Can what?" Laura questioned. "Win more battles? We've been fighting with Stelmond on and off forever, and it's gotten us nowhere. Even after you mercilessly decapitated one of the generals and threw his head at King Ordain." Merrek just sat in silence as she continued, "Or, go straight to

King Haldair and let loose with that temper of yours? A lot of good that's done for us either."

Merrek looked away with some small sense of shame. Try as he might, Laura was right. Nothing had been working; this was a viable option and a welcome one in most respects. As much as Merrek hated Aldrich, he hated seeing his sister suffer more in their current situation. *This is the only way.* Laura's words echoed in Merrek's mind as he sat there thinking about it. The more he thought about it, the more he conceded to it.

"And yes," Laura began after a moment's silence. "I have grown…fond of Wully. But he isn't of noble blood, so it would be frowned upon even if the debts were not in the picture."

"Nobility," Merrek scoffed. "Nobility doesn't come from a bloodline. It's character. Wully is far nobler than that Prince Aldrich will ever be."

The two sat there in silence again; Merrek turned to look out the opposite side of the carriage. He noticed a small tear running down his sister's cheek as he did. "Anyway," Laura said, wiping the tear away after seeing that Merrek noticed. "It doesn't matter," she continued. "This is what we must do, and I am willing to do it. Regardless of what I may be losing in the process."

Merrek exhaled heavily, "I'm sure we can figure something out."

"We've tried Merrek," Laura's tone grew more annoyed. "We have been trying to 'figure something out' since our father died, and it's gotten us nowhere. This wedding is the only option, and we are out of time. The wedding is tomorrow." As she finished speaking, Laura turned to look out her window. Merrek realized that he had pushed too far and dropped the issue…

"The road is clear," Wully said as he and his men reached the exit to the forest trail. "Let's rejoin the caravan."

"Yes, sir," the three men acknowledge in unison.

The three men galloped ahead as they turned back, but Wully held back a moment. He exhaled hard and leaned back on his horse, gazing up into the trees and letting the sun dance across his face, embracing the cool breeze. As he glanced ahead, in the distance, Wully could see the castle's peak in Stalbak; the sun shone off it like a great beacon. After a moment, he slowly turned to look into the woods; his men had just left his sight around the corner in the road.

"Something troubling you, young knight?" an elderly voice spoke out, breaking the silence.

Wully turned sharply, almost throwing himself off his horse in surprise. He quickly caught himself and drew his sword, "What is your business here?" The old man said nothing and remained unfazed. *Where did he come from?* Wully thought.

The old man had a long gray bread and had no weapon nor belongings save the clothes on his back and a wooden staff for walking. Wully could see the man's face and eyes through his hood. He felt forced to pause as he looked into them, he couldn't explain it, but the longer Wully looked into this man's eyes, the longer he wanted to.

The man's eyes were full of life, as were his face and other visible physical features. If he hadn't known better, Wully would've guessed that he was trying to appear older and worse for wear than he was. But his eyes, rich green emeralds that, while they held life and youthfulness to them, there was also a deep sense of knowledge in them. It was almost like these eyes had seen everything since the beginning.

"Your heart is troubled," the man said, ignoring Wully's question. "But even at the brink of great loss, your spirit remains strong."

"Sir?" Wully questioned.

"You are a good man, Wulfred Siggard. You will play your part well."

The captain's face went white. "Sir!" he tried more aggressively, but his voice was taken by the questions that ran through his mind. "As protector of the baroness of Frosbike, you will need to step aside."

The old man chuckled. "Yes, and you will be more devoted to that task than any other before the end." He stepped to the shoulder of the road. "No one here is in any danger from me. I will leave when I see her."

"Who?" Wully asked.

"The beginning of a cursed future," the man said quietly.

Before Wully could protest, the sound of the approaching soldiers and carriages overtook them. Wully glanced up to see his men rounding the corner, then turned back to the old man on the side of the road. He was gone.

Wully suspected a trap, he moved his gaze across the area in search of the man. Nothing. As the caravan reached Wully's location, one of the soldiers paused, "Is everything alright, sir?" Wully said nothing.

"Captain?" the soldier asked again.

"What?" Wully snapped quickly.

"Uh, yes." Clearing his throat and regaining his composure, he replied, "Yes, carry on."

The guard nodded and got back into his spot in line. Wully observed as the procession of troops and carriages paraded before him. Still thinking about the stranger who knew him. Then looking ahead again to the shimmering castle in the distance, Wully muttered to himself as if finishing his thought out loud, "It's nothing."

Chapter 6
It Was a Good Plan

Stelbeck Keep, the Coastal Outpost of Althalos, in Vasalia.

Collins scanned the area as the enemy assault team worked their way up the winding road from the beach. His men were ready; each man tucked into the rubble and along the top of what still stood of the southern wall, holding steady and waiting for his signal to let loose their arrows. As Collins glanced into the fort, he met Wilkins's gaze and nodded softly. The commander returned the gesture before turning his attention toward the city to the west.

Alkeroth had little time to prepare appropriately, and though they had greatly assisted during the initial siege, Collins wondered if they had enough fight left in them for what was coming. He watched as the city guard lined up along the city's edge near the fort. It was a simple, yet effective plan. Once the berserkers got close enough to the fort, Collins would have his men pin them down with arrows. Wilkins and his men would take on those that managed to get through the barrage of archers and the, albeit crudely, barricaded gate in the courtyard below. Finally, the city guard would flank the remainder of the attacking force, coming in from the rear.

Dark clouds hung over the fort and the city, which maintained a dreary feeling over the area. Collins looked down the road toward the river; the berserkers were charging up quickly but steadily. They wore lightly weighted, dark-colored armor with the red scorpion sigil on their chests. Small round shields were fixed to their left gauntlets, with large spikes protruding from the right. Fear began to set in as he watched the oncoming army.

Each man carried a short sword; their helmets were light with large eye openings. This was done as a scare tactic, which Collins had to acknowledge as he felt a tinge of fear as the red eyes of the berserkers got brighter when they approached. Collins' thoughts broke as he felt a tap against his thigh. "Yes, soldier?" he asked. The man didn't say anything in response, but his face gave Collins everything he needed to know. "We only need to hold them off till the drug wears off," he said, resting his hand on the man's shoulder. "By then, our help will come."

The soldier nodded sheepishly. A horn blast broke the sound of the marching men, and Collins and his sergeant's eyes snapped forward. The berserkers were closing in now. Collins gave Wilkins a final nod. Wilkins stared past the barricade to the oncoming horror, "Don't be ashamed. We're all scared. But we must be steady. Dig deep and find your courage!"

The south gate was only partially intact and had been reinforced with whatever the men could find to add additional support. The barricade is a mix of rubble, large boulders, bodies, and timbers piled up against the remnants of the gate. Wilkins's men stood silent behind him, waiting as the ground began to shake beneath their feet. Then he gave Collins a final nod of affirmation.

"Ready," Collins said firmly as he raised his left hand and waited momentarily. He wanted to ensure the most use out of the archers. "Fire!" Collins yelled, and he dropped his hand quickly. A volley of arrows rained down on the first wave of enemy troops as they approached the gate.

Dozens fell where they stood, making those behind slow down. Collins had his men ready for a second wave. Collins's hand signaled again as the next section of troops approached and climbed over their fallen comrades. Another large number of berserkers fell, adding to the pile-up at the base of the wall.

Behind the gate, Wilkins and all his men listened as the onslaught of berserkers took place outside. He peered through the partially damaged gate and smiled to himself; the plan was working—for the moment.

Collins breathed a quick sigh of relief as it seemed the berserker army would be stuck in the arrow storm. But his relief was cut short as the next wave of troops moved faster and harder, pushing through the fallen and injured in front of them. He quickly grabbed his bow, "Fire at will! Let the rain fall!"

All the archers took to their own as they fired arrow after arrow at the advancing troops. Several dozen more berserkers fell under the rain of arrows. But it wasn't enough. Many of the berserkers had taken two or three arrows and still charged forward since the drugs and cloth wrapping reduced most of their feelings of pain at the moment.

What initially looked like a smooth victory quickly turned against Stelbeck. Collins's men continued their barrage of arrows, but more took their place for every man they took down. They all watched in horror as the other charging men and injured berserkers pushed through the dead bodies of their fallen comrades.

The enemy widened their charge as the road in front of the gate filled up. Fear gripped Collins as he watched a group of men move to the eastern wall along the cliffside. If the wall were to be breached, that would be its weakest point. "Wilkins!" Collins cried out as he directed his aim to the advancing group. "The southeast corner!"

Whatever sense of victory Wilkins had felt was immediately gone, and he quickly set his archers to help deter the advancing berserkers. "Send a volley!" Wilkins yelled as he headed to the damaged part of the southern wall. He positioned himself in some of the rubble and watched his men's arrows do their job. Collins' archers over their part of the wall had already engaged the oncoming force. However, even combined with Wilkins' archers, the berserkers were not deterred. "Pour it on them!" Wilkins cried out as he unleashed several arrows into the advancing troops.

Admiral Mortem was stationed in the bow of his ship, watching intently as his men charged up the road from the beachhead. As he watched, a smile grew across his face. His men were making progress despite the countless dead and dying there, and the fort would soon be his. "Captain!" Mortem called out.

"Yes, sir," came the quick reply as Captain Lyso shuffled to the admiral's side.

"Give the signal," Admiral Mortem said with a smile. "Have the men break formation and push harder into the fort; we don't have time to waste with this pathetic game Wilkins thinks he can play."

Captain Lyso bowed low as a smile grew in response, "Yes, sir."

Wilkins had returned to the barricade gate to assist his men there. So far, only one or two of the berserkers had reached the barricade and tried to hurdle it, but Wilkins' men made quick work of them with their spears. However, the wall was starting to fail. The berserkers were piling up. Still, that didn't hinder them as much as Wilkins had hoped.

"Hold them here!" Wilkins called out as he made his way up to the top of the wall to meet Collins and assess his strategy.

A horn blast echoed across the area as Wilkins reached the top of the wall. "We're getting low on arrows, sir," Collins said as Wilkins came. Before Wilkins could respond, another horn blast swept through the area. Wilkins turned his head to the coastline and source of the sound.

"I think we're in trouble," the words barely got out of Wilkins's mouth when he and Collins realized what that horn meant.

The berserkers moved faster and split into two factions. The first wave pushed hard right up the middle of the road. This group was met with more resistance as they climbed over and plowed through the dead bodies advancing to the gate. The second wave came directly from the troops still positioned along the river. This group pushed through the trees and into the clearing around the fort pressing hard against the southeast corner.

Collins looked frantically at Wilkins, who was trying hard to hold his resolve, "Sir?" he questioned as he launched more arrows at the advancing men.

The sounds of the gate breaking could be heard below them. The archers above the broken part of the southeast corner were now engaging the enemy troops as the berserkers used each other to climb up over the rubble. Wilkins briefly dropped his head before responding, "We must hold a while before we call the others." Collins nodded in response and mustered himself as he encouraged the men with him.

As Wilkins reached the ground near the barricade, he stumbled back as the gate was finally breached. A lone berserker jumped through the opening at Wilkins, who went down in the tussle, taking a hard fist to his face. Wilkins shook off the impact as the berserker grabbed one of the nearest soldiers and pummeled the man into the ground.

One of the other archers dropped his bow and unsheathed his sword, immediately stabbing the berserker in the back. The berserker dropped to his knees, howling in pain. Wilkins then took his sword and stabbed him through the chest before pulling it out and, with a clean stroke, removing the berserker's head from his shoulders.

Upon the wall, the berserkers scrambled up the pile of rubble, rock, and dead bodies to reach the broken section and get into the fort. Collins and his archers continued to pick them off, but they kept pressing forward more and more. As he went for another arrow, he realized his quiver was empty. Then, seeing the enemy get through the weak spot on the southeast corner of the wall, "Swords, men!" he yelled out as he unsheathed his own and made his way across the border to assist the others.

Collins men dropped their bows and unsheathed their swords. As the berserkers continued to push over the broken section of wall, Collins' men clashed with the berserkers in a last futile attempt. The berserkers barreled right through them. Fear struck Collins and his men as the berserkers gained ground; injuring them didn't slow them, and they hit Collins' men like ragdolls, throwing them off the side of the wall.

Before long, the berserkers had also completely breached the barricaded gate and began to pour into the courtyard, immediately engaging Wilkins and his men. Wilkins directed his men to create a funnel to limit the onslaught as the enemy charged through them. For a moment, it seemed to work, "Wilkins!"

Collins's voice broke through the surrounding chaos. Wilkins cut down the berserker he had engaged before looking up at Collins, who was frantically trying to maintain the southeast corner of the wall.

Wilkins quickly redirected a handful of men to assist Collins, but it was too late. When the first few enemy troops got over the rubble, dozens more poured in. "Collins!" Wilkins called out as he cut down two more. "Sound the horn! Spring the trap!"

Collins didn't hesitate as he quickly chopped off the arm of a berserker who had one of his men by the throat, then, with a quick slash, decapitated the enemy as he pushed up to his original position. Once he reached his station, he quickly grabbed his horn and blew hard; the sharp sound brought a slight hesitation to the berserker force, which Wilkins and his men used to their advantage, striking down several more of the enemy troops in that instant. Another horn sounded in the distance; Wilkins and Collins both felt slightly excited as they knew then that city guards were in place and would move in to assist.

Collins looked out briefly to see the city guard force, approximately a hundred men, joined with another hundred or so of the city's reserve force. Collins watched as they marched in from the western edge of the town; following Wilkins's request, the troops moved up from the river to flank and subdue the berserker force.

The Vasalian men charged quickly, keeping their form in one large row. Armed with large pikes and full-body shields, they managed to pierce right through the berserker ranks and encircle them there. Relief swept over Collins and his men as they watched from the wall as the berserkers seemed cornered. Collins then called a few soldiers to join him as he headed to assist Wilkins in the courtyard.

"Collins," Wilkins said as he cut down another enemy troop. "How goes it with the reinforcements?"

"I think we may last out the day, sir."

Before Wilkins could respond, a giant berserker swinging a morning star instead of their usual short sword punched through, knocking two of Wilkins's men dead to the ground with one swing. Wilkins and Collins stepped back and braced themselves as the crazed berserker charged them, hitting a few more of Wilkins's men to the ground. Wilkins and Collins paused when they reached what was left of the eastern wall, which was now open to the sea.

Wilkins smiled at Collins as he glanced behind him; Collins understood, and as the berserker got close, he lunged at the men. Immediately as he jumped forward, Wilkins and Collins split to each side, letting the drug-crazed man jump off the cliff's edge. The men turned to watch their foe fall a few dozen fathoms to the rocky beach below. The men's relief turns to sudden despair as they realize that only part of the berserker force had left the beach initially, and now the rest of the army was quickly making their way up the road to reinforce the others.

Collins sighed, "They won't get here in time."

Wilkins glanced up a the Althalos flag in the northern tower; then he turned to look at Collins, "To the last man." Collins nodded, and the two men returned to the courtyard's center.

Admiral Mortem continued to watch the battle as best he could from his ship through the telescope; Captain Lyso stood nearby, waiting for further instructions.

"As I said," Mortem commented, "An enemy who doesn't give up. Admirable, but proven foolish."

"If they have pulled reinforcements from the city, I fear who else may be coming to help," Lyso said.

Admiral Mortem shot a questioning glance at his captain, "Your fears are misplaced, Lyso. He promised us the battle would be an easy victory," he said as he turned his gaze back inland. "A few extra bodies from Alkeroth or the rest of Vasalia isn't anything to worry about." A smug smile crept across Mortem's face, "It just means that we won't have to kill them later when we move to take Alkeroth itself."

"Yes, sir," Captain Lyso said as he bowed slightly. "Apologizes, sir."

Wilkins and Collins continued the fight; screams and cries of pain and death echoed throughout the fort and the city. The rest of the berserker force that came up from the beach punched through the city guard's flank and quickly headed into the city, leaving the remnants of Wilkins's men to continue fighting the ongoing barrage in the courtyard.

Wilkins looked around in desperation at his dying force, trying to devise a plan to minimize the loss. There was nothing to be had. The berserkers would completely overtake Stelbeck Keep before too long. It would likely be too late if additional aid were coming.

Chapter 7
Reinforcements

Admiral Mortem watched as the defense of the south wall was broken. The city's guard force had been taken over, and the berserkers began to ransack the town. From what he could see through the demolished eastern wall, it appeared to Mortem that Wilkins's men within the fort would also soon be overtaken.

A smile sat wide on his face as he continued to watch the fighting that ensued. Body parts of Wilkins's men could be seen thrown around as his troops more directly engaged. A few of Carnheller's troops had made it up the northern tower in a crazed attempt to kill the men there and dismantle the flagpole, removing the flag of Althalos in the process. A demoralizing move, there was no real power in removing the flag, but Admiral Mortem liked to show his enemies that their hope was lost before utterly destroying those who were left.

After a while, Admiral Mortem called out, "Captain Lyso."

"Yes, sir," Captain Lyso responded quickly as he came up from the main deck.

"How long has it been?"

"Nearly two hours, sir," Lyso answered.

Admiral Mortem smiled again, "Prepare the infantry. The battle is nearly won." Lyso acknowledged his orders and immediately set about his tasks. Mortem's gaze remained fixed on Stelbeck. He knew that his berserkers would soon work through their drug-induced adrenaline rush, so whatever remained of Wilkins's men at that time needed to be dealt with. *Let's not give them a fighting chance now,* he thought.

Most of the longboats that dropped the berserkers on shore had returned to their respective ships and were immediately reloaded with the rest of Carnheller's infantry. While significantly less in total number than the berserker force. These men were better armored than their berserker counterparts and were undrugged, as they were used to clean up after the berserkers had done their part.

Mostly comprised of chainmail and leather, each soldier was armed with a small dark shield, the bright red scorpion sigil painted on the center to match their small chest plates. Each man had a helmet that covered their entire face and a short sword at their hip with a spear in their hand. As the men were taken to shore in the longboats, they were calm and collected, very different from the raging howls and grunts of the berserkers. Tough and rugged, even though these men usually only came in near the end of a confrontation, they were still expert killers.

Wilkins continued his fight near the eastern wall of the fort. Using the rubble and cliffside to his advantage, he held his own against the oncoming hoard. As he cut down another berserker, Wilkins looked around the fort; most of his men were dead, already weakened by the night before and prior injuries; they were no match for the brutality of the enemy force.

Wilkins glanced at Collins, who had just beheaded another enemy troop on the southern wall. He was relieved that his friend was still alive; his armor was gouged and dented, blood soaked into his fabric, staining the white and blue colors he wore. Wilkins checked himself and noticed that he was no different.

"Wilkins!" Collins's voice rang out, breaking his thoughts. "We're not going to make it."

Wilkins gathered his strength and braced himself as he looked around. The fort was almost entirely taken. Then he looked up at the berserkers who reached the flag, then around the courtyard, "Follow me."

With Collins on his heels, Wilkins shoved his way past everyone to reach the tower stairs. Then Wilkins felt a sharp pain in his head, which caused him to fall. "Wilkins!" Collins's voice could be heard over the screams and yells of everyone else. The commander collected his wits as Collins pulled him up to keep him from getting trampled. On the ground where Wilkins fell was the body of one of his men.

Together, the men continued to press through the slaughter. It was slow going as each man would fall to the ground numerous times, getting beaten and crushed before finally reaching the northern wall. The two men barely got to catch their breath before a lone berserker came out of the fight and charged them. Wilkins blocked the initial strike as Collins thrust his sword into his body, making the berserker fall.

"Was it just me, or did it go down easy?" Collins asked quickly.

Wilkins looked around, briefly noticing that his men were now gaining ground, and the berserkers seemed to be moving slower, "They're getting tired. The drug is only good for a few hours." He then looked at the tower steps, "Let's go."

Collins followed as they ascended the stairs to the tower. As they reached the first open floor, Wilkins looked over the battlefield. The ground was covered outside the southern wall as the berserkers lay dead from the archers earlier. To the west, smoke rose from parts of the city as the berserker force pressed past the city guards' position and further into Alkeroth. To his left, Wilkins looked out through the remnants of the eastern wall to the sea.

Wilkins dropped his head; he had forgotten that the standard infantry always followed the berserkers with Carnheller's battle tactic. Whatever hope they had quickly left as more longboats were bringing additional men ashore. Collins stepped up and put his hand on his shoulder. "And if this is the end?"

Wilkins looked out at the water again, then up at the side of the tower to the flag above them. "Then it will be our greatest."

Collins nodded in approval, "Let's do it."

Together both men charged up the staircase to the top of the tower. Wilkins took the lead as they reached the top, cutting through the berserkers still on the stairs. Collins leaped out from behind, and after dismembering one of the other berserkers, he quickly sliced through, removing his head. The final soldier lunged at Collins, but Wilkins intercepted with a body shove against the edge wall, sending the berserker down to the courtyard below.

Several of the berserkers down on the ground saw the falling comrade, and as quickly as he hit the ground, they charged up the tower. Wilkins smirked at Collins, "Well, I suppose they can't make it easy for us."

Collins chuckled as he turned, poised and ready to face the threat. The overall space was small, but Wilkins and Collins figured they had a better chance of staying where they were than trying to fight back down. "It's been an honor, my friend," Wilkins said.

Howls of the oncoming berserkers could be heard echoing up the hollow tower stairs. Collins smiled softly and bowed his head, "Captain."

Wilkins gripped his sword with both hands and held it to his head. Collins did the same next to him. When the berserkers reached the top step, they clashed. Wilkins and Collins quickly made short work of the initial rush. They were using the steep staircase and the exhaustion of the berserkers to throw them off balance. They either cut them down or shoved them over the side of the tower to fall to their death in the courtyard below.

After a few minutes, one of the berserkers managed to get onto the tower platform. He swung frantically as the men did their best to defend themselves from the others that made their way up the stairs. Wilkins finally broke free, cut down the berserker he was engaged with, and rushed at the other, trying to remove the flag.

Wilkins clashed with the giant berserker while Collins maintained his position at the top of the stairwell. During the fight, Wilkins took a fist to his face, which knocked him down, causing him to lose his grip on his sword. The berserker reached for the flagpole, breaking it off near the base. Still dazed and exhausted, Wilkins tried to shake off the disorientation.

The berserker stepped forward and raised his arms to drive the pole down into Wilkins's chest. Wilkins braced for an impact, but before it happened, a shriek of pain came from the berserker as he grabbed his leg. Wilkins saw that Collins had thrown his knife before re-engaging his foe. Using this moment, Wilkins reached out and grabbed his sword and plunged it through the gut of the giant berserker.

The flagpole fell out of his hands as the berserker dropped to his knees before collapsing completely. Wilkins grabbed the knife and assisted Collins in slaying the last of the enemy that had been in the stairwell. Here, the two men continued to hold them off, covered in blood and almost drained of their energy, Wilkins and Collins either drove the berserkers back down the stairs by using the recently slain to assist, or they pressed until they drove the enemy troop off the side of the tower.

After what felt like an eternity, Wilkins and Collins had beaten back the remaining berserker force trying to take the tower. Wilkins breathed a sigh of relief as the last body fell to the ground below, and Collins chuckled a little. "I really thought…we weren't going to make it," Collins said between breaths.

"Well," Wilkins chuckled, "We still have to finish the ones down there," he said, gesturing to the ground below.

Collins nodded, "Sure, but…" he took a deep breath. "Can we take a break first?"

Wilkins didn't respond as he picked up the flagpole that had fallen to the ground. Collins took the cue and began pulling out the broken end still nestled in the placement within the tower floor. Once Collins removed it, Wilkins limped over and slid the pole back into its home. "Sir," Collins inquired. "Your leg?"

Wilkins shrugged, "Oh, I'll be alright," and gestured to the fallen berserker at the tower's edge, "Bastard kicked my knee out."

Collins sighed, "The other rider won't be out of Vasalia until morning. Even if Ivan sends help, it'll be too late for us."

Wilkins stepped up next to Collins and looked out over the sea. The sun was finally starting to break through the cloud cover that had lingered over the area since the fleet arrived. "This army may get past us," he said grimly. "But their advance will be stopped. King Leoxtra won't give up. Besides," Wilkins gestures to the countless dead enemy troops around them. "There's not much left."

Collins chuckled softly and gestured out to the oncoming force from the sea, "How many of them do you think we can take?"

Wilkins followed Collins's gaze but then paused before answering, "Wait," he said after a moment. "Did you hear that?"

Collins turned around, trying to find what Wilkins supposedly heard, "No, what?" as quickly as he finished, the sound came over the city. "Wait, yes. What is that?"

Wilkins smiled, "Reinforcements."

"King Leoxtra?"

Wilkins held his smile as he looked out over the western wall, and there, coming through the city, was King Leoxtra and his army on horseback. Moving through the city, they aided the soldiers and quickly worked out what was left of the army there.

Admiral Mortem watched intently as his men were being sent ashore when Captain Lyso stepped up to address him, "Captain?" he questioned.

"Sir," Lyso said, standing at attention. Then, pointing to the tower in the fort, "Look."

Admiral Mortem followed Lyso's gesture and observed Wilkins placing the flag back upright. "It matters not," he said as he brought his gaze back to the other troops headed for shore. "Victory is still ours."

"Captain!" Collins cried out as they were about to descend the tower stairs. Wilkins didn't respond but continued to limp down the stairs. "Captain, look!"

Wilkins paused and turned back to see what Collins had been pointing at. *Wind*, Wilkins thought to himself. Since the land battle had begun, he hadn't paid it much thought, but as he stood there, he waited, and sure enough, a soft breeze was pushing through the area. The flag of Althalos, though tattered and torn, was swaying gently in the draft.

Wilkins laughed and quickly limped up the few steps and across to the far end of the tower. Collins quickly followed, eager to see what Wilkins was excited about. It didn't take long for both men to see it. A massive wave of relief swept over them as they watched; just coming into view from around the cliffside was the full might of the Vasalian fleet coming across the water.

Admiral Mortem stood poised as he had been all morning. When suddenly, a cry came out from one of the adjacent ships. It wasn't long before the admiral noticed a panic moving through his men. "Captain! Report!"

Captain Lyso didn't respond immediately as he and his men were frantically panicking as the Vasalian fleet came into view. "Move the ships out!" Lyso called out to his first lieutenant, "We've got to draw their attack away from the longboats."

"Captain Lyso!"

"Sir!" Lyso said as he hurried past Mortem, pointing to the north.

Admiral Mortem followed his gesture until he saw the fleet himself: "No, no!"

"Admiral, what are your orders?" Captain Lyso asked.

"He won't let us get away with backing down."

"Sir?"

Admiral Mortem's jaw tightened, "Fight to the last man," he snapped. As Captain Lyso hurried about with the others, Admiral Mortem returned his gaze to the fort. That's when he noticed it; the cloud cover was receding, and the sunlight was getting brighter. Screams of pain and explosions in the water broke the admiral away from his thoughts.

The Vasalian fleet had already engaged his own. Several of the longboats had already disappeared beneath the water. Vasalia's fleet launched several catapult attacks using smaller groups of stone, shattering the ships on impact. His victory was hopeless now, and he had to face whatever punishment for failure awaited him. "Captain, Lyso!"

"Yes, sir!"

"We have to retreat," Mortem said earnestly, "Turn the fleet around."

"Admiral," Lyso began to say, and the ship before them took a direct hit. "They're already encircling us; we have nowhere to go!" Admiral Mortem looked at the enemy fleet and saw that they were forming a single file line, circling the other side of the Carnheller fleet to prevent them from returning to open waters.

King Leoxtra and his general moved through Alkeroth quickly with their troops. With the berserker men near the end of their drug-induced run, they were of little consequence for the horse-mounted force. Though few men were left, Wilkins and his team held their own in the fort courtyard. The berserkers were slowing down, which made their movements sloppy.

When the enemy force realized they would lose, they rushed for the beach. Those that got past Wilkins's men and the mounted cavalry of King Leoxtra were met with a disheartening sight as the fleet of Carnheller was all but destroyed and surrounded.

As the berserkers left Stelbeck Keep, Wilkins surveyed the carnage surrounding him. Still limping, Wilkins walked over to the eastern wall and breathed a sigh of relief at the sight. Carnheller's ships were taken, and the sun shone brightly now that the clouds had left.

"Guess we made it after all." Wilkins turned as Collins's voice came from behind.

Wilkins smiled again and glanced at the tower's flag, "Indeed we did."

Chapter 8
The King's Stag

The King's Stag Inn and Tavern, Stalbak, Althalos

Oswald and Aldrich walked into the tavern entrance. A notable inn and tavern of its type that sat just outside the castle walls in Stalbak. It was a pleasant place for anyone who dined or utilized its other services. But the primary purpose and the reason it was so popular was that this tavern catered to the nobility of the castle. The King's Stag, it was called.

Usually, the royal family stayed within castle walls. However, the castle's staff, guards, and guests often wandered out, searching for a more regular and down-to-earth setting. So, it came as no surprise to the people within the tavern, nor the staff when one of the generals and the prince walked through the front doors.

"Hey! Ha-ha!" A tall, lanky, yet muscular figure called out above the rest of the crowd as the two men entered the inn. "My friends!" Oswald immediately piped up and smiled big as he gestured to the prince to follow him.

"Looks like someone started the party without us, eh Thomas?" Oswald asked sarcastically. Thomas was one of Oswald's good friends and technically subordinate since Thomas was more commonly known as Captain Fendrell, lead captain of the King's Army, serving under General Oswald.

Thomas slammed his empty tankard on the table and smiled big, "Maybe?" Oswald joined in the laughter and pulled out the seat at the table, gesturing for the prince to sit as well. Oswald was more prominent than Thomas in size and stature, though that didn't deter any fear of the man. Despite his appearance with his messy sandy blond hair and matching colored stubble now growing on his face combined with his drunken state, Oswald knew as well as the prince that Thomas was a formidable fighter.

In all reality, Captain Fendrell was thought to be slipping into some kind of insanity. This, of course, was just rumors through the ranks of his men. But Oswald knew to take it seriously since the incident in their last war together where Oswald watched the horror of an ambush gone wrong which led to the burning of the Great River, where then General Fendrell lost several of his men due to the cowardice of a few. Oswald had grown up with Thomas since they were little, and both had seen their fair share of bloodshed at an early age. But as the years went on, Oswald was always cautious with Thomas and worried about the toll the wars took on his mental state, especially since his demotion from that incident after watching most of his men burn to death.

As the waitress brought a pint for Thomas' guests, he raised his glass, "Tonight, my friends, we shall drink until the dawn takes us." A smile grew across his face as he finished. "Or the drink does." Oswald and Aldrich raised their glasses and laughed.

As the night went on, the tavern got more crowded and louder as more wedding guests arrived at the castle. As he scanned the crowd, Aldrich wondered if every place was as packed as this one. Wanting to let off some steam and relax after their respective trips, it was not uncommon that places like this would be filled up and busy tonight.

Later that evening, Aldrich began to feel more and more wasted as he downed pint after pint. When Aldrich chugged the most recent one, Oswald pulled the tankard away from the prince, "Okay, I think you may have had enough of this now."

"Exactly what I was thinking," Thomas exclaimed through his slightly slurred speech. He stood to wave down the waitress. As he did so, he ended up falling back on the table the three men were seated at, causing a loud uproar of laughter from those that saw it. However, this commotion got the waitress's attention, so Thomas counted it as an intentional action.

As the waitress approached, Oswald was already protesting since he knew what the captain was planning. "No, Thomas."

"Stop babying the damn boy," Thomas said as he carefully seated himself back in his chair. He grabbed Oswald's shoulder and gestured to the prince, still grasping the empty tankard. "Look at him." Oswald turned his face away from Thomas with sharp disdain as his foul breath hit Oswald's nose like a brick wall. Thomas wasn't fazed by this and continued, "Raised in a palace. Tortured with many years of bitter wine and fine champagne."

Oswald gently removed Thomas from his personal space, "I'm fairly certain those are the same thing."

Thomas took the hint and leaned back in his chair, "Most likely. But what a sad, sad existence," he said as he shook his head sarcastically. Aldrich said nothing and just stared at Thomas with slight amusement. Perhaps, Aldrich thought, *I should get everyone drunk around me. Find out how they really feel.*

"But tonight!" Thomas exclaimed suddenly, surprising the group. "He tastes the drink of the common man!" He turned his gaze to the waitresses who had come over to check on the commotion after Thomas' incident. "My usual," he tells her, holding up three fingers. "The Fendrell Special."

The waitress gave Thomas a flirtatious smile, and Thomas gave her a quick wink with his cheeky grin in response.

"Oh, shit," Oswald muttered as he dropped his head.

"What?"

"He still needs to be able to walk tomorrow, Thomas," Oswald said, gesturing to the prince. "That's what."

"And he will," Thomas said, still laughing. "He just won't know what hit him for the next…eh…several hours." Oswald couldn't tell if Thomas was being facetious or genuinely thought the young prince could handle his concoction after all the beer he'd already had.

The waitress poured three steins of beer almost to the top, then dropped in some more potent liquor until each was full. As she set them down in front of the gentlemen, Thomas gave her another cheeky smile. "Thanks, love. I'll come to see you later for the other 'usual'." As she walked away.

Thomas reached back and gave her a playful smack on the rear end, and she giggled playfully before walking back to the bar. "I'll be looking forward to it as always, Thomas," she said, walking away.

"Hey, what did I say last time?"

The waitress paused, turned back to the table, and bowed in a mocked curtsy, "My humblest apologies." She stood, giving a mock salute, "Captain."

Thomas chuckled, and the waitress, still smiling playfully, turned and resumed her duties. "See you then, love," Thomas said, raising his glass toward her. As he turned back to the table, Thomas caught Oswald's look of disdain.

"What?" Oswald shook his head, and Aldrich stared blankly at the two. "I prefer to use my rank when I'm out in the field." Thomas finished in what Oswald could only guess was a poor attempt at seriousness. When Oswald rolled his eyes, Thomas scoffed and turned his attention to Aldrich, "You ready?" then more sarcastically, "My lord?"

Aldrich nervously stared at the oddly colored mystery drink in horror that was before him. "What's in it?"

Thomas brought his own pint up to his lips, "Paradise."

"You must be drunk if you think I'm drinking that," Aldrich complained.

Thomas set his mug down and laughed, "Oh, my dear sweet prince." He slid the drink closer to Aldrich, "I'm always drunk." Thomas leaned back in his seat, "Besides," he continued. "I think you are drunk enough that you will."

Oswald sighed, and he pulled his drink closer to him. "I'm going to need to pregame this." He prompted the waitress to bring a mug of standard ale, which he chugged to completion in one breath despite the trickle of excess running over the sides of his mouth. As he finished, Oswald slammed the smaller tankard on the table and belched loudly, "Okay. I'm ready."

Oswald picked his tankard up. He and Thomas both look at Aldrich. The prince slowly picked up his mug to match their toast, "To being a married man, I guess…"

Thomas pressed first, clashing the mugs together, "To the end of a man's freedom." The crowd watched intently as the three men showed their might in this battle of the constitution. Thomas was the first to set his mug down, empty. Oswald wasn't far behind, and the two men burped loudly. Aldrich tried to give up after about two-thirds of his drink and began pulling the mug back, but Thomas quickly reacted. "Oh no, you don't, you cheeky bastard."

Thomas quickly leaned forward and forced the mug upwards and thus forcing Aldrich to swallow the rest of the drink, laughing hard as he did so. It didn't go quite as planned, however, as the prince partially swallowed it, but when he pulled away, Aldrich sloppily spat a good portion of it back up all over himself and the table. Thomas then rolled with laughter so hard he nearly fell over and had to use Oswald for support.

"Ugh," Aldrich stammered while coughing vigorously. "Asshole."

Oswald joined in the laughter with Thomas and roughly slapped Aldrich on the back to ease the coughing, which only made Aldrich vomit into his mouth, nearly losing everything a second time. Thankfully, Aldrich would retain his composure and keep himself from making a mess as he wiped the runoff from his face. After he calmed down, the prince began to join in, and laughed with the other two.

After the three calmed down, Oswald leaned onto the table, "You know. Even though you'll be a married man, my friend, and one day a king, I hope you never forget us little folk and this glorious tavern."

Aldrich leaned in, "Well if the stories from the women around here are even close to the truth. Then you, my friend, are no little man." He finished as he gestured to Oswald's pants.

"Oswald?" Thomas burst out. "Ha-ha. What woman told you that?"

"I'll have you know I've seen my fair share," Oswald stated defensively.

"Oh, yeah?" Thomas questioned. "Give me a name," he winked at Aldrich before continuing. "I probably know her and all her sisters."

As Thomas laughed at his joke, Oswald said, "Yeah, I bet you're really proud of your escapades."

"I most certainly am, General," Thomas said now that his laughter had subsided. "I most certainly am."

"Yes, well, unlike you. I pick my moments."

"So do I," Thomas said. "It just so happens that I pick…every moment." The three men laughed together for a time, and the conversation carried a few topics as the night went on.

As Aldrich began to sober up, he used the conversation break to comment, "In all seriousness though…"

Thomas slapped Oswald's shoulder and joked, "Shh, shut up, Oswald. The prince is getting serious." Aldrich sat in silence as Thomas laughed off his mock and then tried to force a stern expression which only made him laugh more.

Oswald finally calmed Thomas, and the two men listened as the prince continued, "I couldn't forget this place…or these people. Any of them." He softly gestures around the tavern, "They helped raise me."

Thomas nodded in agreement, "That I did." Then he raised his tankard to his lips only to find it empty. Waving down the waitress again, he yells, "Another!"

Oswald, ignoring Thomas, leaned in closer to Aldrich and put his hand on his shoulder, "I hope so, my friend. I hope so."

Aldrich nodded and smiled in return. He understood the importance of their primarily unseen and often misunderstood friendship, as did Oswald. "Well," Aldrich finally says, breaking the awkward silence. "I need to piss," he said as he very clumsily got out of his seat.

He stumbled but held his own as he wobbled to the door. *Ugh, Thomas.* Aldrich thought as he paused to rub his head. *I think whatever was in the drink is starting to hit me.*

"Hey, Aldrich," Thomas' voice echoed over the crowd. Aldrich was, for a moment, thinking he had muttered his thoughts out loud and was going to get a sassy comment in return. As he carefully turned back to face the table, Thomas chuckled and said, "You might want to go out back instead."

Oswald was intrigued and looked around at what Thomas might be referring to. As his eyes fixed upon the same thing that Thomas saw, Oswald joined the captain in laughter. "What?" Aldrich questioned, slightly annoyed and still very drunk.

The tavern got quiet. Aldrich turned around to see Merrek standing in the doorway; his face was rigid. Aldrich looked him in the eyes for a few seconds, realizing what was happening. Then, before he could stop it, the prince vomited all over the floor between him and Merrek. Merrek's gaze methodically studied Aldrich up and down. *What a pitiful sight,* Merrek thought as he watched in disgust; *I can't believe this slob is marrying my sister.*

"Merrek!" Thomas roared, breaking the silence. "Come on in. Let me buy you a drink!"

Chapter 9
Family Secrets

Castle Stalbak, Althalos

Aldrich's head was still throbbing slightly from the previous evening's events. It took two additional servants and several extra minutes to get him cleaned up and fit into his ceremonial outfit this morning. After which, Aldrich headed to his father's study for some peace and quiet from the bustling chaos of the rest of the castle in their final wedding preparations.

The sun shone through the partially stained-glass window as he sat his crown on the desk. The rays danced across Aldrich's chainmail shirt; each link glistened brightly as the light hit it. The ceremonial outfit was more decorative than practical; however, it was still a sure way to stop a sword. Made of almost pure lavianite, Aldrich's chainmail shirt had a blueish hue under soft light. But when the sun hit it directly, it refracted the light like glass which gave way to all sorts of colors that would reflect off it.

White pants with black dress boots polished to a shine. The chainmail was woven together with blue and white colored linens, which allowed the clothing to be better fitted. His short Auditore cape was across his left shoulder as it often was, but today it was fastened with golden clasps in the shape of crowns. His hair was tied back against his neck with a golden ribbon, and his white gloves were tucked into his belt.

Aldrich stood tall and proud, staring continuously at the golden sword above the mantel. The pain in his head returned sharply, causing Aldrich to pinch the bridge of his nose and rub his temples. Breaking his thoughts momentarily, Aldrich wandered around the room casually, fiddling with the fit of his clothes.

His fingers grazed across the books on the shelf as he walked past, pausing only after he reached the map table in the center of the room. He studied the maps for a few minutes before the pain in his head came back. Taking a deep breath and shaking off the throbbing headache, he stepped before the fireplace and fixed his eyes on the Golden Sword.

He couldn't tell if it was fear or curiosity, but the more Aldrich looked at it, the more he became drawn to and afraid of it. He stepped closer, almost pulled to it. He couldn't tell if he had finally recovered from his hangover or was numb. It was of little consequence. *Why does my father fear using you anymore? Are you not the most powerful weapon in the realm?* Aldrich's thoughts echoed in his head, almost as if he was expecting the sword to answer. As he stepped closer, an energy reverberated off the blade. Was it calling him? Did it hear his questions?

Before any thought or reason passed his mind, Aldrich, as if guided, reached up and grabbed the sword off the stand. Immediately he felt a force in him, moving unseen yet powerful. After a moment, Aldrich smiled as he suddenly felt better and stronger. He swung the sword playfully as he stepped around the room. With each swing, Aldrich felt the sword radiate energy almost as if it was connected to himself. The sword felt weightless yet swung with such force that he felt he could break a hundred men.

Aldrich stopped swinging the sword around and looked at the pure reflection on the broad side of the blade. As he twisted the sword in his hand, the reflection showed Ivan standing in the doorway behind him. "What are you doing?" Ivan asked firmly. Aldrich turned around, startled. "What have I told you about that sword?"

"Father, I…"

Ivan stepped forward and held out his hand; Aldrich sighed as he bowed his head and hesitantly presented the sword to his father. As Ivan took it, he paused; Aldrich brought his head back up and looked at his father, who was looking at the sword. *Sadness?* He thought to himself, *or was it fear?*

Ivan was dressed in his best ceremonial dress. But as a king his outfit was much more elaborate, with decorative gold chains and lavianite woven into the fabric of his tunic and pants. His full-length cape today differed from the one he wore for regular occasions. The colors were brighter, and the central golden crown was gold mixed with lavianite around the edges. He wore his standard crown over his tightly bound hair, secured by a gold ribbon-like his son behind his neck. The crown looked more polished than usual.

Ivan placed the sword back on the mantle, and as he stepped back, he breathed heavily. Aldrich noticed but said nothing. Perhaps the blade is heavy for those who are not worthy of it. This thought made the prince smile slightly. Then seeing if he could get some information from his father, he asked plainly, "Why do you fear it?"

"Only those who've never seen war crave it. A misguided view of glory that doesn't actually exist," Ivan said, still facing the mantle. Then he glanced over his shoulder, "You don't understand, Aldrich," he sighed, and turned back to face the sword, "My hope is that you never have to."

"Understand what?" Aldrich asked. Ivan didn't respond. He waited silently, patiently at first, then grew more annoyed. Oswald and Thomas had told Aldrich the war stories they were involved in with King Ivan.

He couldn't dispute his father's exploits and how they had helped the kingdom greatly over the years. For this reason, Aldrich maintained a small level of respect for his father. However, his secrets and recent behavior have started to pick at him. The longer it went on, the more and more he couldn't wait to be out of his father's shadow and make his own legacy.

If he were ever to say anything now, Aldrich would've been dismissed. Even Oswald and Thomas, as much as they supported him, supported the king more. Aldrich knew this; he also knew that if he would ever have the full support of any decision he made as king, his father would have to be gone.

Ivan turned to face his son squarely now. Aldrich was almost taken aback by his father's sudden change in countenance. Ivan's serious and nearly sad features when he first arrived were gone. His face was brighter, and a full smile was across it. "I heard you had a fun night."

"Father, I'm sorry," Aldrich began to stammer, still catching up to his father's quick change in attitude. "I made a fool of myself. I understand that with times like these," he dropped his head. "That I can be a disappointment to you."

"No," Ivan interjected. He stepped up and put both his hands on his son's shoulders. "No, my son. You are a young man. It would not be right to view your young behavior as shameful. As a prince, I had my fair share of drunken exploits; just ask your uncle." Ivan chuckled as he stepped back.

After regaining his composure, he continued, "Your grandfather was… well, he was quite harsh. I've tried to be better than that, to raise you better than that. But today…today is the next step. And I need you to be better. Better than him. Better than me. Better than yourself," he quieted and stepped in close. "Take what you've learned from me and make it better, don't relive my mistakes and never follow in my footsteps; learn from where I've been so you can walk a better path than the one before it."

Aldrich's posture changed slightly. He slowly stood straight and rolled his shoulders back, giving his father a proud smirk. This was a side of his father that Aldrich rarely saw.

"So, be better than you," he commented. "Got it."

Ivan laughed, "Now, don't get cocky with me, son," he said as he waved a finger in Aldrich's face before brushing a strand of hair falling out behind his son's ear. "You should get your crown; it's almost time."

Aldrich turned to the desk, grabbed the crown sitting there, and sat it on his head. "How do I look, Father?"

Ivan scanned him up and down and thought for a brief moment. His face fell slightly as if suddenly lost in deep thought. He quickly recovered and replied, "Fine, Aldrich. Just fine." Ivan's tone changed again, trying to lighten the mood. "So, how do you feel about the wedding? Excited? Worried? Nervous?"

"All of the above?" Aldrich responded questioningly.

Ivan smiled as he patted him on the shoulder, "Well, that is to be expected. Come now," he said as he led them out of the room. "We mustn't keep anyone waiting."

Chapter 10
Forbidden Love

Castle Stalbak, Althalos

Laura was standing in front of the window of her room, which faced east, overlooking the city. In the distance, she could see the faint outline of the distinctive purple mountains that lined the bordering country of Vasalia. The sunlight danced across the cityscape, each ray of light more beautiful than the last as they refracted and beamed beautiful colors across the entire view.

It would take some transitioning, *but I could get used to it.* Laura thought to herself as the handmaidens continued to work on her dress and appearance. Laura was significantly thinner than they had initially anticipated, so it took some extra effort to make sure the seams fit correctly. During the process, Laura apologized a few times, but the handmaidens insisted it was fine. To which Laura finally conceded.

Truthfully, Laura didn't know if she had given them the wrong size beforehand or if she had lost weight since then. She and Merrek hadn't been able to eat as well as they were previously accustomed to, partially due to the family debts and the loss of their land but also in part due to the stress of the current events. The title of Baroness was mere that to her anymore; King Haldair still needed regional leaders, so Merrek and Laura would still do their jobs. However, everything was given to them as an allowance as the family debt was paid to the king. Having her family's debts finally paid in full and allowing her brother to rule as a proper baron was something that Laura viewed as a more than fair exchange for her hand in marriage.

Apart from the early apologies, Laura remained quiet and steadily stared out her window at the view. After a moment, she began to think of Wully and her home, and before she could stop it, tears were already softly falling from her eyes. *Maybe I won't get used to this after all, she thought.*

"Are you alright, Milady?" One of the maids asked when she noticed the tears.

Laura quickly wiped her face, "Yes," she smiled and faced the maid kindly, "Yes. I'm afraid I was lost in thought, and the sun made my eyes water." The maid nodded and resumed her business, arranging the bust of the dress on Laura.

Laura turned away from the window to glance at the wall mirror. Upon seeing her reflection, a sense of pride and admiration came across her face that surprised Laura. She had not gotten a good look at herself since the preparations began earlier that morning. But now, the pure white dress form-fitted her figure. The fabric was woven with lavianite in decorative swirls that started down the train and worked up to her waist. The swirls became more intricate there as they wrapped around her torso and across her chest, finally meeting the shoulder straps seamlessly. These shoulder straps were wide, covering her shoulders completely, and were made of pure lavianite.

Her light-colored hair was intricately braided in several small braids on the sides of her head and connected to one large braid running from the top down the middle to her shoulders. A small lavianite tiara was tucked under the braids, making it seem like part of her head. White flowers were woven throughout, a silver jeweled necklace around her neck, and white matching gloves pulled up over her elbows.

A knock at the door broke Laura's thoughts, and she regained her strong composure and resumed her previous gaze out the window in front of her. "Come in."

"We should never have agreed to this," Merrek said as he entered the room purposefully; Wully was silently on his heels. "The man is a blundering fool." He stopped as he reached the middle of the room. Laura was in no mood to argue again and kept her gaze outside.

After several moments of silence, Wully finally stepped up and whispered to Merrek, "Leave her be. She's going through enough."

Merrek ignored Wully's comment and stepped closer to Laura, "Where have you been all morning?"

Laura turned and gestured sarcastically to the maids around her, "Where do you think? And why do you care?"

Merrek responded with a puzzled look, "This shouldn't have taken that long. Other things need attending to this morning before the ceremony."

Laura rolled her eyes and turned back to the window, "Merrek," she said firmly. Her tone surprised her brother; she had never used her authoritative voice with him before. "The dress required several last-minute alterations, which was easier done with me. I'm sure you and King Ivan can figure it out independently, whatever else needs to be done. I can't do everything for you."

"Laura," the word almost didn't make it out of his mouth. It could've been the tone. It could've been seeing his sister in this beautiful setting, maybe even sadness for what was coming. Perhaps it was all three, but Merrek suddenly felt ashamed, whatever the reason. His sister stood before him like a fine work of art, glistening in the sunlight like everything in Stalbak.

Laura bowed her head to hide her expression. Merrek waved away the handmaidens, who took the cue and left the room. Laura softened as the firm hand of her brother lifted her face to meet his. "My dear, dear sister."

"I can do this, Merrek. We can do this," another tear fell from Laura's eye.

Merrek opened his arms to Laura, and the two embraced in a long silent hug. As they pull away, Merrek felt tears forming in his eyes. He quickly blinked and inhaled to hold it in. Laura saw it but didn't say anything, only smiled and kissed his cheek.

"I'll wait outside while you finish up," Merrek said as he walked away. "And I'll make sure that everything else is done. The ceremony is about to begin."

"Thank you, Merrek," Laura's soft voice sank in deep as Merrek reached the door.

Merrek stopped before exiting and turned to Laura, "You are truly the most beautiful sight today, sister." He sighed softly. "I wish I could've seen you like this under better circumstances… Aldrich doesn't deserve you."

Before leaving, Merrek looked at Wully, standing next to the door since the handmaidens left. The two locked their eyes for a moment; neither one said anything. Merrek and Wully had never openly discussed it, but they knew each other well enough that they didn't need to. Merrek knew of Wully's desire to be with his sister. Wully knew that Merrek knew that as well.

Merrek's eyes glanced back at his sister and then at Wully, "Stay with her," he finally said. Wully nodded, and with that, Merrek left the room.

Wully and Laura stood in silence for a while. Laura's gaze never left the window, and Wully never moved from where he had been near the door. After some time, Wully decided it might be best for him to leave and stepped forward to give his formal farewell, "I should," he stammered a bit as he spoke, "I should probably get going then." It took a moment, but Wully managed to muster up the courage to finish. "I will see you at the ceremony," he finished so fast as he turned away, even though he could barely understand himself.

"No!" Wully stopped and turned around; Laura turned to face him. "I don't want to be alone."

Wully's composure softened, "I'm sorry, Milady," he said almost painfully. "I'm sorry this burden has to be yours to bear."

"I knew this was in my future from a young age. Eventually, I would be married off to someone of strong nobility." Laura turned to look out the window again, and Wully stepped beside her.

"Noble blood, sure," Wully said. "But I believe nobility comes from a person's character and not their heritage."

Laura laughed, "You've been spending too much time with my brother."

Wully chuckled in response, "Perhaps, but are we wrong?" Laura gave him a smirk, and he continued. "If I am to be compared to anyone, Merrek would be an honor." Wully turned to face Laura, "Your brother is a good man with good intentions, even if his emotions sometimes cloud it."

Laura touched his cheek as she stepped closer to the window. Wully looked in awe as the sunlight shone off her dress, giving remarkable clarity to her already sharp features. "Our father was a good man, too good, actually. That's how he accumulated all his debts, and sadly we must suffer for it."

"I wish things could be different, Milady…"

Laura turned around sharply, but her face was full of sadness and love, "You don't have to use formalities with me, Wully. At least not until I am…" She paused and looked down, almost ashamed to say it before him. Because that would make it real to her, and she didn't want that. But she must face this reality. Laura raised her head to look directly at Wully, "Future Queen of Althalos," she finished.

Wully walked up to her and gently took her hand in his; she didn't shy away and grabbed his hand in return. This isn't the first time they have been this close. Wully knew what she meant, but it hurt to hear her say it. "I don't want to lose you," he said softly. "Soon, I'll head back to Frosbike, and you'll be left here with Aldrich, with no one to watch over you."

"I can manage," Laura said, choking back tears. "But I must admit that the thought of losing you is the biggest pain I am facing today."

"Then today, we share that pain."

They looked into each other's eyes for a few sad yet beautiful moments. Finally, Laura moved in and kissed Wully. They held each other in the embrace for a few seconds of eternity until a knock on the door echoed through the room. The pair quickly jolted back, and Laura gently wiped her face, "Who is it?"

"It's time," Merrek's voice echoed through the door.

Laura looked at Wully with tears beginning again, "Well," he said. "At least tears are expected at a wedding."

Laura chuckled, "Joy or sadness, only we will know."

Wully smiled and stepped back toward the center of the room as Merrek opened the door and led the handmaidens in behind him. Wully watched in graceful awe as the final touches were applied to the gown and then, with Merrek's permission. Wully offers his arm to escort Baroness one last time. As they leave the room, Wully and Laura cherish the moment. Hoping that this would not be the last time they would be together.

Chapter 11
The Wedding

The Great Hall, Castle Stalbak, Althalos

Wully was still escorting Laura with Merrek one step behind them as they approached the Great Hall. Once a meeting place of the old gods. Now, in all its splendor, it was used for various ceremonies that Castle Stalbak would play host to. The Great Hall was separated from the central part of the castle footprint but still a part of the grounds. It was built like the rest of the castle and the city, with its completely smooth walls reflecting the sun.

A bell toll rang softly in the distance. Laura gripped Wully's arm tighter as the ringing continued. He drew closer as they continued to walk across the castle courtyard to the Great Hall's entrance. The square was eerily empty, but it was no surprise since everyone was either waiting in the main hall for the trio or rustling about elsewhere for the reception party afterward. Though most of the city could not be here in person, they were celebrating from their homes.

The group paused near the entrance, and Laura looked up at its grandeur. Apart from the smooth reflective walls, the Great Hall had several full stained-glass windows of intricate and ornate designs. Now that they were closer, she could see the decorative swirls of lavianite within the walls, adding depth to the overall view as the sunlight shone in from the glass windows in the ceiling.

"So, this is where the old gods used to meet?" Laura asked plainly. Merrek, glancing around the grounds uneasily, brought his gaze to Laura in curiosity.

"So, the stories tell us," Wully replied casually. "Athalon was always good, and I hope that he's still around somewhere."

It had only been a couple generations since the Great War against the gods ensued. Most of the current population of Kralavia only knew of fragments of the old stories of the old gods and times past since the records during that time were lost. By the time King Ivan had gotten his throne in Althalos, the Great War was over, but the other nations remained in turmoil, fighting over territory and thrones. Until Ivan, through a blood-filled season, finally brought peace to the region. Laura's eyes remained fixed on the architecture, "Do you think the others still exist?"

Merrek stepped up beside his sister opposite Wully. "No," he said quickly. "And frankly, I'm thankful." He began to open the large doors to allow the bride to enter.

Laura looked at Wully, "And you?"

Wully paused, then glanced at the horizon, "I used to think not."

"And now?"

Wully brought his gaze to Laura, "Now, I'm not so sure." He hadn't said anything about the strange visitor on the trail as they arrived the day before, but truthfully the encounter never left his mind. Although, honestly, no one would've believed him even if he had said something.

While Wully purposefully kept his response vague, his answer seemed to suffice whatever Laura sought as she smiled and released his arm to follow Merrek up the steps. Wully watched as Laura ascended and smiled warmly to himself. He started to recall some of the more personal times he and Laura shared in the past and hoped that if he could focus on those, he wouldn't feel so bad about the present.

As Laura entered the Great Hall, Wully slowly climbed up behind her. *"Wully!"* A voice cried out in his head, causing Wully to turn around quickly. He stood firmly for several seconds, looking around. When nothing else was heard, he continued onward. *"A cursed future,"* the voice echoed in his head again. Wully stopped and looked out toward the woods in the distance; this time, the voice was recognizable, and Wully remembered the remark made by the strange old man on the forest road.

"Wully," Merrek's voice broke through his thoughts. He turned to face Merrek standing at the top of the stairs. "It's time."

Wully nodded sadly, and his expression remained grim as he reached the door. Merrek noticed the rough face, touched his shoulder, and whispered. "It's not over yet." Wully made a puzzled look, and Merrek glanced further inward at Laura and then back at Wully, "I have a plan." Wully was about to protest, but Merrek was already walking away as the ushers gestured them to their spots. The royal historian stood at the room's far end, with Prince Aldrich on his left.

With no gods since their fall, Kralavia had no worship or religion. Though people would still talk as such, and certain customs were held onto and adapted to fit their more modern views. The cleric or historian for the realm would officiate the royal family ceremony and appoint deputies throughout the city districts to help with the rest of the kingdom.

The Great Hall could accommodate a few hundred people comfortably, and Laura knew, based on how many were present, that it was close to its total capacity. Laura stood firmly at the front of the building, ready to walk down the center marked by a gold and lavianite woven carpet. The light shone through the stained glass, reflecting a soft golden hue on the inner walls and floor.

At the far end of the building, around the outer edge of the stage, stood the nine old gods of the times past. Each statue stood from floor to ceiling, was made of solid gold, and stood between the windows along the wall, looking down at the stage. Laura never understood why the humans revolted. The old scrolls and history books she had read each gave their own account of the early days leading up to the war, but anything during that time was lost. Some said one of the Unatari was too evil, and the humans took over, creating a rift between the rest of the gods and mankind. Others said humans were eager to lead themselves and sought to get rid of the gods peacefully. The gods, however, would not go without a fight, and so the humans reluctantly fought back to gain their freedom.

Whatever the reason, Laura always thought it strange. However, she was alone in her suspicions since that entire generation had died during the war. Any attempt to get the truth of the matter was now distorted through passed-down stories and biased texts. Still, though, the history of the gods intrigued Laura, and she continued to stare intently at the prominent golden resemblances of the gods within the Great Hall.

Centrally located was Athalon, the leader of the gods. He is depicted here, fully adorned in his golden armor, with a golden sword at his waist. On his head was a beautiful crown with nine gemstones, one for each of the gods and their realms. The sword and crown were passed down to King Ivan since they belonged to the god of his realm.

Laura noticed the statue of Denesious to Athalon's left. Denesious was the old god of her home, the nation of Valkos. With a tall and slender build, Denesious never wore armor but a simple green tunic. In his hand was his spear and weapon of choice. Rumor was that the spear, like all the gods' weapons, was pure Althinian and would take the form and appearance of whatever the god desired. So, even though it looked like plain wood, the spear's handle was just as strong and deadly as the tip.

The other gods stood just as majestically. Valenear and Alynia, the sisters, stood next to Denesious. Valenear was rather scantily clad with her simple deep-cut robe barely reaching past her hips, save for a single piece that draped directly in front of her and behind in the same manner. On her exposed leg was her dagger. Alynia was more practical in her appearance, and the statue did her true justice. With golden braids and a firm stance, Alynia stood with her bow, ready and watchful. The other gods were posed in similar ways.

Each of their weapons, unique to them, was highly sought after. However, none could be found except for the Golden Sword of Athalon since it was rumored that Ivan's grandfather laid the killing blow against him and claimed the sword immediately afterward before dying mysteriously when the war began. Afterward, Ivan's father claimed the blade and the crown and pushed back against the rest of the gods—or so the story goes.

For better or worse, the humans won; most believed it was because Ivan's father was using their own weapon against them. A possibility, but only a few years after the war, Ivan's father also died under mysterious circumstances. When Ivan took the mantle, he led without mercy and launched several small but effective war campaigns to settle and help establish the other kingdoms. Some will say it was excessive, but in hindsight, Ivan's campaigns brought a sense of true peace to the part of the continent they inhabited east of the Dead Lands.

As Merrek stepped up next to her, Laura only moved her eyes to acknowledge him, "I didn't expect this many people."

"Neither did I," Merrek said. "But they do things differently here in Althalos, I guess. King Ivan sent out several invitations to random citizens, as is his custom, to allow them a presence here and in the royal court from both his kingdom and ours." As he finished, the music in the room changed, and the guests turned to greet the bride.

"Shall we then?" She said, raising her arm.

"If we must," Merrek mumbled, taking her arm and escorting her down the path to the back of the room where Aldrich was waiting. The walk to the end seemed longer, with everyone staring at them. In the front row to his right, Merrek spotted Wully, closest to the aisle, with Oswald and Thomas behind him. The pair wore something similar to the royal family, with lavianite weaved in and the blue and white kingdom colors throughout.

Behind the cleric on the stage, King Ivan stood further back behind his son, as was the custom, with Haldair standing across from him. The sunlight glistened off every piece of the lavianite in their outfits. As they got closer, Haldair stepped forward. Merrek and Laura bowed, and Haldair returned with a slight bow of his own.

Merrek turned to Laura, and they bowed to each other before he stepped back, joining Wully and the others. Haldair then stepped forward, took Laura's hand, and escorted her to the center of the stage across from Aldrich before returning to his previous spot.

Laura smiled at Aldrich, who returned with his own soft and loving smile. Before the music stopped, Laura glanced around the room; her eyes paused at Wully, who met her gaze until she finally broke it away when the music ended.

As the cleric began to speak, Laura and Aldrich turned to face him hand in hand. Thomas was starting to zone it out, so he quietly took a small flask from his vest pocket and took a quick swig. Oswald elbowed him gently but hard enough that it made Thomas grunt.

"Oh, sorry," Thomas whispered sarcastically, "Want a swig?"

"Give me that," Oswald said as he took the flask from Thomas and quickly stuffed it in his coat pocket so he couldn't drink anymore. "Be respectful, please?"

Thomas gave Oswald an initial sharp look but softened it quickly as he pulled out another small flask and proceeded to drink from it. Oswald rolled his eyes and then turned to Merrek, who had stepped beside him beside Wully. Merrek didn't return his gaze but fixed it on his sister's soon-to-be husband.

After a moment, Oswald touched Merrek's shoulder and leaned close, "She'll be alright."

Merrek sighed as he finally turned to meet Oswald's gaze. "So many battles…" he turned to look back at his sister onstage. "So many times, I've fought out of a hopeless situation. But now, I can't change the one thing I really need to change."

Oswald stood back up straight and waited a moment before responding. He was aware of the tension between Merrek and Aldrich. He had fought with Merrek in the past and knew what Merrek was looking for in a husband for his sister. But Aldrich was still a friend, and Oswald raised him in some respects, though that would do nothing to ease Merrek's mind now.

"The union of these two great kingdoms…" The cleric, Gathar, could be heard echoing throughout the building.

"Aldrich has his…well, some qualities. Good and bad, as do we all," Oswald said as Merrek turned to face him, Oswald kept his gaze fixed on the prince, "But I think he's a good man overall." Then turning to Merrek, "I trust he'll keep her safe."

Merrek didn't respond to Oswald's statement; he moved his gaze back to Aldrich as the Magistrate continued his speech in the background. "… This union of families, the Prince of Althalos and the Baroness of Frosbike…"

Wully stood still, lost in thought, as he watched the ceremony. He took his eyes off Laura and began to scan the statues that loomed overhead. Obar, Athalon, Denesious, Dolos, and the others were all there in majestic golden form. As he glanced across each sculpture, Wully almost unwillingly paused at the image of Denesious.

The longer he stared at the face of the god, the more familiar it felt to him. Then, without warning, the face of Denesious turned to look at Wully directly. Wully blinked quickly to verify what he saw, but when his eyes returned to the statue, it had returned to its original position. Wully brushed it off and brought his gaze back to Laura and Aldrich.

Merrek looked at Wully; he was unaware of what had just transpired. Merrek observed as Wully's firm, almost expressionless face was fixed forward. A well enough façade for anyone, but Merrek knew better of the pain Wully was hiding behind the tall man's eyes. As hard as it was for Merrek to deal with this disrespect for his sister and household, he knew it must be even more challenging for Wully and Laura's love for each other.

Although Merrek had never had anyone to care for in that way, he imagined how it must be for them. His military life and other duties had always made him too busy for such things personally, but secretly Merrek longed for the connection that Wully and Laura had. But he knew that this sacrifice of his sister and Wully was much stronger than his own and realizing that gave him a stronger sense of humility. Then, turning back to Oswald, "That doesn't change what I think of that man, though."

Chapter 12
The Reception

Castle Stalbak, Althalos

It was after midday when the wedding ceremony finally concluded. At that time, all the guests followed the wedding party from the Great Hall across the castle courtyard and into the ballroom. Like the exterior part of the castle, the interior walls of the ballroom were a perfectly smooth and bright color with decorative pillars around the room, all leading up to the intricate designs in the architecture of the ceiling that met in the middle. From this point hung a giant chandelier made of solid gold and strung with lavianite crystals cut into ornate rose shapes that reflected the light and made it dance across the room.

On the far end of the room, large wooden double doors opened up to a stone balcony that overlooked a low spot of the city, giving any who stood there a full view of the rooftops over that part of the city. Opposite the balcony was a small stage where the band was already playing. Around the edge of the room were several long tables already full of the feast for the wedding guests.

Laura smiled as she took Aldrich's hand as he led her out to the center of the ballroom. Per the tradition of Althalos, the bride and groom would dance first at the wedding party. As the guests gathered around the room's outer edge, the rest of the wedding party took their positions around the prince and his new bride.

The band briefly paused the song they had been playing to transition to the music for which the first dance was arranged. The pause was brief, but the transition to the next song was so smooth that Laura took notice of the graceful and eloquent switch. As the dance began, each lady briefly interchanged with the men; when the song reached its central peak, the dancing couples smoothly stepped across the floor to meet up with their original partners. Once Laura was wrapped in his arms, Aldrich asked softly, "So, how do you feel?"

Laura blushed lightly and glanced down, "Well, as the baroness of Frosbike, I am accustomed to being the center of attention or at least part of the center." She returned her gaze as she finished, "But I admit that it's different being here, having the wedding, and the entire event is around my presence with you."

Aldrich chuckled softly as he glanced around the room at the guests. Most watched intently as the group danced; others had already found their seats and were helping themselves to the food laid out for everyone. "I suppose my father went a little overboard."

"Perhaps," Laura giggled, and the two danced silently for the rest of the song. At the start of the next one, others in the crowd stepped up and joined on the center floor. Aldrich and Laura held their positions centrally; each one smiled at the other as they joined in the next dance.

"So," Aldrich said finally. "Are you excited about our wedding holiday?"

Laura smiled and nodded; she was excited, though perhaps not as much as some others would be. After the ceremony, the wedding couple would take a fortnight to enjoy each other's company in the new marriage. Locations for this varied across the country and on social status. But being the newly named princess of Althalos, Laura and Aldrich's destination was set to be a private stay on one of the beautiful small islands on the south coast of Carnheller.

The islands were officially part of Carnheller's territory. Still, they were more exclusive to tourists and visitors, which never bothered King Valtor much since it generated significant revenue for his nation. Laura didn't mind the location, as it was known for its beautiful beaches and crystalline waters. It mainly was King Haldair's idea, of course, which meant that King Ivan went overboard and paid out to have the whole island emptied for the time Aldrich and Laura would be there. Personally, Laura would've liked a little more say in the location of her wedding holiday, and as much as she genuinely didn't mind that she would be with Aldrich, there was someone else that Laura would have preferred to be with.

Wully, Oswald, Thomas, and Merrek had taken one of the tables near the balcony entrance, which gave them a full view of the ballroom floor. Wully and Merrek sat with their backs facing the wall to observe the dancing, while Thomas and Oswald sat opposite them.

After a while, Thomas chugged the rest of his drink, "Well, gentlemen," he said as he placed the mug back on the table. "It's been very nice conversing with you all," he glanced at Merrek and Wully, who had been silent since they sat down. "Well, at least one of you," he said, shifting his attention to Oswald.

Then, standing up rather quickly, Thomas used the table to steady himself, "I think it's time I go find myself a pretty little thing to dance with."

Oswald laughed as Thomas slowly staggered toward the dance floor, "Do try not to step on her toes." Thomas was about to say something, but the only thing that came out was a large belch. "Or throw up on her," he finished.

As Oswald returned to the others, he noticed Merrek staring into his drink. "Good drink, good food, and fine music, eh?" He asked, attempting to start a conversation.

"What do you think, Oswald?" Merrek asked, finally breaking his silence.

Oswald ignored Merrek's question and directed his attention to Wully instead, "How about you?"

Wully didn't respond; he was lost in his head, replaying his conversation with the old man in the woods, the voice that called out to him before the wedding, and Denesious' statue moving. *What does it all mean?* He thought.

"Wully," Oswald said a little louder to garner his attention.

Wully snapped out of his daydream and stared blankly at Oswald.

"Leave him alone," Merrek interjected.

"Just trying to lighten the mood," Oswald said.

Wully looked at Laura dancing with Aldrich as his thoughts took over again. *Wully*, the same voice echoed in his head again, much more intensely than before. Wully shook his head and stood up abruptly, "Excuse me. I need some air."

Oswald and Merrek watched as Wully made a beeline for the open balcony, "Poor chap," Oswald said.

"Oswald! Merrek!" Haldair's voice boomed as he approached, taking their attention off Wully's strange behavior. "This is truly a fine wedding. You should be proud, Merrek; despite your family's hardships, you managed to have the most beautiful sister," he said. "Aldrich will be pleased, I'm sure," he nudged Oswald.

Oswald chuckled, "Yes, I'm sure he will be." Merrek scoffed in response, got up, and walked out to see Wully outside.

Haldair sat next to Oswald, and the two turned to watch the couple, who were still dancing. King Ivan had joined in and was dancing with one of the noble women that came with Haldair's entourage. "I haven't seen my brother like this in a long time," Haldair said.

"He does seem happy today," Oswald acknowledged.

"Has he not told you?" Haldair asked. Oswald shot him a perplexed look. "He hasn't told you, has he?" he confirmed. "I should have expected that, actually, knowing him."

"What is it," Oswald asked earnestly.

Haldair sighed. "Ivan, he's…" he began. "He's a very ill man, Oswald."

"Ill?" Oswald asked, "Is it…"

"Fatal?" Haldair interjected. "Of that, I am not certain. When you've seen as much death and destruction as my brother and I…" He paused as he watched Ivan continue to dance. "Well, sometimes it's not any sort of mortal man's everyday disease that finally snuffs you out. Eventually, everything in your life catches up to you, and you can't fight the retribution it seeks for your past sins."

Oswald followed Haldair's gaze and watched Ivan dance. He had a bright smile and a chipper in his steps. You wouldn't know that he was sick by looking at him. "Does Aldrich know?"

"There's no telling how long. But I foresee the end coming sooner than we would hope," Haldair said, ignoring the question.

Before he could clarify his concerns, Oswald felt a hefty slap on his shoulder as Merrek sat beside him with a fresh drink. Oswald turned his attention to Haldair, "Why are you telling me all this?"

"I know my brother has always been fond of you, Oswald; so have I," Haldair explained. "Ivan doesn't trust anyone; he trusts you, not even Aldrich. You are the only person I can tell this to. If Ivan were to perish, I fear the consequences of his successor…"

"Aldrich?" Oswald inquired.

"Yes," Haldair said. "I love my nephew, but neither his father nor I am confident in his abilities as a future king, especially if he becomes such at a young age, which may come to pass." After taking a short drink, he continued. "Ivan has talked about appointing someone else to run the kingdom until Aldrich is fit for the crown's weight."

Merrek glanced over his shoulder and saw Aldrich and Laura; the newlywed couple had left the dance floor and were socializing near one of the banquet tables on the far side of the room. Anger was boiling up inside him. Merrek roughly grabbed Oswald and pulled him close, "You said Aldrich was a fine man. You said she'd be safe."

Oswald tried to calm Merrek, but it was of no use. Merrek got up and stormed over to Aldrich and Laura. "Merrek, don't. Merrek!" Oswald said, calling after him. He intensely looked at Haldair, who matched Oswald's grim expression with his own.

Aldrich and Laura were casually conversing when Merrek stepped up, "Laura," he said as he stepped between the couple. "I need to talk to you now."

Aldrich, shyly, took a half step back, "Merrek, what a pleasant surprise."

"Aldrich, will you excuse us for a moment so I may speak to my sister privately?" Merrek said as he kept his gaze fixed on his sister.

This response bothered Aldrich, leaving him confused and slightly offended at Merrek's tone. It took only a moment for Aldrich to muster his courage as he stepped up next to Laura. He was married now and would be king; he couldn't allow himself to be pushed around so haphazardly.

"Well, Merrek," Aldrich said, putting his arm around Laura. "Your sister is now my wife. So, whatever you feel you need to say to her can be said to both of us. If it concerns her, then it concerns me." Merrek stared at Aldrich; his eyes burned intently.

Laura smiled softly and put her arm around Aldrich, "Merrek, if this isn't something you can say to us now, then it can wait." Her voice was smooth yet firm. She couldn't have Merrek making a scene here and now. "I won't have my wedding party disrupted by such childish behavior."

Those near the group stepped back to give them some space. Thankfully, and much to Laura's relief, the rest of the party went on unfazed by the slight commotion. "Merrek!" Oswald's voice echoed loudly over the rest of the bustling noise. *Well, so much for that, Laura thought* as Oswald's voice began to draw additional onlookers. "There you are," Oswald said as he touched Merrek's shoulder. "What are you up to?" He asked playfully.

"Not now, Oswald."

Oswald removed his hand and stepped in closer, speaking in a hushed tone, "You want a pint? Let's get a pint. We should find Thomas." Oswald grabbed Merrek's arm and directed him away from Aldrich and Laura. Most of the guests watching have now moved on to other business. "Thomas!" Oswald called out.

"Oswald," Aldrich said, stopping them short. "It's okay, Merrek just came over to say," he began, "Oh, actually, what was it you wanted to say to my beautiful wife and me?" He pulled Laura in tighter and gave Merrek a smug look.

Merrek tuned and faced Aldrich squarely, a stern expression across his face. Oswald looked at Laura, who matched his concerned expression with her own. Oswald quickly glanced around the room. The musicians were still playing, and several couples were dancing in the center of the room. Ivan was mingling on the other side of the room near Haldair. Wully and Thomas were nowhere to be seen. Short of a significant disruption, it seemed there would be no way to end the coming conflict.

"Well, go on," Aldrich said as Merrek remained silent.

A smile crept over Merrek's face, and Aldrich suddenly regretted his firm stance against him. Fear had crept into Aldrich, though he could not show it. "I was just coming over to see if the Crown Prince Aldrich…" Merrek stated with added sarcasm in his tone. "Would you be interested in a duel?"

Those close by, listening in, suddenly began whispering to each other. This caused others standing nearby to be drawn in, adding to the commotion. "A…a duel?" Aldrich stammered.

"Merrek," Laura pleaded. "Not here."

"Don't worry, sister," Merrek said as he placed his hand on Aldrich's shoulder, "It's just a little competition between brothers now." Aldrich didn't say anything. "Because that's what we are now, right?" He asked. "You said it yourself; you married my sister. We're family now, right?"

Aldrich nodded, "I did."

"I don't know if that's a good idea," Oswald said. "Why don't we all just have a drink? Relax."

"Nonsense, Oswald," Aldrich said. "Just a friendly contest. We're family now."

Merrek smiled, "Absolutely! Shall we step outside?"

"Lead the way."

As the two proceeded to the balcony, Merrek glanced back and smirked at his sister. Her face was stern and angry, but she said nothing. Oswald shook his head disapprovingly; Merrek winked at him and continued on.

As Merrek and Aldrich reached the balcony, Merrek decided to move the duel down to the courtyard, "That way," he said. "We don't have to worry about the bystanders." Aldrich agreed and took his position in the courtyard's center. Most of the other guests had gathered on the balcony to observe.

Aldrich looked up at them; Oswald was closest near the stairs, his face still holding the same disapproving look he had before. Laura stood next to him, more concern than anger in her expression. Then he saw his father, Ivan. Aldrich paused briefly when their eyes met, but Ivan gave no sign nor smirk of anything; he simply watched as a neutral bystander. Aldrich shrugged them off as he readied himself.

Merrek stood across from Aldrich, calm and collected, "Do you have much experience with the sword, Aldrich?"

"There's no denying your battlefield experience far exceeds my own, Merrek," Aldrich said plainly. "But I am versed in the art of swordplay. My father's tutors have trained me."

Merrek chuckled, "I'm sure." The two men removed some of the more decorative pieces of their outfits and got in their ready stances. Merrek unsheathed his sword, twirling it quickly before letting it rest casually at his side. "At least I won't have to go easy on you then."

"I'd have it no other way," Aldrich said as he pulled his sword out. Aldrich also twirled his sword but added a few steps and spins before holding his stance. Aldrich knew that Merrek was the better fighter in a war scenario, but he figured that he could catch him off guard by showing Merrek what he knew, then he could find a weak spot in Merrek's fight. "What are the terms?"

At least he has good form, Merrek thought. *This may prove to be a bit more rewarding than I initially expected.* "Well, I wouldn't want you to soil your wedding outfit," Merrek stated after a moment. "Shall we say… first one to knock the other off his feet?"

Aldrich twisted his feet to get them firmly placed on the ground, "I hope you're ready."

"Oh, I've been ready," Merrek muttered.

The tension rose as the men stood in silence for a few moments. More spectators from the wedding party began to fill up the balcony. Aldrich slowly stepped forward, inching his way to Merrek, who remained calm and motionless. Once Aldrich got within a few paces of him, Merrek twitched, and Aldrich immediately froze up.

Merrek took the opportunity and lunged forward, closing the distance between him and Aldrich in a single step. Merrek's strikes were hard and fierce, but Aldrich held his own, carefully blocking each blow. Merrek was slightly surprised by Aldrich's skill, so he increased his fighting intensity.

After a while, the two locked blades briefly before Merrek sent Aldrich sliding backward from a swift kick to the stomach. Aldrich staggard back but managed to stay on his feet. Aldrich stood up straight, having quickly recovered himself. Merrek casually stood a few paces away, "You're not ready to quit, are you?"

Aldrich smiled, "No, no, not yet."

Merrek smirked and lunged forward again. "You know, Aldrich," he said as the pair re-engaged. "It was complicated for me to bring my sister here, give her away to a man I've never truly gotten to know personally."

Aldrich scoffed and shoved Merrek back so he could re-center himself. "I want to know the man my sister has married," the baron said as he closed in again. His strokes were quick but light; he wanted to play with Aldrich for a while.

"Well," Aldrich asked as they clashed again. "What do you want to know?"

"I want to know that if it comes down to it, I can trust you with her life."

Aldrich scoffed as he spun around Merrek, bringing his sword across to strike Merrek in the back. Merrek saw this coming and turned his sword behind him to block it. Once the swords clashed, Merrek grabbed Aldrich's collar and pulled him close, "Impressive."

"Your sister is safe with me," Aldrich snapped back. "You can trust me with that."

"Oh, can I?" Merrek asked rhetorically as he shoved Aldrich away from him. "Because the only thing I have to go on," he said as he lunged at Aldrich again, "Is your vomit on my feet."

Aldrich felt shocked as Merrek's attacks grew more intense with each hit; his hands were already numb from the vibrations. For a moment, Aldrich thought Merrek would surely win. Finally, Aldrich found his opening and put distance between them. Aldrich watched the crowd; Oswald, Laura, and his father still held their positions but were now easily lost in the group of faces that filled the area.

"Come on Aldrich," Merrek teased. "Show me how you'll protect my sister." Merrek then gestured to the crowd on the balcony, "Show all these people how you'll defend them as their king."

Aldrich stood still for a moment; his anger was boiling. He would not just beat Merrek; he would humiliate him. He would kill him. Aldrich roared and charged forward, almost catching Merrek off guard. The two continued to fight, almost gridlocked in the duel, with neither man gaining any real ground.

Laura watched as the two continued to fight, "Oswald, this can't go on."

"I agree," said Haldair, who was behind her. "This is disgraceful."

"My lord," Oswald said, bowing his head. "Stepping between Merrek and his opponent means you'd turn this ceremony into a funeral."

Laura leaned in and whispered to Oswald, "If someone doesn't step in, there may be a funeral anyway."

"No," Ivan's firm voice interjected. "Let Aldrich fight it out. This is his own doing, and he needs to see the consequences."

"Don't worry, my dear," Haldair said to Laura. "As disgraceful as it may be, Merrek won't hurt the boy, but he is in for a rude awakening." Haldair shot a questioning glance at Ivan before returning to the spectacle below.

Aldrich and Merrek continued exchanging blow after blow. "Oh, look at that," Merrek joked. "Last night, I saw the little prince turn green, and now, he's turning a shade of red. Tell me, prince, how many other colors can you take?"

Aldrich pulled back and then started laying blow after blow upon Merrek. Merrek just laughed them off as he blocked Aldrich's rage-filled strikes. Aldrich made one final fury attempt but missed Merrek by a hair. As Aldrich stumbled to regain his footing, Merrek seized his advantage and quickly disarmed Aldrich. Aldrich watched as his sword hit the ground some distance away; immediately, Merrek swung his foot and tripped Aldrich, causing him to fall.

Some of the crowd began to disperse; others remained with Ivan, Laura, and Oswald out of curiosity, eager to see if anything would come of the beaten young prince. Haldair tapped Laura's shoulder gently before proceeding to go back inside. Merrek stepped up and loomed over Aldrich, who was still catching his breath.

"I would say that I'm disappointed," he said as he sheathed his sword, "But my expectations have been met quite accurately." As Merrek turned and walked away, Aldrich, still enraged, sat up. "We'll have to do this again sometime," Merrek said over his shoulder.

Aldrich watched as Oswald and Laura proceeded to come down to them; his father, however, remained on the balcony with the other guests that stayed; his neutral yet firm expression was still on his face. Still enraged, Aldrich pulled a small dagger out of his boot. As he stood, Oswald saw this and quickened his pace to the young prince. "Hey, hey, hey!" Oswald said as he embraced Aldrich in a huge hug and discreetly grabbed the knife. "It's alright. You have to stop now." Oswald grabbed the prince's neck and whispered, "It's over."

Aldrich submitted to Oswald's words and let him take the knife. Merrek, unaware of what Aldrich had attempted to do, turned to see Oswald comforting the lad. Merrek smiled and continued up the balcony steps. He paused when he reached Laura, "I hope you're happy with yourself," she snapped. "Thanks for ruining my wedding." Merrek didn't respond but continued on his way.

As Aldrich gathered his sword, he looked up at his father on the balcony. Ivan only met his son's gaze briefly; he wasn't upset that his son had lost the duel. He was concerned that he would try to cheat in the end. The king sighed before he turned back to enter the ballroom. Some of the other guests that were still present began to whisper to themselves as they went inside. Aldrich guessed that they, as well as his father, saw what had happened. *I'm sure I'll hear about that later,* he thought.

As Oswald helped him clean up, Aldrich looked at Laura, who remained on the stairs. Their eyes met, and Aldrich could tell that though she looked okay, his gut told him she was not. Laura's head dropped, and she began to make her way back inside.

"Help! Help!" a voice cried out, breaking the silence.

"Wully?" Laura exclaimed as they turned around to see Wully leading a horse with a rough-looking rider upon its back.

"Wully," Oswald said. "Where have you been? What is this?"

"I have…a message…for King Ivan," the rider said in-between breaths.

"Laura," Aldrich said quickly. Laura nodded and turned to get King Ivan from the ballroom. "Help him down, gently now." Aldrich and Oswald assisted Wully in helping the man off the horse and laid him gently on the ground.

Within moments, Laura returned with Ivan and several castle staff. "Easy, lad," Ivan said calmly. "What's happened?"

"Stelbeck Keep…" the man muttered as he drifted in and out of consciousness. "Under…attack." As the man finished, he passed out.

Ivan stood, "Take him to one of our guest rooms and call the doctor. I want him watched until he wakes up and can tell us more." Without hesitation, several people around him began to carry out the instructions. Then turning to Oswald, Ivan said, "Get to the messenger bird room and find out why this news hasn't reached us already."

Oswald bowed and ran off.

Ivan looked at his son before heading back inside. Nothing was said, but Aldrich knew what his father was thinking. "Father, I…" Aldrich started to say. But Ivan ignored him and turned to walk away.

Chapter 13
The King's Orders

Castle Stalbak, Althalos

Ivan stood quietly in his study. The murmurs of the guests as they dispersed for the evening softly echoed outside the door. After Aldrich's folly in the courtyard with Merrek, most of the guests had taken the cue to leave; Ivan firmly but respectfully dismissed the others after the messenger arrived from Stelbeck Keep.

Ivan remained motionless, staring at the golden sword on the mantle. Visions of his past flashed in his mind, and reflections of the flames danced in his eyes. The screams of dying men echoed in his head as he recalled the dozens of battles after the Great War, but he was a much younger man then. At eighty, Ivan had only reached the middle of his life span, as was the norm for those in Kralavia. Ivan was about twenty when his father died mysteriously, and the power of the Golden Sword was given to him. Though technically an adult, in hindsight, Ivan realized that he was still much too young to lead.

Ivan's memory showed him standing alone on the battlefield; hundreds of dead men and soldiers lay around him, and the golden sword in his hand glowed brightly. Ivan recalled his feelings then, with the Golden Sword and a hot vengeance, he picked up where his father had left off and brought peace to the region in the aftermath of the Great War. The people loved Ivan's zeal and quickness to end the fighting. However, getting the kingdoms re-established and ceasing the infighting was less accepted by the populace. It wouldn't be until long after the domains were established that they accepted Ivan's methods and choices.

Ivan winced as he remembered the whispers in his mind at the time. overboard, went overboard; he was too young to understand there was more to ruling than wartime victory. Ivan recalled the time he finally set the sword on the mantle—much to his disdain. Years passed, and now he was married, and his son was due to be born soon; the continent was at peace and had been for almost a decade. There was no more need to wield the Golden Sword. The sword and he were connected, but as Ivan grew older, he started to feel the accurate weight of his reign.

The sword had aged him, though he didn't look it on the outside; mentally and emotionally, Ivan felt death creeping in the more he used the weapon. So, with his son on the way, Ivan retired the sword. Initially, he felt relieved and hoped the effects would reverse, but the damage was already done. The queen died in childbirth, but Aldrich, Ivan's son, survived.

Ivan's thoughts broke momentarily as a log from the fire broke free, dropping hard against the grate at the bottom. Ivan stooped and began to stoke the fire slowly. He felt something trickle down from his nose and caught it with his finger, blood again. In the almost twenty years since Aldrich was born, Ivan has worked hard to ensure that his son would not have to begin his rule with life-or-death choices. Hopefully, it was enough.

Ivan wiped his face and stood slowly as the knock at his door brought his attention to the present time. "Come in."

Oswald stepped in with an elderly man behind him. Closing the door, Oswald stepped forward, "My lord."

Ivan turned to greet his guests directly, "What happened?"

"I have received no birds regarding the attack of Stelbeck Keep, Sire," said the elderly man.

"Have any birds come through?" Ivan asked.

"Yes, Sire." The elderly man replied. "I have received several congratulations on Aldrich's wedding and other casual things that I set to be read to you at our usual meeting tomorrow."

"I searched the cages and paper clippings myself, sir," Oswald said. "Nothing about Stelbeck."

Ivan turned back to the sword on the mantle, "Interesting. That'll be all, Neilith." The elderly man bowed and took his leave.

Oswald waited until the door was shut again before speaking, "I have other information."

Ivan nodded but said nothing as he grabbed one of his large maps, unrolled it on the table in the center of the room, and began studying it. "I stopped by the messenger's room on my way here."

Ivan didn't take his eyes off the map, "Has he said anything else?"

"His name is Amias," Oswald began. "But he has no further information about the attack because they sent him out early on, and they hadn't identified their attackers then."

"Carnheller," Ivan muttered.

"Sir?"

"The only nation able to bring a surprise attack to Stelbeck Keep would be Carnheller," Ivan said.

"Are you sure?" Oswald asked. "Could it be someone from further across the sea? There's so much unknown to us in that part of the world, apart from our direct trade partners. And what about the Five Crown Alliance? Surely King Valtor would dare to break such an agreement."

"It's possible. But even still, Carnheller would've been in the way or at least known of their presence. They either knew of it and did nothing or are directly involved somehow." Ivan explained.

"So, what's your plan?"

"Send a message to King Leoxtra," Ivan said, looking at Oswald now. "If he hasn't heard by now, then we will tell him and let him know we will be moving. I want my troops armed and ready by first light tomorrow. You, General Ulrich, and Rollins will lead. Whoever is behind the attack will get no further than they already have."

"Very good, Sire," Oswald acknowledged. "Shall I have your things readied as well?"

"No," Ivan said softly. "Where is Aldrich?"

"I believe he is in his quarters with Laura."

"Tell him his honeymoon will have to wait," Ivan said as he grabbed some paper and began writing something. "He will go in my stead; I think he needs time to reflect on his actions tonight." Ivan rolled up the small paper and placed his seal on it. Then he handed the paper to Oswald, "Your instructions," Oswald bowed his head and tucked the sealed paper into his belt.

"Are you sure you don't want to be there yourself?" Oswald asked.

"I've seen enough war," Ivan replied. "Besides, Aldrich must learn, and you will help him."

Aldrich stared out his window at his reflection. His appearance was much more modest as his wedding adornment was traded for more comfortable evening wear. Aldrich repeatedly replayed the fight with Merrek in his head; there were a few spots where he recognized his failure and replayed it with various ways in which he could've won that duel.

Aldrich's thoughts broke as he saw the reflection of Laura in the window entering the room behind him. They had not spoken directly since the incident. She showed no signs of anger toward Aldrich, but he could tell, based on her sullen expression, that she wasn't pleased either. "How are you doing?"

"Better than you, I suppose," Laura said softly. Aldrich fought to hide his expression as much as her candid response and lighthearted comment humored him. Aldrich wasn't sure yet if she meant to insult him or not.

"Indeed," Aldrich said finally, playing along to see if Laura would reveal more of her thoughts. But Laura only smiled as she stepped behind the Shoji. Aldrich turned back to the window to allow her some additional privacy. He thought about dropping the issue and directing the conversation toward anything else. But Aldrich's pride got the best of him, "Are you happy your brother won?"

Laura stepped out from behind the Shoji, tying the blue and white robe as she did, "You were both idiots."

"See, that's the…" *Knock, knock.* Aldrich's response was interrupted by the rap at the door. "Come in," he said, stepping closer to the door with Laura at his heels. "I suppose my father has come to give me his formal tongue-lashing about what happened tonight."

Laura chuckled.

To Aldrich's surprise and relief, it was not Ivan in his doorway, but "Oswald?" Aldrich exclaimed, "Is there something wrong?"

Aldrich half hoped that the shock of his actions earlier would've sent his father into such a mental frenzy that he would get sick and be unable to continue his rule.

"I apologize for the disturbance," Oswald said. "But your father has said that in response to the attack at Stelbeck Keep, we are leaving at first light tomorrow."

Aldrich rolled his eyes and turned to Laura, "So much for the honeymoon."

Laura kissed him gently on his cheek, "We've still got tonight."

Aldrich smiled and turned back to Oswald, "Does the king have any direct order for me concerning this mobilization?"

Oswald nodded and smiled, "To lead it."

Aldrich's face froze as he began to process the many emotions that ran through him. "Seriously?" he asked when he managed to find his voice.

Oswald nodded again, "Indeed. You are to lead as representative of your father, King Ivan. I will be your second in command, with Generals Ulrich and Rollins leading the troops."

Aldrich could hardly believe it. *Finally,* he thought.

"I'll leave you both to it then," Oswald said as he bowed and left the room. "Milady." Laura bowed her head in response.

When the door was closed, Aldrich held Laura tightly for several minutes. "Let us enjoy this night," he said as they released their embrace.

Laura smiled, "Let us enjoy each other."

The following day, Aldrich stood near the window of his room admiring and adjusting his armor. It took all of his effort for him to conceal his excitement. There wasn't much more to the information from the night prior. They had no direct word on whether Stelbeck Keep was victorious, in ruins, or holding fast. Whatever the case, Aldrich was eager to finally get his chance to lead as a king and an army.

Aldrich's thoughts broke when he felt a soft touch on his neck from behind. Turning to look, he saw Laura standing there in a beautiful gown of blue and gold. "How do I look?" he asked, turning around to face her.

"Like a king." A familiar voice said from the doorway. Both Laura and Aldrich moved their attention to the visitor.

"Oswald!" Aldrich greeted. "Well, what do you think? It was father's, a long time ago."

Oswald admired the prince for a minute before noticing the belt and sword on the table nearby, "I think you fit the part well," he said as he handed the sword to Aldrich.

Laura helped secure the belt. Then Aldrich drew the sword as the others stepped back to observe. Aldrich and Laura exchanged a loving glance as he playfully swung the sword getting a feel for the weight and his new armor. As the prince sheathed the blade, Oswald smiled.

"Well," he said, "I won't have to worry about watching your back after all."

The trio chuckled, "You better," interjected Laura playfully. "I want my husband to come home from this endeavor."

Oswald bowed sarcastically, "Of course, milady."

The laughter ended abruptly when there was a loud knock in the doorway. The three looked in silence at the new arrival. Merrek. *Of all the people*, Aldrich thought.

"They are preparing to leave," Merrek said.

"Thank you, Merrek," Oswald said.

Merrek turned to leave but paused momentarily as he eyed Aldrich up and down. "Hmm, cute."

Aldrich stepped forward, but Laura and Oswald stopped him as Merrek left the room. "Ignore him, Aldrich; there are more important things to have on your mind right now. You are the future king of Althalos, and this is your first test of authority outside of the castle keep; best to start planning ahead, my friend."

"Thank you," Aldrich said quietly. "Thank you for being there. You've always been there through everything." He chuckled, "Well, been there to bail me out of trouble mostly."

Oswald laughed, "Every time."

"Thank you for always having my back."

"Always," Oswald said. "You would only ever do the same for me if you had the chance."

Aldrich got serious and gave Oswald a nervous nod. Oswald gives Aldrich the same nod in return. His nervousness was replaced with pity. Oswald had grown up with Aldrich and had been waiting for this moment. But Haldair's words from the night prior still echoed in his mind.

Now that he knew Haldair didn't think Aldrich was ready to be king, Oswald started questioning his judgment of the young prince.

Is it possible that Ivan himself didn't think Aldrich was ready?

Chapter 14
Unknown Horizons

Ivan's army was getting assembled outside the city walls. The sun was rising, and though it had not yet peaked above the Purple Mountains, the light reflected off the soldier's armor brilliantly. Aldrich, Oswald, Thomas, and a small part of the King's Guard assembled at Stalbak Castle. Once they departed, they were to meet the rest of the military troops in Alpine Forest near the base of the Purple Mountains and, from there, proceed to Stelbeck Keep.

"Uuuuggghhh," Thomas moaned as he climbed on his horse.

"What's the matter?" Oswald chided. "Drink too much last night?"

Thomas shot Oswald mockingly, "I was supposed to… It was a wedding, after all."

"Oh yeah," Oswald said. "Because you need more reasons to drink than you do already." Thomas chuckled as he acknowledged defeat in Oswald's argument. Oswald mounted his steed and trotted to the small group of the King's Guard soldiers nearby. "Lieutenant," he barked.

"Yes, sir," came a firm reply from the man within the group of soldiers.

"Take your group ahead. We'll meet you at the city gates and proceed from there." Oswald ordered.

"Yes, sir," the lieutenant replied. He then mounted his horse and ordered his men to do the same and move out.

Oswald positioned himself next to Thomas, "Where is the prince?"

"Not sure," Thomas interjected quickly. "But he can take his time." He yawned. "The longer he takes, the longer I get to sleep."

Oswald rolled his eyes and glanced up at the castle. He had not seen Aldrich since they met briefly in his chambers earlier. Come to think of it, King Ivan was also scarce this morning. *Maybe Ivan is giving Aldrich one final set of instructions?* Thought Oswald. He then felt his belt and gripped the still-sealed paper that Ivan had given him the night prior. Make sure to read this before you arrive at Stelbeck Keep. *Make sure you tell no one save for King Leoxtra about it should the need arise.* Ivan's instructions still echoed in Oswald's mind…

"You must understand it is with the utmost uneasiness that I am allowing Aldrich to go along with you," Ivan said as he stared intently into the fire. With the guests gone, the castle was now completely silent, save for the crackle of the wood in the fireplace of King Ivan's study.

Standing in the center of the room behind Ivan, Oswald looked puzzled, "My lord, I know his outburst last night was certainly not the most respectable look for a man of royal stature, but I assure you he is ready."

"I'm not worried about his image, Oswald. He's already set on fouling that up," Ivan stated as he turned and faced Oswald. "I'm worried about who he is. There is a darkness inside of him. Anger and bitterness seem to cling to that boy. I fear the man he may become… It reminds me too much of myself."

"Is that a bad thing?" Oswald asked. "You are an honorable man."

Ivan glanced down and chuckled softly, "Honorable," he muttered. Oswald stepped forward to protest, but Ivan returned to the fire, "Perhaps. But I wasn't always, and a lot of people suffered."

Oswald had no response. He understood better than most about the romanticism of war and how the history books only recorded so much. There is always a more profound and darker side to every conflict, and within every general and king, the same deep and dark notions exist—the heart's true intentions.

"I may be worrying over nothing," Ivan said, breaking the silence. "Let the prince lead and guide him as he makes decisions and leads these troops. I need to know what kind of man he is when I'm not there."

"Yes, sir."

Ivan turned to face Oswald again. "You have my document, and I will send the other to King Leoxtra. Don't worry."

"I'll look after him."

"I know you will."

Before long, Aldrich's figure could be seen exiting the castle's main doors, and his horse was being led by one of the stable servants already prepped and ready.

"Are you ready?" Oswald asked cheerfully.

Aldrich nodded and said nothing as he mounted his horse next to Oswald. As the group left, Aldrich asked, "Where is my father?"

Oswald was slightly taken aback by this question. Thomas, however, merely sighed and bowed his head to his chest. "I thought he was with you?" Oswald replied. "I haven't seen him all morning."

Aldrich seemed to accept this answer and shook his head, "Neither have I," he said quietly as he glanced back up at the castle towering over them.

"Did you and Laura get a chance to get a proper goodbye?" Oswald asked.

Aldrich didn't respond right away, lost in his thoughts. "Hmm," he said after a moment. "Yes, yes. Let's go." Several eyes watched as the three departed the castle grounds and rode through the city to the eastern gates.

As the three proceeded through the city streets, Aldrich glanced over his shoulder back at the castle and then down at himself as he shifted in his saddle. "Relax," Thomas said gently. "Just be yourself and remember what you've learned."

"Indeed," Oswald cut in. "Just be who you are. Nobody can do that better than you."

"That hasn't gained me the biggest favor from anyone lately."

"Well, sometimes that's the price you must pay," Oswald replied. "You'll be king one day. Not everyone will support you or your decisions the same way. Not everyone supports your father's."

Aldrich nodded in agreement, "Well, some of my father's recent decisions have certainly not been worth supporting."

There was a moment of silence before Oswald glanced back at Thomas, "Any help here would've been nice." Thomas chuckled softly and waved his hand. Then turning to Aldrich, Oswald said, "Aldrich, your father is one of the greatest men in all of Kralavia. Nothing he says or the decisions he makes should be taken lightly. He is a wise man."

Aldrich laughed, "Wise as he may be, most people think he seems to be losing that at his age."

"Physically, maybe," Oswald confirmed. "But his mind is still sharp. He knows more about what's going on in Kralavia than most."

Aldrich pondered this momentarily before changing the subject, "Will you support me, Oswald?"

Oswald smiled at the young prince, "I already do."

Ivan stood in the east tower, looking at the brightening sky over the horizon. He watched as his son and the others started on their journey. He turned to Neilith, who was tending the messenger pigeons at the room's far end. "Send a bird to Carnheller. Tell King Valtor I wish to meet."

Neilith bowed his head, "Yes, Sire." The birds fluttered around as Ivan strode past to leave. He needed to move quickly if he was to have any chance of getting ahead. He began to recall the pieces of history he could remember. That, along with his own experiences through and after those times, helped Ivan put together the possibility of what was coming and the bigger picture of it all.

"Do you think our past is returning to haunt us?" Ivan asked, his face was solemn. Haldair had yet to move from his seat at the main table in the dining hall. A partially eaten breakfast of cakes and eggs was before him.

Ivan stood motionless near the table as Haldair leaned back in his chair and stroked his beard. Crumbs began to fall from it but clung to his clothes' jeweled chains and decorative pieces. The chair creaked slightly under Haldair's plump figure as he shifted.

"Well, I suppose I must head back home then and rally the remaining members of the Five Crown Alliance." He rose, "Don't worry, Ivan, if it is Carnheller, they were easily beaten before, and we'll crush them again."

"Will you return alone?"

"No, if this is true and we rally the five kings for this, I'll need my general and best fighter," Haldair said. "Where is Merrek anyway?"

"If I can be of assistance," Ivan began.

"No!" Haldair exclaimed. "I am no fool, Ivan. We both know what that sword has done to you. I fear if you use it again, it'll be for the last time."

Almost instinctively, Ivan brought his hand up to his face; he thought he felt blood running down his face again. The king was relieved when nothing was there. Haldair eyed him suspiciously. Try as he might, Ivan could not keep up the façade much longer.

"Perhaps you're right," he said, sighing. "I know that you only have my best interests at heart. But I don't think the rest of the world shares your concern."

"Perhaps not. But you do your diplomatic thing with Valtor if you can," Haldair said. "But if you can't, and Carnheller refuses to cooperate, and Aldrich finds them truly behind the attack on Stelbeck Keep, then we'll be ready. Hopefully, it won't come to that. But now, I must find Merrek."

Merrek was slowly walking down the upper corridor of the castle by himself. His head was down as he strode along the hallway. His armor glistened in the rays of light that shone through the windows as he walked past them—a red tunic and short cape that displayed the black falcon as the sigil for Valkos. In one hand, he carried his helmet, etched with falcon wings on each side.

Memories of last night played in his head. He knew Aldrich was a petty boy, no better than a spoiled child, but he had not considered that underneath that whiny temperament was the gall to try to kill someone, much less murder them. Merrek had to admit that had it not been for Oswald, Aldrich might've succeeded.

"Sir," came the familiar voice from a nearby doorway.

Merrek suppressed his thoughts, lifted his head, and smiled when he saw Wully standing there, "Wully."

The two exchanged a brief greeting, and Merrek mentioned how nice Wully's armor looked. "But you won't need that this time," Merrek said.

"But you and Haldair will be leaving shortly," Wully exclaimed. "Where you go, I will follow."

Merrek smiled, "Wully, you have followed me long enough." He glanced down the hallway to Laura's room. "You will be staying here in Althalos," he said as he put his hand on Wully's shoulder.

"Sir?"

"You heard me."

"Sir, I promised your father I would protect the family and the estate," Wully argued.

Merrek stepped in closer, "Laura will need you here more than I will. Things are stirring up now, and I know I can care for myself. But I can't watch over her when I'm gone. You must look after her for me."

"But Ivan…" Wully started to protest. But Merrek silenced him. After a moment, Wully dropped his head.

"Hey," Merrek said. "Look at me." Wully brought his gaze back up to Merrek's. "If anything happens to me today, tomorrow, twenty years from now. I need you to take care of her." Wully nodded. Merrek stepped back and placed his helmet on his head. "Should Aldrich fall, take care of her in his stead." Wully shot a questioning look at Merrek, who smiled and walked away.

Laura observed as Aldrich and the others trotted off the castle grounds and through the upper levels of the city. She had no reason to question the safe return of the men; Ivan's army was grand and well-trained. But why did she have this sinking feeling in her stomach about it?

"Milady," came a firm voice from the doorway.

Laura turned and softly smiled as Merrek stepped in. "Haldair and I must head home," he said grimly.

Laura raised a brow, "Oh? What happened?"

"Haldair is going to rally the alliance together. Ivan plans a diplomatic approach, but we must be ready."

"Strange," Laura said. "Are we even sure exactly who opposed us?" She walked back to the balcony and gazed out over the city. Merrek remained silent and still. "So, am I to lose my husband and brother all in one moment?"

Merrek sighed and stepped forward, "Laura, I…" His voice trailed off when he noticed that Laura wasn't listening. Her back was still to him, and her gaze remained intently on the horizon. "Milady," he said as he bowed and left.

Laura didn't move. It wasn't that she couldn't handle Merrek leaving, and as happy as she felt initially with her marriage to Aldrich, she wasn't overly concerned about his safety either. Bits of history started to enter her thoughts as he stood on the balcony alone.

Carnheller wasn't supportive of Ivan's rule; not many had been. Laura had very little knowledge about the lands to the east, so, on principle, she dismissed the thought of them unless further proof was presented. The only other nation that caused any kind of consistent trouble was Stelmond. A recluse country was full of proud and arrogant people. It was recorded that Stelmond was the last kingdom to yield to Ivan and remain peaceful after the Great War.

King Ordain was an old man; Laura figured him to be one hundred and twenty years old if her memory was correct. King Ordain was one of the few who could recall the world's events directly during the Great War and what led up to it. He wouldn't ever share that information; he was too proud to interact and engage with the rest of the kingdoms for anything.

The average lifespan for Kralavia was around one hundred and fifty years. However, most died young in the Great War, and in the few decades since, few remain that could recall the time of the Unatari's reign before the war. King Ordain only submitted to Ivan because of Ivan's weapon—as was the case with many of the kings of old. That said, Ordain refused to let go entirely and has been a thorn in the side of Laura's home country of Valkos ever since. The more Laura thought about this, the more plausible it became that they would also be involved.

Laura recalled all the moments when King Haldair called Merrek off to fight against Stelmond. Sometimes it was a minor skirmish. Other times, it was a full-scale war. Thankfully, Valkos always held its own. As one of the largest kingdoms in Kralavia, by sheer numbers alone, it was a formable force against anyone who dared oppose it. King Haldair, Merrek, Laura, and King Ivan all agreed that though it was never said, Stelmond's push against Valkos was only because King Ordain sought to get to Althalos and King Ivan. King Haldair just happened to be in the way.

As long as Haldair had no trouble in keeping Stelmond in check, he and Ivan agreed that Ivan should never get involved or call upon that weapon in war again. Laura was unsure of the details, but she guessed that using that sword caused much strain on Ivan, and Haldair was trying to protect him in the long run. Her thoughts then shifted to focus on the more pressing matter. She attempted to find a correlation between the attack in Alkeroth with Stelbeck Keep and the possible involvement of Carnheller or Stelmond. No strong connection came to mind; Laura decided she didn't have enough information and let the thoughts go.

Later that afternoon, Laura was reading in the garden. The sun was shining, and the beautiful colors of the flowers shone brightly against the brilliant castle walls. Laura paused her reading as a shadow was cast over her. Looking up, she saw the dark silhouette.

"Wully?" she questioned.

A smile could be seen as her eyes adjusted, "Yes, milady." The figure said, stepping out of the sun and sitting beside her.

"I thought you would've left with Merrek and King Haldair," Laura said.

"I was supposed to," Wully began to say. "But I was given different instructions." He smiled as he finished.

Laura smiled shyly, and the two sat awkwardly silent for several minutes. Laura knew that Merrek had arranged this, and while she tried to be upset, she couldn't bring herself to those feelings.

"So, how was your wedding night?" Wully finally asked awkwardly.

"Is that really what you want to talk about?"

"I suppose not," Wully replied, looking at his feet.

Laura smiled and pretended to read, "It was good." Laura carefully glanced over the book to see Wully's expression. Nothing. Wally's gaze remained fixed on the ground. "We've already had this conversation," she said more seriously. "Aldrich is a fine husband, and I am as happy as possible."

Wully sat up straight and slowly lowered the book as he looked directly into Laura's eyes. "Are you sure?"

Laura's smile slightly faded as she recalled the rush Aldrich was in this morning when he left. Truthfully, everything was good. But something about Aldrich's attitude this morning sat uneasily in her mind. "He didn't say goodbye," she said without realizing it, so soft it was almost a whisper.

Wully knew what she said but asked her to clarify anyway.

"Never mind," Laura said sharply as she got up to leave. She had already said too much. It was too soon to tell if she would be happy, but all signs indicated she would be. Despite his actions last night, Aldrich seemed to be a fine man to her overall. *It's just because he left so suddenly right after the wedding,* Laura thought. She was a little upset with Ivan for sending Aldrich on this errand and with Aldrich for being so willing to go. But those are no reasons to talk inappropriately about them to anyone else.

Suddenly, Laura stopped. She felt a firm hand on her arm that held her firmly in place. Turning around, it was Wully holding her. "I'm sorry," he said softly. "I was out of place; I just wish to remain friends, as we have, and follow Merrek's request for my duty in his absence."

Laura bowed her head and accepted his apology. Wully released her arm and bowed in return.

Chapter 15
Visions

Later that evening, Wully found himself wandering the castle grounds. Ivan had been taking councils that day, and Laura was at the start of her city tour as the future queen. She needed to become familiar with the needs of the people and greet them—as best she could—in person to give a sense of care and familiarity.

As the evening wore on and the sun-lit display of Althalos's beauty began to fade, so did Wully's thoughts. The night became relaxed but comfortable. His shadow bounced in front and behind him as he walked past the torches along the steppingstones that lined the garden walkways. A shadow grew in his mind. He didn't realize he had quickened his pace as he strode through the several acres of garden.

After some time, Wully paused when he found himself in front of the bench where he and Laura had been earlier. His heart grew sad, and his chest felt heavy as he recalled the conversation and the love he felt for her. He sat down slowly and gazed across the dimly lit garden. Spread across the green were various-sized flowers and other plants. During the day, he remembered they seemed very normal for what plant life would be here. Then, he realized that Althalos was dazzling in the daylight and at night.

In the dark, as the shadows grew, the Cradinlings glowed. Wully stared in amazement and almost forgot his sorrow as he wondered about the display. The Cradinlings were a typical flower with several species within the plant's group. Usually, each species would glow differently; some would be a different color, others, a different pattern. However, Ivan arranged them so that each plant was woven in on itself or with others to make beautiful works of organic luminescent art.

After taking in the beauty of the display, Wully finally closed his eyes to rest a bit and think. "Wully." He shot up when he heard it. The voice in his head again, almost like a whisper this time, but clear as it could be. "Come out!" he cried, "I'm not playing this game anymore. What sort of power lets me hear you in my mind?"

His voice echoed faintly against the stone of the castle walls. Still, Wully was alone. The leaves began to stir gently as he felt the wind pick up. A mist was moving in around him. Wully spun on his heels, still looking for the man he had heard moments before. He paused when a cold chill ran down his spine. Then he heard it again. *This way, Wully.* This time, the voice rang from a distance; Wully stopped and looked carefully toward the call.

The Cradinlings around him still glowed their bright colors in beautiful shapes. But it seemed to Wully that the castle grounds beyond the garden were darker, almost like the torchlight was straining to penetrate the shadow of the night around them. Wully was about to follow the sound back through the garden when he suddenly felt his resolve return and asked aloud, "Why should I follow you?"

Silence.

Wully grasped his head in pain as the voice pierced his mind. *"Destiny never lies in hindsight, only ahead of you."* After the voice was done speaking, Wully gained his breath and carefully proceeded forward.

"This way," the voice would whisper as Wully reached a corner. Questions began to form as he walked. *Why am I doing this?* Then, as if the voice heard his thoughts, it would answer. *"Your time has come."* Wully winced again in pain as the voice called out to him. Who are you? Wully thought as if in reply. No response came after that. He stumbled through the garden growing weak, dizzy, and almost confused. The colors of the plants started to blur around him, becoming more and more distorted. Wully blinked hard to shake off the feeling, but nothing worked.

"Sir!" A voice called out. Not the same voice. This one was different. This one was real. Wully shook his head and blinked hard as his view focused on the face of one of the castle guards. Wully sat up; he didn't remember falling. Looking around, he was outside the garden and in the courtyard. In front of him, only a few feet away, was the entrance to the Great Hall. "Sir, are you okay?" the guard asked again.

"Yes, yes, I'm fine," Wully said as he stood. "Just…needed to clear my head."

"Of course, sir. Do you need anything?"

Wully shook his head, "No, thank you." The guard nodded and turned to leave. "Actually," he called out, still looking at the Great Hall. "Is this…?"

"The Great Hall, sir, yes." The guard interjected. "Are you sure you're okay, sir?"

Wully was about to answer when he heard the voice again, *"Wully, in here."* There was no pain this time, but even though Wully heard the voice in his head, he knew, deep in his gut, that voice came from inside the towering structure.

"May I go inside?"

"Of course, sir, it's not locked." The guard paused before leaving, "Are you looking for something?"

"I think I already found it," he muttered as he ascended the stone steps. The voice so entranced him that Wully hadn't noticed that the guard had heard him, shrugged, and walked away.

The front doors looked less brilliant in the night light. However, a sense of overwhelming came over Wully as he approached the doors. As he pushed them open, Wully was suddenly met with visions of the Hall, filled with people and bright light. Wully closed his eyes and sent those feelings away, for he saw Laura's wedding as a memory. Too real to embrace just yet. When he opened his eyes, the room was dark and empty again as it should be.

As Wully walked further into the main room, the moonlight shone brightly through the ceiling glass and refracted off fixtures, spotlighting each of the nine gods' statues that adorned the room's far end. Each figure glowed softly in their spotlight and from the windows that separated each one around the curved wall in which they stood. *Why do I feel I'm not alone,* Wully thought.

"Because you're not alone." Wully shot a glance toward the front again, then he saw him. A hooded figure was sitting at the base of Athalon's feet. Another chill runs down Wully's spine. "Don't let the chiseled gold and stone frighten you, Wully." The hooded figure raised his head, looking at Athalon, "Even in life, he was of a good nature."

"You're the man from the woods," Wully stated firmly, finding his resolve.

"Ah, good, you remembered."

"How did you get here?"

"For all the things on this world be,

A man, a bird, an ocean, a tree.

I only care that before I decease,

I may sit in a room under a blanket of peace."

Wully is taken aback slightly at this riddled response but recovers quickly, "Who are you?"

"I'm old if my beard doesn't give it away," the man chuckled.

"What manner of magic is this? Sorcery and witchcraft have long been gone from this world."

"There is no sorcery here," the man said as he rose. "And there never has been. Only truth."

Wully reached for his sword, only to find it gone and in the hands of the old man, "No more of this old timer. I need clear answers, not riddles."

"With the passing of time comes all answers to all questions."

As his sword was returned to him, Wully held it up at the man in frustration. "That is the exact opposite of what I just said."

The old man did not flinch, "The answer was clear, just not the one you wanted."

"Tell me what you want, then I may allow you to leave."

"What I want is beyond what is capable. So, I'll settle for what needs to be done at this time."

"And that is?"

"The eastern sea runs with blood as the south burns with war." He stepped closer and continued, "And you need to see, Wulfred Siggard. You need to see what may come to fruition and play your part in this string of destiny."

Wully took a moment to think; his sword was still firm in his hand at the visitor. Finally, he sheathed the blade and lowered his head, "Show me."

The hooded figure stepped directly in front of him and Wully glanced slightly upward as the old man was taller than he was. His green cloak is battered and torn, and in his right hand is his staff. Though the appearance of frail fingers gripped it, Wully imagined a hidden strength in those hands that he did not see. As quick as he moved in, the old man tapped his staff on the stone floor, it rang out and echoed a metallic ring, but it was deeper, heavier, maybe?

There was no time to process these questions because as soon as the man got face to face with him, Wully was locked in his green eyes. Deep under the hood and in the dark, these eyes glowed bright and strong. Wully searched inside himself for some sign of feeling; there was only calm. No fear, no anger, only calm…and pain. The man extended his empty hand, "Come with me."

Wully hesitated but then slowly reached out and grabbed it tightly.

As fast as he did, Wully was taken to another place. Darkness around him; he wasn't in the Great Hall but couldn't tell where he was. He knelt and felt the floor, the material was firm as a stone, yet it didn't feel like stone. Then, a mist appeared and a light within it. Soft at first, but it quickly grew. The old man was nowhere to be found. Wully tried to call out, but no sound exited his mouth. Fear began to take over.

Then suddenly, the mist took shape. Within the fog, Wully could see something. The smoke moved strongly as if pushed by the wind, yet Wully felt nothing as he watched intently. Before him, Wully saw King Ivan within the blurry image. He watched as Ivan fought before him against a massive army. Ivan's eyes were glowing pure white, and he wielded the Golden Sword. No man could touch him; Ivan effortlessly removed a dozen men with each swing.

The mist changed as quickly as it came. Another vision was presented, and Wully observed Aldrich in the Great Hall at the foot of Athalon, being crowned king of Althalos. The mist changed again and showed another blurry image of Oswald and Thomas on horseback, armed for battle.

In the following change, Wully saw Laura with Aldrich in Stalbak Castle. She was holding a child in her arms. Wully winced at the image, suddenly feeling sick to his stomach. The following picture was of himself, but older, his black hair now had a little gray throughout, and his beard was fully grown. Laura approached him, more aged as well yet still beautiful. She was holding the hand of a young boy with black hair. Laura looked at Wully with deep love and care, but her eyes had no joy, only pain.

The mist faded again, and Wully screamed into the nothingness. A futile attempt, as no sound escaped his mouth again. He reached out before the image was gone to grab the one he loved. But as fast he held Laura's appearance, she faded away.

As Wully fell to his knees, the mist retook its shape. He saw General Oswald, older and angry, with his sword drawn. No, not his sword, but Merrek's. Oswald held the falcon hilt tightly as Wully watched the sword, who's blade was now woven with blue veins and blood dripping off the blade as he walked through the empty halls of Stalbak Castle, no longer wearing the blue and white colors of the realm.

When the mist changed again, Wully smiled and stood. This time the vision was crystal clear; he saw Laura through it. She lay in bed with an older image of himself sitting beside her. This time, he had a stern face, a full head of gray hair, and a white beard. Wully stepped forward until he was almost next to the bed himself.

Laura began to cry. *"Take care of him, Wully, please."* The older version of himself responded, *"I will, my love. He is yours; he will be everything to me. He will be all I have left of you…"* Laura lethargically put her finger to Wully's frail lips. *"He is ours, Wully. That's what I want for him; I want him to know…"*

Wully stumbled back as he observed what was taking place and fell to his knees as the image of that moment faded. BOOM! Another rush of wind pulled the mist open in front of him; red is all that Wully can see now—swirling around him within the fog.

A glimpse of Oswald, older still from the last vision. He was fighting a very young man. Another image flashed of a man on a ship wielding two swords and holding his own against the entire crew.

Wully attempted to stand, but a great earthquake kept him kneeling as another vision appeared. He looked out to see nine flags before him, each with the coat of arms of the Kingdoms of Kralavia. Each flag lit up with fire and were quickly consumed. He saw the crown of Althalos on the ground. The burning flags fell around the spot where the crown lay, then it shattered. The crown in the center of the ashes, broken and bloodied.

As the image faded, Wully slowly stood. Suddenly, a dark figure appeared in front of him. Fear filled him as the figure wore back armor, grew large, and towered over Wully.

The dark-armored figure raised his weapon and struck. Wully let out a cry for help as he stood frozen. This time, his voice worked, and as fast as he released his cry for help, it stopped. Wully opened his eyes and saw the old man standing before him. The hooded man looked younger and more vibrant. His beard was shorter, and his staff was now a full-length spear. Newness also returned to his clothing, as the color and worn look were now that of the figure of authority. Wully glanced up and saw the man holding his spear aloft as if blocking a blow from above.

Wully let out a breath he didn't realize he held, "What was that?"

The old man set his spear down; the metallic clang echoed softly as it hit the floor. "That…was the cursed future." As fast as he spoke, the man was gone, leaving Wully alone in the Great Hall, with only the statues of the Unatari as company and questions in his mind.

Chapter 16
Valkos

The Valkos Countryside, Outside Terrowin

Terrowin, the capital city of Valkos, was several leagues directly south of Stalbak but an easy road to travel. The main roads were wide and smooth like most of Kralavia, as they were used by many and regularly for trade routes and others who wished to travel across the countryside. The productivity and growing economy for Valkos were partly thanks to the close friendship that Valkos shared with Althalos.

The alliance between the two countries grew stronger when Haldair, the second son of King Animas, was married off to the only daughter of Hagar Forrend, the previous king of Valkos. King Hagar was never blessed with a son, but the law of Valkos stated that any man of noble birth could take up the mantle of the king if appointed by the current king. If the current king could not make such an appointment, the barons of Valkos would meet and present a vote on the available candidates.

King Hagar had one daughter and no sons. So, he ventured to strengthen the union with Althalos by having Animas' second son marry his daughter. Prince Ivan, the oldest, was set to take the throne from his father, so the fact that Prince Haldair would also have a throne of his own intrigued Animas. At the time of the union, the world was near the end of the Great War, so King Animas heartily agreed to the marriage in hopes he could strengthen his forces against the remaining gods and the men that followed them.

Haldair and Ivan both showed extreme promise of good fortune and men of honor, so King Hagar had no disagreements with Haldair being king in his stead. So, at the end of the Great War, Haldair was finally married to Jasmine and pronounced Valkos' King to Be. However, less than a decade after they married, a plague ran through many parts of Kralavia and claimed the life of Jasmine and her father, King Hagar. Haldair was crowned King of Valkos, but he never remarried, and despite earning the crown of Valkos, he went into a deep depressive state. He became less physically active and gained weight. He relied heavily on the current barons to run their territories, and for a long time, most of the people of Valkos never saw their king.

Only his brother Ivan, having recently lost his wife in childbirth to Aldrich, could pull his brother out of the pit of despair. Haldair was an excellent king despite his depression, and though he never lost weight after his recovery, his mind was as sharp as ever.

Haldair looked out the window of the carriage at the passing fields. Valkos was a very open land, spacious with more green fields than woods or mountains. This landscape made farmland the biggest commodity in the kingdom and became the most prominent form of outgoing trade for Valkos. Valkos was the largest Kralavian kingdom based on land and population, it was not the wealthiest, but it was actively well run thanks to Haldair's leadership.

Given that the land was so vast, the system of government was different in Valkos, there was Haldair as king, and he had six barons who each had a section of land to manage and care for under their king. Merrek was one such figure.

Haldair adjusted his plump figure in the seat of his beautifully adorned carriage; it was a well-made ornate piece fit for a king. Merrek, who sat across from him, idly gazed out the window. Most of the trip was silent. Several times Haldair wanted to say something but didn't. He knew Merrek was displeased by his decision to marry off his sister to Aldrich. But he knew that it was what was best and had to be done in the long run. Merrek had been invaluable to Haldair over the years, but the debt that the baron's father owed was far more than Merrek could ever hope to pay off.

By Haldair's reasoning, it had been a mercy for Laura to marry Aldrich and have Merrek's family debt paid. He knew that Merrek would resent him for the decision. However, he also knew that Merrek would never reach his full potential under the weight of that debt.

"What are your plans now that we are returning home?" Haldair asked, trying to break the awkward silence.

Merrek remained quiet for some time. Haldair thought about repeating his question. But, before he could bring himself to do so, Merrek answered plainly, "I plan to help you assemble the Five Crowns for a possible attack on the invasion in Vasalia, and if I am no longer needed, I plan to return to my estate in Frosbike."

Haldair could feel Merrek's resentment in his answer but didn't let it show. "What if there is war, Merrek? I'll need you by my side."

"You have other barons, and they all have armies," Merrek's gaze remained fixed out the window. "You don't need me."

"Well," Haldair said, "It is a well-known fact that The Baron of Frosbike is the best warrior in the Valkon army." He hoped that would help ease the wound a bit.

Merrek sat back in his seat and folded his hands in his lap, "Everyone needs a break, Sire, sooner or later."

Haldair leaned back in his seat and relaxed the muscles he hadn't realized were tense. He knew that if the need arose, Merrek would be there, regardless of his feelings. Haldair had always trusted Merrek, and Merrek had never given any reason to doubt that trust. He didn't know if Merrek ever realized it. But Haldair was grooming him to become his successor for the throne, so Haldair had Merrek spend more time in Terrowin than in Frosbike. This favoritism wasn't without problems, as the other barons often resented Merrek for his position with the king. *He could be a good king one day; he needs some time to grow up, but he would undoubtedly make a great leader.* Haldair thought as he glanced around the carriage, the city of Terrowin on the horizon.

Terrowin was the capital city of Valkos, a vast city that almost rivaled the size of Stalbak in Althalos. It was a solid city; the walls were thick and tall and made of a robust tan-colored stone common in Valkos. The city was also stable but not nearly to the status of the towns in Althalos. Financially, the middle class in Terrowin were only as wealthy as the lower poverty levels within Stalbak. Despite this, the people of Valkos still enjoyed their lifestyle and comfort since the kingdom was well run, and everyone remained fed through the amount of open farmland utilized by the country.

Haldair looked up and down his walls, as his coach approached the front gate. He always marveled at his brother's kingdom and the home of his birth, but he loved his city, the citadel here in Terrowin, and he loved his country and served them well. Haldair was a good king, and he had the respect of his people, which gained him favor within the Five Crown Alliance, even more than King Ivan.

Part of this respect was also since Haldair's past was not nearly as bloodied as Ivan's, however useful it was to establish the kingdoms in the aftermath of the Great War. That said, Haldair was no novice when it came to warfare. Valkos had always been on the brink of war with the kingdom of Stelmond to the south. Thankfully, it never really went that far.

Stelmond occasionally hosted attacks and raids on the southern border of Valkos, which Haldair would defend with little effort. It had been like this since the Great War generations ago. Haldair never really went on the offensive because, for the most part, Stelmond's attacks were the equivalent of small waves upon the rocks, so he defended when he needed to but left the country alone otherwise. There had been several attempts to reach out for peace talks to King Ordain, but King Haldair was met without response each time he sent a letter to Ordain's castle in Gordost.

Home, Haldair thought as his attention was drawn to the looming city gates that were drawing closer. Merrek was looking out the other side window. The expression on his face told Haldair that he was not as pleased to be home. As the carriage got closer, Haldair's face grew grim as he noticed that the usual bustle of the city's entrance was…non-existent. Usually, the city gates were open to the public during the day for the farmers and outlying villages that wanted to come and go for business and the trades that came through daily. Terrowin's gates, since before Haldair was king, had only ever been shut at night *or in times of war,* he thought.

As the carriage approached the main gate, Haldair had forced his whole head out of the window to better see what was happening. Merrek, too, had noticed the strange sight and leaned closer to his window for a better look.

"Open the gates!" came a loud voice from above the doors. "Open the gates for King Haldair." Loud metallic groans and wooden creaks echoed in the doorway as the massive doors slowly opened.

The doors stopped wide enough to allow Haldair's entourage through before closing immediately behind them. "What is this? What's going on?" Haldair asked as he exited the carriage. Merrek stepped out behind Haldair; his hand was ready on his sword. None of the guards responded right away. "What happened?" he demanded, much louder this time.

"My lord!" a faint call came down the nearby street.

"Leon?" Merrek muttered.

"General Harris," Haldair stated. "What is the meaning of this?"

Leon paused briefly as he stood next to the carriage. Leon Harris was one of the barons of Valkos. His territory was in the northwest corner of the country. Leon had been a baron for several years since the passing of his father and was given the title of General as was the standard practice. Though he was fifty, General Harris was strong, athletic, and second only to Merrek on the battlefield.

"You haven't heard, my lord?" he asked. "We sent three birds…"

"Obviously, I haven't heard," Haldair snapped, cutting him off. "What has happened?"

Leon looked nervously at Merrek, then back to Haldair, "Valkos is under attack, my king," his voice wavered. "Handon has fallen, and Baron VonGarth has been publicly executed."

Haldair's eyes grew large; he glanced back at Merrek, whose expression matched his. "Wh… What?"

"It's Stelmond, milord," General Harris said, his voice regaining strength. "I don't know how they amassed a strong force, but our numbers have been nothing against them."

Haldair's fingers twitched, but he held his composure, "Handon is the closest territory to our capital city. It's damn near the center of the entire kingdom!" he stepped closer to Leon, who retreated slightly as Haldair approached. "Explain to me how an army of that size got that far through Valkos without being stopped or even seen?"

"I don't know, milord," Leon replied. "I was riding to Handon to meet with VonGarth and his son about a potential marriage to my daughter when I crested the hill and saw his estate was in flames. It was from one of the stragglers of the attack on Handon that came here that I heard of VonGarth's execution. I came directly here, and when I saw that you were still gone, I sent the birds to you and sent birds to the other barons to collect the armies. That is all I know, milord, I swear."

Haldair started to calm down as Leon explained, "Thank you, Leon. You've done well and reacted appropriately." He stepped back a few paces and asked, "Have you gotten any responses from the other barons?"

"No, my king. The birds were sent days ago, but no response as of yet."

Haldair turned to Merrek, "It seems birds are proving to be more and more useless these days." Then, he returned to Leon, "Send riders at once to the other barons. Until further notice, no birds are to be used for communication."

"Yes, Sire," Leon said, bowing slightly before he left.

Haldair and Merrek stood in silence as the guards that had been present were shuffled back to their posts. "I guess you won't get that break you talked about after all."

Chapter 17
The Remnant

The Dead Lands—West of the Nine Kingdoms, Kralavia

The Great Desert, if it were once rich and full of life, no one today would know. The placement of the area didn't dictate the weather, yet it was as if the sun was hotter and the ground dryer than the rest of the continent. Although parts of the known regions of Kralavia had dryer conditions that were less green where the soil was less rich, no land was more desolate than this.

The people of Kralavia called it "The Dead Lands," for within it, nothing grew, and beyond it, it was utterly unknown. With little to no natural life and scarce water sources, no one dared attempt to navigate these lands. The wildlife that called this place home were starved and scattered, much like the people forced to live there.

Near a small stream, one of the only water sources in this area was a small village of humans. Remnants of a once-growing nation of people until the Great War.

Serrek knelt beside the stream to collect some water that ran through it. As he stared at his reflection, he sighed; how long has it been? His hair was long and matted, his beard full and unkempt, and his clothing was more animal skin than cut threads. Dirt and grim covered his body. After he collected the water, Serrek sat for a moment under the shade of the small tree nearby. The Dead Lands had several pieces of plant life that grew throughout; however, most of it held neither leaf nor fruit, save for a few along the stream.

He glanced up at the sun and squinted. His people tell themselves that this place is cursed, and no life may thrive in this area. Perhaps it was true, perhaps not. Serrek did not care for any truth of it, only reprieve from it. His grandfather, for whom Serrek was named, was the first governor of the tribe since their banishment to this god-forsaken place. Initially, the people followed Serrek's grandfather and embraced their fate, holding their faith in old gods and believing they would be restored for their commitment and devotion. But it never came.

When Serrek's father took over the governing authority, the people had already begun to lose hope. What was once a proud people numbering in the thousands now counted less than a few hundred. Consistent malnourishment and harsh conditions had brought the people of this region to their knees and, as even Serrek had begun to do, abandoned the idea that gods still existed or cared.

Their initial devotion to the gods got them banished by King Ivan's father, who had ended the Great War. During this time, any who still favored the gods were made to accept the new order of kings or, in the event of a rebellion as Serrek's people had done, face defeat, humiliation, and banishment.

As Serrek rose to leave, he spotted a wolf across the way, starved and worn; he watched as it made its way to the stream on the bank across from him. The wolf collapsed before it made it. Serrek's eyes met the wolf's as it strained slowly to get something to drink. In one last exasperated sigh, the wolf was still, and life was removed from its eyes. He stepped across the stream and, after ensuring the wolf was dead, threw it on his back and made his way home.

On the way, he passed a mostly rotten and eaten horse carcass. This was no surprise to Serrek, for his horse lay there. It had collapsed some time ago on his hunting trip. Needless to say, the meat he brought home that day was an easy take.

When he returned to the village, Serrek walked through the main path lined with fur and brush tents. This is what his people had been reduced to, nomads and homeless. All the people here looked as rough and well-worn as he did, using whatever they could to survive. The few out and about paused their activity and bowed slightly as he passed. Whatever the conditions, they knew he was doing all he could, and the people still respected him as their leader.

Near the far end of the encampment, Serrek entered the final tent. His son was sitting next to his bed, and on it was his dying wife, the boy's mother. There was a new sadness in his son's eyes as he approached. The boy said nothing but returned his gaze to his mother on the bed. Serrek sighed; he knew what had happened. His wife was gone. A series of emotions flashed through his mind. He had been preparing for this day for some time, but it wasn't the same as having to experience it firsthand.

Later that day, Serrek stood at the gravesite with his son next to him. There was no funeral or ceremony. There was no need for such things. Death was so common in this area that each member took care of their own in this regard. Near his wife's grave were the modest graves of several others, all members of Serrek's family. Serrek pointed out a few of these graves to his son, who listened but said nothing.

Serrek gestured to the surrounding graves, "Their mothers and fathers… their brothers and sisters…back and back and back the generations go… but they're all buried here. Empty promises and broken treaties. A raped land and forgotten people. Now we're all that's left of it." His son still said nothing.

Serrek looked up at the sky and took in the view of the sun, trying to pierce through the clouds. It often looked like rain, but it never came. He then slowly turned to look his tearful son in the eye. After a moment, Serrek turned his whole body toward his son and placed both hands on his shoulders, "I love you, son, and I will not bury you here. No more of us will be buried here."

Chapter 18
Deep Thoughts and Near Death

The Purple Mountain Foothills, Althalos

The journey east had been pleasant overall, considering the circumstances in which they were forced to be headed that way. For most of the trip, Aldrich, Oswald, and Thomas rode in the quiet. Generals Ulrich and Rollins, who shared command with Oswald, joined the trio at the front early on.

The afternoon sun was bright, and the army was making good time thus far. Technically, it was only half of the full force of Althalos, but at ten thousand mounted troops, it was still a formidable force to be reckoned with. The emerald greenery of the countryside looked especially beautiful in the afternoon sun, with the light reflecting off the Purple Mountains in front of them. Unfortunately, no one was able to stop and enjoy the view.

They planned to stop for the evening in a forest clearing called Weldrake Meadow, which sat at the base of the mountains. Here, Ivan's father had made the clearing (as well as several others across the known realms of Kralavia) as troop-stopping areas. These points were essential in the effective movement of troops during his reign as the armies of Althalos moved across the countryside in the aftermath of the Great War.

"Ahh," Thomas exhaled after a large swig from his flask. "Nothing like a fine drink in the fine outdoors."

"You drink everywhere we go," Oswald chided.

"Yes. But!" Thomas exclaimed. "I most prefer it in the outdoors."

"Is that so, Captain?" Ulrich asked. His voice was as rough as he looked. Ulrich had broad shoulders and a tall stature, which, combined with his armor, gave an initial fear to those he met on the battlefield. He had long dark hair and a full, thick dark beard.

"Indeed, it is, General," Thomas responded casually.

"Well," Ulrich said. "According to the stories I hear at the Stag, you prefer it in the…"

"Mere tall tales to sully the grandeur of my escapades," Thomas interrupted. "I prefer many things, though most are lost in translation." Ulrich chuckled to himself as Thomas followed his statement with another drink. Then, Thomas turned to offer a drink to Aldrich, who politely refused. Thomas shrugged and put the flask away.

"Well," he said. "I'm sure our dashing young prince found out what he prefers last night, eh?"

Aldrich shook his head again, "No, no. I shouldn't."

"Oh, come now," Thomas chuckled. "You're a married man now. A king to be!"

Ulrich and Rollins exchanged a brief glance of annoyance, and Oswald, who began to feel awkward for Aldrich, shifted his horse closer to Thomas, "Thomas, he doesn't want to."

Thomas shot Oswald a questioning look, "Let him tell me that then."

"He already did."

"Well, if he really wants me to, maybe…" Aldrich began sheepishly.

"My prince," Oswald snapped. "It's not the time."

Aldrich said nothing and instead directed his gaze elsewhere. He didn't like that Oswald needed to stand up for him. Thomas was right. Aldrich was soon to be king, so why didn't his words have any weight? Do they not respect his authority? Is this why his father sent him on this errand with them to earn the respect of the other leaders? But how was he supposed to do that if Oswald continued to treat him like a child prince?

Aldrich's thoughts were interrupted when Oswald called out, "Ulrich! Captain Fendrell and I are riding ahead. Take the lead with Rollins and Prince Aldrich."

"Ugh," moaned Thomas, "What for?"

"You and I are going to scout the clearing ahead so the army can make camp safely," Oswald said firmly. "I don't want to lead the garrison into any unwanted trouble."

"If Thomas doesn't want to go, I can take his place," Aldrich said, now a part of the conversation.

"Stay with the men, Aldrich," Oswald said. "Captain Fendrell and I can manage."

"But I…"

"A king leads, Aldrich," Oswald said. His toned had shifted from a snapped command to a pleaded request. "He does not scout." Aldrich was about to protest further, but Oswald gave Aldrich a brief smirk and winked. Aldrich reluctantly smiled and nodded in understanding.

A moment later, Aldrich watched as Thomas and Oswald rode off ahead. "Don't mind it, your majesty," Ulrich said, riding beside the prince. "You have more support than you may realize."

As Oswald and Thomas got deeper into the woods, Thomas began to notice Oswald's demeanor, and despite a few futile attempts, Oswald would not become amused. "Okay, what?" Thomas finally said after his last round of chiding.

Oswald continued to glance around the woods, thinking of the recent conversation and the wedding night in the tavern, which began to get lost among all the other times Thomas pressed his influence on the young prince. "I don't want him drinking. Not now."

"But he's a man."

"Yes, he is," Oswald said as he stopped his horse. "And I don't want him taking more drinks from a child."

Thomas stopped next to Oswald, "He's not taking a drink from a child. He's taking a drink from…" Thomas cut himself off as he realized that Oswald was referring to him. Oswald smiled at Thomas in brief silence before proceeding on. Thomas shook his head and slowly followed.

The two rode silently for a while, and Captain Fendrell began to notice an unusual number of dead animals. All kinds, in all stages of decay. "Oswald!" Thomas shouted as he paused to look at one animal in particular.

Oswald rode up to Thomas, "What is it?"

Thomas pointed at a half-decayed carcass of a large raven on the ground. "Looks like one of the messenger birds, doesn't it?"

Oswald eyed the animal for a few minutes, "Possibly," he said. "But there isn't any way of knowing for sure. There are a thousand ravens that aren't in captivity, and hundreds that get as big as the ones the kings use for message sending."

Thomas didn't take his eyes off the dead animal, "Maybe," he said softly.

Eventually, the pair reached the clearing near the center of the woods. The Weldrake Meadow, it was called. The clearing spanned over half a league in diameter, and the ruins of the large stone monastery were in the middle. Once a place of gathering and meeting with the gods of old, now little more than a floor with portions of the walls still standing. The meadow surrounding the ruins had gone from a neatly cut and groomed landscape to an overgrown grassland with a few wildflowers that had taken over.

Oswald and Thomas split up and briefly walked around the perimeter; everything appeared as it should. Thomas arrived at the monastery first. After stepping through the remnants of the structure, he made his way through the primarily overgrown parts of the garden next to it. "I think we'll be okay here tonight," Oswald said as he approached.

Thomas nodded but said nothing. Instead, he knelt and carefully caressed a few flowers that had sprung up among the weeds and grass. His fingers carefully felt the silky petals as the luminescent hue of blue began to glow around the edges.

"It's a beautiful thing," he finally said, keeping his eyes fixed on the flower. Oswald said nothing as he stepped closer. "The trees, the grass, the animals. They all work together. Everything is born here, and everything dies. But they return to the ground, and their cycle starts over." Thomas sighed and stood before continuing. "This forest has been here for thousands of years. It just keeps going and going and going. It feeds off the old and creates something new. There is no end, not like us. There is an end for us."

"Perhaps not," Oswald said, crossing his arms. "Who's to say a dying man cannot fertilize the birth of new life the same as a dying bird or squirrel will fertilize the roots of these trees and these flowers."

"Because I've seen the fate of a dying man, Oswald. I've seen the fates of hundreds upon thousands of dying men, many of which I delivered that very fate. The destiny of man is to suffer. Bleeding out in the mud. Left to rot in the sun. I see that end for all of us…except for me."

"And why is that?" Oswald asked.

"Because my destiny is already at hand. I am already enduring my suffering. My life is death." Thomas turned and looked at Oswald, "I am the reaper."

Oswald stared blankly at Thomas momentarily as he tried to process what his friend had just said. After a moment, A smile broke across Thomas' face, and hearty laughter began to echo in the clearing. Oswald smiled but was taken aback by Thomas' sudden change of demeanor.

When he finished laughing, Thomas took a long drink from his flask before offering Oswald one, "Do you find my words false?"

Oswald accepted the flask and took a quick swig, "Very well, to a certain point, I guess."

"To what point?"

"To hell, if I know, Thomas," Oswald said as he returned the flask. "I barely understand what the hell you're even talking about. How did we get on this topic?"

"This topic is always on my mind, Oswald. Our lives were set into motion by two dead men that we never found…tends to weigh on you after a while. The realization that they died meaninglessly and rotted away, alone and lost. And realizing that you most likely share the same destiny."

A grim look grew across Oswald's face, "Don't bring them into this." Memories flashed through his mind. Memories of a life that had long since passed.

The Second Age—5,990 A.C.

"Thomas, hurry up!" Oswald cried out.

"I'm coming!" came Thomas' lighthearted reply.

Thomas and Oswald could often be found together growing up. Their families had farms nearby, so the two would often join together to do their chores and find a reason to play as they went. The boys had seen a large caravan approach the farmhouse and were eager to see who was there and why.

Today, they were supposed to fix some fence lines near the field that had fallen into disrepair. However, after an hour or so of working on the fence, adventures of grander things came to mind. The boys found themselves running through the pasture, slaying the foul beasts of vivid descriptions that came from the rumors of the few who dared—or claimed—to have traveled north beyond the Great Mountain Ridge into the uncharted lands.

That is, until a large caravan of troops and carriages was seen approaching from a distance. The flag of Athalon was flying high on the poles. A dark flag with a golden sword standing erect within the center and around the blade, a crown of the same. The gold in the soldiers' armor reflected brightly in the warm sun that day. The boys had seen it several times before, as their home was in the western farmlands of Althalos.

"… Times have changed," came a sharp response. The boys arrived at the house after the caravan had, and they carefully approached from the rear of the house as they tried to hear what was going on without showing themselves.

"But you can't," Oswald's father argued. "It'll be harvest soon. I need to be here. The war has been hard enough on my family already."

"King Animas makes the call," said the soldier from his horse. "I only deliver and enforce. All able-bodied men between fifty and a hundred years of age are to report to Castle Stalbak before the new moon. Any who refuse will be counted as traitors to the crown."

"Only the Unatari wear the crowns," Oswald's dad cut in.

"Not for much longer. Athalon has been gone since before the beginning of the war. Killed or shunned, it matters not since we wield his weapon. Obar is the same, though his weapon remains hidden. Borden has been defeated along with Alynia. Their weapons shattered with the last beat of their hearts. Renibaun and Kilith have engaged our forces in Ornion. Denesious, Valenear, and Dolos have retreated into hiding but won't stay that way for long."

Silence followed; Thomas and Oswald held fast as they watched intently from their hiding place around the house. They knew about the war; it was impossible not to. It had started before they were born, about fifty years prior. Thankfully, it never reached their peaceful area directly; the same could not be said of most parts of the continent.

Oswald's father did not move; his mother remained at his side, solid and unmoved. The soldier then held out a sealed roll of paper. Oswald's father slowly reached out and grabbed it. "Fine," he muttered between his teeth.

"For the good of Althalos and the good of Kralavia." The soldier said. As he left, the caravan of troops behind him followed suit.

Once the army was out of sight, Oswald and Thomas joined his parents with a giant group hug. "Thomas," Oswald's father said. "Run home quick. I have a feeling that your family is about to receive the same news." Thomas nodded and ran off after saying goodbye.

Thankfully, the new moon was a few days away, giving Oswald and his parents time to prepare for it. Oswald and Thomas didn't see much of each other since his family also received the same orders. When the time came, Oswald and his mother said goodbye, and he watched his dad head out for his assignment. Who knew it would be the last time they saw each other?

Weeks turned into months, and months turned into years. Soon, over a decade had gone by, and the Great War was over. King Ivan had succeeded his father Animas and was busy maintaining the blood-fueled fury of his father. After Thomas' mother died of a sickness, he joined Oswald and his mother, and the friends grew together as brothers. Both remained hopeful that word would be sent that their fathers were alive and well and that they would be coming home. Nothing ever came.

As the land found peace in the wake of Ivan's blade, new kings were established, and unique banners and colors to mark their thrones, a symbol of the new regime. But Oswald and Thomas grew more and more anxious about their fathers. By all matters of reason and thought, they had to accept that they had been killed in some battle and were never identified or recovered. Still, once Oswald and Thomas reached twenty and were able to, they enlisted in King Ivan's army voluntarily in hopes that they might get some closure.

The two fought bravely and well under Ivan's lead and soon earned their leadership positions. The more bodies they stacked up, the more

Thomas began to drink. He wouldn't talk of the faces. That part wasn't real, he would say. But Thomas would recall the aftermath, when the adrenaline was gone, and you alone are left on the battlefield to gaze over the bloodied corpses of your fellow man.

Oswald understood. He was there each time. For reasons unknown, however, Oswald didn't seem as fazed by it in the long run. He never enjoyed it, but he never regretted it. Deep down, Oswald knew that he was on the right side, and it was for the better, and so far, he had been right. Oswald figured that Thomas, regardless of how just the cause, couldn't really bring any justification in his own head about it.

Perhaps he should've been more careful with Thomas, but who was to know? Every time a battle came up, Thomas fought with strength, cunning, and vigor. Oswald couldn't count the times that Thomas had saved him in one way or another. They never found their fathers or any word of where they might be.

Maybe it'll just work itself out over time…

Present Day…

"What do you see for yourself then?" Thomas asked again.

Oswald blinked hard; he hadn't meant to zone out, "What do you mean?"

"Your end. Every man thinks about it. Even if he says otherwise." He turned to face Oswald directly, "What do you see?"

Oswald sighed, "I don't see anything, Thomas. I live here and now. I follow orders, fight my battles, and don't question whether or not I deserve to survive. I don't question whether or not I will continue to survive. I accept what I have been given, and I accept what I will be given. As long as the cause for which I fight is just, nothing else matters."

Thomas' face grew a curious expression, "Interesting. Even you can't make the lies sound convincing."

"You asked, and I gave you my answer. What do you want to hear me say?"

Thomas glanced around the area before responding. "I think I chose the wrong words. If you could choose your end, what would it be?"

"Choose?"

"Yes," Thomas answered. "Choose whatever you want. How does the story of Oswald Cromwell come to an end?"

Oswald stood in silence for a moment. He'd never had to think about that choice before.

Thomas began strolling around the ruins while he waited patiently for Oswald's answer. "All that I can ask, Thomas," he said, breaking the silence. "Is that I hope I get it before you do. I'd rather die before my time, knowing that I did everything I could in the time I had to protect the ones I love, rather than surviving long enough to be alone and realize that I failed every single one of them." He paused briefly, waiting for Thomas to answer, "Does that suffice?"

Thomas nodded but didn't say anything.

Then he took another drink from his flask and offered it to Oswald. "You're such as ass sometimes," Oswald muttered as he took the flask and downed a long drink. After he tossed the flask back to Thomas, who caught it one-handed with incredible skill, given his drunken state, Oswald mounted his horse.

"I don't want to talk about this. I'm returning to the troops to let them know it's clear. Stay here and make sure it stays that way. Maybe try to scrounge up some food for everyone."

As Oswald began to ride off, Thomas gave a mock two-finger salute, "As you wish, General." He followed that with another drink from his flask. Oswald rolled his eyes and rode on. Thomas' face grew serious as the general got out of sight. "I'm sorry."

After a few minutes, some rustling in the brush line on the far end of the clearing got Thomas' attention. He stood to get a better view when he noticed it was a deer stepping out into the clearing. Carefully, Thomas reached for his bow from his horse, but the deer caught the movement and was gone.

Grabbing his bow, Thomas ran after it into the woods. He tracked the deer for several minutes, following tracks and broken shrubs. Thomas stopped suddenly as he heard a deep growl, followed by a strange whining before all went silent. Nothing moved, and neither did Thomas. A strong scent of rust reached his nostrils. Thomas followed the smell and stepped gently to investigate. Whatever it was that got his deer was still a threat to him.

He followed the hoof prints until they stopped in a big pool of blood. Thomas studied the area and saw that the trail continued, but instead of hoof prints, it was a trail of the deer's blood. *Curious,* Thomas thought. *Not many creatures here could drag that deer away.* Some other tracks were seen in the area, but Thomas couldn't make them out in all the mess.

As he carefully and quietly moved forward, Thomas paused near a large tree. As he peered around it, he noticed three giant wolf-like beasts. *Dire Wolves!* Thomas had only ever heard about them. Wolves in overall appearance, but as tall as a small horse but more robust and fiercer. They supposedly roamed the area during the recorded First and Second Ages. Since then, none have been seen in any kingdom. Some have said that the wolves, like the other strange and foul beasts of that era, moved north of the Great Mountain Ridge and remained there.

Thomas strung an arrow and began to think about a good approach. His aim was true, but the repeated draw speed for multiple shots worried him. Additionally, there was no telling exactly how tough the skin of a dire wolf was.

As he continued to think, Thomas reset his footing to get a good first shot. *Crack!* His foot caught a weak twig on the ground. Immediately all the wolves caught his attention. "Fu…" Thomas barely got the words out as the first wolf lunged at him. Quick as he could, he drew the arrow and released it. The first wolf dropped mid-stride; Thomas' arrow had found its mark.

However, there was no time for celebration as Thomas ducked behind the tree to string another arrow. He stepped out and released it quickly. The wolf staggered but didn't fall. With no time left to try again, Thomas started to run, throwing his bow over his shoulder and drawing his sword. As the second wolf caught up to him, he spun quickly, connecting his blade against the wolf's neck: two down, one to go.

As the second wolf dropped, the third reached him before he could react, knocking him back. Pinned down and unable to find his sword, Thomas pushed both hands as hard as possible at the wolf's throat to keep his long fangs away. But that didn't stop the claws from tearing at his arms and chest.

As he strained under the pressure of the wolf's assault, Thomas gagged as the rotting stench of the wolf's breath reached his nose. After a few moments, Thomas' arms weakened, and the wolf's mouth found its mark. The pain was excruciating. The long fangs pierced his left arm deep into the tissue. Frantic now, Thomas scanned the area around him, hoping to find his sword. Nothing.

He punched the wolf's head and nose, trying to get it to let go, but that only made the giant beast angrier and grip tighter. After several strikes, the wolf loosened its bite on Thomas' arm. Instantly, he lunged forward and punched his right arm down the wolf's throat, choking it.

The wolf released a muffled whelp of pain as Thomas forced his arm deeper. The pain was intense as the wolf's teeth buried into his upper arm while he still forced it down its throat. With his other arm—as useless as it was—he braced himself, rolled up, and moved the wolf down on its side.

He fed his arm to the beast, pushing it forward straight as an arrow, and plunged it farther and farther down the wolf's throat. Through the slime and fluids, Thomas noticed that the wolf's mannerisms slowly changed as it suffocated. At last, the dire wolf relaxed and died.

Thomas shoved the wolf to the side as he retracted his arm from its throat. After he glanced around, he found his sword a few paces away and retrieved it. Standing over the giant beast, the wolf didn't react. "Don't worry," he said to the dying animal. "You're suffering is not like my own…yours has a purpose. And I will not let any of you go to waste." And with that, Thomas plunged his sword deep into the beast's heart. He exhaled heavily, not realizing he was holding his breath yet.

The woods went silent.

Then a whimper was heard. He walked toward the sound and found the wolf he shot first, still clinging to what little life it had left in it. Thomas knelt next to it and stroked its fur as it lay there. He turned around and sat with his back against the dying beast. Blood still oozed from the bite on his left arm, and his right was still covered in blood and bile. Then, when the wolf breathed its last breath and the woods went silent again, Thomas began to sing his favorite wartime lullaby. It was a song he had learned early on while serving, though it wasn't until a few years ago that it took on a different meaning for him.

Come here, come close, my youth,
Come hear my tale of pain.
Listen close to tales of death,
And of storms, without the rain.

Come one, come all, to battle we go,
We fight and die as one.
We fight, we fight until the end,
When all is said and done.

We move, we move ever more,
We move so close to death.
We move, we move farther we go,
Until our dying breath.

Come forth, come forth, soldiers of strength,
Come forth all arms to fight.
Come forth, protect all you love,
Not all survive the night.

Come here, come here, die free, die fair.
For we all shall die alone,
The dead, they call you to their lair.
The dead, they call you home.

He glanced up at the sky, peeking in from above the trees. He almost wished he could be up there. His hands shook as the adrenaline wore off, but they would be steady enough if he decided to do it. Thomas sighed to himself as he looked at his reflection in the blade. No, as much as he wanted to be above the trees, floating in the air, above all the suffering, death, and chaos that continued to plague his world.

He can't. Not yet.

Chapter 19
Hard Words and Soft Lessons

Weldrake Meadow—Althalos

What was a large open meadow quickly turned into a cluttered, filled space as Aldrich and the army of Althalos began to pile in and make camp. It was nightfall when everyone settled in; blue and white tents filled the area with two large fires near the center monastery ruins. Other smaller campfires were littered throughout, though truthfully, the only reason for large fire pits was the feast of the evening, thanks to Thomas.

Oswald glanced around the camp from his perch on a partially ruined upper window along the crumbling monastery wall. Three giant Dire Wolves, skinned and prepped, were roasting on the open fire. Cheers and tense talks filled the air, and Thomas' name was tossed around like something from the legends. Rightfully so in this instance. There had only ever been rumors and tales recorded from times past about Dire Wolves and other such beasts. *But that's all they were,* thought Oswald, *rumors and stories.* His gaze remained fixed on the scene below as he processed this turn of events.

"AH!" Oswald's thoughts broke suddenly as Thomas' sarcastic pain filled voice echoed from below. He smiled softly; at least Thomas was in good spirits. Considering what he went through on his own today. Even with his wounds, Thomas' account of what happened was so far-fetched that neither of the generals nor Oswald believed him. That was until the bodies of the animals were dragged out of the woods.

Oswald walked down to the ground level after taking one final look at the camp. Aldrich and the other generals had taken command within the monastery, doubling as the medical station. As Oswald approached, some other officers admired the wolves' skins hung against the wall. They had been discussing the events and comparing notes about different stories and possible explanations that might explain the reality of what they saw.

In the far corner, Oswald saw Thomas on a cot, moaning with the dramatic flair of his pain. "You know, Thomas," he said as he reached the bed. "I didn't think we'd need to set up a surgery until after we got to Alkeroth."

"Ha. Ha. Ha," Thomas sarcastically replied. "And I didn't think I'd spend my afternoon shoving my arm down a wolf's throat," he said, shaking his bandaged right hand in Oswald's face. "Guess we're both having a bad day."

Oswald did feel bad for Thomas at first. But after he was bathed, changed, and getting his wounds cleaned and wrapped, he looked far better than his initial appearance. After the surgeon finished putting Thomas' wrapped left arm in a sling, he gestured to Oswald and pulled him aside. "He's doing far better than most men would be in his situation."

"Well, Thomas is tougher than most men."

"Yes, well, perhaps his will is stronger than his body," the surgeon said. "The left arm is all right; it should heal in a few weeks and return to normal. But there's some severe nerve damage on his right. It took most of the force of the attack. I gave him something for the pain; he's stabilized…but I fear that arm will never be the same."

"Will he still be able to use it?"

"Well, yes, that's why I didn't amputate," the surgeon answered. "And we got to it before it could turn gangrenous. But even once his ability to use the arm returns, the pain will remain to some extent. I've seen it a few times before."

Oswald looked at Thomas, who was finally calm and lying peacefully in the bed. "Have you told him?" he asked. The surgeon shook his head. Oswald nodded and placed his hand on the surgeon's shoulder, "Let me do it." The surgeon agreed, and the two parted ways.

Oswald stepped up to Thomas' bedside. "Well, Captain Fendrell. Let's get you on your feet."

"Ugh, what fo—?" Thomas moaned as Oswald reached down to him. He slapped his hand away, "What for?"

Oswald ignored the slap and kindly shoved Thomas off the cot while gripping his shoulder. It took a few steps, but Thomas found his footing as the effects of the medicine were wearing off slightly. "They didn't get my legs," he said, shoving Oswald away. "I can walk."

"I know. I'm just making sure you're going in the right direction."

Thomas stopped, "Oh? And which direction is that?"

Oswald crossed his arms in annoyance, "We are going to find you something to eat."

"I don't want food. I want something to drink."

"Well," Oswald said as he grabbed Thomas' arm. "You're getting food. It's kind of like drinking, but you eat it instead."

"Kind of like how my ass and your face are different yet share very similar looks."

Oswald smiled, "Yes, Thomas. Exactly like that." Then he gently slapped Thomas on the back of the head. "That's for you," he said, gesturing to the crowd. As they headed through the camp, several men stood and held their drinks aloft, saluting Thomas on his hunt.

"They have drinks."

"Shut up."

"When this stuff wears off," Thomas said. "I'm going to ensure you're the next patient in that medical bed."

"I'm looking forward to it."

A few minutes later, the pair find a spot around a smaller fire with Ulrich and Prince Aldrich. "Ah! Hahaha," Ulrich said. "There he is. The man of the hour." Thomas didn't respond as he sat down. "A fine kill you've got yourself here, Thomas. I didn't think you had it in you."

"Ignore him," Oswald said as he motioned for a nearby soldier to bring two plates.

"Here," Ulrich said, ignoring Oswald's comment. "I made a little souvenir for ya." Once Thomas made eye contact, Ulrich tossed something over. Thomas carefully caught it between his arm and chest in the sling wrap. When he pulled it out, he saw that it was a necklace made from all the claws and teeth of the three wolves neatly tied on a thin rope.

"Not my finest handiwork, but I figured it's the least I could do to pay you back for dinner," Ulrich said. "If there's any more of those bastards lurking about, they'll fear the scent of Captain Fendrell, the wolf slayer."

"So, what was it like, Thomas?" Aldrich asked.

Thomas remained silent for a moment as he stared at the necklace. "Oswald," he finally mumbled. "I think I'd like to see where my bed is tonight." As he finished, he stood and walked away.

Oswald got up after Thomas, "Yeah, sure."

Aldrich turned to Ulrich, "I didn't mean to offend?"

"Don't worry about him," Ulrich said.

Oswald guided Thomas through the maze of tents, "I've got your tent set up over here."

"This doesn't make any sense," Thomas interjected.

Surprise took Oswald, and he stopped, "What doesn't?"

"I've read about Dire Wolves," Thomas explained. "They haven't been seen in this region for hundreds of years. I thought they were extinct or a rumor from time past. Back when there were also drakes, dragons, scorpios, and basilisks."

"No one believes that stuff of legend," Oswald scoffed as he tried to lighten the mood, "Besides, I didn't know you could read."

Oswald couldn't imagine what Thomas was going through. That, combined with his medicine, while sober for the first time in years, must be taking a hard toll on the brave captain. "Oh, that's funny, Oswald," Thomas sneered. "That's really funny." He stepped forward and shoved Oswald in the chest. Oswald laughed it off initially as he tried to get Thomas to calm down. "You know what else is funny?" he continued. "The fact that I was almost eaten by three animals that shouldn't exist anymore, I think that's hilarious! Don't you?"

Thomas shoved Oswald again, harder this time. "You must also think it's funny that I was left to take those wolves by myself. I hope you're satisfied; I followed orders just like you, *General,*" Thomas said mockingly. "I scrounged up some delicious food, so stuff your gullets; it only nearly cost me a couple of arms and my face!"

Oswald nearly missed the fist that suddenly came at him, and he quickly blocked the second while he shoved Thomas to the ground. Oswald let Thomas fall on his back to avoid further injury to his damaged arm. "I'm sorry, Thomas. Now come on, stand up."

Oswald reached to offer Thomas assistance getting up, but Thomas just slapped it away, "Get away from me." He retracted his hand and knelt beside Thomas as he brought himself up to a seated position. "You don't know what it's like, Oswald," he said. "You never have. I've always been strange, unstable…weak to you."

Oswald's expression grew solemn, "I have never once told you that."

"Well, you can tell quite a lot from a man who never tells you much. You've always been the stronger one. You've always been able to…keep it all inside." His voice grew weak as tears formed in his eyes as he spoke. "I can't do this anymore, Oswald. I'm seeing things clearly for the first time in a while, and I can't handle what lies ahead."

Oswald placed his hand on Thomas' shoulder, "Thomas, you're sober. It's rare, I know, but it's just some intrusive thoughts being let in. Just ignore it."

"They've always been there. I've been ignoring thoughts for ten years. It was just a matter of time… I'm dying, Oswald."

"Thomas. You're okay."

Thomas shook his head and took a deep breath, "I'm dying." He pointed to his head, "I'm dying up here." Tears started to drop down his face, and Oswald began to realize that this was the real Thomas speaking. "Up here with all my wasted life's demons, regrets, and sinful actions. I can't even keep it straight anymore. I want to die, Oswald…I *want* to die."

Other soldiers in the area started to gather, and Oswald quietly sent them away as Thomas continued. "But I *can't* die. I can't give up. I won't let myself give up, which means I can't do it myself, and I can't just yield a fight. I hope tomorrow is it. I really do. I hope we find Alkeroth in flames and an army numbering in the hundreds of thousands standing before us tomorrow. I'll draw my last breath there. Perhaps an arrow through my chest or maybe decapitation, swift, painless, I won't even know what happened." Thomas paused as he looked up at the stars that shone overhead. "Yes…yes, I think tomorrow will be quite exciting…I think tomorrow I will finally feel… I don't know."

Oswald waited as he put his thoughts together. He needed to be kind and uplifting, but sometimes life is what it is. He had never really thought about it beyond that. "I hate to tell you this," he finally said. "But you're not going to be able to die tomorrow. I won't allow it," Thomas chuckled. "You're not weak. Do you know who got the two of us out the door all those years ago? You did. You were the one who encouraged us to leave to try and find our fathers. I was content to stay on the farm and just accept it."

"But…" Thomas started to say.

"You know who saved my life during the scorching of the Great River?" Oswald interrupted. "You did." Thomas thought back; Oswald was right. That was a time he did a great thing and saved his friend. But it was also the beginning of Thomas' downslide.

The Great War was over, but several skirmishes remained throughout Kralavia. King Ivan had been on a bloody rampage to bring peace between the human kingdoms. Toward the end of this expedition, Oswald and Thomas had been promoted to General, and together, there was not a better fighting force in Ivan's army.

They were dealing with an uprising on the southwestern corner of Althalos, remnants of Ornion. Generals Oswald and Thomas had been sent to quell the insurrection. The fight was long and bloody. The enemy's guerilla fighters used the woods to their advantage and brought countless death to Thomas' and Oswald's troops. In a final desperate attempt at victory, Thomas ordered his men to burn the woods.

Thomas' plan worked…too well. The entire woods were in flames in minutes, and the oil and tar burned the water. In the chaos, some of their men got caught in the blaze with the enemy. Thomas rushed through the woods to save any he could find, and that was when he found Oswald. Suffocating in the smoke, Oswald was near dead when Thomas reached him and got him out.

In the aftermath, both sides took a heavy hit and lost significantly. It would be days until the fire burned out and the smoke would clear the sky. But it took even longer for the Great River to return to normal, as the scorched woods, burned oil, and tar would remain and taint the water for months. Thomas was demoted for his reckless action, which he took personally and never truly recovered. Over time, Thomas' consistent drunken stupor brought about his second demotion, returning him to the captain rank.

Thomas blinked a few times to clear his eyes as he remembered. "It was because of me that the trees along the Great River are now little more than tall black sticks that fall over at the slightest touch. Because of me, the river itself was filled with chard corpses. The locals said they found bodies all the way over at the harbor outside Stelbeck." He looked at Oswald, "Maybe we'll see some tomorrow. Ha-ha."

Oswald felt his heart drop, "You're the best soldier I've ever been privileged to have at my side." He then pulled a small flask from his tunic and handed it to Thomas. "I figured one day you finally run out."

Thomas' eyes got big, and for a moment, Oswald thought his youthful spark had returned. "Is it?"

Oswald nodded, "Pure Terrowin Ungelded Brandy." Thomas' favorite and one of the strongest percentages you can find in Kralavia. "Bartered some off of Haldair at the wedding. Drink up," he continued, "keep those voices at bay."

Thomas was hesitant initially, but then he took the flask and drank in large gulps. When he finished, Thomas' eyes practically rolled into his head. Oswald was sure for a moment there it looked as though a faint bit of steam rolled out of Thomas' nose and ears.

"Ugh," he finally said, taking a breath. "That's better than a woman."

Thomas offered Oswald a taste, but he refused and helped Thomas to his feet. When the two reached the captain's tent, Oswald opened the flap and gestured to Thomas. As he entered, Thomas paused and looked back at Oswald, "Don't leave without me."

"Never," came Oswald's soft reply. "Try and get some sleep, Thomas."

As he walked away, Oswald stopped and glanced back at Thomas' tent. Concern began to creep in as Oswald realized that some of his suspicions about Thomas were true. Others were much deeper than Oswald ever considered. Additionally, he wondered if he should've just come out and told Thomas about his arm and how it'll never fully heal. But then again, perhaps it was best that he didn't say anything…yet.

When Oswald returned to the primary fire, Ulrich and Aldrich were still there. Oswald initially paid them no mind as he cut some meat off the roasting animal. "What's gotten into Thomas?" Oswald tightened as Ulrich's voice rang out.

"It's been a long day," Oswald said as he grabbed a mug of ale and sat across the fire. "And I don't think your gift or the new name for him was exactly helpful."

"Long day?" Ulrich jeered. "Ha-ha, we're soldiers! Every day is long, and all he did was take out a few wild dogs."

"Lay off him, Ulrich," Oswald snapped.

"Why should I?"

"Because I know what you're doing."

"Oh?" Ulrich asked. "Do tell?"

"I don't have to. You already know," Oswald responded, keeping his tone mellow. Oswald knew that part of Ulrich's resentment toward Thomas was for his role in the scorching of the Great River. Ulrich lost three brothers that day and never let Thomas forget it. It didn't help that Ulrich saw Thomas' demotion as little of a punishment. More than once, Ulrich remarked that death was how it should've been handled.

Nothing more was said as Oswald finished his food. When he rose to leave, "As you've said, Ulrich. Every day is a long day for men like us. Every day comes with its own difficulties. The best we can do is move on from them, and you need to learn how to do that just as much as Thomas does." Oswald turned to Aldrich and bowed his head. Aldrich bowed in return, and with that, Oswald left to find some solace in his tent, leaving Aldrich to sit in awkward silence with Ulrich as he finished his food.

Oswald's walk back to his tent was slow, having to nod and address every group of soldiers as he passed. But the most frustrating part of his walk came when he was just about to reach his destination, "Oswald!" he froze and sighed to himself. Oswald knew that voice and had hoped to avoid it as much as possible.

Oswald smiled and turned to face the caller, "General Rollins. How are you this evening?" He didn't actually care. Rollins had been in the king's service for less time than the others, and the two never quite got along.

Oswald casually strolled over to the bench Rollins had claimed for the evening. He was propped up against a barrel with a full mug in his hand. Once Oswald was closer, Rollins offered him a drink. Oswald cautiously agreed and took it. "Easy, Oswald. I mean no offense to you tonight," he said. Then, he stood, grabbed another mug, and filled it from the barrel he had been using as a backrest, "How's Thomas?"

Oswald finished a large swallow, "He's alright. He'll be back to normal in a few weeks." Even as he said that he didn't believe it. But he wasn't in the mood to discuss anything further tonight, much less with Rollins or Ulrich.

Rollins caught the slight tremor in Oswald's voice; he knew more was going on than Oswald let on. Rollins knew Thomas just as well as most but less than Oswald. Nevertheless, it wasn't hard to see that Thomas was slipping. Seeing that Oswald wanted to ignore the topic, he offered to change the subject, "You think this is enough men? We don't know the exact size of what we're walking into tomorrow."

Oswald handed back his empty mug, "Don't think about that. There's nothing we can do about it now. Just remember, we're men of Althalos, Rollins. We serve under the weapon of Athalon himself. We can take anything."

"Are you sure about that?" Rollins asked as he glanced toward Thomas' tent.

Oswald ignored him and turned to leave, "I'd try to get some rest if I were you. We leave at first light."

Meanwhile...

The guys had finished eating, and Ulrich was cleaning his sword with the soft embers of the dying fire. Most of the troops had called it a night, knowing they were continuing in the morning. It wasn't necessarily a hard road up through the Purple Mountains, but it was tiresome, and they would still need their strength when they arrived at Alkeroth to assist in whatever was left of the attack on Stelbeck Keep.

Aldrich sat nearby, watching the small flames dance in the dark. Memories flashed in his mind as he recalled the duel with Merrek in the courtyard. He replayed the fight repeatedly and Aldrich would imagine a different outcome each time.

Ulrich noticed Aldrich's glazed-over stare and nudged the prince with the hilt of the sword he was cleaning. Aldrich blinked as his thoughts faded, and he was left to stare dumbfounded at Ulrich, and the sword outstretched in his hands, "What?"

"Take it," Ulrich said.

Aldrich gently grabbed the sword and sat up as he swung it out over the fire. He had only swung it a few times before he felt the strain in his forearm, and Aldrich had to let the blade hit the dirt at his feet. "It's heavier than I imagined. My sword is lighter."

"Is it?" Ulrich's face cracked with a large smile. He took the sword from Aldrich and playfully swung it around in several large sweeps and flares. "In its wielder's hands, the sword can be as light as a feather, my dear boy." Aldrich doesn't respond.

Ulrich sat back down and sheathed his blade, "I saw what happened at your wedding." Aldrich had a flush of embarrassment rise through his cheeks. "You had good training."

"Not enough, apparently."

Ulrich stroked his beard as he watched Aldrich stare back into the fire. After a moment, he stood and told Aldrich to do the same, "Come," he said firmly. Aldrich shot him a questioning glance as he followed Ulrich to a small clearing near the ruined monastery. Ulrich took his stand and drew his sword. "I have witnessed your fighting ability. Now, let me experience it."

"Wait, now?"

"Show me what you know," Ulrich said, unmoved. "Then let me fill the gaps."

Aldrich hesitantly drew his sword; what caution he had initially was gone. Ulrich was here to teach, and Aldrich knew that he could never get rid of those feelings about his loss unless he got better. The king had provided Aldrich with all the finest training, but even the prince knew there was something to be said for more practical experience. *Perhaps Ulrich can show me something,* he thought, taking his stance opposite Ulrich.

"Just a quick round before we call it a night."

Aldrich nodded and readied himself, "On you."

Ulrich smiled and lunged forward; Aldrich stepped forward and blocked the first strike. The force was strong, and Aldrich winced momentarily as he tried to hold it back. "Very good," Ulrich said as he returned to his original position. "First lesson, never block a full attack unless you have to. There's no sense in trying to out force someone, especially if they are bigger. You won't win."

Aldrich paused as he contemplated this. During his fight with Merrek recalled several moments where Merrek got the upper hand because he had tried to stop Merrek squarely. "Got it," he said as he readied himself again.

Ulrich remained poised as he stepped in again, attacking differently. This time, Aldrich side-stepped and deflected the blow, forcing Ulrich to lose his balance slightly. "Very good," he said as he lunged again. "Use my force against me, more deflection to ready yourself for a counterstrike."

Aldrich smiled as he danced around with Ulrich. Though it was far more controlled and playful than his duel with Merrek, Aldrich could see the errors of his previous ways as Ulrich guided him further. The teachers that Ivan had to help train Aldrich were good by any standing, but they were clearly lacking in some areas. That said, perhaps Aldrich didn't pay attention enough during his lessons, or maybe they didn't want to upset the prince, so they kept it easy and let him think he passed and was doing well. Aldrich scoffed in his head at this thought.

As Ulrich and Aldrich continued, a hooded and cloaked feminine figure sat in Ulrich's seat. Her legs crossed, exposing her purple tinted skin through the slits along the sides of her fitted robe. A seductive smile could be seen as the firelight danced in front of her. No one noticed or cared to notice, but she sat and observed nonetheless. She watched as the first pieces of her plan were unfolding. Whispers in the dark. She had chosen well. It would work…it had to.

Ulrich didn't care that he was a prince. He didn't care to get Aldrich upset for failure and trained him as though he was just another young man. The two began to draw a small crowd of nearby soldiers still out and about. Swords clanged, and a couple of soft cheers and playful mocks came from the audience. Aldrich didn't care. He loved it; hearing the support as he went gave him a new focus.

The duel was finally stopped when the pair reached an impasse. Aldrich looked up at Ulrich as he held the tension on the blades. Ulrich smiled, "Excellent job, my young prince."

The two relaxed and sheathed their swords as small applause came from the crowd before it dispersed. "I wish I had you to train me before," Aldrich said. "I feel so behind now."

"Nonsense!" Ulrich exclaimed. "You were excellent. Even in your fight with Merrek, most had bet that you'd fall out much sooner than you did. Merrek's very good, but you held your own. And that last-minute sneak attack," he chuckled. "Impressive." Aldrich shot him a startled look.

"Don't worry," Ulrich reassured. "Your secret is safe with me." He put his hands on Aldrich's shoulders, "Sir, you will always have my support. I am happy that it is you that will take the throne. You're not afraid to get things done. I like that. If there's anything you need, let me know."

Aldrich smiled, "Teach me more."

Chapter 20
Unusual Happenings

The Purple Mountains, Althalos

The sun glistened off the reflective purple rock that made up the mountainside, and for a few beautiful moments of the morning, a soft purple hue covered the area in the open parts of the woods below. Aldrich and his generals led the way as the army proceeded up the stone and dirt path that cut into the mountain and provided the main thoroughfare for travelers and traders between Vasalia and Althalos.

The prince glanced at the sky around the top of the mountains; despite the sunlight reflecting off what parts of the western side it reached, a dark shadow of clouds still hung over the top. "Does that look normal to you?" he asked Oswald, who was riding beside him.

"No, but Amias mentioned that a storm proceeded the attack. Perhaps it has made its way here."

"Strange for this time of year, don't you think?"

"Possibly," Oswald responded. "Perhaps it'll clear up as the day passes."

Aldrich shrugged in agreement and gave the signal to press on. Oswald, Ulrich, Rollins, rode beside him with the army in columned rows behind them. With a wide girth and stable shoulders, the road up through the mountain was usually easy. However, as the military drew to the top of the mountain pass, what should've been a relief as the trail leveled out and gave a view of the vastness of Althalos and Vasalia, was now covered in frost and cold.

The temperature began to drop quickly as they neared the center of the peaks atop the mountains. Thankfully, the men had some light from the sun. Though the clouds and snow partly concealed it, it was light enough to keep the army on the main road.

Then, they saw it. "I hold to my question from earlier," Aldrich said. He and the generals had come to a halt in front of a wall of a blizzard. They had just experienced the remnant of the storm outside its core.

The wind and snow blew hard and fast, holding itself still. Ulrich got down from his horse and stepped up to the barrier. He reached his hand through and then pulled it back. His gauntlet and glove were covered in frost. "What devilry is this, Oswald?"

Oswald sat in silence, trying to hold back his shivering. They hadn't even entered the worst of this yet, and already he was struggling to hold himself together. "I think…"

"What, Ulrich?" Rollins's voice rang out. "Just a bit of morning chill."

"Just a morning chill?" Ulrich exclaimed. "It's a wall of blowing snow. My sword is already frozen in its scabbard."

"Well, that's the first good news I've heard all morning," Oswald chided. "I feel much safer with it there." Ulrich sneered and muttered to himself as Rollins and Oswald chuckled.

Aldrich's firm voice broke through the noise, "Mount up, Ulrich. Natural or not, cold or not, we must get through."

The general nodded, and Oswald glanced at Thomas, who had been unusually quiet thus far. "Thomas!" He called out. Thomas didn't respond. Oswald shifted closer and noticed that he looked more pale than usual. His slung arm was held close to his chest while the other barely had the reigns.

"Let's go!" Aldrich yelled.

Aldrich and the generals led the way marking the road. Before Oswald could get close enough to Thomas to help, they were all shuffled forward. Each man had to stay close so no one would get lost or left. Cold death instantly gripped them as they crossed into the hard pounding snow. Oswald kept turning around to see if Thomas was okay. "Thomas!" he cried again, though the wind took his voice as fast as he spoke.

"I'll check on him," Rollins offered. "Stay with the prince at the front." Oswald nodded, and Rollins pulled back to get near Thomas. "Are you alright?" he asked when he got within earshot. Thomas didn't say anything. Instead, he held up his flask and tipped it over. Only a tiny drop came out. Rollins smiled.

"I feel sick," Thomas finally said.

Rollins chuckled, "Just that morning hangover." Before he pulled away, Rollins realized that Thomas probably felt more miserable with his wounds than the others. He reached into his pack, pulled out his extra cloak, and tossed it at Thomas with a wink. "Hang in there and keep that arm warm." Thomas nodded and wrapped himself in the shroud to cover his injured arm.

"Is he alright?" Oswald asked as Rollins returned to his position.

"He's sober."

Oswald glanced back at Thomas, "For any other soldier here, I'd be happy to hear it."

As the army trudged on, nothing changed. The wind and the snow blurred everything. What should've been a peaceful, beautiful view of the purple rock formations was all shades of gray now as the clouds blocked the sun.

"I don't like this," Rollins said. "We should've picked the southern route."

Oswald shook his head, "There was no way to know this storm would be here. Besides, the southern route would take too long since we had to cross the Great River into Valkos before heading east again to Alkeroth."

The top of the Purple Mountain pass stretched a few miles across, and though it was wide and level, it was anything but straight. Tall peaks and fragmented cliff sides that dropped to unknown depths within the mountain littered the area. The group glanced around as the wind died for a moment. The small streams from underground springs that once rushed across the road's edge and other mountain paths were now trickling as the water began to freeze over.

As they neared the center point, the distinctive Roseust Tree, with its large thick limbs and pale red, almost pink-colored leaves, was covered in snow and barely seen. The tree would bud twice a year with bright white miniature flowers. Though now its beauty was masked by the weather. Thomas stopped briefly as he glanced at the hunter's shack nearby. Torn to pieces from the storm, this shack was used by many during their travels through the mountains. As he got closer, He saw two bodies frozen on the porch, and sighed before pressing on; *death for nothing, death for all,* he thought.

As the army marched on, they reached a bottlenecked part of the path, with pieces that had steep shoulders on both sides that dropped off quickly to several fathoms below. The wind began to pick up again, and the snow blew, which obscured their view as they went. "Careful!" Rollins called out. "It narrows out up ahead!"

As Rollins led the way through the rugged terrain, Oswald was behind Rollins, along with Aldrich and Ulrich. The wind blew hard, and it took all their strength to hold themselves in their saddles. Suddenly, a loud crack was heard in the wind. Rollins looked back at Oswald, who was already looking up at the rocky peak to their left. "Look out!" he cried as he and the prince stepped up their pace forward. The rest of the army backed up slightly, but it was too late. A large chunk of snow and ice broke free and fell down the mountain. Three men were taken down over the side of the cliff edge with the falling snow, while two others were crushed beneath it.

Oswald watched in horror as the snow covered the area, "THOMAS!"

Aldrich, Rollins, and Ulrich's eyes followed Oswald as he dropped from his horse and trudged through the mound of snow to the edge, where it dropped off into the narrow ravine. From his point of view, Oswald couldn't tell if Thomas was crushed or pushed by the snow. All he knew was he saw Thomas on his horse at one point, but the next moment, neither Thomas nor his horse was there.

Ulrich and Rollins dismounted and began assisting the others caught in the snow. Oswald carefully sifted through the deepest parts of the snow, careful not to slip off himself. "Anything?" Aldrich's voice called out. Oswald stood and shook his head.

"Help!" Oswald perked up as he heard the faint cry coming from the cliffside.

"Thomas?" he cried out as he stepped closer.

"Yeah."

There, clinging to a small outcropping just over the edge of the road, was Thomas and one of the other soldiers that went over the side. Oswald reached down but lost his grip and began to slide forward. Frantic, he began to grab at anything he could, to no avail.

"I got you!" Rollins said as he grabbed Oswald's leg and braced himself against the rocks. Oswald then grabbed the less secure soldier and pulled him first. "Little help?" Rollins asked as he glanced at Aldrich, who was with Ulrich on the other side of the road.

Oswald struggled to get a good hold of the soldier with all the snow. The cold began to numb his fingers as he attempted to reach for the soldier's hand. Aldrich stepped over to assist, but as he got there, the ice came loose, and the man fell. "No!" Oswald cried; he reached forward as the soldier cried out in fear, but it was useless. The soldier's voice went silent in the darkness of the crevice below.

Thomas was still holding on with his one good hand. Strain and fear filled his face. Oswald shifted over as Rollins braced him. "Hang on, Thomas," he said, trying to hide the panic and anxiety in his voice.

As Oswald shifted over, Thomas began to relax. He looked down into the darkness of the crevice beneath him. It wouldn't be difficult; all he had to do was rest a bit more. It's not like they'd be able to pull him up anyway. No, he thought. His muscles tensed. He wouldn't give in; if he were to die, he'd die fighting.

"Thomas!" His thoughts came back as he heard Oswald calling him. "Grab my hand!"

Thomas looked down at his limp arm. There was no other way. He pulled it out of the sling and reached to let his injured arm get caught in his friend's hand. Oswald gripped it tightly, and Thomas winced in pain as he let himself be pulled up by the damaged limb. "I've got him," Oswald called back to Rollins as he began to pull Thomas close.

Rollins nearly lost his grip on the pair as the two were brought up. Had it not been for Aldrich coming to his aid with Ulrich at the last minute, Thomas and Oswald may not have survived.

The wind howled and blew across the path around them. Some men had finished clearing the fallen ice that created the whole fiasco. Rollins, Thomas, and Oswald lay on the ground and tried to catch their breath. Aldrich and Ulrich gathered the horses and had another one brought up for Thomas, whose original horse was not so fortunate as he.

After a few moments, Oswald got up to tend to Thomas, "His shoulder is dislocated," he said as he examined his right arm. Thankfully, the left and most damaged had a little added injury to it.

"Pop it back in," Rollins said as he got up to help.

The pair got Thomas up and braced him, "Okay, Thomas. This will only hurt for a moment." Oswald reassured.

Thomas took a deep breath to brace for the pain, but Ulrich stepped in and roughly jerked Thomas' arm back into place before Oswald could set it. Thomas cried out in pain, but Rollins quickly covered his mouth and let Thomas sit back down.

Oswald and Rollins each shot a questioning glance at Ulrich, who merely shrugged, "You were taking too long. We got to get moving."

Oswald turned to Thomas, "Are you alright?"

Thomas nodded, "Thank you."

"I would never leave you."

After Thomas was placed on a horse and wrapped back up, Oswald directed his attention to the wounded and the few dead found when they cleared the snow off the path. Those few men were placed along the cliffside, and Oswald went by and gathered their personal belongings from each of them.

As the soldiers gathered the last belongings and cleared the path, one approached Ulrich, "Orders, sir?"

"Get the wounded on horses and wrapped up warm," Ulrich replied. As the soldier departed to follow the directive, Ulrich caught his reflection in the frozen blood on the trail. He tried to find some way to blame this on Oswald and take this road to Alkeroth and not the southern road. He finally conceded with himself when he realized there was no way to know that this storm was here. It shouldn't have been. Despite this recent event, they had made good time and hopefully would again once they exited the mountains.

Ulrich looked up as he saw Aldrich approach, "We should bury the dead, General." The prince said, nodding to the bodies at the road's edge.

"Of course, milord," Ulrich said. "We'll fetch some shovels."

"No!" Oswald snapped.

Aldrich and Ulrich turned to face the other general. "What?" Ulrich asked.

"You already said we were taking too long," Oswald explained. "You were right, and this will only make it worse."

"As it is, Oswald, I think we've already taken quite the detour," Ulrich said, his anger growing. "Besides, the prince has spoken."

Oswald ignored them and directed his attention to his lieutenant, "Get the wounded on horses, then leave the dead."

"Leave them? We can't just leave them," Ulrich exclaimed.

"We'll retrieve the bodies on our way back to Althalos," Oswald said casually as he mounted his horse.

"There won't be anything left of them."

Oswald mounted his stead, "General Ulrich, you know as well as I that we have to keep moving."

Ulrich mounted his horse and reluctantly rode up behind Rollins. Aldrich said nothing and followed in behind Oswald and Rollins. He was just as uncomfortable as the others but saw Oswald's point. There was no need to argue over it. The sooner they could get to Vasalia, the sooner they could get this over with. Thomas, though on horseback, stayed near the primary columns of troops until they cleared the narrow part of the mountain pass.

The rest of the journey was uneventful, as it was only a matter of hours before the cold lessened, and the storm was settling as the troops made their way out of what appeared to be another wall of snow and wind.

Almost immediately, the sky was brighter as the clouds were fewer. The warm rays were melting the snow as fast as it came, and the Purple Mountains once again held to their name. Aldrich paused as the troops marched to the road that took them down the mountain and into Vasalia. He looked up at the storm wall and pondered the possibilities briefly. Nothing obvious came to mind.

As the prince looked ahead, he moved back up to the front as excitement began to brew within. A sense of pride came to him as he rode with his generals and the troops behind them. The unison sound of boots hitting the ground gave Aldrich a feeling of power.

This, he thought. *I could get used to this.*

Chapter 21
Over My Dead Body

Haldair's Castle at Terrowin, the Capital City of Valkos

Haldair was sitting at the head of a large table in his gathering room. Around him sat his five barons, the local governors of his kingdom territory. Merrek Frosbike was seated immediately to Haldair's right, and Leon Harris of the Crysanta Estate sat opposite him. The others were Jacob Devons from the southernmost Haywood Estate. Clayton Conrad of Germond and Ivor Borlaug of Kamdon. For Haldair, these barons also served as generals for their portion of the king's army.

Haldair had called all his barons together to discuss the situation of the army moving north through his land. What he did not expect was that no sooner had everyone gathered when arguing and infighting started to ring out among them. With rumors and accusations being haphazardly tossed around the room. Haldair sat in silence for some time, hoping that some truth would be revealed during the discussions; however, the longer it went on, the less likely this option seemed.

Finally, the king shot an annoyed yet questioning look at Fendon Runar, captain of the king's personal guard, standing nearby. Captain Runar gave a subtle nod of acknowledgment, and Haldair directed his attention back to the men at his table. "Enough!" He snapped loudly, silencing everyone. "Has anyone heard from VonGarth?" he asked as he pointed to the empty chair.

No response came. "Fine then. Has anyone been to VonGarth's estate in Handon to see what happened? Or is this all just hearsay? I know what Leon here has already said, but does anyone else here have any information that could be used in this witan?"

Cayton Conrad was the first to speak, "I believe that we just assemble the Valkon armies and say the hell with the rest!" Murmurs of agreement came from around the table. Only about thirty years of age, Cayton was one of the younger of the group. His youth, combined with his hard-headed attitude, made him brash at times but truthful.

Haldair raised his hand to silence them again, "It will come to that, I'm sure, Clayton. But we need facts first, and a plan must be made. And we cannot do that without knowing their numbers or exact position." Haldair motioned to Captain Runar, who grabbed a map and laid it on the table.

The map was centered on Valkos and showed the various cities and terrain. "So, what do we know?" he asked.

Clayton stepped up, saying, "We know they are in Handon. And we know that it's Stelmond who commands the army. That's enough information to know we can beat them on the battlefield as we have been doing since the end of the Great War!"

As Clayton sat down, Ivor stood. He was much older, almost seventy, though you wouldn't know it from his appearance. With a calm voice, he spoke, "But we don't know how they could travel across Valkos unseen and also take Handon, which was apparently in less than a day. Otherwise, someone would have heard something and reported it."

"Germond borders Handon," Clayton snapped. "If we don't move now, my people could be at risk of being the next target!"

"I need not remind you, Clayton," Haldair interjected firmly. "That your people are also my people. All the people of Valkos are at my highest consideration. So please, calm yourself and let us move forward more sensibly."

Clayton shifted in his seat awkwardly.

Ivor nodded to the king and continued, "I motion that we first try to figure out how they got an army large enough to take Handon in less than a day and get to the center of Valkos without being seen or heard."

Everyone turned to look at Jacob Devons at the end of the table, who had been silent through the whole ordeal since his arrival. Even though he was the youngest of the barons, Jacob was a good man and a strong leader at just over twenty years old. He was never very direct or outspoken; however, Haldair knew that Jacob was never one to be afraid to speak his mind if he had something relevant.

"Devons." Haldair addressed. "Haywood is our most southern estate. How did they get across your land unnoticed?"

"I… I don't know, milord," Jacob stammered. "We have not seen nor heard even a loose sword in Haywood."

"Then perhaps, Baron Devons, you should be keeping a closer eye on your lands," Clayton said. "Or were you offered something in return for letting them pass?"

Jacob's nervous expression turned to shock at Clayton's words. "I would never…"

"How much did they pay you?" Clayton interrupted.

"If I was sided with the enemy, why would I come when summoned by our king? If I were on their side and promised security, I would have stayed at my estate."

"I'm not buying it." Clayton snapped.

Haldair stood from his seat, "Clayton Conrad, say nothing more on that matter. Jacob Devons may be many things, but I don't see him as a traitor to the crown or the country. And he also has a point, why would he even bother to come here if his safety was secured." He then turned to Jacob, "There is still the matter of how they got passed without you noticing. Are you not supposed to keep a rotating guard over the southern border?"

"Yes, milord," Jacob said. "I've had a rotating watch that I've doubled because of recent events…after the stories, I've been hearing…and now… what I saw on my way here."

An eerie silence sat in the room momentarily as they all leaned in to hear what Jacob had to say. "Well, Jacob, what did you see?"

Jacob swallowed hard and took a deep breath, "You will all think I'm crazy, but my scouts have seen bad things. Things of legend and folklore."

"Spit it out, man. What have they seen?" Merrek asked impatiently.

"At first, I thought nothing of it," Jacob began. "One lone scout over a month ago claimed to have seen a pack of Dire Wolves on his southern border patrol. But it was just one man, and I assumed he had been drinking or mistaken it for bears or regular wolves and thought nothing of the matter. But then more men started coming forward, more stories of the same beasts. Then I started losing men…" he took a drink and another deep breath before he continued. "Three went missing on a scouting mission south, and we have yet to hear anything. We lost two fishing ships at sea last week without there even being a storm, and then one man made it back from a southern watch by the roots of the mountains…but he was a dead man walking."

"What do you mean by that?" Leon asked.

"He could walk and move, but barely; he couldn't speak and seemed to have lost all communication abilities. He was frothing at the mouth, but he had no scratch save for what looked like an arrow wound on his shoulder," Jacob explained.

The archives of Althalos are among the best in the region. Growing up, Haldair and Ivan were schooled from those old scrolls and books telling of a time before, through the First and Second Ages. Haldair listened as Jacob recalled more specific events about the recent sightings and incidents that had happened to his people.

The continent of Kralavia was vast, and only a small portion had been explored beyond the nine kingdoms. There were tales, Haldair recalled, that talked of strange beasts and dangerous things that emerged in the early parts of the Second Age. However, as the time of the Great War neared, tales and accounts of these creatures got fainter and fainter, until there was nothing left but legend and myth. After the information gap immediately before and during the war, there was no more talk of these beasts. The Third Age began, and civilization excelled.

"Then it really set into me when I saw it on my way here," Jacob said. "As you know, I had to travel around Handon. While not far from the lands while I was camped, I was taking a walk before bed, I looked up into the night sky, and I swear on my life, I saw a creature like none other."

Merrek rolled his eyes, "What did you see?"

"Probably just a hawk," Clayton said. "Valkos is full of them, and at night in the shadows, they can look bigger than they are."

"It was large enough to block out the moon and cast its shadow over the fields like nothing I have ever seen," Jacob responded.

Haldair said nothing, nor did his expression give any slight shock and awe as the others did.

"Fine, I'll just say it," Jacob finally said. "It was a Drake or a Dragon. I know it's just stories and songs, but I swear I saw something evil in that night sky."

"Aren't they the same?" Clayton asked.

"No," Ivor said. "Drakes are about the size of horses, and they only have back legs as their front arms and wings are one and the same. Their fire breath is just intense heat, according to the stories. On the other hand, dragons were rare and as large as a standard house, with four legs and large wings. Its fire breath was liquid and stickier on impact."

The conversations and knowledge of these beasts got more intense as it went on. Each man shared what they had heard, seen, or read somewhere they were sure was the more factual story. After a few moments, Haldair stands up again, silencing the room. "Fairy tales and folklore had to come from something, am I right?" No response. "There were once gods and creatures of magic in our realm, in case you have all but forgotten, during the days of the Unatari. We will move on with how to go about dealing with the invasion now, but I am not inclined to drop the idea that there may be something larger at play here."

"I second that motion," Ivor said calmly.

After nothing more was said, Haldair spoke, "Then we move on." He turned to Leon, "You have sent the riders to each of the Five Crowns, correct?"

"Yes, milord."

Haldair nodded, "Then their aid will be arriving, I'm sure. I was going to request them to be ready for the battle in Vasalia, but…" he trailed off. "Hopefully, Leoxtra and Aldrich can handle that on their own. And as reluctant as I was to do so, I personally sent a messenger with a letter to my brother in Althalos, and I'm sure he will waste no time coming to our aid."

"Will he bring the weapon?" Clayton asked eagerly.

"I hope not," Haldair answered. "I did not give that inclination in my letter. But until then, we must be ready. I need each of you to return to your estates and raise your armies. We will meet in the Field of Denesious. The Alliance of the Five Crowns was instructed to meet us there." The others verbally agreed.

"Tomorrow," Haldair said, "You will all leave. We must be ready for battle in no less than a week. I'll be damned if I ever let Stelmond get through my kingdom, with or without creatures of legend."

Chapter 22
Alkeroth

Alkeroth, Vasalia

The remainder of the journey had been a smooth and uneventful one. The main road through Vasalia was well-maintained but had little for civilized stops. Most cities and homes were further back and secluded by one of the many rocky outcroppings. This silence only added to the speculation about what they would find once they reached Alkeroth and did nothing about easing the nerves of the troops as they marched through. As they moved across the country, Oswald and Aldrich glanced back at the Purple Mountains. The storm clouds could still be seen faintly across the top. It made no sense to either of them or the soldiers with them. The Purple Mountains had always been a peaceful place to travel, unlike the Great Mountain Ridge to the north of Kralavia, which blew snow and cold constantly, making it treacherous.

The sun was setting behind the mountains in the distant west as Prince Aldrich and his army reached the plains just outside the city. Aldrich, Oswald, Ulrich, and Rollins stopped the march as they observed the scene. Nothing. No smoke, screaming, nor war cries could be heard. It was as if the war had never happened.

"What do you think?" Rollins asked, breaking the silence.

Oswald pulled out his spotting scope, "I'm not sure," he said as he scanned the area. "I can't see Stelbeck Keep from here. We'll have to move in."

Aldrich nodded in agreement and then turned to the bannerman riding behind them, "Let them know we're coming." The soldier nodded, grabbed his horn, and blew hard. After his initial blast, the others across the army echoed with him for a second. As the third horn unison sounded, Aldrich and the other generals began moving toward the city.

When Aldrich and his men got closer, several riders came out from Alkeroth's center and quickly approached them. "They are flying Vasalia's banner," Ulrich said.

"Perhaps there is no need to fight?" Rollins speculated.

When the Vasalian riders arrived near Aldrich, the men exchanged greetings and were informed that the battle was over, and King Leoxtra was the victor. "King Leoxtra is eager to speak to King Ivan," said one of the riders. "Is he here among your company?"

"No," Ulrich said firmly. "His son, Prince Aldrich, is here in his stead."

The riders gave a brief look of surprise and then bowed their heads in respect, "Very well, prince," the rider acknowledged. "If you'll follow us then."

Aldrich ordered most men to remain outside the city and camp there. Then, with his generals and a few soldiers as personal guards, He led the way into Alkeroth, following the other riders. "This is ridiculous," Ulrich groaned.

"Why?" Aldrich asked.

"There's no fighting. I was looking forward to getting my blade bloodied."

"Not all of us are so eager to spill blood, enemy or not," Oswald added. Ulrich scoffed to himself and remained silent as they entered the city.

When the group reached the city center, they were greeted by King Leoxtra's lead commanding general, Thaddeus Omarr II. "General Cromwell! We are pleased to see you have arrived in short order."

Oswald smiled and nodded, "General Omarr. I see you didn't save any fighting for me."

Thaddeus shrugged, "You know how it is, General."

Oswald laughed, "Indeed I do." Then he cleared his throat, "General Omarr, may I present Prince Aldrich Ventril, son of King Ivan Ventril of Althalos."

Thaddeus bowed respectfully, "It has been many years since I've seen you, young prince. I hope your father is doing well."

Aldrich bowed his head in return, "He is. Thank you for asking, General. You remember my other generals, Ulrich and Rollins."

"Of course," Thaddeus said. "I see you brought your best for this."

"Well, the messenger made it sound more urgent than it apparently was," Ulrich said.

"Messenger?" Thaddeus asked. "Did you not receive our birds."

Aldrich shook his head, "No birds have come from Vasalia in recent days."

"Interesting," Thaddeus remarked.

"It's probably that freak storm on the mountaintops that threw them off course," Ulrich commented.

"Wait, what storm?" General Omarr asked.

Aldrich and Ulrich took turns describing the events in the Purple Mountains. Oswald noticed that Thaddeus kept an inquiring yet puzzled look on his face during the accounts of the story. "Thaddeus, if I had to guess, I would say that this mysterious happenstance of nature is not the first that you've seen in your time."

"Correct you are, General Cromwell," Thaddeus said.

"Well, speak up, man!" Ulrich cut in.

Thaddeus paused before he turned to a nearby soldier, "My horse." Promptly the soldier brought out General Omarr's horse. As he mounted, "I think it's best you speak to King Leoxtra. Things here…have been strange since this fight started."

Disappointment grew over Ulrich's face as he silently complied and followed Thaddeus through the city with the others. "I must say, General Omarr," Oswald said, trying to break the awkward silence. "This is not the sight I expected upon our arrival."

"Nor I, honestly," Thaddeus agreed. "Your lads at Stelbeck put up a good fight. They held strong. The Carnheller's fleet never reached the inner parts of the city."

"So, the battle is won then?" Ulrich asked.

"Indeed," Thaddeus replied. "Most of their fleet sits at the bottom of the bay just outside the harbor. What few remain, we're using as temporary holding for the prisoners."

"You're sure it was Carnheller?" Aldrich asked.

Thaddeus nodded. Aldrich and Oswald exchanged brief glances. Oswald wasn't sure if Ivan had expressed the same ideas to his son, so he didn't say anything. However, he couldn't help but wonder what Ivan knew beforehand that brought up such speculation before it was known. Much less, have that speculation be correct.

Ulrich moved closer to Oswald, "So, our enemy was defeated days ago, probably when the messenger arrived. Which means this trip was for nothing. You got those men killed for nothing."

"You dare hold that against me?" Oswald snapped back. "These are circumstances that neither I nor any of you were aware of." Ulrich's sudden shift in blame didn't sit well as Oswald pondered its possible reasons. None immediately came to mind, but it still seemed strange that even though it was no one person's fault, why was Ulrich directing his anger at him?

"You got several of my men needlessly killed," Ulrich stated. "And then you left them there. You're damn right. I would hold that against you."

Oswald gave Ulrich a cold, hard stare. "They were my men Ulrich," he said coldly. "Do not tell me how many I lost. I know." Realizing Oswald was right, Ulrich drew back and left the conversation alone. Aldrich,

Rollins, and Thaddeus remained quiet for a few moments, not wanting to worsen the tension.

As the men approached the keep, they had to make their way around the piles of enemy bodies, weapons, and rubble being gathered outside what was left of the fortress walls. "My lord!" Thaddeus called out as the men reached the staging area for those in charge of the clean-up. King Leoxtra stepped forward from the small group of men he had been conversing with near the main tent. Thaddeus gestured to the others with him, "Prince Aldrich of Althalos, my lord. And his generals, Oswald, Ulrich, and Rollins."

"General Oswald!" Leoxtra called out. Oswald dismounted, and the two greeted each other with a warm embrace. "It has been too long. If I had known that by joining the Five Crown Alliance, there would be even more peace in the country, which would mean I never get to fight again alongside my favorite men, I would never have done so."

Oswald laughed, "Well, it seems your desire was granted. But you beat them before I could arrive."

The others dismounted, and Aldrich stepped up to King Leoxtra, "King Leoxtra," he greeted.

"Prince Aldrich," Leoxtra replied. "Last time I saw you, you were but a wee child." He stepped forward and shook the prince's hand. "Good to see you've grown into a man. You have your father's look about you, son."

"Thank you, sir."

"I'm glad Ivan sent his best. Such a shame there is no battle left to be fought."

"I wish we had gotten here in time, but I'm afraid the rider did not arrive until a few days ago," Aldrich said almost shamefully.

"You did not receive my raven?" Leoxtra questioned.

"None, Sire," Oswald chimed in. "No ravens reached Althalos from Vasalia."

"We suspect it has to do with the weird storm on the Purple Mountains," Aldrich added.

"Most peculiar," King Leoxtra noted. "We sent several here, to Stelbeck, as well, to warn them that we were coming to reinforce the defense with our fleet but...the same result."

"No messages are getting through then?" Aldrich confirmed. Leoxtra nodded, and Aldrich looked back at his generals, all with the same puzzled look. Oswald particularly remembered Thomas had pointed out the dead and half-eaten raven in the woods just over the mountains. Was there a connection?

"No. None of them," Leoxtra confirmed. "And such a large fleet moving into our waters unseen…Something very strange is going on here. I haven't known Carnheller to have the strength or boldness to launch an attack of this scale. Nor the desire for that matter."

"What are our losses?" Oswald asked as he looked around the carnage.

King Leoxtra motioned to another soldier nearby, who promptly brought a small parchment page to him, "So far, we've counted two hundred twenty-two men of Althalos," he began to read aloud. "Seventy-eight of my men between the city guard and the forces I brought in," he caught the grim and solemn looks on the faces of Aldrich and the others. "So far," he continued with a small chipper in his voice.

"Almost a thousand of the Carnheller troops are counted among their dead, most of them part of the berserker unit, as you can see here. They also lost six ships, with two others crippled in the bay. Including the men aboard those, and estimated fifteen hundred Carnheller troops dead, with many more injured and prisoners."

The moods of Aldrich and his men brightened slightly at this news. Aldrich began to take a closer look at the aftermath of the battle. Of the five kingdoms joined in the Five Crown Alliance, Vasalia was his father's favorite in battle. Vasalians were more violent and brutal in their nature of war, and with King Ivan's blood lust the way it was early on, they had made a great union. King Haldair may be a brother to King Ivan and very well handled in wartime efforts, but King Leoxtra, at least for the early years, was Ivan's favorite.

Aldrich grimaced as he watched the Vasalian troops do what they often did in the war. Several enemy troops were missing fingers, eyes, and other small parts of their bodies, often taken and made as trophies. Aldrich had heard about what war looked like and what certain countries would do as part of their customs and dealings. However, he had to choke back his feeling to vomit at the sight of some Vasalian troops using an enemy head as a kicking ball.

As Aldrich continued to scan the area, he noticed that the enemy troops and the men of Althalos had been stripped of armor, weapons, personal belongings, and valuables. Oswald, Rollins, and Ulrich seemed less fazed about this; having fought beside Vasalia before, they were accustomed to their treatment of the enemy in life and death. Although confused, Aldrich said nothing and returned to where Oswald and the others were still conversing with King Leoxtra.

"Were there any survivors from our garrison?" Oswald asked as Aldrich approached.

"Less than a dozen, I'm afraid," Leoxtra answered. "But you'll want to speak to Captain Wilkins and Collins. They led the fight when Commander Gregson died early on."

Oswald perked up when he heard this, "Yes. I would very much like to speak to them."

"This way," Leoxtra said as he led the way up into the remnants of the keep. A tent had been set up as a point of contact for the clean-up and accountability of the men and the fight.

"It's not easy for a defense like this to be your first command," Oswald said. "I pity them."

Leoxtra chuckled, "I pity the Carnheller troops. Well…somewhat."

As the group approached, they could see Wilkins sitting in a cot with one leg up and braced around the knee. They had set up a small desk for him to review the reports and records of what happened and delegate from there. Collins was standing nearby. Dead and wounded were brought to him for identification and status, which he then would dictate to Wilkins. Leoxtra and Oswald were the first to arrive in the entranceway as a gurney was brought in and set before Collins.

Oswald could see it was one of their men by the colors on the armor, but the man's face was bludgeoned so badly that identification was impossible.

"Such a strange thing," Collins said, thinking out loud. "Perhaps a few days ago, I knew this man… I knew them all… Now I don't know any of them."

"You know me," Captain Wilkins yelled from the back of the tent.

"Yeah," Collins joked. "You're the crazy bastard who led me into certain death to save a flag."

Wilkins laughed, "Hey, you followed me." Collins laughed but grew somber as he returned his gaze to the soldier before him. "Stop looking at him."

"I know," Collins remarked. He motioned the men to remove the body and bring in the next. He turned to Wilkins, "Before this, I wanted to be a tailor."

"Yeah," Wilkins chuckled, "And I want to get back to my nap, Collins. So, let's hurry this up."

Collins smiled and turned to the entrance to summon the next one in. He stopped short when he saw King Leoxtra standing beside him, "General Oswald!"

When Wilkins heard this, he snapped up in his seat. "King Leoxtra," he greeted. "Prince Aldrich," he and Collins both bowed their heads, "My lord."

Aldrich held his hand up, "No need for that here."

Oswald and Aldrich stepped forward with Ulrich, "Captain Wilkins," Oswald said.

"Yeah," Wilkins said as he looked at his knee. "What's left of him."

"I was told you were in charge of the defense of Stelbeck during the attack."

"I did my best, General," Wilkins said modestly. "They showed up out of nowhere. Some strange storm camouflaged their fleet."

"What was strange about it?" Aldrich asked.

"No wind…no rain," Wilkins replied. "Just thunder, lightning…and pure darkness."

A moment of silence was between the group as Oswald and the others reflected on the uniqueness of the storm in the mountains. "Have any of the prisoners spoken about the purpose of this invasion?" Oswald finally asked Leoxtra.

"Not at the moment," the king answered.

"Who was in charge?"

"Admiral Mortem, sir," Thaddeus answered from the front of the tent. "He has been undergoing questioning for several days since we captured him. But he hasn't said anything yet."

"Let me at him," Ulrich said as he rubbed a fist in his other hand. "I bet I can make him talk."

"Indeed," said Aldrich. "Where is this admiral?" he asked General Thaddeus.

"He's being held in prison in Alkeroth. I'll take you to him."

The group said their goodbyes to Wilkins and Collins, and then General Thaddeus led the way as Leoxtra, Aldrich, Oswald, and Ulrich followed. As they went down the hill to their horses, Aldrich turned away from the small talk conversation to the open field nearby. Several Vasalian troops were laying out the bodies of the dead soldiers of Althalos after being seen by Wilkins and Collins for identification. Aldrich paused briefly as he noticed that after the body was brought there, the men stripped the armor and other personal valuables before placing the body with the others for burial.

"Hey," Aldrich called out as he quickly approached the men. The others with him stopped and turned to look at what was going on and why Aldrich was suddenly walking away.

The Vasalian soldiers said nothing nor stopped what they were doing.

"Hey!" Aldrich said again, louder this time. Still no response from the men he directed his attention at. "That is one of my father's men, my men." Aldrich snapped as he got closer.

One of the Vasalian soldiers stood up and faced Aldrich directly, "Well, now he's just another dead body. Getting ready to take his home in the ground." Aldrich was slightly taken aback as the soldier stooped down and removed the rings from the dead body's fingers.

"Those aren't yours to take."

That same soldier glanced at his partner, then stood up again and squared himself with Aldrich, "And I don't think he'll be missing 'em. Now go on about your business and leave me to mine."

Aldrich was about to protest further when the soldier spat in his face. Without thinking, Aldrich backhanded the soldier and attempted to draw his sword. Oswald promptly reached the young prince and held his arm, stopping him.

"Aldrich," Oswald said firmly. "We are guests here."

Aldrich quickly slammed the partially drawn weapon back into its scabbard. "These are our men," he snapped back. "Why must we allow them to be treated as such? These items should be returned to give to their families."

Oswald was about to answer when King Leoxtra cleared his throat loudly, "Perhaps I can answer that question, my young prince." Aldrich turned around to face Leoxtra directly as he continued. "The agreement made between Althalos and Vasalia when your father brought peace and we set up the Five Crown Alliance was that everything, be it friend or foe, from any soldier that fell on Vasalian soil, is to be claimed by Vasalia."

"What?" Aldrich exclaimed. His gaze turned back to Oswald. "Why was this detail left out of my schooling?"

Oswald sighed, "This is the information you would be briefed on as king. Besides, an act of war was never taken before, allowing Vasalia to use that part of their agreement." He placed his hand on the prince's shoulder, "This is the first hint of war in decades; many things are about to be seen that had not been before. And this is hardly the time nor the place for this conversation."

Aldrich scoffed and knocked Oswald's hand away, who then directed his attention to the king. "King Leoxtra, please forgive the prince. He is young and has not yet become fully accustomed or informed about the different cultures of our allies in times like these."

"It's alright," King Leoxtra replied. "I understand in some way. Prince Aldrich, you are welcome to take the fallen men back to your country to be buried there. Otherwise, they will be buried here in our soldier's cemetery with our men and the honor they are given."

Aldrich said nothing and stormed past King Leoxtra. He stopped at Ulrich, who nodded in approval of Aldrich's statement. "Have our men wrapped and prepared for the trip home," Ulrich said to the soldier, still rubbing his face from Aldrich's hand. "We'll send them home with a few men when they are accounted for."

The soldier looked at King Leoxtra for approval; the king nodded and then turned to the rest of the group, "Well if there are no further complications. Let's go see this admiral."

After the group started moving into the city's center toward the centrally located prison, Oswald noticed the sour expression across Aldrich's face and gently inquired about it. Aldrich said nothing initially, which bugged Oswald. Oswald and Aldrich had been friends a long time, and they never had any bad blood or relationship, no matter how bad the disagreement seemed. But, Oswald thought, *maybe Ivan was keeping the direction of anger off himself.* Only time will tell.

As Oswald thought more and more about the turn of events since departing Althalos, he remembered the note that Ivan had given him should Aldrich's leadership decisions begin to crumble. "Why are you like this now?" Aldrich's voice snapped Oswald back to the current moment.

"Like what?"

"Ever since this trip started, you've done nothing but undermine me, ignore me…and now you're keeping secrets from me?"

"I have kept nothing from you. I was unaware you would have such a strong reaction to it."

"Of course, I did," Aldrich snapped. "And I still don't understand why you're willing to sweep our casualties under the rug. First up in the mountains, now this. Oswald, they are stripping our men like slaughtered cows. How could I be okay with that?"

Oswald rolled his eyes slightly, "Okay, that's a bit of an exaggeration," he said plainly. "The different kingdoms make their money through different methods, just as they all obtain supplies through different methods. Your father understood that which is why the agreement was made in the first place."

"Just how many other agreements has my father made as king?"

Oswald sighed and glanced back at the others. Once he was sure that they were otherwise engaged in another conversation, he continued.

"Once you are King, you will also be forced to make decisions, Aldrich, and those decisions might not always be the most desired, but rather, the most necessary."

"Like the decision you made to abandon our dead?"

"I have made many difficult decisions as a soldier, and I try not to dwell on any of them… I don't need you or anyone else dwelling on it for me."

Aldrich realized that Oswald had politely closed this topic and decided not to press it further. "So, what exactly is it between you and General Ulrich?" he asked as he glanced back at others briefly.

"He's a corrupted man, Aldrich," Oswald replied. "I don't want him getting too close to you."

"Corrupted how? Did he also disagree with your decisions?" the prince asked, almost sarcastically.

Oswald smiled, "I'm sure he disagrees with many of them. But one, in particular, he's held against me for a long time."

"What was it?"

Oswald sympathetically looked at Aldrich, "That's not my story to tell."

Aldrich said nothing, but Oswald could tell that wasn't the response he was looking for. After a moment of silence, Oswald continued. "I know you probably think I'm treating you like a child. But you're like a brother to me, Aldrich. I just want what's best for you. I'm trying to teach you what I can, and I'm sorry I'm not always very good at it. But you don't have the most experience, so if I'm saying no to one of your suggestions or Ulrich's, just assume I have a good reason behind it."

Aldrich nodded but remained silent.

The group continued into Alkeroth and was met by one of Oswald's lieutenants. "Sir," the lieutenant greeted. Oswald returned the greeting and asked for a status update. "The men have made camp outside the city limits," the lieutenant reported.

"Very good," Oswald replied. "How's Thomas?"

"The captain made his way into Alkeroth after things were set up with other men."

"Of course, he did."

Chapter 23
The Raid

Greebold's Trench, Althalos

Greebold's Trench was a small, pleasant village on the western borders of Althalos near the Great River. Here, the terrain was shaped by the soft rolling hills of the grasslands that covered this part of the country. The village sat comfortably in the valley of several of these hills and thrived on producing and supplying farm goods shipped out to most of Althalos and some of the harbor cities along the Great River to the north.

The village was founded by Arthur Greebold, who, before the Great War, had set up his homestead in the area. The most significant boom in this small area came during the war. Despite being located on the Great River; this area had been relatively untouched by the conflict during or after the war. This peace made it an excellent spot for those citizens looking for relief from the fighting. The homesteaded area then became an established village and was thus named Greebold's Trench in honor of the first settler and his family.

It was early evening, and the sun had just passed the horizon when Alfred Trench walked the main street through the village as he often did with his mother, Olivia, and brother Douglas.

Though they were brothers, Douglas and Alfred were very dissimilar. Alfred was tall and lean, with short light brown hair and a few days stubble he kept on his face, and at thirty years old, still considered very young. Douglas, however, while younger than Alfred, was taller and looked much older, with a full beard and long black hair. The trio had been discussing various topics, from national politics to local ones, which led to a conversation about family. Alfred had just announced that he and his wife were trying to have another child.

"Just don't stretch yourself too far, Alfie," Olivia said. Alfred always hated that name she used. "Your father and I could hardly handle you two boys, let alone three!"

"Father was gone for most of our childhood. He was a soldier, Mother," Alfred replied. "I'll admit, though, when he was home for a time, he couldn't have been a better father."

"I'm aware," she snapped. "So don't you and Douglas get any ideas like your friends Oswald and Thomas. I don't need you two galivanting across the country waiting to die the next time a battle occurs."

Alfred smiled. He knew his mother worried more than she needed to. But neither he nor Douglas could blame her. Like many men around Kralavia, their father had been recruited to the army for the Great War. Even though their quiet place never saw actual combat, the effects of war were a different story. Many of the husbands and fathers taken out of this area never came home. Alfred and Douglas' father was one of them.

"Neither Douglas nor I here plan to leave Greebold's Trench mother; this is home. Being in the town guard is enough for us." He and Douglas exchanged a brief smile. Olivia smiled softly; her white hair glistened in the stone street's torchlight. "And don't worry, Mother," he finished. "We're stopping at three children..."

"Remember," Olivia said, almost chuckling as she did. "You don't need a son despite what your father always said, so don't keep trying until you get one."

"I don't care much about what I have as long as I have it," Alfred said. "And besides, I've got to make up for Douglas..." Alfred shot him a playful look as he finished.

Olivia nodded, "Oh yes, such a shame you don't want a family, Dougie."

"I'm too busy for a family," Douglas stated.

"Your father wasn't," their mother noted.

"Lot of good that did him, huh?" Douglas quipped without missing a beat. As fast as he spoke, he regretted it. They all stopped before Olivia stormed off alone.

Once she was out of earshot, Alfred turned to Douglas, "That was uncalled for."

"Yeah, well... She shouldn't have called me 'Dougie'," Douglas said, trying to defend himself.

"You'll need to apologize."

Douglas looked at his mother's figure as she continued down the street. "Another time, perhaps." Alfred nodded, and the two began to walk again, heading in the direction their mother had just gone. Suddenly, Douglas stopped and listened intently. The sound of a horse's hooves beating the ground grew louder and closer. Douglas and Alfred strained to see into the darkening horizon to see who was approaching.

"What's this?" he asked aloud to no one in particular.

In moments a lone rider appeared. Douglas and Alfred watched as the hooded figure rode hard until he suddenly stopped near them in the center of the village. Alfred and Douglas stepped closer to the rider as he dismounted his horse. A stench of death hit the nostrils of those nearby and watching intently.

As they got closer, Douglas noticed the horse was thin and sickly; the rider had the size and stature of a man but had a hood and scarf covering his face. The wind sent a small gust that carried the stench heavier than before, forcing Douglas and Alfred to choke back their throats to avoid vomiting.

The rider stepped forward and glanced around at the few people lingering in the area. Douglas and Alfred continued to walk toward the rider, and when he locked eyes with the pair, he stopped and addressed them directly. "I request an audience with whoever is in charge here," the rider said. He sounded masculine, but his voice was frail, and he breathed heavily, almost strained to speak.

Douglas took a half step forward from the position that he and his brother had stopped, "I am the commander of the town guard. My name is Douglas Trench, and this is my brother Alfred," he said as he gestured to Alfred.

"Welcome, stranger," Alfred greeted.

"What is your name, rider?" Douglas asked. "And what is your business here?"

"My name," the rider said mockingly. "Is of little importance. I'm certain you'll forget you ever had the pleasure of this meeting."

Douglas scoffed, "I wouldn't be so sure of that," he said as he rubbed his nose. "I already find no pleasure in this meeting." Alfred, next to him, remained expressionless. Something wasn't sitting right with him about the whole encounter.

"I speak for my chieftain, Serrek son of Sedrick son of…" the rider began.

"You can skip past the formalities, please," Douglas interrupted, waving his hand.

The visitor stood and stared in silence. Douglas and Alfred remained unmoved, and naught but the wind and distant wild animals were heard. Then, the stranger finally spoke again, "We believe you have something of ours."

"We do?" Alfred questioned.

"Indeed, Mr. Trench."

"Well, I assure you…messenger," Douglas said. "That we have nothing of which your people nor your chieftain are owed."

"Where are you from that such a demand is made of us?" Alfred asked firmly.

"Oh, no. Good sir," the rider said, ignoring the question. "I assure you, in fact, you have exactly what we are owed in your possession. Notice the grass beneath our feet," he gestured his hand around him. "The rocks and twigs used to build your homes. The trees all around us, all of it is stolen land, stolen from my people by the fathers of your fathers. An agreement made was broken, and now…now we have come to reclaim it."

"Well, messenger," Douglas stated. "Give this message to your chieftain. You are in Althalos; all the lands belong to King Ivan and his heirs. Now…you have no claim here, none. So, I suggest you get on your horse, turn around, and ride home."

After a long pause, the rider mounted his horse. He then pulled his hood down with his face shroud, revealing an old, weathered face. The man smiled, and the brothers were close enough to see that his teeth were a deep yellow and black. The man guided his horse in the direction he came, "We are home." He stated more clearly than he spoke before. Douglas and Alfred said nothing, and with a heavy breath, "Ya," the man galloped off into the dark.

Alfred relaxed when the man was out of sight, "Was that wise?"

"Don't lose sleep over it, brother," Douglas reassured. "I've never heard of this 'Serrek' he speaks of. The man's probably insane." He took a deep breath, "Still, it wouldn't be a bad idea to assemble the town guard, though, and have them keep a watch all night."

Douglas had no sooner finished his statement when the brothers heard soft thunder in the distance. "Do you hear that?" Alfred asked. The sounds grew louder before it became clear.

As the men began to recognize the sound, Douglas muttered, "What have I done?"

The sound became more distinct, and the pair realized it was not thunder but horses. Alfred looked in the distance toward the direction of the hoofbeats. Panic had started to set in the villagers, the boys' mother among them. Alfred pressed forward to reach her, but it was too late.

Dozens of horses barreled through the streets with no regard for person or thing. "Wait!" Alfred cried out before he got sideswiped by one of the riders. Mass panic took over as the riders continued to run through the village, slaughtering all they saw. Alfred carefully pulled himself up and continued to move toward where his mother was last seen.

In the commotion, Alfred staggered slowly, trying to avoid the riders as they charged through. Screams of pain echoed in the valley, almost as loudly as the rider's war cries. He tripped and fell again, looked at his feet and practically gagged. It was the young boy's body, head nearly cloven off with blood collecting in the street. He tightened his resolve and reached where his mother was. She was dead. Her body lay there, with her severed head nearby.

"Alfred!" Douglas' voice cried out in desperation. Alfred quickly drew his sword and returned to the village center.

The horse riders had broken off and continued to raid the surrounding area as Alfred went to Douglas, who was engaged in a fight with a man in black armor and a dark cape; his face was covered by a thick helmet, wielding a war hammer. Screams of terror still filled the area. Suddenly, a burst of bright light and Alfred saw flames licking the roofs of some of the buildings. Quickly, more and more small fires grew as the homes and other structures rose in flames.

Alfred watched Douglas as he was knocked down by his opponent's blow to the chest. He quickened his pace only to be stopped by a rider who had been nearby and moved in to deal with the lone guard. Alfred slashed at the horse's legs without thinking, causing the rider to fall and sent his sword through the man's head as he did so. "Douglas!" he cried as he ran to aid his brother.

Douglas was pinned on the ground. Blood was gushing from his nose. The assailant had been pressing the hammer down to crush Douglas' head, but Douglas held his own as he blocked that attack with his sword.

Alfred took a few more steps before getting caught in a small crowd that ran before him. Frantic now, Alfred pressed through the villagers to reach his brother. He watched in horror as the armored warrior casually crushed several of the villagers that were within arm's reach of him. Douglas, still dazed, struggled to get up. Alfred began to run, but again, he was too late.

The opponent had swung the spiked end of his war hammer and impaled Douglas' gut as he sat on the ground. Alfred froze briefly before he took to his heels and ran the other way. *Home,* he thought as he watched the fires burn all around him, lighting up the sky. Alfred carefully ran through the city, bodies littered the streets, and most of the buildings were engulfed in flames if they were not being ransacked.

When he reached his home, just on the outskirts of the village, Alfred dropped to his knees as he saw the horror; the flames completely swallowed his home. In the front of the house, clothed in flame, were three charred bodies. Tears began to form in his eyes as he watched the fire continue to eat away at his family and home.

More shouts and cries of pain were heard in the distance, but Alfred's thoughts broke as he listened to the panicked sounds of his horse in the stable nearby. Quickly, he sucked up his tears and ran for the barn. There was nothing more he could do here; all that mattered now was to get to safety and find a way to get help and inform the king.

Alfred hastily saddled his horse, and with a firm, "Ya!" he rode hard out into the east toward the small guard station, Fort Elias. The fort was set some distance from the village and held a small garrison of the king's men to oversee most of the western side of Althalos, including Greebold's Trench. Alfred had to cut out the sounds of his people being slaughtered behind him as he rode. At one point, he glanced back; the night sky glowed red across the hill-scaped horizon, and smoke blocked the stars in the area.

Is there even a village left to save? He wondered.

Meanwhile
The Village Square, Greebold's Trench

The fires were burning out, and the smell of smoke and blood filled the air. The black armored warrior was pulling the sharp end of his war hammer out of another man on the ground; by his armor, it looked to be another city guard. The hooded rider that had initially contacted the villagers casually rode up to the warrior and dismounted his horse.

"Victory is ours, Dynius," the man said. His voice strained as it always did.

Dynius wiped the blood off his weapon, "Yes, Whistler." His deep voice echoed from within the helmet he still wore. Whistler was about to speak further but was interrupted by another rider who had approached. "Captain Mencis," Dynius greeted. The captain nodded but said nothing.

"Shall we…" Whistler began to ask. His voice squeaked. "Shall we press our attack to the fort?" Dynius said nothing but nodded in acknowledgment. Whistler smiled crudely, his yellow and rotten teeth fully exposed. "Shall we…attack the fort?" Again, Dynius said nothing and nodded. "Men!" Whistler shouted; his voice cracked with every word. "To the fort! Kill them all!" Those around him and Captain Mencis cheered and called as they rallied around the village center and began to make their way to the fort. "Forward!" Whistler squawked, leading the way.

Chapter 24
Deeper Truths

Alkeroth, Vasalia

There was a little chipper was in his step as Thomas walked down the city street. The men had made camp outside the city, and since there was no telling how long they would be there and no war to be fought, Thomas had made his way to the town for some of the more luxurious things.

However, his first stops were more practical, visiting the bathhouse and the medical shop. There Thomas got himself cleaned up and his wounds re-bandaged. Most of his strength and mobility had returned to his left arm, and only minor wrapping was needed as the wounds had already begun to close up. His right arm now required no bandage. However, it was still painful to grip heavier items with it. His hair was trimmed up, and so was the beard that had grown in the last few days on the road.

As he walked along the street, Thomas felt like a new man. That said, what his heart truly desired was something strong to drink. He walked with purpose but slowly as he viewed the world differently now. Being completely sober was a strange feeling, so the local sights looked different to him than at other times. Thomas could smell the ale and food as he approached his destination. He chuckled as he recalled when Oswald had started a conversation about that very thing some time ago.

"Everything smells like food and booze to you," Oswald chuckled. They had been on the road for several days back from aiding the Northern kingdom of Halika. A small resurgent force of Dun-mar had come out of the Great Ridge Mountains to the north. Very little has been known about the Dun-mar since the beginning. They have always remained underground.

The Unatari Kilith and Broden were the only ones these people—if you could call them that—would listen to since they were created by those two Unatari specifically. Small and wiry in stature, these Dun-mar always kept to themselves unless provoked. However, they would occasionally venture out and attack the kingdoms of Halika and Taureau.

They posed no actual or significant threat, and no reason was ever given for the random attacks, but since Halika was part of the Five Crown Alliance, Ivan had sent his two best generals to assist the minor kingdom.

"Well, Oswald," General Fendrell said, "It's amazing what one can do while lacking the basic necessities of life if you can enjoy a few luxuries."

"Well, Thomas," Oswald remarked. "We have ways to go before we get either necessity or luxury."

Thomas sighed, "I'm aware; just trying not to think about it."

"Smelling food and booze in the air when there shouldn't be isn't helping you know." The two laughed softly and continued their journey home…

Thomas' thoughts came as he reached the pleasant aroma's source. On The Rocks tavern was one of his favorites in all of Kralavia. Set back into a small rocky protrusion from the ground in the city, this particular tavern had access to a unique water spring that, according to the locals, made for the best ale in the land. Thomas agreed.

He found a small, open table in one of the far corners of the room and sat down with his back to the wall. The tavern was dimly lit, though the front of the main room also gathered some light from the two front windows that faced the street.

Thomas got himself comfortable and relaxed as the damp smokey air hit his nostrils. He had waited not a few moments when one of the young serving maids greeted him and asked what she could get him. "A pint of your strongest ale," Thomas said. The maiden nodded and began to walk away. "Your strongest," he repeated.

As he waited, Thomas pulled the dire wolf claw necklace from his pocket and began to play with it in his fingers as his eyes glanced around the room. He blinked abruptly as the pint of ale was set before him, "Can I get you anything else?" the maiden asked.

Thomas took a sip of the pint and exhaled. "Food," he stated.

The young lady's soft blue eyes went from bubbly to annoyed, "Anything in particular?"

"Look," Thomas sighed, "I've been on the road for a few days, and I'm bound to return on the same road at any moment. What I want is some real food. A meal."

The young maiden's eyes softened with the rest of her complexion. "I'll bring you the chef's special."

Thomas nodded and placed a few coins on the table, "And another ale, please." The waitress nodded as she walked away. Thomas took another long, slow drink and exhaled heavily as he savored the taste. Then, after a moment, he slammed the remaining pint down in one long gulp.

Meanwhile

The city prison was simple and crude but effective. No jail, save for the stronghold beneath Stalbak Castle, was more secure. Because of all the rocky outcroppings in the country, Alkeroth built its town hall into one such landmark and carved its prison into the rock.

Oswald, Ulrich, Aldrich, and Rollins let Thaddeus and King Leoxtra lead the way through the damp hallways into the basement of the town hall building. Since most of the building was carved directly into the rock, the walls were one solid piece of stone, unmoved in their placement.

The guard at the prison entrance stood as King Leoxtra greeted him before unlocking the doors. There, the group was led into a more brightly lit hallway. On each side sat the cells holding various criminals that somehow went against the king's law. In the end, in the most prominent cell sat "Admiral Mortem," King Leoxtra greeted. He hoped to interrupt whatever peaceful sleep the admiral might have been trying to enjoy. No luck, however, as Admiral Mortem's acknowledgment was quick and straightforward.

The group paused a few paces away from the cell door. Thaddeus turned to the men with him and playfully asked who was first. Ulrich stepped up before Oswald put his hand up to stop him. "General Ulrich, we need him alive and conscious enough to be able to talk," Oswald whispered. Ulrich scowled, "Now look," Oswald said. "I'm not trying to be disrespectful by saying this, but please…just stay quiet and let me and Leoxtra talk for now."

Ulrich began to protest, but Rollins agreed with Oswald, "Ulrich, Oswald has had just as much experience getting information from enemy soldiers. Give him his chance, and if they fail, you can use your…more creative techniques."

After a moment, Ulrich conceded, and Aldrich sighed through his nose, "All right."

Oswald nodded to Leoxtra as they approached the cell; Admiral Mortem was already standing by the door, arms crossed and an annoyed look on his face. Chains draped from his wrists and ankles locked to the bolts in the cell's floor, giving just enough slack to allow the admiral to reach the straw mat and chamber pot.

"Admiral," Leoxtra chirped. "We have another fun day to get through." Admiral Mortem didn't move. "I have a few gentlemen here who want to speak with you."

Mortem's gaze looked over the men outside his cell and locked on General Cromwell. "Well," he said, with a blood-filled grin. "Pleasure's all mine, General." Oswald smiled, and Mortem glanced around the men's faces again. "Who's the lad?" he asked, gesturing at Aldrich.

"None of your concern," Oswald said quickly. Mortem eyed him suspiciously. "What can you tell me about your purpose here?" he asked, ignoring Mortem's gaze.

Mortem straightened up, "That depends on how detailed of an explanation you're looking for."

"The attack on Stelbeck. Why?" Oswald demanded.

Mortem chuckled, "Why not?"

"Because while I don't think much of Carnheller and its people," Oswald said. "I've never once thought of them as stupid."

"You should," Leoxtra quipped.

Oswald smiled but asked Mortem, "You can't tell me this was a last-minute plan." He began. "The number of ships and manpower you brought. For what reason did you attempt this invasion?" Admiral Mortem's smile grew into a full chuckle. Oswald's patience grew thin, "You realize if you don't tell me anything, you will be dealt with by the Vasalians." He threatened. "They are a far more savage bunch than we are."

Mortem caught his breath and responded, "Funny. I haven't had that impression so far while dealing with them."

King Leoxtra was nearly offended by this remark, "Well, from now on, you'll be dealing with me personally, sailor boy."

Mortem's jaw tightened, "Sailor boy? I am ready to die for the cause."

"You will try," Leoxtra snapped back. Then, stepping closer to the bars of the cell, "I won't let you die."

Oswald stepped forward to calm the king, "Admiral, what cause? Who is involved? And what are they after? As part of the Five Crown Alliance, you've already broken numerous parts of the treaty. What did you hope to gain from this?"

"Althalos will burn," Mortem sneered. "Vasalia and Valkos will burn with it." His smile returned, "You're all going to die."

Leoxtra lost his patience and told the guard to open the cell. As fast as it was open, Leoxtra jumped in, landing a firm blow to Mortem's face. "Your fleet is in shambles, son," the king snapped. "I'll take you down to the shoreline. You'll see a bunch of masts poking up out of the water like little sticks. That's what's left of your cause." Mortem spat out a wad of blood and possibly a tooth. Oswald couldn't tell. But more would come as with each silent stare, Leoxtra would pound the admiral's face again. "Look at me!" he finally said, grabbing the admiral's face.

"Your Highness," the admiral mocked.

King Leoxtra's face went tense, "The only thing that's going to burn is your balls when I stick them with a branding iron. Tell us what we want to know, and I'll just give them a quick snip instead."

Admiral Mortem laughed manically. When he finally stopped, "You know nothing. Ha-ha. This attack may have failed, but it has only prolonged the inevitable. You are all going to die."

Leoxtra readied his arm for another punch, but Oswald stepped in and grabbed his arm, "Leoxtra!" Ulrich, Rollins, Aldrich, Thaddeus, and the guard, remained silent. "King," he said, bowing his head. Leoxtra relaxed and faced Oswald, "If you break his jaw, then he'll never talk."

Leoxtra scoffed, "It'll heal."

"You can break every bone in my body if that gets you off," Mortem taunted. "I've already said everything I'm going to say."

King Leoxtra stepped forward and held Mortem's face up by his hair, "Give it time, Admiral." Mortem coughed hard as a firm fist was plunged into his gut. Oswald stepped back to avoid the blood spray from the admiral's mouth.

"General Omarr!" Leoxtra called.

"Milord," the general said as he stepped forward.

"Bring me some hot irons. We'll be needing something for cauterizing wounds."

As Thaddeus ran his errand, Oswald glanced back at Aldrich. He could tell the young prince was nervous about what he was witnessing but doing his best to hide it. Ulrich was smiling and had a hand resting on the prince's shoulder. Oswald and Ulrich had been generals with Thomas and Rollins for some time. And as tough as Ulrich talked, Oswald knew he was a 'yes-man'. But more than that, Ulrich was hungry for power and control and would do everything he could to maintain his position and good standing with the king. Ivan was less caring about such things than Ulrich hoped for. However, Oswald knew that if Ulrich could win over the prince, Aldrich would do what Ulrich wanted, not what his father wanted.

Oswald looked back at Mortem, who was barely standing, blood oozing out of his mouth. King Leoxtra stood nearby, waiting for Thaddeus to hatch whatever evil torture he had planned. King Ivan's instructions came back to Oswald's mind. He understood that he was given them to keep Aldrich from having strange ideas. *But,* he thought, *maybe it would be used against King Leoxtra's ideas.*

Later

Thomas had long since finished his food and had been enjoying several rounds when his peaceful solitude was interrupted by an unexpected visitor. "Ulrich?" Thomas questioned most annoyedly. "To what do I owe the…whatever this is."

Ulrich sat across from Thomas and flagged down one of the staff, "Wench!" he cried out and gestured to Thomas' drink. "Whatever he has." Then he turned to Thomas, "Captain Fendrell, what a lovely surprise to bump into you here."

Thomas groaned aloud, "No, General, I'm afraid it's simply a surprise." Ulrich chuckled. "Besides, aren't you supposed to be with Aldrich and company? Where are they anyway?" he asked as he looked around the room.

"Yes," Ulrich replied as the lady brought his plate and ale. "I was. However, the interrogation of Admiral Mortem is going…less than ideal, and I got sick of waiting for nothing. General Rollins left to attend to the men at the camp, and Aldrich and Oswald stayed there with Leoxtra to see if anything more would come of it."

Thomas nodded, "So what do you want, General?"

"Can't two friends just sit and enjoy a drink together?"

"Yes," Thomas answered. "But we both know that we're not."

"Oh, come now, Captain. No need for such a harsh claim."

Thomas shrugged as he brought his pint to his mouth, "Hm, could be harsher."

"Yes, I'm sure you could, Thomas," Ulrich agreed as he drank. "I would like to apologize for what happened in the mountains. I didn't mean to offend."

"Thanks?" Thomas remarked.

"Do you accept my apology?"

Thomas firmly set his tankard down and groaned aloud again. "What do you want, Ulrich? What're you doing here?" he questioned. "You hardly ever drink. From what I've heard, you prefer not to. You enjoy looking down on those who do, especially people like me. So have you come here to humiliate me?"

"Of course not. You do that quite well yourself," Ulrich teased. "I just wanted to make sure there were no hard feelings."

"That's the pot calling the kettle black on hard feelings. Me apologizing for what happened on the Great River has never changed how you feel about me. Are you still pushing for my execution, or did you finally give that up?" Ulrich didn't say anything and took a few bites of his food. Thomas realized his mug was empty and asked if Ulrich would actually drink his. To which Ulrich slowly took a sip while he kept eyes locked on Thomas, who had flagged down the waitress again.

After the additional mug was brought, Thomas took a long gulp before he spoke. "So. Tell me about your brothers."

Ulrich almost choked on his food, "What?"

"Tell me about them. I figured I should get to know them since so much of our relationship rests on the loved ones taken away from you that day because of something I did."

Ulrich chewed and swallowed his food. "Well, there was Isaac. He was the second oldest after me. Very timid and quiet, he kept to himself mainly. My mother and father weren't attentive to him growing up, and I think he was somewhat stuck in my shadow… But he was a good lad."

"Yes, I'm sure," Thomas said. "And who was the third oldest? I believe his name was Alexander, am I correct?"

Ulrich seemed pleased, and his mood lifted slightly as he continued. "Yes. Alexander. He was, ha-ha, he was a funny little boy growing up. Unlike Isaac, instead of being quiet, he went the other way. He was loud and mischievous, always getting into trouble and hatching schemes with his friends. I often caught the strong beating of my father's belt."

"I know that feeling," Thomas said and raised his tankard in salute to that.

"Ugh," Ulrich recalled. "And then there was Reynold, the youngest. He was the son that finally changed my parents' tune. After the delinquent Alex turned out to be, they wanted to get child number four to turn out right. They wanted him to be like me…and he was. He was so much like me. I was sure that one day he would become a general." Ulrich went silent, and Thomas' eyes remained fixed on his with a cheeky smile. Ulrich began to stiffen up as he realized he'd already said too much. "They were good lads," he finished plainly, downing the last of his pint.

"Yeah," Thomas noted. "And all dead."

Ulrich's soft features hardened quickly. Despite the past events and the differences, he never hated Captain Fendrell. But Ulrich began to feel something more was brewing in Thomas' mind. Something that he was not going to like.

"You know," Thomas said. "Funny thing about perception. It's so different from person to person. For instance, you may remember your brothers as the wonderful, timid, kind, and mischievous little rascals they were growing up. I, being their commanding officer then, saw them only as the cowards, rapists, and thieves that they had become…"

Ulrich was speechless. He couldn't tell if he wanted to leave or punch Thomas.

Thomas continued without pause, "I remember years ago, my company and I were sent to settle a border dispute between Althalos and Alnirya. A few days prior, an Althalothian village was sacked by a local baron from Alnirya who claimed the village sat partially on his territory. King Tiberious, may he rest in peace, gladly turned over the baron who had initiated the attack, saying he acted independently against the king's wishes. We were to bring him back to Stalbak to face trial. So, we arrested him along with a few of his captains. Everything went smoothly, with no complications. But the night before we returned to Althalos, your brother Alexander and several other men went to the baron's house, assaulted his daughters and his wife, killed everyone after, and hung his sons from the ramparts."

This information caught Ulrich off guard. He had not heard this tale, nor was any full record shown to him concerning that event. He recalled it happening afterward, as Ivan had him elsewhere. Was it all true? Or was Thomas embellishing the details now because of the conflict between them after burning the Great River?

"And Isaac," Thomas said after taking a quick drink. "Oh, that quiet little boy Isaac. A real sadistic bastard, he was. I once caught him trying to feed a captured enemy soldier his horse. I remember that man pleading, crying…screaming about how he'd had that horse since it was a foal and loved it like family. Your brother just dropped its decapitated head in his lap. The man went into shock and passed out…and your brother…I've never seen a man laugh harder in his life."

Ulrich's face went from firm thought to red with anger as Thomas continued, "Oh, and last but not least, although in this case, he is the least, Reynold! That sweet little boy that you said was so much like you. I'll set the scene for you. There we were, the banks of the Great River, our favorite location for a story."

Ulrich's fist clenched his mug tighter.

"I had divided my company between the left and right flanks of the river while Oswald was to bring his entire company up the middle, and we'd all push across. All was going according to plan until Reynold, who was ordered to hold our left flank, broke formation and attempted to retreat once the enemy committed an unexpected counterattack. The defense was crumbling quickly. I had to act fast…so we set the forest on fire…it got out of hand. Friend and foe alike lost in the flames." Thomas paused. Sober or not, it was always a hard memory to recall.

Still, he pressed on, reliving every detail as it happened. "Oswald's company was almost completely engulfed. I ran into the flames… searching…searching every single body I found, getting as many wounded out as I could even as the smoke burned into my eyes, and I could barely see any longer. Many soldiers continued trying to fight despite the hopeless situation, hacking each other apart, not caring whether it was the enemy or their own compatriots. I finally found Oswald and got him on his feet, and then there I saw him. Your brother, shoving past his own troops, trampling wounded. He is just trying to get himself out of a situation he caused. He tripped and twisted his ankle. I left him. I left him there to die. And I was so pleased to learn that the other two received the same fate. I've often told myself I wish that day ended differently, but honestly, I think I'd do the same thing every time if it meant I was going to cook those little bastards."

Ulrich stood up so fast that Thomas had no time to react. The table flipped, and Thomas fell back as the dishes went flying. Ulrich stepped over the mess, but Thomas was already up, sword drawn. "Come on, General," Thomas chided. "Come on, old boy. Make your brothers proud. Avenge them."

Everyone in the tavern stopped, and they all watched to see how this confrontation would unfold. Ulrich didn't move, his hand clenched tightly around the hilt of his sword, but he never drew it out of the scabbard. A voice in the background called for someone to get the city guard, and another said to take the fighting outside. But no one moved.

"Do it," Thomas demanded. His voice grew louder as he spoke. "I'll give you a fair fight if it makes you feel better. Hell, you can say I swung first. Just do it."

"My brothers were…" Ulrich started to say. His voice was shaky. Whether it was the anger for the lies or tears for the reality, he couldn't tell. "My brothers were good men."

"Your brothers were scum through and through."

Ulrich finally gained his resolve and drew his sword. The two men square up, ready and waiting for the other to make the first move. At that moment, two Vasalian guards rush in, "Hey!" cried the first guard. "Do we need to intervene here?"

"This is a private matter," Thomas said, not taking his eyes off Ulrich.

"Put your weapons down," said the first guard firmly. "Or this private matter will be settled in the stockade."

Ulrich was the first to sheath his blade. Without a word, the general made his way to the door, "Hey!" said the second guard as he stepped in and blocked his path. "Stop."

The guard patted Ulrich and attempted to redirect him back inside, "Unhand me!" Ulrich yelled, and he punched the guard square in the nose. The guard slumped to the floor. The first guard stepped in, but Ulrich pulled his dagger and held it at the man's throat. "I am a General for the Althalothian army," he scowled. "Do not touch me again, or I will take your head off."

The guard backed away and tended to his unconscious partner. Ulrich glanced back at Thomas, who had also sheathed his sword, then stormed out.

As he returned to the town hall, Ulrich thought long and hard about what Thomas had said. Those details had never been revealed before, and whether they were true or not, he couldn't know. But internally, Ulrich was determined to increase his influence with Prince Aldrich. Then, he could be rid of those that sought to question his authority and, more importantly, ensure the version of the stories that needed to be shared.

"Sorry about the mess, love," Thomas said sympathetically. He had helped the young gal reset the table and chairs and collected the dishes thrown around in the scuffle. As the last of them cleaned up, Thomas turned to the girl and asked, "Could I have another, please?"

As she turned to leave, Thomas winced as pain shot through his right hand. He opened and closed it several times, and each time it was uncomfortable. He began to massage his forearm and palm as he got comfortable in his seat. Strange, he thought, as the pain went away.

Chapter 25
War Has Begun

Alkeroth Prison, Vasalia

Oswald and Aldrich watched as the torture and questioning from King Leoxtra continued. Still, Mortem held his silence. Aldrich thought this was a pointless gesture. Now that he knew who was at fault, killing the remaining survivors and sending their bodies to the bottom of the sea made more sense.

Ulrich and Rollins had left some time ago; Aldrich couldn't blame them. Ulrich had gotten annoyed that he couldn't do the job himself, and Rollins felt he was better needed elsewhere and went to check on the men at the camp. For a moment, Aldrich had to agree with their attitudes; this was the first time he had witnessed such cruelty, and he almost wished he could've left.

After the initial beatings didn't work, Leoxtra pulled fingernails and small incisions mixed with the hot iron. Aldrich thought for sure that this would make any man talk. It appeared he was wrong. Blood began to pool at Admiral Mortem's feet. The man grunted and groaned in pain with every strike against him, but he never yielded.

"This is only continuing by your own choice, Admiral," Leoxtra said as he wiped his hands off. "Answer our questions, and it can all end."

Mortem snorted and spat on the ground at Leoxtra's feet, "Never."

Leoxtra nodded, "Very well." He gestured to Thaddeus to bring the hot iron again. Mortem gritted his teeth and hissed as the hot metal seared the flesh of his arm. Leoxtra stopped and turned to Oswald and Aldrich, who had been observing outside the cell. "Any other ideas?" he asked them.

Oswald shook his head. If Mortem didn't talk now, more pain wouldn't work. Aldrich stood silent and motionless for a moment before he finally spoke. "His motives are irrelevant at this time," the prince said as he shifted his gaze to the admiral. "Kill him." Everyone present shot Aldrich a questioning stare. "Kill them all," he finished calmly.

"But…" Oswald began to protest.

Aldrich held his hand in silence; he had had enough of this. "As punishment for their crimes against Vasalia and Althalos. For violating the agreement as a member of the Five Crown Alliance, striking against an allied nation without cause. The sentence for the leader, and all those involved, is death."

"Now see here," Leoxtra snapped. "This is my country, and I will make that call here."

"My prince," Oswald interjected. "This is not what your father would want."

Mortem's gaze met Aldrich's as the prince stood silent momentarily. Fear? Or resilience? Either way, Mortem's eyes gave Aldrich a feeling of power. He didn't much care why Carnheller attacked anymore. He would return all the heads to King Valtor and show him exactly what happens when you cross the line. "General Ulrich was right, Oswald," Aldrich said as he gazed at the confused general. "You always were too soft."

"I have only ever done what I've been commanded," Oswald said defensively.

Aldrich ignored his comment and said to King Leoxtra, "I expected more from you."

"General Thaddeus!" a guard shouted from the entrance, "We have a visitor. Your presence is requested." Thaddeus gratefully returned to the surface, eager to rid himself of that conversation's presence.

"Send his head home with the rest of them!" Aldrich demanded. He had grown impatient and bored of this conversation already. His father would not have met such backlash, and this thought infuriated Aldrich.

Mortem groaned from his cell. The trio turned to face him, "If I must die," he said weakly. "Then you should know that this was only the beginning. War is coming, and all will burn." He coughed and chuckled as he finished.

"By order of my father, King Iv…" Aldrich started to say.

"Is not that," Oswald firmly interrupted. Leoxtra and Aldrich watched as Oswald produced a small, rolled note. Oswald handed the letter to Leoxtra, "King Leoxtra," he said. "In the instance where Prince Aldrich was to make an unwise or potentially grievous error in his judgment. King Ivan has sent me these specific instructions as his wishes for this occasion."

King Leoxtra smiled and took the paper from Oswald as Aldrich turned red. Leoxtra read them aloud. It said:

King Leoxtra,

In the event that my son does not follow my example and teaching as king, I hereby give this memo, through my trusted General Oswald Cromwell, my specific instructions.

All prisoners are to be treated fairly and kindly until the matter of 'why' is resolved with the aggressing nation. I have speculated that Carnheller and King Valtor are involved somehow. If that is the case, we will only decide what to do with his men after we speak to Eric. Carnheller is still part of the Five Crown Alliance, and Kralavian citizens should be treated as such, regardless of their foolhardy and brash actions. I have already sent word to Eric to meet with us and discuss this matter. I will send word to you once I have confirmation.

If Carnheller is not involved, we must be extra cautious. Very little is known about the nations across the sea and what they could gain from this attack; I am still determining. If this is the case, we must be careful not to provoke something greater unless necessary.

I hope my son will not veer too far from this direction, but if he does, General Cromwell has been directed to give this to you.

King Ivan Ventril, king of Althalos

King Leoxtra finished reading and flashed the King's Seal at the bottom of the page so Aldrich could see it. "I'm sorry, son," he said as he tucked the paper in his belt. A large smile formed as he continued. Leoxtra didn't necessarily agree with Ivan but was more than happy to accept any instruction that would put a thorn on the prince's side. "Your father has spoken, and I agree with him." He turned to Mortem, "Lucky for you. Or perhaps, not so lucky." He chuckled, "This means I get more quality time with you."

Mortem only groaned in response.

"I'm sorry, Aldrich," Oswald said.

"Save it." Aldrich snapped as he stormed out.

"King Leoxtra," Oswald said quietly as he watched Aldrich leave. "Thank you. I really hoped I wouldn't have needed to use that." Leoxtra nodded. "When you question Mortem again," Oswald continued. "Press on what he meant by his attack only being the beginning. What else is coming and why?"

Just then, General Thaddeus came rushing down. "What happened to the prince?" he asked, trying to catch his breath.

"Pay him no mind," Leoxtra said. "What is it?"

Thaddeus straightened up, "Milord, a message from Valkos. Stelmond is attacking, and at Haldair's request, the assembly of the Five Crown Alliance."

Mortem laughed through short coughs of blood, "It is only the beginning."

Leoxtra turned to Thaddeus, "Assemble the men. We will ride today." Then he turned to Oswald, "Better find your prince and tell him. No doubt Ivan will want his army to head that way."

Oswald nodded, "Where are we to meet?"

"The Field of Denesious," Thaddeus stated. "It appears that Stelmond is moving north to Terrowin. Haldair hopes to stop them before then."

"If Haldair calls for the Five Crowns to join him, this is far worse than we imagine." Leoxtra pointed out. "We must help him." The trio left the prison, and Oswald ran off to find Aldrich while Leoxtra and Thaddeus assembled their men.

Oswald didn't have to do much to find Aldrich. With their lavianite armor, any Althalothian stood out among the other kingdoms, the prince more so. Several people saw him headed to Stelbeck Keep, and so Oswald pursued him.

"Well, look who it is," Oswald stopped as he recognized the voice that called out over the crowd in the streets.

"Thomas!" The general greeted when he spotted the captain sitting at the tavern's outside table. "What have you been up to? I see you're looking better now that you got cleaned up."

"Thanks," Thomas replied. "And just the usual."

"How many?"

Thomas shrugged, "I lost track."

Oswald chuckled, "Well, get back to camp and tell the others to assemble, war has come to Valkos, and King Haldair is calling the Alliance to help." Thomas straightened up, "Have you seen the prince?"

Thomas nodded, gesturing to the keep, "He headed up there." As Oswald started to ride on, Thomas continued, "You might want to be the one to tell General Ulrich. I don't think he'll listen to me."

Oswald stopped and rolled his eyes, "Why's that?"

"He came looking for a fight."

Oswald pinched the bridge of his nose, "Thomas, what did you do?"

"I didn't do anything," Thomas said, raising his hands in defense. "I simply gave him some information that he was previously unaware of, and he didn't take it well."

"His brothers?" Oswald asked.

"Perhaps."

Oswald's eyes rolled so hard he thought they could be heard, "Today of all days," he muttered quietly. "Athalon, give me strength. Get to the camp and tell General Rollins and Ulrich that we move out today." Thomas playfully nodded as Oswald rode away.

"Are you alright?" Aldrich asked as he watched Wilkins limp across the tent. He looked exhausted, like he hadn't slept well or at all in days. The prince had returned to visit with the survivors to try and grasp his father's instruction. It was easy to make decisions from his castle, but if the king had been here and witnessed the slaughter and maltreatment of the men's bodies and the stubbornness of Mortem, Aldrich wondered if the instructions would've been the same.

"I'll be alright, Sire," Wilkins said, "I can't help but think that if I shut my eyes and go to sleep…they'll come back."

"You're safe now," Aldrich said. "You needn't worry any longer."

Wilkins nodded.

"I'd like you and Colins to return to Stalbak when we leave," Aldrich said. "And the other survivors."

Wilkins looked shocked, "But, this is my post, sir."

"Stelbeck is destroyed," Aldrich stated. "We will rebuild, but let's take you home now. A hero deserves to go home."

Just then, Oswald came riding up, "Prince Aldrich!"

Aldrich rolled his eyes and exited the tent, "What, General?" He was in no mood to chat with Oswald at this time.

Oswald relayed the message from the rider from Valkos and explained what he planned to do with Rollins and Ulrich. Aldrich was taken aback by the news. "We leave today." Oswald finished.

Aldrich stood and thought for a moment. Then, he got an idea. "Yes, General. We will take the southern road along the Great River south of the Purple Mountains. Then, you and the other generals will take the army to Valkos and meet with my uncle. I will take a small escort with these survivors here and head to Stalbak. Send a rider ahead to ensure my father knows I am coming home first." Oswald nodded and promptly left Aldrich alone with his thoughts, "He and I need to talk," he muttered.

The city had a large bustle as King Leoxtra's men and Ivan's army gathered and prepared to move out. The thought on everyone's mind was the same, would they get there in time? It would be a few days' ride to the Field of Denesious. What would they be marching into?

Captain Frendrell had, as instructed, informed Generals Ulrich and Rollins about the change of plans. While still angry at Thomas for his conversation earlier, Ulrich pressed his feelings down deeper as the thought of actual battle pleased him. He was also pleased to learn, through the whispers from the men, that Aldrich and Oswald had a little bit of a falling out. Over what exactly hadn't been shared, but he was pleased to get a chance to step in with Aldrich and find out. He hadn't counted on an issue rising between the two, but Ulrich would be a fool not to take such an opportunity when it presented itself.

Later in the afternoon, the troops finally crossed the Great River entering Valkos. Questions ran through everyone's mind. Who? Why? To what end? Oswald pondered these questions and needed answers. Perhaps all will be made clear once they engage Stelmond? Maybe it will only get more twisted?

As they rode, Oswald watched as Aldrich and Ulrich carried on in long conversations together out of earshot of the others. He tried not to let it bother him, but he couldn't help it. Whether or not he did the right thing wasn't the concern; King Ivan had a request, and Oswald followed through. What Oswald did wonder, though, is if he should've told Aldrich about it ahead of time and saved the whole situation. Ultimately, Oswald had to let it go and hope that Aldrich would see that Oswald only did what he was told. Besides, there were other things at hand now.

War had begun.

Chapter 26
Fort Elias

Fort Elias, Althalos

Alfred rode quickly, ignoring the winding road and cutting across the open fields and small hills to get to Fort Elias as fast as possible. He was careful to avoid the clusters of people on foot running away from the village and surrounding areas so as not to trample them. Mass panic filled the air around him as he watched the farms and smaller settlements outside Greebold's Trench empty in fear of the coming threat. The dark of night had fully settled in; however, the area was still well-lit by the fires that burned in the wake of the attacking force that pushed through behind him.

Soon, Alfred could see the lights of the fort in the distance; hope filled his heart as he thought about the safety of the remaining villagers that could be found there. "Quickly now!" he shouted to the people near him.

Alfred paused as he glanced around the mass of people. So many familiar faces, yet none of them were of people he was close to. Did none of his family or friends survive?

"Alfred!" a voice called above the crowd. Alfred turned his horse as he searched the area for the source. "Alfred!" the voice called again.

Then, Alfred spotted him, "Marty! Marty McFarland!"

Marty pressed through the crowd to Alfred, "Alfred! Where are the others? Douglas and Olivia? Amelia and your children? I searched the crowd as I ran, but I haven't seen them."

Alfred tensed as he held back his emotions. "They're gone," he said coldly. Then, changing the subject, he asked, "Where's Billy and Bolger?"

Marty glanced back toward the village, "They were at Bolger's Stead when I last saw them. I left them there when I went to the village to investigate the commotion and…" A loud horn blew in the direction of the village cutting him off. War cries and screams of terror filled the air.

Alfred turned his steed back to the fort, "It's too late to worry about them now. We have to keep moving."

As they pressed forward toward the fort's gates, Lord Elias and his lieutenant, Lucas Grant, stood above them. They watched as the flock of villagers got closer, crying out for help and safety. "Shall I open the gate, sir?" Lucas asked.

Lord Elias remained silent. His stern, emotionless face remained fixed on the approaching crowd. Behind them, he could make out the oncoming riders that only stopped to slaughter those caught in their path. He wondered if any would even make it to the gates alive. "Sir?" the lieutenant asked again.

"No," Elias said finally. "We cannot risk this fortress's safety during an attack. The gate must stay closed."

Concern crept over the lieutenant's face. "But, sir."

"Not another word," Elias interrupted. He stepped closer, though he was nearly the same size as the lieutenant. Fear made the lord's figure tower over him. "My decision is final, Lieutenant Grant." Lucas nodded and then looked out at the coming mass of people.

Alfred reached the gates and looked up at the walls of the fort. People had already been gathering, yet the gates did not move. Behind him, he can see the raiders killing those that had fallen behind or were slow. They moved quickly and without mercy through the remnants as they pressed forward. Alfred glanced up and saw the soldiers at the top of the wall. "Lord Elias!" he called out. "Don't let your people suffer!" No response came from the fort.

Alfred got angry as he looked around for a way to save the people. None could be found, save the fort itself. "He doesn't care about us," a small voice said nearby. Alfred looked around and saw a small lad next to his horse. Tears had already formed in the young man's eyes.

"And why should he?" the lad continued. "We are peasants in comparison."

Alfred's face grew red with anger as he called up to the fort again, "It is his duty to care for his people, to give us leadership and protection! King Ivan would have opened the gates and had an army ready to fight the attackers! He would not hide behind his walls while his people suffer!" Still no response from the soldiers above. Then, turning to the young lad, he asked, "What is your name, friend?"

"Sam," he replied sheepishly. "Sam Gable, sir."

"This will not be your grave, Sam Gable," Alfred said firmly.

Upon the wall, Lieutenant Grant listened to the cries below; he heard Alfred's call. Lord Elias remained next to him, emotionless and silent. Lucas glanced at the approaching threat and again at the helpless people below. After a moment, he mustered his courage and ran down to the courtyard below. He knew what he must do. "Lord Elias!" he called up from the square. Elias turned to face him from atop the wall. "If you don't order the gates to be opened. I will do it myself."

Elias's face grew red, "You dare defy me?" he bellowed. "That is an act of treason!"

Lucas drew a deep breath; he had finally had enough of Lord Elias's cowardice and cruelty. "It would be treason if I did not, sir." He firmly stated. Lucas nodded to the soldier near the gate mechanism. The guard nodded in return, and Lucas approached.

"Lieutenant!" Elias shouted. "If you open those gates, I'll have your head."

Lucas stopped and looked up directly at Elias, "If you had kept to the orders of King Ivan, that village would not have been slaughtered! I recognize those riders, and I know that you do as well. This attack on these people is your fault!"

"I am your lord!"

"You are an old man without honor!" Lucas snapped. "King Ivan has my loyalty and would not stand by to see his people slaughtered needlessly." As he finished, he stepped toward the gate controls.

"Stop him!" Lord Elias ordered. No one moved. "I order you all to stop him!" None of the soldiers moved from their positions.

As Lucas began to work the gate lever, he shouted, "To anyone loyal to King Ivan of Althalos, to anyone loyal to our land and our people, come with me! The villagers will need protection as they move into the walls." All at once, the guards within the fort assembled. Those on the wall positioned themselves with their bows, ready to send a volley. Others gathered near the gate, prepared to rush out and aid those who sought safety there.

"You will not open that ga…" Lord Elias was cut off as his body suddenly slumped down. Behind him, a soldier had hit him with the hilt of his sword and was sheathing the weapon as Elias fell where he stood. Lucas glanced up and smiled as he continued to raise the gate.

"Men," Lucas called out as the enormous metal and wood gate creaked and groaned as it was lifted. "Prepare yourselves. May Athalon greet you with honor should you fall here today."

As the gate began to open, Alfred had the people give way to allow the guards to get out and to their rear before the people rushed to the door. It didn't take long for the guards to exit in their formation. Once they were out, Alfred directed the others inside. "Quick now! Into the fort!"

Alfred waited as the crowd entered the fort. As he glanced back, he saw Marty and others mowed down by the advancing riders. Alfred sighed and entered the fort with the remnants of the group there.

The guards lined up with Lucas creating a barrier near the entrance. A few stragglers still filtered through the ranks to get inside. "Archers!" Lucas called out as his men lined up. The soldiers on the wall then drew their arrows and held, ready. Lucas waited for a few more distant refugees to get closer to his line before calling the attack. "Now!" he finally shouted.

In an instant, the volley of arrows sailed overhead. Whistler watched as several of his riders went down. Quickly he split up the men and staggered their approach. More arrows rained in; fewer riders went down that time.

"Do not let them breach the walls!" Lucas shouted. His men held firm in their positions. The outside of the fort was open, but it had several barricades scattered around to help break up any incoming force before it got to the walls. Lucas was one of a few of his men on horseback and knowing that they didn't have the numbers to stop all these attackers on horses, most of his men were stationed around these barricades. He hoped the archers would remove enough of them to ease the fight. However, as the riders gained ground, that hope faded, and in an instant, the two staggered waves of the enemy force swallowed Lucas and his men.

Alfred only felt a slight reprieve inside the fort as he watched the gate close behind him. He dismounted his horse and tried to calm the still frantic and afraid people. Alfred couldn't blame them but needed them to get inside safely. "Ladders!" Alfred heard a guard shout from atop the wall.

"Quickly, everyone, get inside the barracks!" Alfred shouted. As he pressed against the crowd to get back to his horse, the mob of people shifted, and his horse bucked violently and kicked him in the chest. Alfred went flying through the crowd and landed some feet away, unconscious.

Chapter 27
Ghosts of The Past

Greebold's Trench, Althalos

His eyes opened slowly before shutting again. The pain was incredible everywhere. Even the sun's light hurt him. He tried to move, but that hurt as much as lying still. Still, he needed to try. After several failed attempts, the man managed to roll on his side, and after a few deep breaths, the smell of smoke in the air began to register in his brain.

He glanced around, though his vision was still blurry, outlines of structures around him consumed in black smoke. Figures lay scattered on the ground around him. As his vision cleared, so did his memory of what happened. The slaughter of his home and all the people. He shifted slightly, and a jolt of pain shot from his stomach. Reactively gripping the source of the pain brought back the reality of what happened to him.

He felt the hole in his gut that shouldn't be there. Then he remembered his demise—the dark-armored warrior. He carefully and slowly shifted to a nearby fallen horse to prop himself up and rest as he collected his thoughts. He felt dizzy, no doubt from the loss of blood. Could he even walk? Maybe. He could still feel his legs, which moved well enough to crawl, as slow going as it was.

Once he was against the dead animal, he paused and took a few deep breaths. His vision cleared a little more, and so did his brain. Taking great care, he glanced around to see if anyone else was up or moving, but everything was still. The only sounds heard were that of the crackling wood from the fires that had been burning all night.

The man carefully removed his bracers and shoulder harness that held the armor piece that covered his shoulders and upper chest. He also removed the rest of his chest covering, which consisted of a woven mail and leather shirt. He examined the hole in his stomach and saw it was black around the edge, though not as deep as it could've been, thankfully. Memories of what happened flooded his mind. He winced as he remembered feeling the impact of the Warhammer against his chest, knocking him down. Although, what came later was more painful. Douglas felt the hole in his gut after he removed his armor. What little protection he was wearing had done its job.

Then Douglas wrapped his wound using some fabric from the saddle of the dead horse he was against. He pulled it as tight as possible to help stop the blood and hopefully buy him some time. He began to think through his few options and decide what he could and should do now. Wait here. Escape and hope to live. Try to get help. No, Fort Elias was nearby, but under the circumstances, the attackers were probably already engaging them as he sat there. Besides, there was no use for him to run through the trouble, not in his condition.

Then he had another thought. Stalbak. It was only a day's ride, and if he was careful, he could get there without passing Fort Elias directly. He'd have to go through the forest road to the south. It wouldn't add more time to his trip. But first, he would need a horse and the strength to ride.

An hour later, Douglas had carefully crawled to a stable nearby. When he got nearer, he found two horses standing at the far end of the fenced area outside the structure—no doubt where they had been all night. Thankfully, the fire wasn't so bad here that they jumped the fence. It was one of the few structures that weren't totally burned through.

It took another hour to grab some water and saddle the frightened horse. But once he was up in the saddle, the horse settled and followed his lead. The man took another deep breath and gripped his stomach with one hand and with the other, the reigns. *Here goes nothing,* he thought as he began to ride east.

The western side of Althalos was heavily forested, with beautiful trees of all colors. The arrangement of Harvest Flowers marked all the roads on this side of Stalbak. These flowers got their name because they bloomed brightly in various colors throughout the spring and summer. The flowers would then turn a dark midnight purple in the fall for two weeks before opening up and showering their golden pollen over the area. Some parts of Kralavia would hold small celebrations as people would gather to witness the Harvest Flower open up to reveal its golden pollen.

Memories flashed in Douglas' mind as he rode through the small, wooded area. He wouldn't have time to enjoy the view today. It was hard enough to keep his focus on the road as it was. No sound was heard; not even the animals stirred in the leaves today. He glanced out to the north as he exited the woods. Smoke billowed on the horizon. *Fort Elias,* he thought to himself. Was he already too late? He took a few deep breaths and winced with every inhale; the pain in his gut grew stronger the longer he tried to remain upright. But he must press on.

A few hours later, the tall, thick gates of Stalbak were before him. As Douglas rode through the gate, the guards briefly stopped him. After he recounted briefly what happened, the guards quickly sent him on to the castle with an escort to get through the city faster.

The guard with him shouted out as they entered the castle courtyard. Wully, outside at the time, raced over. "What is it? What happened?" he asked hurriedly.

"Greebold's… Trench…attacked," the man tried to say. Before he could finish, he slumped over and fell to the ground.

Wully quickly stepped up, caught the man, and helped ease his fall. "Come now, help me get him up." He cried out to the guards nearby. Several other spectators had begun to show up in the distance as the commotion gained attraction from those within the castle grounds.

"My village," he said suddenly.

"What?" Wully asked. But the man's eyes had already rolled back. Wully gently slapped his face, "Sir! Who are you? What happened?"

Suddenly the injured rider took a deep breath, "The king! I must see the king!" Douglas coughed up blood before passing out again.

Wully looked at the guards with him, "Let's get him to the medical ward and summon King Ivan." The guards responded respectfully, and within moments the doctor was on site as they carefully moved the man inside the castle.

The medical ward of the castle was an add-on from the time of the Great War. It was a large open room that could comfortably house a hundred men on cots. Several fireplaces lined two walls along the cots to aid with boiling water and to cauterize. During the war, this room bustled with activity and was a godsend for the troops that needed to be seen before they could return home or battle. Today, however, as all days now, it remained empty.

Douglas was laid on one of the cots near the door, and immediately the doctor began to work. "Can you save him?" Wully asked.

The doctor shook his head, "Too soon to tell."

Moments later, King Ivan arrived. The two guards fetched him at his heels as he entered the room. "Who is he?" he asked without breaking stride.

Wully shook his head, "I don't know yet, sir. He rode in, demanding to see you. Something about a village attack." Wully gestured to the cot behind him where the man lay, "But as you can see, he isn't in the best shape."

King Ivan nodded and sent his guards away, closing the doors behind them. "Then I guess we'll have to wait and see," he said as he walked over to the window.

"I suppose so," Wully agreed. He was surprised that Ivan chose to stay. "You don't have to wait here, your highness. I can stay with him. I'm sure you have other duties to attend to as the king."

Ivan chuckled, "What duty does a king have if not to care for his people?" Wully smiled, unsure of how to respond to that. He had spoken to and been with Ivan on several occasions before and, of course, in recent days, had spoken to the king many times. Yet, at that moment, Wully realized that he genuinely didn't know Ivan as king apart from a king's commands. "I know I haven't always been that way as king," Ivan said, trying to fill in the silence. "But I've done my best to regain my honor and to be someone people can follow until the end."

"There are many things you are and many things you aren't great at, my king," Wully said, finally finding the words. "But I've never known you as anything but the most honorable of men."

Ivan glanced out the window and sighed quietly, "I wish that were the case." Ivan looked back at Wully, "But I appreciate that," he said, suddenly changing his tone. "My brother has gotten to you, hasn't he?"

Wully smiled, "King Haldair has a lot of influence."

Ivan smiled again, "That he does." Douglas coughed suddenly, and both men watched as the doctor continued to work. "I always envied Haldair for how well he was accepted in Valkos, being a foreigner put into the throne, and how well he ran his country every day since then."

Wully nodded, "He has the full respect of his people, which I'm sure you do as well, your highness. I've seen no indication of anything else."

"My brother crafted a great kingdom without all the poorly made decisions I had as a king in my youth." Ivan smiled as he thought to himself. "Perhaps he learned from my mistakes before he made them himself."

"King Haldair holds you in the highest respect. That is something I do know for certain."

"I know he does," Ivan replied. "It just makes all my past mistakes harder to deal with." Then he changed the subject. "You were Merrek's man, correct?"

Wully nodded. "Yes, Sire. My father served his father, and I now serve him."

"What do you think of Merrek?" Wully's face grew solemn as he was taken aback by the question. Ivan smiled, "You can answer me honestly. I'm not trying to corner you."

Ivan sat near the fire and folded his hands in his lap. Wully sat down across from him and thought for a moment before answering. "Merrek is a good man and leader," Wully started. "He has the respect of those above him and those below. He sometimes has moments and difficulty controlling his anger, but he is a good man and a furious warrior."

"Interesting," Ivan paused as he glanced toward the doctor still working on the man on the table. "I always wondered why my brother chose to take him under his wing. I know he will eventually need a successor for his crown, but Haldair seems to have a bit more of a personal attachment to this man."

"Haldair sees Merrek more as a son than a successor."

"I know that's the case," Ivan said as he relaxed in his seat and sighed. "My brother was heartbroken at the death of his wife, so much so that he nearly lost his kingdom. To this day, he refuses to remarry, but I know he always wanted his own children."

"I don't think I've ever known a better ki…" Wully stopped himself short as he realized what he had just said. A tinge of fear crept into his eye as he wondered how Ivan would respond to such a remark, even in his presence. "Oh, king, I didn't mean…"

Ivan chuckled, which slightly softened Wully's concern, "Don't stress over it, Captain. Ha-ha. I take no offense, and I actually agree with you. I have never known a better king than King Haldair."

The two continued to laugh together and exchange a few war stories until the doctor finally summoned them to the table. "He has regained consciousness, and I have stopped the bleeding. But he still needs constant attention and try not to strain him too much with questions."

Ivan nodded and stood over the shifting man uncomfortably, "Lie still; you're safe here."

"Ivan…" the man said weakly.

"Yes," Ivan said as Wully stepped up next to him.

"What is your name?" Wully asked.

The man's eyes moved quickly around the room before focusing again on the two men next to his bed, "Douglas, Douglas Trench." Ivan and Wully glanced at each other briefly as the man continued. "My father was Manus Trench," Douglas looked at Ivan, "He served under you."

Ivan nodded, "That he did, and a good captain he was."

Douglas coughed again, and blood oozed out of his mouth. The doctor quickly grabbed a rag to clean it up and urged Douglas to stay calm and stop speaking. Douglas shook his head, "Milord, my village Greebold's Trench, it was taken! We need help!"

King Ivan leaned in, "When did this happen, and by whom?"

"Last night," Douglas replied. Memories flooded back into his mind, and Douglas gasped as he recalled the pain of seeing his people slaughtered. Then, he remembered being struck in the stomach again and began grabbing at his waist. "They're all… They're all gone."

"By whom?" Ivan insisted.

"I didn't recognize the banner," Douglas said. Then he remembered something else, "Death," he said. "They smelled of death."

Ivan straightened up and stepped away. Wully followed and asked, "What does that mean?"

Ivan said nothing momentarily as the doctor attempted to calm him down. Then, without warning, he left, storming down the castle hallway out of the medical ward. Wully quickly followed and asked again what the cryptic message of Douglas meant to the king. Ivan stopped near the main entrance and looked at Wully squarely, "It would seem that more of my past is coming back to haunt me."

Wully shot a questioning glance at him. "Perhaps I did it wrong before," Ivan muttered to himself before he resumed walking. Wully followed until Ivan stopped again near his study. As he entered the room, Ivan glanced back at Wully, "Fetch me, Neilith."

Wully bowed his head and stepped back before turning away; at that moment, Wully saw the Golden Sword brightly displayed above the fireplace within the room. He watched as Ivan intently stared at it for several seconds before stepping further into the study. As Wully began to leave, his vision of Ivan several nights ago in the Great Hall appeared in his head. Fear took over as he quickened his pace.

When Wully returned with Neilith, Ivan was pouring over maps and records. "Milord," Neilith said as he bowed.

"Any news from Fort Elias?" Ivan asked.

"No, Sire," Neilith said. "But I have received word from Aldrich that your army is to move south to assist King Haldair since King Leoxtra had already defeated the attackers, which were confirmed to be an army from Carnheller, as you predicted, Sire. No word yet from King Valtor, Sire. I have sent the additional birds on time as you requested."

"Why does Haldair need Ivan's army?" Wully asked. "We've taken Stelmond on before."

"I had already received word that Haldair had requested the aid of the Five Crown Alliance," Ivan said. "Moving my army south after any conflict in the east was resolved was already expected. But I'm pleased to hear that Leoxtra already took care of the attack on Vasalia. Saves me the trouble." Then he directed his attention to Neilith, "Anything further?"

Neilith nodded, "Aldrich is unhappy with how things turned out in Alkeroth with Carnheller's Admiral Mortem. He says he will be coming here to speak to you before joining the army south. Based on the timing of the message, he should be arriving tomorrow."

Ivan took a deep breath, "Thank you, Neilith. Send a bird to Fort Elias and ask for an update. See what kind of response we get." Neilith bowed and left.

Wully asked Ivan, "What do you plan to do?"

"I will wait for my son and plan my visit to Fort Elias," Ivan said calmly. "Then," his face grew solemn as he glanced at the Golden Sword on the mantel, "I finish what I started."

Wully recalled his vision again and said nothing. Too many unknowns yet, and he still needed to figure out what his part was to play in all this. After a moment of silence, Wully dismissed himself and went back to check on Douglas Trench; then, he needed to talk to Laura; perhaps with more information, he could shed some light on the mysterious circumstances that seemed to be circling Castle Stalbak.

Chapter 28
Not a King Yet

Stalbak Castle, Althalos

Laura was enjoying a stroll in the sun in the castle gardens. It was a pleasant break from all the show-and-tell she had to do with the people as their new queen-to-be over the last several days. As much as she loved to get out with the common folk, working and talking among them, it was nice to enjoy peaceful walks on such quiet days. "Milady," Laura almost jumped in her skin when she heard the voice behind her.

"Oh!" Laura gasped, half surprised. "I haven't seen you for a few days. I thought maybe I scared you off after our last conversation here, Wully."

Wully stepped forward and blushed a little as she said his name, "My apologies, milady." He bowed his head slightly. "I have been…distracted. Not by our conversation," he turned and looked at the Great Hall, which loomed across the courtyard. "But something else these last few days."

In question, Laura tilted her head slightly, "I beg your pardon?"

Wully shook his head and smiled, "Nothing. Would you like some company?" Laura smiled and held out her arm. Wully grabbed it as they walked together, "So, how has your visit through the kingdom been?"

"Good," Laura said. "But long. It's nice to have a day or two to relax finally."

"I'm sure those busy days are just practice for what's in store for you as queen later."

Laura laughed, "Let's not get that far ahead of ourselves. Ivan still has many good years ahead of him." Wully smiled briefly before he winced in pain as a flash of the vision of the crown of Althalos broken on the ground came to memory. They stopped walking, and Laura turned to him, "Are you okay?"

"Yes," Wully nodded as he pinched the bridge of his nose. "I'll be alright." Laura was skeptical but continued walking with him, nonetheless. "Actually, I do have a few things on my mind."

"Tell me."

"The war in the south isn't going as planned," Wully explained. "King Haldair has called for the Five Crown Alliance to join him." Laura's expression grew solemn, but she said nothing. "Additionally, it seems that King Leoxtra was successful in his defense of the coastline and that Carnheller was the invading force."

"What of King Valtor?" Laura asked. "He would've been summoned as part of the Five Crown Alliance, but what now?"

Wully shrugged slightly, "I'm not sure. But Prince Aldrich has already sent his army south with Vasalia to aid in the threat. He'll be coming here first to speak to his father." Laura felt her heart skip. She was glad she could see her prince sooner than she thought, but some part resisted it.

"Stelmond has never posed a great threat to us before. I'm curious what changed that has King Haldair requesting aid." Laura sat down at the bench they approached, and Wully followed suit.

"I don't know much more than that now," Wully said. "And I'm not sure what King Ivan will want now that he is also dealing with raids on his western border." Laura turned and looked out across the horizon to the west. She couldn't see very far, with the castle and city walls blocking most of the view and several treetops that dotted the landscape. "What?" Wully asked when he noticed she was distracted.

Laura shook her head, "Nothing."

Wully nodded and relaxed in his seat. He wanted to tell her about the strange man and his visions. Over and over, they played in his mind, especially the ones with Laura. But what did they mean? Doubtful, she would know anyway, even if he did share them with her. In the silence, Wully decided to keep the visions a secret yet. He didn't want to worry anyone else about them until he had more information and knew his place in them.

"You said Prince Aldrich is coming here?" Laura asked, breaking the silence.

Wully nodded, "Yes. That is what I heard. Are you excited, milady?"

Laura blushed a little, "Yes, I suppose I am a little excited. It will be nice to see my husband before he goes off again, even if it is brief. What is it you said this is? Practice?" she chuckled. "I imagine the duties as king will take my husband across the continent often. I shall have to get used to it. Absence makes the heart grow fonder, does it not?" Even as she spoke, Laura didn't believe all the words she said. In Aldrich's absence, her heart did grow fonder, just not for her husband. She and Wully had not had much time together since the prince's departure, and though she could not admit it, she had enjoyed Wully's company very much.

"That is what they say," Wully agreed. Laura smiled and looked around the garden. She could not betray her husband; she had no reason to, and even still, as queen-to-be, there was an image that was required to present. She pushed the thoughts out of her head for now. Once she saw Aldrich again, it would be fine.

At Laura's bidding, the two got up and walked back through the garden to the courtyard and into the castle. They continued to chat about little things, from the weather to life in the court and some superficial parts of politics. Wully expressed concern over the call to assemble the Five Crown Alliance to protect the north. With the kingdom of Halika called to join King Haldair in Valkos, the elusive Dun-mar might finally call out with enough numbers to threaten the safety of the lands near the Great Mountain Ridge.

Laura had made a good point that King Gallant in Taureau would not let that happen. Taureau may not be part of the Alliance, but they were still part of Kralavia. "Besides," Laura said. "Queen Vetrina Dogas is not likely to leave her kingdom completely unguarded in her absence. Halika will be fine, and the Dun-mar won't be of any issue."

Wully nodded in agreement as he stepped onto her balcony overlooking the castle grounds. Laura walked up behind him as they heard a horn sounding in the distance. Wully looked out at the castle gates, "Looks like our young prince is home," he said, almost saddened by that fact.

Laura quickly headed back inside her room, "You must leave."

Wully bowed respectfully, "Milady."

Meanwhile

King Ivan was in his study, and a few servants were securing his armored breastplate as he stood in front of his fireplace. After he dismissed them, Ivan stepped over to the mirror in the corner of the room. His long dark hair was untied and complimented the dark pants and boots he wore with his bright lavianite armor. While the rest of the King's army wore full suits of armor pieced together to cover most of the body, he was not. Ivan only wore a breastplate and had lavianite woven into his pants and boots, not as good as the plate armor, but better than nothing, allowing him more freedom of movement.

The sunlight shone through the window behind his desk and reflected off the breastplate, shining into the room. The intricacies of the molded armor as it reflected the light became clearer. Each decorative swirl of lavianite within and each fold of the metal as its form fitted his chest. Clasped to the shoulders was his cape, on which was the blue and white checkered pattern with the golden crown in the center. At his waist, an empty sheath.

Ivan looked at the Golden Sword on the mantel. He didn't want to use it and hoped he wouldn't need to. However, Ivan also knew he must ensure his son would not have to use it. As Ivan grabbed the sword, he felt the power surge through him. He had almost forgotten what it felt like. He held it out, almost as if to get his arms to remember its weight, but of course, there was none. The sword became part of the wielder and, as such, carried no weight. Slowly, Ivan sheathed the sword and exhaled hard. As quickly as the blade was out of his hand, the strength and power that came with it left him.

Ivan walked over to his table and took a few minutes to breathe and restore his strength. Then, he began to pour over the maps of the lands. King Valtor and Carnheller had remained unresponsive since the attack on Vasalia; Ivan made a mental note to deal with that insurrection later. First, his priority was the raids in the west.

Ivan knew his kingdom well. In fact, as he settled most of the nine domains after the Great War, there was little within those kingdoms that Ivan was unaware of. Greebold's Trench was a small village near his western outpost Fort Elias. An outpost that, other than doing its regular job of keeping peace and defending the border of the west, had only one task.

Ivan studied the maps further and took to memory the layout. The Great River ran south along his western edge, marking his kingdom's end. Across it was the Dead Lands, a rough desert with little in the way of habitable areas. Apart from Greebold's Trench, several farms and other small villages sat along the river. Some, further north where his kingdom bordered Alnirya. Ivan honed in on this area. Several points along the Great River allowed for travel across it; one of the main ones was at the junction of Althalos and Alnirya. Ivan ran through several scenarios and possibilities in his head. Each depended on what he would find when he reached Fort Elias.

Just then, a horn sounded faintly in the distance. Ivan smiled; his son was home.

Prince Aldrich rode up and stopped directly before the castle's front steps. The personal guard he had with him continued to the stables. Aldrich didn't acknowledge the boy who took his horse as he dismounted, only tossed him the reigns and stormed up the stairs. Two days on the road, Aldrich had run through every possible conversation he could think of for why his father had General Oswald hold his instructions and let Aldrich only believe he was in charge of the mission.

Aldrich's nerves began to twitch as he entered the castle. He asked the first person he saw where the king was; the servant pointed toward King Ivan's study. He should've known the king was often found in his research.

The prince's rage began to boil as he prepared for his opening line to his father. Though that rage was quickly abated when he saw, "Laura," he said, half-startled. He had rounded the corner into the side hallway leading to the study when she stepped out and greeted him.

"My prince," Laura said gracefully, "It's so good to see you. I'm glad your trip to Vasalia was not as intense and war filled as we expected."

Aldrich's smile faded as Laura's words sank in. "Yes," he said coldly. "Aren't we all so happy?" Laura stepped in and embraced him. Aldrich accepted and returned with his embrace. "We'll talk later," he said as he broke away. "I need to speak with my father."

Laura nodded and stepped to the side, allowing Aldrich to pass. As he walked away, Laura watched and thought. *Not quite the welcoming I expected for a newly married couple.* Laura looked around and then carefully proceeded to Ivan's study, hoping to learn what took her husband's attention so thoroughly. When she reached the doorway, Laura stepped aside to hide from view as she listened to the conversation inside.

"Then why send me if you were going to declare your orders anyway?" Aldrich demanded. His voice quivered a bit.

Ivan stood in front of the fireplace with his back to Aldrich. "It was a test to see if you could lead as I have. If you would seek answers and keep the peace over creating more chaos," Ivan explained. "This was for me to see if you were ready to be a king. I don't expect you to do everything like me…" Ivan paused as he looked over his shoulder. "I wanted you to be better. But your choices have shown me otherwise."

"How is it I'm expected to act like a king when at every turn I get undermined?"

Ivan turned and stepped toward his son, "You are a child! You talk of acting like a king but still acting like a child." He dropped his head and returned to the fireplace, placing his back to Aldrich once more. "You will come with me to Fort Elias; there, maybe you can learn from me better how to act as a man and as a…"

"I'm sick of being treated like a child!" Aldrich shouted, interrupting his father. *We have your back and are ready to follow you.* General Ulrich's words echoed in the prince's head. He quickly drew his sword. "I am going to be king!" Laura's eyes went wide as she couldn't believe what she saw. Would Aldrich really try to challenge his father?

In a flash, Ivan turned and drew the Golden Sword from his sheath. The light in the room around him dimmed, and his eyes glowed pure white. As he swung his sword, Aldrich saw it begin to shine. He tensed, ready for the impact, but before the Golden Sword would touch his, the prince's sword shattered in his hand, leaving nothing but the hilt. Ivan flicked his wrist and held the sword parallel to the ground and the tip at his son's neck. Then Aldrich, still in shock, felt pressure against his body, and his armor shattered like his sword had. "But you are not a king yet!" Ivan's voice echoed deep within the walls, chilling even Laura to her very core.

Aldrich dropped the hilt from his hand and looked at the ground around his feet. His face was white as he stood frozen in fear over what his father had just done. Small pieces of his pure, supposedly unbreakable lavianite armor lay on the floor. Aldrich had never seen the Golden Sword used in any capacity. By the time he was old enough to remember, Ivan's post-war campaign had ended, and the nine kingdoms were as they have been since. They were all stories to him.

Ivan's eyes softened as they returned to their natural state, and the glow of the Golden Sword dimmed as he sheathed the sword back at his waist. The room brightened, and the air seemed less tense and heavy as Ivan stepped back in front of the fireplace.

"You will come with me to Fort Elias," he said calmly. His voice had returned to normal. "From there, we will join my brother and our army with the others in Valkos."

Aldrich gulped silently, "Of…of course, Father."

Ivan turned to leave the room. Exiting, he said, "You'll need new armor and have my Bronwyn notified that we leave within the hour. The remainder of my troops are ready."

Aldrich bowed his head, "As you command."

Ivan stepped out of the study and glanced down the hall; he saw Laura walking several paces away. He paused and looked at her. Laura also stopped walking and glanced over her shoulder at the king. Neither said anything, merely acknowledged each other's presence with a slight nod. The two then continued in their separate directions.

Aldrich stood for several minutes in the same place he had been. The broken pieces of his sword and armor were still strewn about on the floor. He saw his father pause outside the room but paid it no mind. He figured Ivan was giving him a final chance to say something. But what was there to say? Not only had he been humiliated in Vasalia, but even now, as his father drew the sword against him, Aldrich's hate boiled in him for what the king had just done. Despite these feelings, Aldrich relished the thought of wielding such power when he took the throne.

The prince knelt and picked up a piece of the armor from the floor; part of the etching of the Althalothian crown was still visible in the metal.

"Not yet, Father," Aldrich said quietly. "But soon."

Chapter 29
Aid in The Darkness

Fort Elias Prison, Althalos

He could see their faces in his dreams. He could always see their faces now. In his mind's black, dark recesses, they appeared, like ghosts in his head, haunting him.

Alfred rolled silently in his cot; the room's darkness was as dark as his dreams. He blinked several times, trying to find some bearing on the place he lay. His body ached as he sat up and rubbed his temples, "Amelia, mother," Alfred winced. "My kids," he exhaled heavily. Then, the memories came back, and in an instant, he felt sick to his stomach as the image of his mother being cut down and his wife and children hung and burned came back.

"The dead can't hear you, Alfred," said a soft voice. Alfred looked to find the source, and his eyes fell upon a frail-looking older man in the room across from him.

"Who are you?" Alfred asked. "And where am I? This looks like…"

"Yes," said the old man. "Relax, though. You've been out for a while."

Alfred painfully got up and walked to the entryway. His fear was confirmed; he was in the Fort Elias dungeon. Small torches lined the hallway, and through the crude iron bars that made the door to his cell, Alfred could see several others from the village in the cells across the hall.

"Hello!" he called out. "There's been a mistake! I'm from Greebold's Trench. I'm not an attacker."

No response.

"And that," said the old man from his bed. "Is the reason for which you are here."

Alfred turned to face the man. He appeared crippled, his features were older, and his long green cloak was well-worn. *Slam!* Alfred jumped in his skin as one of the guards banged his spear into the cell door bars. When Alfred gathered his wits, he realized that the guard was one of the attacking forces that ransacked the village.

The guard smiled menacingly at the pleasure of scaring Alfred. Behind him, other guards were dragging a woman down the hall closer to him. The guards dragged the woman into the cell across from Alfred, where a man was lying on the floor, seemingly unconscious. The woman, bloodied and beaten just as bad as the man had been, still had enough strength to catch herself as they threw her in.

"I hope I get my turn tomorrow," said the one guard.

"Nah," said the second. "Whistler hasn't left her alone. Makes me less inclined to want any part of that spoil."

"You'd think the old man would've given in by now," said the third as they began to leave. "Some father he turned out to be." The others agreed and laughed as they continued down the hallway.

Alfred started to put the pieces together from the guard's conversation and, after further inspection of his cell, realized that the two prisoners across from him were Lord Elias and his daughter Alisson. "Lord?" he asked carefully. Elias did not stir.

"He was a lord, but no more," said the old man from his cot behind Alfred. "He is nothing more than a prisoner, like you and I."

Alfred ignored him and returned to the cell across the hall. "*Lord, what can we do?* We have to do something." Lord Elias remained unresponsive on the floor of his cell. Alfred glanced up at Alisson, curled up in the corner of the cot, softly sobbing.

"They've found his weakness, Alfred," the old man said. "He has run his course."

Alfred turned to the man in his cot, "How do you know my name?"

"The same way you do," he replied.

"The same way I, what?" Alfred asked sharply.

Alfred turned back to the cell across from him, and nothing changed. Lord Elias remained on the floor, his daughter crying in the bed. "Denial eventually becomes acceptance," the old man said. "It always does. He knows his daughter's fate as much as he knows his own. And when a man learns of his fate…he is a man no longer."

Alfred returned to his cot across from the old man, "Now listen here…" he paused as he realized he didn't know the man's name. "What's your name?"

"My name is of little importance."

"What?"

The old man smiled, "If you need to call me something, call me Egbert." Alfred shot a questioning glance. The old man maintained his smile and continued, "Egbert, Johnson, Rowen, Hew…Amelia. Names are only as important as the owner, and I have long passed my prime, Alfred."

Alfred flinched at the sound of his wife's name. Who was this old man? He thought. As far as Alfred could remember, this man wasn't from the village nor the refugees coming to Fort Elias. As much as he wondered about these details, there was something peaceful about this man. His features were mostly obscured in the dark, but when the light flickered, he noticed the man's eyes. Bright and green as emeralds reflected the light and almost glowed.

Alfred was about to inquire further when the sound of metal clanging in the distance broke his thoughts. Alfred stepped up to his cell door to see what was going on. Several men approached, then it hit him, that same smell of death that he smelled in the village when the messenger arrived. As they got closer, he noticed that Alisson's tears got more intense, and she huddled tightly in the corner.

"Well, well," Whistler hissed. "Welcome back to the land of the living, Mr. Trench."

Alfred winced and gagged at the stench, "Only to send you to the grave you smell like."

Whistler chuckled, "Captain Mencis."

"Yes, sir."

"Bring the good lord," Whistler commanded. Never taking his eyes off Alfred. "He has an appointment to keep." Immediately, Mencis and his men open the cell across from Alfred and drag Lord Elias to his feet. Elias began to moan and blinked several times. Whistler led the way as the group drug Lord Elias out of the cell and down the hallway.

"Hurry up, Captain," Whistler said. "It's not every day that we get to see the execution of a lord."

Alfred looked at the cell and Alisson within. Her sobbing had stopped, and she simply stared at the wall. In the dim light, he could see her eyes still wet with the tears she had shed, now glassed over in a steady daze.

"She has been broken," said the old man. "Like her father." He sat in his cot and looked at Alisson in her cell. "Though she still has some life left in her."

Alfred returned to his cot across from the old man and massaged his aching arms and chest. "Wait a minute," he said. "My chest, I was kicked by a horse." Suddenly more memories came back. "Marty had just died; the people were panicking and…"

"You're welcome, by the way," the old man said.

"What?"

"I kept you alive," the old man smiled, and his eyes brightened. "I expect no payment nor reward. Of course, if you'd feel the need to do so, I wouldn't object."

Alfred stared in disbelief, "You kept me alive? A cripple?"

"Yes. Why is that so hard to believe?" the old man said. "You don't need legs to help a man."

"Then why not heal yourself?" Alfred asked.

"I prefer to provide aid for others," the old man said. "I am content with my state."

Alfred nodded, "Well, thank you. How long was I out?"

"A few days, maybe more. It's hard to tell here," the man said as he gestured around the room.

Alfred gestured to Alisson in her cell, "And she? They've been using her to get to Elias, I suppose. They must've finally got what they wanted then."

"Do you know who's responsible for this?" the old man asked.

"I remember that squeaky bastard said something about Serrek," Alfred recalled.

"Ah, yes," the old man said. "Serrek, mighty chieftain of the Dead Land's tribes. So, he has finally done it. He's come for his revenge."

Alfred tilted his head in confusion, "Against who?"

"Against you, Alfred. Against your brother, your children, your wife, your mother, and your village."

"Why?"

The old man shifted in his cot and propped himself against the wall, "Because people in power are seldom not tainted by corruption."

"I don't understand."

The old man sighed, "In a world full of humans. Sometimes the hardest thing to find is humanity." Alfred remained silent. "Elias broke an agreement; the attack was justified."

"What?" Alfred exclaimed. "Our Lord Elias wouldn't…"

"Our?" the old man interjected. "Elias is no lord of mine. The only one with that privilege has long since gone from this world."

"How did you end up here?"

The old man thought for a moment, "You know. I've quite forgotten now." After a pause, the old man whispered, "You have tasks ahead of you."

"What?"

"I have remembered something. Did you know this cell is on the edge of the fort?" Alfred shook his head. "Well, it is. And it is also right next to a cave system," the old man explained. "Before I was crippled, I spent some time building an escape tunnel through it. This tunnel may be useless to me now but to you…"

Alfred perked up at these words, "Are you being serious? There's a way out?"

"Aye. Under my bed here."

"Then why don't you use it."

"Because I was supposed to be here for this."

Alfred looked puzzled again, "I don't understand."

The old man smiled, "I didn't expect you to." He motioned for Alfred to move the bed quickly. Alfred followed the prompt and revealed a hidden trap door on the floor under the man's bed. "I'd hurry now, Alfie; the guards will return once they finish killing Elias."

Alfred stopped as he stepped into the hole, "What about you and Alisson?"

"Worry about yourself, Alfred," the man said as he looked at Alisson in her cell. "My job here is not done yet."

"Where shall I go?"

"To King Ivan," the old man said. "There is someone in Althalos you need to see."

As Alfred stepped further into the trap door, the old man exited the bed with youthful vigor. Alisson, who had broken out of her daze at the mention of her name, then asked, "I thought you were a cripple?"

"People say things all the time," the old man said as he pushed the cot back over the trap door. "But they hardly ever mean them."

"So, you're a liar then?" she snapped.

"I say what I have to for the greater good of mankind," he said as he crawled back into his cot. "Such is my task in life."

Alisson got up slowly and walked to her cell door, "If you can walk, then why are you here? Wait. Where did you send him?"

The old man smiled, "He has a role to play, Alisson Elias. He's the kind that should not be in cages when they could be flying." He paused briefly, "Douglas Trench is only holding on to live to see his brother once more, even if he doesn't know it yet."

Alisson thought momentarily about what the man said to her, "Who are you?" she finally asked.

The old man said nothing for some time, then spoke softly, "I am nothing more than a person. Crippled in this life long ago. Until my task is done…nothing else."

Alisson shakes her head and returns to her cot in the corner of her cell. "Nothing else," she muttered.

Chapter 30
The Field of Denesious

The Field of Denesious—Valkos

Haldair stepped out of his tent; he had slept well the night before, considering he didn't have his bed chamber and his comfortable feather mattress. He opened his eyes as they adjusted to the fresh light of day, and he looked over the field and saw nothing but white tents and the red flag of Valkos flying over each one. King Haldair had, unarguably, the largest army in Kralavia as far as sheer numbers go. Ivan's army was more powerful, though, primarily due to the vast supply of valuable resources they had access to and the lavianite ore in their weapons and armor that gave them an edge over any of the other known countries on the continent.

The hustle and bustle of soldiers moving about echoed through the camp as Haldair walked on the main path between all the tents. He stopped at a clear area atop the crest of the hill along the left flank that sat near the Emerald Lake. Here, the king had a good view of his troops. Haldair gazed over a sea of tents and flags. *The barons have done well,* he thought as he began moving toward the council tent. His baron's armies and his own had already amassed and settled the day before, but he was anticipating the arrival of the rest of the Alliance, and he wanted to see if there was any news.

The gathering army was loud but well organized. Everyone seemed to know their place in the camp and what they needed to be doing. Haldair looked at his men with awe; he hadn't seen an army this large gather since the end of his brother's conquest for peace; times had been different then, easier even, until now. Why had this happened? Why now, after all this time? Haldair couldn't shake the feeling of something not being right about it all, but besides the circumstances, he was proud of his army and almost glad to see it all in one place again. If it didn't mean bloodshed would follow.

The king continued to gaze over the area. This place was a pivotal point for Valkos as a country. The last time the Valkon army was here was to fight Stelmond in full force, which was at the end of the Great War. In that war, Valkos had reigned victorious. He hoped this time would be the same.

As Haldair stood, the barons assembled around him near the large tent.

"What news do we have so far about the Five Crowns?" Haldair asked without directly addressing them.

"We have received a rider from King Leoxtra," Leon began. "His army is traveling with the Althalothian army led by Generals Cromwell, Ulrich, and Rollins."

"Oswald?" Haldair raised his eyebrow in interest. He was both surprised and excited to hear that Ivan's forces would also aid them.

"Yes, milord," Leon affirmed. "Stelbeck Keep is under Althalos' control, and the attack had been taken care of. Prince Aldrich rode west to return to Stalbak to meet up with King Ivan, and the generals are leading the army down here with King Leoxtra and his men for our aid."

"When should they arrive?"

"Before noon, milord. The rider wasn't far ahead of the army and arrived early this morning."

"Good," Haldair said, turning to face the group. "We should see them shortly then. Any word on Queen Vetrina?"

"Her rider got here late last night," Leon answered. "We expect her around midday as well. But, with how they ride, I wouldn't be surprised if they beat Leoxtra and Cromwell."

Haldair and Leon exchange smirks. It was well known that the Halikian army were furious riders; they could move a whole army twice as fast as any in Kralavia. That also makes them well known for having the most formidable cavalry in the world. Their horsemanship has yet to be matched.

Haldair breathed and looked over the horizon. The breeze moved the grass gently, and you could see the waves of light reflecting off the blades as they moved with the wind. This field was a beauty to behold, vast luscious green grassland, not a tree in sight. Flowers bloomed randomly among the soft turf adding speckles of color throughout the beautiful field.

"Do you know why this is called the Field of Denesious?" Haldair finally asked, breaking the silence.

The others glanced at each other in question before Leon finally spoke. "Only that it has been the name of this field since the Great War." This answer surprised no one since that was all that could be confirmed about the details of that time and recorded for the history that would remember it.

Haldair sighed softly, "That is because it was never taught in our schools. I'm sure you know why the Great War is commonly taught. You see, humanity despises the gods. When humanity hates something, you'll find that they usually try to hide the good that came from it, make it out to be exactly what they hate even though that may not be so."

Leon looked puzzled, "I don't think I quite understand, milord. Didn't the gods fight us during the Great War?"

"There was a lot more to it than is taught in Kralavia. I know for sure that at least one god didn't." Leon turned fully to Haldair, who was still looking forward to the beautiful field ahead as the king continued. "King Hagar told me the field was named after the last time Denesious, the god of Valkos and its people, was seen. When the war broke out, all the armies of men rose to fight the gods, even Valkos. I was just a boy at the time. We moved our army to this spot where we were to meet him, Denesious. But when they arrived, it wasn't what was expected. Denesious sat alone in the middle of the woods."

"There are no woods here, though," One of the other barons interjected.

Haldair smiled, "He sat alone, and when he saw the Valkon army, it wasn't anger on his face, but sadness. The betrayal broke him of his people."

"Wasn't it the gods that betrayed us?" Another asked.

The king sighed, "What our people didn't know, though, was that Stelmond was moving in under cover of the vast forest that used to grow on this land," Haldair explained. "You see, Valkos at the time was already weakened by the war that was going on, so Stelmond was moving in to take the country while everyone else was busy with the Great War. Denesious stood and faced King Hagar and said through the tears in his emerald eyes, *'The only people that can truly betray you are the people that you love enough to feel it'.*"

The barons listened as Haldair explained that after speaking, Denesious turned around to see the Stelmond army coming in through the trees toward the weaker Valkon forces. King Hagar had tried to rally his men as best as possible, but it took a moment before he realized he wouldn't have to. Denesious walked forward as if he feared nothing, stepping toward the charging Stelmond army as his staff turned into a long spear. Then, suddenly, he began to float off the ground, moving forward still but up above the trees.

Haldair's eyes glistened as he recalled when King Hagar told him, "Even in the sky, the Valkon army could see the pain and sadness that plagued their god and protector," he said. "Then came a boom, a huge earth-moving sound that seemed to echo from the planet's core to the surface. At Denesious' command, the ground opened up, swallowing the entire Stelmond army and the beautiful ancient forest that once covered this land. When that was finally over, and the ground began to close up, the god slowly returned to the earth. As his feet touched the ground, grass grew in his footsteps and spread. The king of Valkos then named this place the Field of Denesious, after the god that created this field, the god they betrayed, and the god that saved their kingdom."

"I… I never knew…" Leon stammered. "I grew up believing the gods were to blame for the war."

"Most things are not as they seem," Haldair said. "Sadly, most people will never know what truly happened, and very few are left that remember."

Everyone stood in silence as they observed the events of the men around them. Then, breaking through the clamors of metal and shouting, a horn blew across the field. Haldair smiled. He knew that horn. "If I'm right, then we should start to feel the earth shake shortly."

Sure enough, not long after the horn was heard, Leon and the others looked down at their feet and could feel the vibration growing under them. "What?" he whispered to himself.

"Queen Vetrina has arrived," Haldair stated.

The men looked over the hill behind the camp and saw the tops of pikes starting to peak over the hill. Then flags and heads, until a massive army on horseback began to pour over the grass, moving fast to the camp.

"Milord, are they going to stop?" Leon asked sheepishly.

Haldair laughed, "She always rides like that. I promise they have more control over that wave of horses than they let on." The horses eventually came to an abrupt halt a short distance from the edge of Haldair's camp line, which more than startled the Valkon men there. "Come," the king gestured as they began to walk down the hill toward the Halikian army, as many of the Valkon men also rushed over to see. "We need to greet our guests."

Halika was not a kingdom like most in Kralavia. They didn't have any castles or large fortresses. The people of the grasslands lived on the road as they traveled their kingdom, only settling in small homesteads and Jarls. The queen had a home in the capital city of Eltalion. However, she never stayed there long, thanks to the occasional skirmishes with the ever-elusive Dun-mar in the Great Mountain Ridge and the ever-on-going patrols across the vast open land. Halika's people were tough and hardened partly by the lifestyle they chose and partly by things they didn't not.

The people were, on average, generally taller and broader than most of the others in Kralavia. Their attire was mainly thick leather and fur, some wearing chainmail over the leather underneath. But, perhaps the most unusual thing about the people of Halika, according to the other kingdoms, was their complete lack of segregation. In Halika, men and women, young and old, were all warriors, hunters, and gatherers. Halika was also the only kingdom in the world with a queen sitting alone on the throne.

As Haldair and the others approached, he bowed respectfully, "Vetrina, a pleasure as always."

Queen Vetrina bowed in return, "It is always an honor, Haldair." As she straightened, the queen thumped her chest hard, echoing back by a chorus of her force doing the same, reverberating that sound across the entire field. "It has been a long time since we have all been called together, King Haldair. You have a lot to explain."

"Yes, we do," Haldair agreed. "But I am glad that the Five Crown Alliance is still strong, even after all these years."

"As it always has been."

"Come, we must speak," Haldair said. Quickly, Vetrina directed her force to gather near the lake as she followed Haldair and his barons. "I…" Another loud horn echoed over the area, cutting off Haldair's words.

"Leoxtra," Queen Vetrina rolled her eyes. "Pompous swine. I had almost forgotten he was part of this."

Haldair chuckled, "Old tensions die hard, I see. But I assure you we are all here on even ground. This is my land, and I will make sure no one steps on anyone's toes."

"If he does, I shall break his."

Haldair winked and stepped up through the thinning cavalry of Halika to greet the forces of the Vasalia that came into view.

Vasalia and Halika were allies politically but on a personal level, the two countries disagreed on most things which led to them, for the most part, not being on good terms. They got along when they chose to but often avoided each other. Some said this dispute was due to a sour relationship that King Leoxtra and Queen Vetrina held, but these rumors have all but been dismissed. Others say that it started after Ivan settled the area after the Great War and that the dispute was over territory in the mountains that Halika claimed, but Vasalia got. Whatever the reason, not many of the other countries in Kralavia took it seriously. Even Haldair, aware of the disagreement, always considered it petty and was known to shrug it off and joke about it to both of them.

Compared to Halika, the Vasalian army was much more organized. All the soldiers were in rank and beautifully decorated and well adorned. The red and white flag of Vasalia flew proudly above each rank of troops. Alongside Vasalia was a large company of Althalothian soldiers, even more elegantly dressed, their armor glistening in the sun from the lavianite it was made with. At the head of the troops rode Generals Cromwell, Ulrich, and Rollins with Captain Fendrell close by.

King Leoxtra heeled his horse to Haldair before his troop reached the camp, and Oswald and Thomas followed suit. Haldair and Vetrina continue to walk through the lush green grass to greet them.

"Leoxtra, my friend!" Haldair shouted. "How was Stelbeck Keep?"

Leoxtra didn't respond but dismounted as quickly as his horse stopped near Haldair, "We need to talk and quickly."

Haldair's concern grew as he glanced around to see the grim faces on the other as well, "Then talk we shall, at once." Oswald directed Thomas to take the army and make their camp along the right toward the center of the field before he joined the other generals, barons, kings, and queen in the main council tent.

Once they got settled, Leoxtra, Oswald, and Ulrich took turns describing the events of the siege of Stelbeck Keep, the strange force at work with the weather, and Admiral Mortem's words, *"Althalos will burn. Vasalia and Valkos will burn with it."*

The group processed this information as the barons of Valkos explained the strange events and creatures spotted in the dark. "And we still received no word from VonGarth or have any word about what happened in Handon and what Stelmond has done. Other than what we've managed to see from a distance," Leon finished.

Vetrina shifted in her seat next to Haldair. "The Dun-mar have been more agitated as of late, and we, too, have seen the Dire Wolves coming from the mountains."

King Leoxtra pounded his fist on the table, "And why have we not heard any of this sooner?"

"Because!" Snapped Vetrina. "I'm too busy keeping the evil off you and your cozy piece of rock!" Leoxtra stood quickly and knocked back his chair as he did. Vetrina matched him, and the two stood opposite each other across the table, locked in a menacing stare, neither one backing down.

It was only seconds, but it felt like minutes before Haldair stepped in and calmed them down. Small discussions continued as the information about what had been going on was further worked through.

Then it came, and the conversations immediately ceased as they all listened intently. There it was again, louder this time, and with a resounding echo that moved over the area. "I know that horn better than any of you," Haldair said.

Chapter 31
Over Life and Death

Fort Elias, Althalos

The ride across Althalos was silent as King Ivan and his son rode on. Behind them was Bronwyn with a portion of the King's Guard, followed by the remaining ten thousand troops from his army. More than Ivan needed for this errand. Aldrich staggered behind his father; he didn't want to make any conversation seem welcome today. Throughout most of the trip, Ivan was aware of this and knew he needed to speak more with his son. However, with the pressing matters of the recent events, he maintained his silence on the journey.

It was late afternoon when they approached Fort Elias. Ivan paused, and Aldrich guided his horse up next to him. Around the fort was aligned with the bodies of the Althalothian people and the slaughtered troops stationed there. Aldrich's stomach turned.

"Did they spare no one?" he muttered to himself as he set his eyes upon the charred remains of children strung up on the walls. Ivan remained quiet as he gazed upon the scene. War no longer fazed him nor the capacity for evil within men.

"Be sure the men keep their swords sheathed," Ivan said. "We don't want to upset our hosts."

"Hosts?" Aldrich blurted out, unable to control his anger. "We should kill the whole lot of them!"

"Be quiet, Aldrich!" Ivan snapped. He was in no mood for his son's impulsive attitude. He then gently prodded his horse forward, making his way around the mess, and approached the fort's main gate.

Aldrich and Bronwyn followed behind. When they reached the gate, Serrek's men began to appear on the wall above. Ivan watched unamused as more and more men began to show themselves. Even as they strung their arrows and readied their aim, he did not flinch. Aldrich signaled the men to equip their bows, but Ivan quickly stopped them, telling them to wait. Aldrich tensed but conceded as Ivan rode ahead.

"I am King Ivan Ventral of Althalos," he began. "Son of King Animas Ventral. I have come to discuss terms with whoever oversees this route." The men on the wall remained as they were; no one moved or spoke.

When the gates finally opened, Aldrich tightened his jaw and gripped the hilt of his sword as a young boy with a worn weathered face emerged.

The boy had no fear in his eyes and approached Ivan without pause. When the young lad reached King Ivan, he glanced around at the others behind him and then back to Ivan. "Come with me." The boy said calmly, "Just you."

Ivan stepped off his horse and signaled his men and Aldrich to wait. Then, he turned to follow the boy up to the fort. As they reached the gate, Ivan saw that Lord Elias's body was strung up in the gateway on one side and his head on the other. He exhaled slowly; the muffled laughter and conversations broke through the air. The boy waved his hand, and Ivan followed him into the open courtyard.

The king scanned the crowd, and dozens of men and women were feasting and celebrating. Though Ivan recognized no one, he remained calm and expressionless as he took in the scene, his left hand casually rested on the Golden Sword, sheathed in his belt.

"Father," said the young boy firmly to the man seated at the head of one of the tables. "King Ivan of Althalos."

The crowd grew silent at the boy's words and the man the boy directed the statement to eyed Ivan up and down briefly as he finished chewing his food. Then, several men jumped up from their seats, swords drawn. Ivan didn't flinch, he gripped his sword tighter, and the air thickened and swirled as his eyes turned white. Hesitation set into the hearts of the soldiers who stood to oppose him.

"Enough!" shouted the boy's father. Immediately the men sheathed their blades, and Ivan returned to his natural state. "Stand down," the man repeated calmly. He gestured at his son, and the boy ran toward the far end of the courtyard. "You arrived sooner than I expected," he said to Ivan. "I'm touched that the affairs of my people have finally managed to fit into your busy schedule."

Soft chuckles echoed around the area as Ivan responded, "Well, we have much to discuss."

"Indeed, we do," the man said as he gestured for Ivan to follow. "Come." Ivan followed the man into the interior part of the fort as the chatter of conversations and laughter grew among his people.

Meanwhile, Aldrich sat uneasily with the other men outside. "I don't like this," he muttered. "We should do something."

"We will do nothing," Bronwyn snapped. Aldrich shot a sneer in return. "That'll do you no good here," he said. "Our orders only come from the king. And if you want to be king, you'll need to relax and wait more. Think. Your father knows what he's doing." Bronwyn smiled, "Trust me."

Ivan followed the man inside the fort into one of the interior offices. "I never got your name," he asked as the man sat in the chair behind the desk.

"Serrek," the man stated as he took a large bite of an apple, he grabbed off the desk. "Here to discuss your surrender, King Ivan?"

Ivan chuckled and sat in a chair at the far end of the room opposite Serrek. "You have a remarkable sense of humor."

"So, I've been told. But I'm not joking."

Ivan sat back and relaxed in his seat, "Well, I'm not surrendering. And I'm not fighting. I don't have time for this petty conflict. There are other matters more pressing than this one at the moment."

Serrek sighed, "I see." He took another bite of the apple, tossed the half-eaten fruit behind him, and grabbed a new one from the bowl. "My people…always the last on the list of concerns. Dealt with quickly…and forgotten…put under the care of greedy degenerates like Lord Elias."

Ivan then confirmed what he had suspected, the people of the Deal Lands were responsible for the massacre. Lord Elias was to continue to provide food and supplies as needed after their banishment in the aftermath of the Great War, most of which were always given by Ivan himself from his reserve. However, Lord Elias had no longer been doing that at some point, and his inaction caused this event to come to a head.

"Lord Elias's neglect of your people was indeed an oversight but…"

"An oversight?" Serrek interjected. He tossed the next half-eaten apple over his shoulder and grabbed another one. After taking a couple of bites, he also chucked it. He repeated this a few times until he got up, grabbed the entire bowl, and threw it at the wall. "I've waited my entire life to do that. For years, we scrapped and saved everything, never having a surplus, let alone enough to get by."

"I didn't know," Ivan said solemnly. "Nothing ever reached me that your people were suffering."

"You were the one who banished us in the first place!" Serrek snapped. Ivan sighed but said nothing. Serrek waited momentarily and then finished calmly, "You look just like him…your father." Ivan winced at the thought. His father was thoroughly taken in and corrupted by the power the sword gave him and, thus, even more bloodthirsty than he had been in his younger years. Ivan suddenly felt the warm drip of blood running from his nose. He quickly grabbed his rag and wiped it. "Well," Serrek said. "Unlike him, you seem to be in good health."

Ivan smirked and showed Serrek the blood-stained rag, "I've been better." Serrek nodded, and as Ivan put away the cloth in his hand, his eye was drawn to the sword at Ivan's belt. He had seen it before, and it did not faze him; Serrek had no fear of it. "Serrek," Ivan finally said. "I need to ask, and despite your feelings toward the people of Althalos, I need you to answer me truthfully."

Serrek shrugged, "I do not need to lie."

Ivan nodded, "Stelmond and Carnheller have united to wage war against the Five Crowns. Are you a part of this uprising?"

Serrek shot a questioning glance and held his hand in defense, "My quarrel is with you. I have no business with the others. Whatever scheme Stelmond or Carnheller have concocted, I have no part to play in the matter."

"I see."

"How do you wish to proceed with this, Ivan?" Serrek asked after a moment of thought. "You won't surrender…you won't fight…our list of options grows thin."

"I want you to take your men and leave."

Serrek chuckled, "And where will we go? Back to the Dead Lands? Back to all that misery? No. I cannot do that."

"I swear to you, withdraw peacefully, and I will do the same. There will be no consequences, I promise you."

Serrek didn't flinch, "I have heard the empty promises of your father. My people will not be fooled again. I will not be fooled again."

Ivan's jaw tensed, "I and not my father."

"Yet you share his name, seed, and lands," Serrek quipped. "For what reason should I expect anything different from you? For what reason should I expect fair treatment or anything less than empty promises?"

"Because Serrek, we are men of a new era that has yet to be forged!" Ivan said. "Our stories are yet to be told. We have legacies that are yet to be left behind. Let us not drown those legacies in further bloodshed. Walk away…I will not ask again."

Serrek thought for a moment before responding. "I have awoken in the middle of the night at the same time every night since I was a boy." He began. "I stepped out of my house, walked to the edge of my village, and stopped at this tree. It was the tallest tree; you would see for miles. I would climb to the very top and look all around me. I looked to the horizon where in the beginning, I saw hope. Despite our hardships, in all directions, I saw nothing but hope; the hope of a future, the hope of a new life beyond that god-forsaken wasteland, not for me but for my people." He paused. "We sent the brave few into the unknown for that better future. They never came back. More and more were sent…and the results were always the same—no word, nothing. Slowly what hopes we had left burned away, and it became the struggle to die peacefully. There is nothing. Nothing beyond the wasteland or out in the unknown; our only hope is here. I didn't want it to come to this, Ivan," Serrek pleaded. "Despite all the hate in my heart, I never wanted this. But we cannot go back."

Ivan sat in silence for several minutes. He had no interest in killing these people even though he had the power to do so. The blood lust of his younger years had long since passed; there should be no need for further slaughter. Ivan removed his crown and glanced up at the wall behind Serrek. There hung a large painting of the Great War, gods and men clashing for an unknown reason for an unknown end. "My father once foretold to me the end of Kralavia," he finally said. "It came to him in a dream many times before he finally spoke of it to me."

"You will see the old fighting in desperation for a society and a belief that is since been outdated. The young and the naive—if there is even a difference—will follow close behind. They know nothing more than what they are told, fighting for mere tricks and lies. But leading them all will be the insane who fight for nothing more than the love of chaos though that love is disguised with a silver tongue and a vision that is simply too good to be true, and in their wake, death. When you see this, my dear boy, it's too late. It is the end."

The king then unsheathed the Golden Sword and held it up. He stared intently at his reflection in the blade. "My father always told me that, with the belief that as long as the bloodline of Althalos continued, Kralavia would be safe," Ivan said. "As long as we held power, Kralavia would live on. Only when our enemies or allies gained too much power would it all crumble. It would all end. But perhaps it's already too late, Serrek. Perhaps it's always been too late. Perhaps there is a hidden truth behind my father's words that even he did not understand. Althalos is just as much a part of the problem as the rest of the kingdoms."

Ivan sheathed the blade. "As a king, you are the silver-tongued lover of chaos, even if you do not want to be. You lead men to their deaths; you lead *generations* to their deaths. And for what? We will say this for many noble and honorable reasons. The old will fight for one cause, and the young will fight for another. But in truth, it's for nothing. All those causes, all those goals to be strived for, they're just empty promises."

Serrek scoffed softly, "Empty promises."

"I'm approaching the end," Ivan said. "I'm done lying. I'm done trying to lead men to some glorious victory because, frankly, I no longer know what glorious victory is. I fight wars. I win wars, and then what? I sleep, and the wars continue in my dreams. It never ends, any of it."

"Victory is to die with the end of your life having meant more than the rest," Serrek replied.

Ivan smirked and nodded, "That's an interesting way of looking at it." He paused for a moment as he pondered this. "Perhaps we could come to an agreement then?"

"What did you have in mind?"

"You stay here. Halt your advance," Ivan said. "Stop this conquest. Stop the bloodbath. Return your prisoners to us and allow the bodies of the dead, especially those poor bastards outside the main gate, to be returned home to their families for a proper burial. You may keep all the land you've taken and its resources. You may build a new life for your people here."

"A kind offer but…"

"Do not let your pride stop you from considering this," Ivan interrupted. "You are not a coward. You are not weak in accepting this deal. You have fought well and done more than enough for them."

Serrek hesitated. He worried about what this deal meant for him and his people. Was there more to it that Ivan had yet to reveal? Specific terms and conditions that would place his people in worse shape than they were before? Did Ivan's words hold more weight than those of his father?

As he thought Ivan waited, he knew how sincere he was. He just needed Serrek to see it and believe him. Ivan slowly got up from the chair, walked over to Serrek, and extended his hand across the desk. "Please," Ivan said. "Be better than my father. Be better than me." Serrek's tone softened as Ivan finished, "I'm trying to be."

After a moment of thought, Serrek stood and shook Ivan's hand, "I accept your offer."

Ivan did his best not to show the enormous relief that swept over him. "I will return in two weeks," he said as he ended the handshake and stepped back. "By then, I would like your prisoners released and free to return to their families and what may be left of their homes."

"Can I trust that this is not a trap?"

"I give you my word. Though I do not know how much weight that holds," Ivan replied. "But it is the truth. Today and from here on…I no longer see you as my enemy. When I return, I will bring aid to help you and your people settle and provide relief for those who have lost at your hand."

Ivan grabbed his crown and began to take his leave, "We are not friends, Ivan," Serrek said firmly. "Do not make that mistake. There are far too many old wounds to be sealed with a single conversation and exchanging of land."

Ivan paused and turned back to Serrek. "I know, but here's hoping this is the first step to a brighter future. Now if you'll excuse me, my men and I are needed elsewhere." He placed his crown back on his head and bowed his head.

Serrek awkwardly nodded in return, "So. Off to fight the armies of Stelmond and Carnheller?"

"Well, Stelmond, at least," Ivan answered as he proceeded to the door. "From what my generals have reported, Carnheller has been defeated at the coastline. Stelmond stands alone."

Serrek smirked and crossed his arms, "So tell me. What is the point of fighting this battle if you do not know the meaning of victory and do not wish to lead your men to such a seemingly pointless triumph?"

Ivan stopped, smiled softly, and glanced over his shoulder, "It is, as you said, Serrek. Victory is to die with the end of your life having meant more than the rest." He explained, "Before I die, I will see the wrongs of my family righted. I will see that for once my kingdom knows a bit of peace and safety…" he turned to face Serrek directly, "For all of us."

"Will you win?"

Ivan thought for a moment about how to answer that. He knew he would win the war, but how he would come out of it was unknown. The king knew what would be needed if he was to put an end to Stelmond's persistence finally. In all his early years of bloodlust and war, perhaps he had been too soft on those that needed the harder hand and was too hard on those that didn't deserve it.

"Our people will," he finally said.

Ivan left the room before Serrek could respond further. Serrek, in his solitude, turned and looked at the painting behind him. He couldn't help but maintain a level of anxiousness about the coming changes, but under all that fear was hope that it was finally ending.

No one acknowledged Ivan as he left the fort. Serrek's men continued their celebration throughout the courtyard as he strode through. He expected more than a few wouldn't be happy with Serrek's agreement, but Ivan also could tell that these people, most importantly, were loyal to Serrek and trusted him. Hopefully, as peace with them continued, they will be more open to the arrangement.

Aldrich and the others were still waiting where they had been as Ivan exited the fort's main gate. "Did they surrender after they saw your weapon?" the prince asked jokingly.

Ivan climbed on his horse, "They are to be left alone." Aldrich chuckled. "I'm serious," he said. "The people of the Dead Lands will occupy this region and become formal citizens of Althalos. Aid and compensation will be given to assist in the transition and help those who have lost property and loved ones." He then turned to Bronwyn, "We ride for Valkos."

"What?" Aldrich exclaimed. He was fuming now at this outrageous plan of his father's—the mere thought of not crushing and punishing them for killing all those people, his people. With no more than a thought, Aldrich knew that his dad could've wiped out everyone and dealt justice with a swift, firm hand.

Ivan ignored his son's outcry, "My brother needs help." The other soldiers nodded and began to follow Ivan.

Aldrich held back at first, fuming to himself as he looked back at the fort and then at the departing troops. He wasn't sure what made him angrier, that justice wasn't given to those that deserved it, or that his father and all the men dismissed him. The prince would lead differently; people would love that he kept his word and honored those who had fallen while ensuring immediate and swift justice came to those who came against him or his people. Thoughts like these ran through the young prince's head as he finally prodded his horse and rode to catch up with the others.

Castle Stalbak, Althalos

Each step echoed in the large empty staircase. The light danced against the cold stone of the torch. Cobwebs hung heavy and low, and Wully carefully maneuvered around them as he descended. The visions of the mysterious visitor replayed in his mind over and over, partly from his own doing as he tried hard to make sure he remembered them. He wondered if he had been doing the right thing by keeping it to himself and not sharing the events with others, especially Laura. But each time Wully was given a chance, he froze inside and could not speak of it.

He had spent the last several days scouring the library for clues to who the old man was and if that would bring any connection or explanation to the visions that disturbed him. Wully had considered talking to Ivan about it during their discussion when Douglas Trench was being tended to. However, like before, Wully froze when he thought of inquiring about the topic. Would Ivan even believe him? What further could Wully learn if he knew so little yet? So, after what seemed like an eternity, he got through what he found in relevant information within the library and found nothing. He finally asked Gathar if there were any other documents and where they might be kept.

Take the stairs down in the far west tower. Any remnant that remains of the history of Kralavia will be there. The man's words echoed in Wully's head as he descended. *Use caution. No one has been there since the Great War. Even I am not sure what may remain.* Wully reached the door at the bottom of the stairs and quickly opened it. The door scraped across the floor, and a cloud of dust blew through the room from the force of air behind him.

The room was extensive, and Wully figured it covered much of the castle's layout. A harsh scent hit his nostrils as he carefully looked around and lit the torches on the wall. As the room became brighter, Wully gasped. The source of the musty ashy smell suddenly became clear. *Gone!* All around him were the scorched remains of whatever texts were at the time stored there.

Books, scrolls, small documents, and letters… It didn't matter. All that remained was burned parchment ash. Wully carefully moved through the room, and at first, it seemed he would find nothing here, but then toward the back of the chamber, his light fell upon some untouched books and scrolls. A mix of relief and excitement ran through Wully as he began to illuminate the room more.

"Now," he muttered to himself. "Where to begin?"

Meanwhile…

Alfred Trench paused as he reached the top of the hill. Heavy gasps came as he tried to rest and catch his breath. He had been running cross-country most of the way, avoiding all roads and cities for fear of being seen and word getting back to Fort Elias. Stalbak sat before him in the distance, and Alfred smiled as he realized he was almost done. Several questions still lingered in his mind, but before he could seek answers, he must first get to King Ivan and tell him what happened. After glancing around to ensure no one was watching or following, Alfred pressed on.

Laura had been strolling the castle grounds when she encountered heated discussions near the main door. "What is this?" she demanded.

"Milady," acknowledged the guard. "This man claims that he has urgent news for King Ivan. But, even after explaining that King Ivan is gone on business, he refuses to leave and will not relay the message for us to pass on."

Laura nodded and eyed the visitor up and down. "What is your name, sir?"

The man wrenched his arm free from the guard's grasp and bowed his head, "Alfred Trench, milady. I have urgent news from the western border at Greebold's Trench."

Laura softened and turned to the guard, "Summon Captain Siggard."

The guard bowed, "Yes, milady."

As the guard left, Alfred caught a quick glare of displeasure before he turned and went on his errand. "Pay him no mind," Laura reassured. "Sometimes they do their job too well." Alfred nodded silently. "So," she continued. "Start from the beginning."

As they walked, Laura listened intently as Alfred recounted the events that had transpired over the last several days. "I'm just not sure what to do," Alfred said at the end.

"Don't worry, Alfred," Laura said as they stopped near a door near the end of the hallway. "The king and his son, along with several of his personal guard, are already heading to Greebold's Trench as we speak."

Alfred's face lit up, "Really? How did they know what happened?"

"I think Wully will be a better person to answer that question," Laura said, smiling as she gestured behind them. Alfred looked to see Wully making his way down the hall.

"Laura," Wully said as he approached and hugged her. "My apologies for the delay, but I've found some interesting information…"

Laura touched his lips, "Shh," she interrupted. "This is Alfred Trench from Greebold's Trench."

Wully's eyes widened. "I thought it best that you show him."

Wully nodded, "Alfred, come with me." He then turned to Laura, "We must talk later." Laura smiled and nodded again. She kept her smile as Wully and Alfred left, but as they got further away, her smile faded, and she placed a hand gently on her stomach before heading back.

"So, what is it that I need to see?" Alfred asked as they reached a room at the far end of the castle. "How did the king know to come to our aid?"

Wully smiled, "Not what," he said as he opened the door. "Who." As the door opened, Alfred gasped. On the bed was his brother Douglas, still heavily bandaged but awake. Alfred was about to rush in when a firm hand on his shoulder held him back. "He's barely hanging on," Wully whispered. "We are surprised he has lasted this long."

Chapter 32
At What Cost?

The Field of Denesious, Valkos
Utter chaos.

The armies of the Five Alliance had fully engaged Stelmond's forces and held their line. Over the course of the day, victory seemed sure. Haldair and Vetrina led their forces forward, pressing hard into the opposing lines. Stelmond had little chance, the emerald-green grass that blanketed the field soon turned blood-red as the soldiers fought.

As the men opened up the initial enemy lines, Vetrina pressed her cavalry into the heart of Stelmond's army. "If our flanks hold, we may have this victory before sundown. But…" she paused and looked ahead to the rest of Stelmond holding back in the rear. "I'm curious about King Ordain's overall plan." King Haldair agreed and watched intently at the forces near the end of Stelmond's army that, under the circumstances, should've been deployed sooner.

Then, without warning, Stelmond blew the horn of retreat, and cheers of victory and relief swept over Alliance's men and women. "Haldair!" he and Queen Vetrina turned to see King Leoxtra riding toward them.

"It appears that victory is ours," Haldair said as Leoxtra drew beside him.

"Indeed," Leoxtra said before acknowledging Queen Vetrina.

"Call in the assault," King Haldair commanded. "We will crush them in their retreat so much that King Ordain never again tries to make a move against us." The others agreed, and the signal was given.

War cries and shouts echoed across the field, and a thunderous beat was heard as the troops ran forward, killing all in their path. As Stelmond's fragmented forces began to reach the rear defensive line, the troops held firm, forcing the alliance army to a standstill. Haldair watched from his perch, he had battled Stelmond many times over the years, and this tactic was new to them. As much as he was sure he could beat King Ordain's army, an uneasiness sat in Haldair's stomach about the setup.

Leoxtra and Vetrina remained beside Haldair on their horses and watched the battle unfold. Suddenly, war cries and shouts turned to pain and fear. The trio looked at the right flank and watched several men fly across the field. Interest turned to fear as all three realized what they were watching. Several large scorpios jumped out of Stelmond's ranks. With large claws and massive stinger tails, these beasts cut through the foot soldiers like ragdolls.

"Signal our men to fall back and form up," Queen Vetrina commanded. Haldair and Leoxtra agreed, and as the horn blew, the Alliance army began to retreat and reform its line at its original position. As they ran back across the field, the scorpios followed and took out dozens of troops as they fled. "Where did these creatures come from?" the queen asked.

Haldair shook his head, "Stelmond has never used them before."

"No one has!" Leoxtra cut in. "Those beasts were never good for anything but killing." Vetrina and Haldair exchanged glances. "Something more is at work here, Haldair. The attack on my country stank of the same strange power."

Haldair looked out at his army. The line barely held as the beasts lunged forward with Stelmond troops behind them. Several of Haldair's men gathered enough courage and worked to distract one of the creatures while others came up behind it and hacked its deadly tail off. Strange sounds of pain came from the beast's mouth as it lashed about in pain. Then a few men managed to jump on its back and, with a loud crunch, pushed their swords through the tough shell and pierced the scorpio's heart.

Vetrina smiled softly as cheers of praise came over the army at the sight of the slain beast, "Clever. Hopefully, we can keep this momentum with the others as well."

Motivated by the first kill, the Alliance army held firm against the remaining dozen Scorpio creatures that pressed into their ranks. However, that strength lasted only briefly as Stelmond's troops pushed forward. The kings and queen watched in horror as the rest of Stelmond's army were released and joined the fight. What advantage they thought they had was quickly taken.

General Ulrich took his reserve units around the right flank and tried to get behind the enemy. Queen Vetrina had the same idea and had King Leoxtra take her cavalry around the left side to do the same. Meanwhile, Haldair restructured his troops in the center, keeping the heavy shields and spears up front to hold back the giant beasts that continued to push into the ranks of the alliance. For a moment, it looked like they would hold their own.

Neither side gained any ground. The flank maneuvers had failed miserably as several packs of Dire Wolves tore out of the woods in the distance. In seconds the cavalry was pulled through. Haldair prepared himself for the fight as he sent in his last reserve unit. Stelmond's numbers were holding. There was nothing they could do against beasts that none thought existed, especially when they seemed trained for war.

"We need to call a full retreat!" Vetrina barked at Haldair.

Haldair shook his head, "All our troops are here. Even if we retreat, we wouldn't have the means to stop them later."

"Let me send word to King Joshua in Alnirya or King Forest in Ornion." The queen explained. "Knowing what we know now about Stelmond's forces, I'm sure they'd see they need to join the fight."

Haldair shook his head again, "They'll never get here in time." Queen Vetrina nodded and conceded that point. Both then looked at the battlefield; they only hoped for a miracle.

As the fighting continued, Stelmond started to gain ground. Haldair, Vetrina, and Leoxtra prepared to send the final messages from the battlefield to the kingdoms, ready to declare their loss. "Wait!" cried Leoxtra. "Do you hear that?"

The others strained to listen over the sounds of the battle nearby. "What?" Haldair asked.

"A horn," said Leoxtra. "And not one of ours."

Haldair turned and faced the northern ridgeline. Then, he saw it. The sun glistened off their armor as they approached. "Looks like Althalos has sent more troops," Vetrina stated.

"Indeed," agreed Haldair. "Looks like Prince Aldrich brought the rest of the army with him." Then, as the additional forces rode in, Haldair's heart sank.

"Looks like King Ivan is with the prince," Vetrina noted.

Haldair nodded in agreement. Indeed, Ivan was with the prince with a small force of additional men on horseback. Haldair quickly rode back to meet them. "I cannot permit you to be here, Ivan," Haldair snapped firmly. "We both know it'll be the end."

Aldrich shot a puzzled look at his father and then at Haldair. Neither one acknowledged him. "Aldrich, take our troops and find General Oswald. Have him get you set up in command," Ivan said while keeping his eyes locked on his brother. Aldrich nodded and rode off.

King Ordain sat on his horse, overlooking the battle before him. His old age prevented him from engaging directly in the war anymore, not that it mattered. The taming of the creatures had been a tremendous gift from her and a benefit for his cause. Sometimes he wondered if it was worth it. But then we remembered what he would have in the end and the revenge that would soon be satisfied. *After all these years,* he thought. *We may finally get our victory.* He watched with pleasure as his troops moved against those of the Alliance. Unsurprisingly, the Five Crown Alliance would join in this venture against him, and King Ordain relished taking out most of his opposition in one fell swoop.

"Shall we send in the rest of our forces?" asked Ordain's general, who was next to him.

King Ordain shook his head, "We cannot show our full hand this soon." The general nodded and continued to watch the fighting unfold. After a few moments, a horn blow in the distance grabbed their attention. Both King Ordain and his general scanned the horizon. King Ordain smiled, "It seems King Ivan has come to us, ha-ha. This will save us a lot of trouble." Then he turned to the general, "Be ready."

King Ivan and Haldair remained near the rear crest overlooking the war. Haldair had convinced Ivan to at least give the troops a real chance before directly engaging in the war. "Your son is a fine fighter," Haldair mentioned as he watched Aldrich move through and direct the troops.

Ivan agreed, "He is headstrong and needs a lot of refinement in the way of leadership and treating people. But yes," he smiled. "He has become a fine warrior."

The brothers watched for several moments as the additional Althalothian troops engaged Stelmond. However, even though they had the numbers, with the giant creatures on their side, Stelmond was starting to make progress. Ivan sat sternly on his horse, observing the events. "You'd have thought King Ordain would've learned his lesson from the last time."

"Indeed," agreed Haldair. "This is very different from my past skirmishes with him, and even those always bothered me because of what happened with our father."

"Do you know where he found and tamed the scorpios and wolves for this fight?"

Haldair shook his head, "Nothing. One of the barons mentioned strange things and sightings of the creatures of old. But nothing has been confirmed until now. Have you received the details of what happened in Vasalia?"

"Yes," Ivan replied. "And the report of the Dire Wolves my men found on the way." He looked up, and his voice grew solemn. "There is something else at work here, and I'm not sure any of us are fully ready to understand or deal with it," Haldair said nothing. Ivan returned his gaze to the battlefield and watched intently as the alliance forces struggled to hold their line. "Okay," he sighed as he climbed off his horse.

Haldair shifted as if trying to block him from approaching the fight. "No, Ivan. Please. I've already lost great leaders here today."

"I will not risk more death and destruction of our people," Ivan said firmly. "Not while I have the power to do something. Enough of my past has returned to haunt me, and I will not let it stand."

"But it will kill you!"

Ivan nodded softly and began walking toward the battle, "So be it then," he said over his shoulder. As the king approached the troops, he drew the Golden Sword; his eyes became white and bright as the stars. Haldair watched in sadness as the air grew dense and the sky darkened overhead.

As Ivan stepped into the ranks, the Golden Sword glowed brightly, and the soldiers around him cheered and stepped back to make way. Though many of them had not seen the sword used before, stories of Ivan's great weapon had spread since his time as king.

The air began to swirl around Ivan as he moved. Stelmond's army charged the king as the alliance army parted. As Stelmond's troops got into range, Ivan attacked without thought or mercy. The first wave fell before they even got close. The Golden Sword shattered armor with each swing, slashing everything in its path.

Aldrich watched as his father's movements seemed to speed up. With each stroke, Ivan's sword cut down all in its wake. he quickly moved through the ranks of the enemy forces. It seemed no one could touch him. For each sword or arrow thrown at King Ivan, a ghostly echo was seen in the wake of every swing and deflected from all sides.

Aldrich stood in amazement as Ivan became surrounded and, with a thunderous yell, stabbed the ground at his feet, causing all the enemy troops around him to fall instantly. The excitement began growing in the young prince as he envisioned all he could do with such a weapon. Even the foul beasts were no match as Ivan effortlessly slashed at them, and with a single stroke, the beasts were slain in two.

Haldair watched with a heavy heart as Ivan continued. He had ordered most of his troops back to hold a final line. Part of this decision was to keep his men from getting caught in the path of his brother as he fought. The other part was his concern for Ivan's health. The Golden Sword took a toll on its wielder, and though it was never confirmed, Haldair and Ivan both had already suspected that their father and grandfather's sudden death was partly due to the constant use of the sword.

Aldrich was beside Ulrich and Oswald with their men on the right flank. Like the others, they had moved back to hold the line away from where Ivan fought to ensure any that got past him were quickly dispatched. This tactic would prove unnecessary in the end. At the sight of Ivan and his

Golden Sword, King Ordain sent in more troops, and they pressed hard on the right flank. Ivan saw this and held out his sword at the approaching force. In an instant, all their armor shattered. Oswald took the opportunity and ordered the archers to send a volley, which stopped any further advancement from the attack on them.

Ordain watched silently as Ivan moved through his troops effortlessly. He was no stranger to the power that the mighty weapon had. He was also aware of the side effects of using the sword. Ordain's general sat on his horse next to the king with fear and concern visible on his face.

"Milord?" the general asked earnestly after watching their last charge get killed after Ivan dispatched them of their armor.

"Ivan has learned to restrain himself," Ordain said, ignoring the general's question. "Better than his predecessors in that regard, then." He faced his worried general, "Perhaps we should push him a little, huh? Send in the others." A wrinkled smile crept across his face. The general nodded and directed men. Immediately, hundreds of soldiers hidden in the woods out of sight charged forward from the tree line behind the king's position.

A mighty horn blast echoed over the field, followed by a thunderous roar. King Ordain smiled. The real battle was just beginning.

King Leoxtra and Queen Vetrina had taken their places beside King Haldair at the rear of the army and watched with concern and earnestness as Ivan took over the battlefield and laid waste to the enemy troops. However, as Ivan's movements began to slow, his concern for his brother's ability grew.

Ivan slashed at some of the remaining enemy troops that charged him before falling to one knee struggling to breathe. His eyes still glowed white, and his armor shined as it reflected the golden hue of the sword off of it. Suddenly, one of Stelmond's troops ran up behind King Ivan and attempted to kill him from behind. As the soldier got closer and raised his weapon to strike, Ivan's eyes got brighter as a ghostly vision of the god came out of Ivan, quickly decapitating the attacker.

Everyone watched as Ivan stood tall afterward. The air moved faster and harder around him. The sky grew darker again as he called upon the full strength of the weapon. Stelmond's forces lay strewn about the field, and what few remained stayed their hand some distance away.

Ivan turned his sight on King Ordain's position as a loud horn was heard, and several hundred men launched from the tree line behind them. Queen Vetrina turned in shock to Haldair and Leoxtra, who shared the same expression. Never before has Stelmond ever held such numbers. But this shock in the next wave of troops was overshadowed by the roar from the trees afterward.

Fear and panic took over the army and kings as several drakes soared out of the woods and high above the tree line, screeching as they flew. Ivan stood firm as Stelmond's army charged him. Then, he turned back to look at Haldair. The brothers' gaze locked together. Tears began to form in Haldair's eyes as he looked at Ivan. Blood was running down his face from his nose, and though his eyes still held their powerful shine, Haldair could see a sadness in Ivan's expression. Fearing what he would do next, Haldair quickly spurred his horse and rode toward his brother, shaking his head as he did. No, no, no, he thought as he attempted to reach Ivan.

But it was too late by the time he got there. Ivan gave one last look at the alliance and paused briefly on Aldrich before he returned his gaze to the enemy forces. In an instant, Haldair was forced to stop, almost thrown from his horse, as Ivan increased the air pressure and power around him. The drakes began to circle overhead, swooping down in targeted strikes against the alliance's army, spewing heat and fire from their mouths. Ivan took a direct hit from one of the drakes, completely engulfed in the flame.

After several seconds of the intense heat, the drake finally stopped as several arrows from the alliance forced it to move on. After the fire went out, King Ivan stood firm and untouched by the flame. He raised his sword and was pulled up by an unseen force above the field. All the drakes quickly turned their attention to him from the troops on the ground and began to attack Ivan in the air. But as soon as they approached, Ivan stretched out his arms, and several echoes of the sword left his body and pierced through every flying beast that Stelmond had unleashed.

Then he pointed his sword to the ground and cried out with a deep voice that carried across the field. Instantly, the armor and weapons of every enemy soldier shattered. Fear and retreat took over the enemy force, but it didn't matter. Lightning cracked and echoed across the area as it struck the army all at once, instantly killing everyone.

Ivan lowered himself and hovered a few feet above the ground. Apart from the sound of the air that swirled around him, nothing else was heard on the field. Nothing else moved. The armies of the alliance stood in silence as they tried to process what they had just witnessed. Then, without warning, Ivan sent himself across the body-ridden battlefield and approached King Ordain.

Ivan paused, and hovered in front of Ordain, "Will you never learn your lesson?" his voice thundered as one that was not his own. King Ordain and his general exchanged a questioning glance before looking back at Ivan. But Ivan wasn't looking at them. His eyes were fixed behind them. Both turned to look but nothing was there.

The expression on Ivan's face grew more intense as he gazed at the ground behind the enemy king. There, a feminine figure stood, her purple tinted legs protruded from the slits in her long, dark robe. Her hood was pulled up, but under the sword's power, Ivan could see right through the shadows, right through the fear. "I see you," he said with a voice that wasn't his. There was a slight twitch of her head before she vanished altogether, leaving even Ivan's sight.

The hovering king brought his attention back to the others. King Ordain remained unfazed. He saw the blood running down Ivan's face and knew victory would be his even in this moment of loss. "You won't kill me, Ivan," he said confidently. "You never have, and you never will. I have seen my end, and it is not here or by you."

"What you have seen," Ivan said, his voice echoing across the area. "Is nothing but the lies of the one you think works for you. But you have been alive long enough to know he will not keep his promise to you. He only lives for himself."

"You think you know so much," Ordain sneered. "There is more going on than even you can know. The end of Kralavia is near, and soon we all know the truth, and only when you finally accept that will you be able to live in peace."

"Peace will not come from him," Ivan boomed. "Nor will it come through you." His figure loomed over Ordain, who remained seated on his horse, unafraid.

Ordain laughed, "You fool. It has never been through me, ha-ha. I am only the beginning. Your time is coming, and you will lose all you have worked for. You are nothing but a sad excuse…"

"No more!" Ivan interrupted. He flicked his wrist in a flash, and King Ordain's head fell from his shoulders.

As Ivan lowered himself to the ground, Aldrich, Haldair, and several others reached him. "Take that man captive!" Haldair commanded, gesturing to Ordain's general, who had slowly backed away in fear and awe of Ivan's power. Ulrich and Aldrich rode on and apprehended the general, who surrendered without a fight.

Once Ivan touched the ground, Haldair stepped up. The sky lightened, and the air calmed as Ivan sheathed the sword and returned to his normal state. As he did so, he turned to Haldair and smiled softly, blood still oozing out of his nostrils and now around his eyes. Haldair smiled in return, and as Ivan began to collapse to the ground, Haldair was there and caught him, letting him down gently.

"Thank you, brother," Haldair said. "It's time to go home now." Ivan mustered a small smile and closed his eyes.

Oswald was nearest to Haldair and rested his hand on the king's shoulder as he comforted his seemingly lifeless brother. As the men began to clear back, Ivan was placed on a wagon to be carried back to Terrowin for medical attention. Out of the corner of his eye, Oswald noticed Ulrich whispering in Aldrich's ear, he shrugged this off at first, but then, the general noticed a smile creep along Ulrich's face as he continued to speak. Anger burned inside Oswald, but he got no more than two steps before, "General Cromwell!" he turned as a firm hand was placed on his shoulder.

Oswald turned and greeted King Leoxtra, "Yes, milord?"

Leoxtra exhaled hard, "I think you should escort your king and his brother. We can handle the clean-up."

"What of the prince?"

"We'll keep him busy," Leoxtra said with a slight chuckle.

Oswald nodded as Leoxtra walked away. Ulrich and Aldrich had since parted ways, but Oswald's uncertainty grew as he pondered the events further. Ivan's power with the sword was known to many, but in all his years of service, it had never been like this. What the king did here today made Oswald ask all kinds of questions. So many things to process, Stelmond's attack, the drakes, and scorpios; Ivan's new power—however short-lived it was.

Chapter 33
Hidden Secrets

Stalbak Castle, Althalos

Wully had been pouring over the old scrolls and texts that remained salvageable from the ashes of the old record room. He needed answers; however, despite the long hours of careful study, he found nothing of value and finally dropped his head in frustration. Images of his visions from the temple flashed in his head again. He tried to pull anything from them that would give him clues on what they were or what to look for in the texts to reference. Nothing.

As the memory of the visions began to fade, Wully closed his eyes as the final image of Laura flashed before him, "What does it all mean?" He opened his eyes and took a deep breath. All Wully had managed to piece together from the scenes that the old man gave him was that, in some way, the gods of old were connected. But how? And to what end? He could only gather that the visions had been pieces of the future, but how they came about or what he was supposed to know from them, he couldn't guess.

With a final sigh of frustration, Wully got up and left his room to clear his head. The halls of the castle had been hushed as of late. With Ivan's army gone, as well as most of his personal guards, the remaining staff had little to do since keeping up after themselves required less comparatively.

As he walked, Wully admired the ornately decorated interior. It wasn't anything he hadn't seen before, but with everything on his mind, he felt a calming sense of relief as he strode along. The lavianite swirls and intricate carvings around the windows and extended ceilings reflected the light in such a way that gave a calming and almost enchanting aura to him.

As he rounded the approaching corner, he froze. The hallway he entered—was the same as in one of his visions. Wully's mind raced as the vision played out, he heard footsteps behind him, and as he looked, Oswald's ghostly figure moved past him. Merrek's falcon sword in his hand, drawn and ready. Wully noticed a detail that he hadn't before. The blade was fractured throughout, with a strange blueish hue coming from the joints of the fractures, like lightning in the metal. The droplets of blood hit the floor echoed in the silence between steps.

"What does it mean?" he cried as the vision faded.

"Wully?" came a soft voice behind him.

He whirled around to see the source of the voice, "Laura." Wully's heart was pounding in his chest.

Laura chuckled, "What thoughts had you so entranced?"

Wully's breathing returned to normal, and the pounding in his chest had subsided a bit, but he wondered if he should share what he had been through, especially the parts about Laura directly. He didn't have the answers he needed yet and was hesitant to involve her since undoubtedly, she would impose her own that would also go nowhere.

"Oh," Laura teased, "Cat got your tongue?"

Her eyes connected with his, and as always, his heart began to melt at that moment. Wully took her hands in his; he couldn't lie to her now; he never had before and probably couldn't if he tried. He glanced down the hallway, "Walk with me, please?"

Laura grew curious as she accepted. She knew something was bothering him. The two had grown close in the past, and it had become easy to read each other over the years. The couple walked in silence through the rest of the castle.

Once they found their way outside, she finally asked, "Wully, what's troubling you?"

Wully ignored her question and kept his gaze ahead. "Remember when we were younger?"

Laura blushed a little, "I remember everything," she said softly, squeezing his hand in hers.

Wully smiled, and the pair stopped outside the entrance to the old temple. Laura followed his gaze up the sides and to the stars, which had begun to shine in the early evening sky. "Do you believe in fate?"

The couple turned and looked at each other. "In some respects, yes," Laura said. "Whether we want it or not, I believe that at some point, all the events of the world bring each of us to a point that is otherwise inevitable." Wully didn't respond as he fixed his gaze on the structure ahead. After a moment, Laura reached up and grabbed his cheek, turning his head toward her, "Wully, what's troubling you?" she asked. "Why are we here?"

Pain and sadness began to show on Wully's face. "Laura, I need to tell you something," he said. "But I don't fully understand any of it, so please, bear with me."

Laura nodded, and at her gesture, they sat on the steps that led to the temple entrance. Wully recounted his experience, and she listened earnestly as he explained the meeting of the mysterious old man in the woods on the way to Althalos. As well as the voice that he heard in his head and the events that unfolded within the temple several nights ago.

When he explained the visions, Wully was careful not to reveal that Laura was seen with him nor of her apparent death. As much relief as it was to share this burden with her, he feared it would only cause unnecessary problems with many unknown pieces. To work around this, when he reached the visions that involved the two of them, he stated that the faces of the other in these parts were blurred and distorted.

Laura processed these things carefully, and Wully explained his search for answers in the records room below the castle and how most of the old texts were nothing but char and ash. When he finished, Wully dropped his head in his hands, "I just don't know what to do now?"

Laura smiled and got up, "Come on."

Wully was puzzled, "Where are we going?"

"To the record keeper."

"Why? It didn't do much good last time."

"You are not the soon-to-be queen," Laura grabbed his hand and led him back into the castle. "I think it's time I start to use my authority."

The recordkeeper was at his desk deep in a large book in front of him, and though Laura and Wully approached, he paid them no mind as he continued to read. The room looked like it always had; most items were organized and neatly placed on the shelves or racks throughout. The rest, however, was more carelessly strewn about the floor in various stacks that, to any outsider, would seem a mess. To the historian, however, each item was cataloged carefully, and until such a place could be found for said books, the floor was their home.

Laura and Wully stood in silence, patiently waiting to be acknowledged. "I know why you are here," the historian said without taking his eyes off the page. "But what you seek, I cannot provide."

"Why?" Wully snapped. "Then why send me down there for nothing?" The record keeper said nothing as he sat up, removed his glasses, and gently stroked his long, graying beard. "What even happened down there that everything burned?"

"Gathar," Laura pleaded, "Please."

Gathar sighed. "In answer to your first question, it was because that was my direction. You'll have to ask my predecessor to answer your second question." His voice was firm despite having a bit of the frailty that comes with age.

"Wait, what?" Wully questioned.

Laura raised her hand to quiet him, "Let him speak." Then, she addressed Gathar, "Explain yourself."

Gathar stood, and though his body was aged, he had strength in his presence. "The history of the old gods you sought, Wully, was ordered destroyed and forgotten by those long gone. Furthermore, what pieces remain," he said as he gestured around the room. "I am sworn to protect and only allow certain individuals access."

"On whose authority?" Laura asked.

"By King Ventril, Ivan's grandfather," Gathar replied. "I took the oath of this office as my predecessor did before me."

"Who is authorized to know this information?" Laura asked. Her voice was firm and surprised Wully a little as he had never seen Laura execute any type of authority before.

"Well," Gathar stammered. He knew what was coming. "Members of the royal family."

Laura smiled. "Then, as wife to Prince Aldrich Ventril and future queen of Althalos. I demand a history lesson."

Wully fought to hide his smile as Gathar bowed his head, "Yes, milady." He led them to an adjoining room and produced a large key from a chain on his neck hidden beneath his cloak's layers. "Apart from what we left in the basement storeroom after it was burned, one book remained." He unlocked the cabinet. Within was a large book with smooth emerald-colored wrap and gold and lavianite trim. "A close friend of my predecessor wrote it, and through a series of unknown events, he died, along with my predecessor and Ivan's grandfather."

Laura gently grazed her fingers across the cover before taking it from the pedestal on which it sat. "What's in it?"

"Pieces of our past," Gathar said. "Whether you find what you seek or not, I couldn't say. But," he said as he closed the doors. "If you need something from the past filled in…this might be a good place to start."

Laura thanked him, and she and Wully returned to his room. Carefully, they opened the book and scanned the pages. Each page was ornately decorated with beautiful transcripts and drawn pictures throughout.

During their initial inquiring, it appeared to have just the basic information on the lineages and the kings and minor pieces of the history of the kingdoms after the war. But, upon inspection, Wully found a rather odd inscription under the section of the gods. "What is that?"

"Some sort of story or perhaps a prophecy?" Laura guessed.

"Read it," Wully urged.

"Laura began,"

In ancient times, a god once reigned,
A power beyond compare.
His people thrived with no fear of pain,
In his world, so free and fair.

His sons and daughters, eight,
Did rule by his side.
But in one's heart was endless hate
And the rules he didn't abide.

Athalon, the god of all,
He knew this to be true.
He knew his son would have to fall.
Before the world could be made anew.

So, one day, without a warning,
Athalon, alone, did leave.
His people did their mourning,
For their god, they did grieve.
For in this time without Athalon
The children eight did rise,
Mortals' freedom now was done.
And the gods they grew to despise.

As the days turned into years
The world began to change,
The people's joy turned into tears,
As war broke out in range.

The world was plunged into deep darkness.
And war was everywhere,
Mortals cried themselves to sleep,
In fear and in despair.

For in those times of myth and lore
The gods and men did clash,
The world was filled with blood and gore,
As swords did ring and flash.

Without their god to keep them strong
The people fell into despair,
And with each passing night and day
The battles became less rare.

The sons and daughters of Athalon
Fought the humans with all their might,
The world was not safe for anyone,
In this world's largest fight.

The grass, once green, turned red
As armies clashed and fell,
The people wished their gods dead
To stop the war's cruel swell.

As Athalon was gone forevermore,
His people left to their fate.
Their world is consumed by endless war,
And darkness, fear, and hate.

A weapon, though, was left,
Perhaps by Athalon alone,
And one man that weapon did heft,
It's power he did hone.

And then a change began to brew,
As that one human grew in might,
The mortals rose up to the gods they slew,
And would challenge them on sight.

The gods were shocked, for they'd never seen,
A mortal with such might,
Scared they grew as he cut them like straw,
His power, to them, wasn't right.

For the gods, the children of Athalon,
They did fight until the end,
But the world they couldn't have won,
For their lives, they did spend.

Laura and Wully sat silently as they finished; neither could believe what was read. Since the Great War, people have speculated that the gods turned against them, but not that it was only one of them. "Why did we fight all eight?" Wully finally asked.

Laura shrugged, and the two flipped through a few more pages but found nothing further on the events leading up to the Great War. "This had to be written sometime after the war ended."

Wully leaned over Laura's shoulder as he examined the pages. She smiled to herself as she remembered moments from a time long past when Wully and her used to be close, and, despite her best efforts, she started to wish that maybe her life could've been a little different.

Wully sighed as he stood straight, "This still has nothing about what I saw in my visions or who the old man was, and now, we have even more questions. Like, why were the others killed for this? What was so bad that no one else could know this? And who killed them?"

Laura shook her head, "I doubt even Ivan knows those answers."

As she turned the page, Wully leaned in again. On it were drawn pictures of each of the old gods. Wully slid his fingers over the rough texture of the paint; he paused when he reached Dolos, the god of Carnheller. As always, the god was depicted in armor; however, this time, the armor and cape matched something Wully had seen before.

He gasped. "So, it's true."

"What?"

Wully's mind was racing as he tried to remember more of what he heard the old man say and do. The last vision replayed in his mind. Dolos, it was Dolos. The Guan Dao weapon was too engrained in his head to be mistaken. "It was him."

"The old man you saw?"

"No," Wully replied. "In the last vision, you remember, when a giant figure tried to kill me, and the man intercepted. Dolos was the figure! Which means…" Wully paced the floor quickly as he processed, "I bet it was Dolos who was the evil god." He paused, "But to what end? And what does it mean for what's happening now?" he stepped back to the table and hunched over Laura again.

"All the gods are gone, Wully," Laura said. "If this is correct, Athalon left first, and the others were destroyed."

"Are you sure?"

"We have nothing to confirm anything with…other than what's been told to us." Her voice softened as he spoke. Laura almost didn't believe her own words. But what good would it do, even if they were right? Who would listen? And to what end? Did it even matter anymore? "What about the old man?" she asked. "Would you know him again if you saw him?"

Wully's eyes had been fixed on the picture of the gods, but this time, it wasn't Dolos' image that drew his attention. A green hooded man with a long spear, Denesious, god of Valkos, their home country. "I know I would."

Chapter 34
The Shadow of Greed

The ride back to Terrowin was long and silent as Oswald and Haldair sat with Ivan. Both remained deep in thought about the current events and the possible future needs under the circumstances. Ivan's breathing was soft and irregular. He would occasionally cough, spewing small amounts of blood as he did so. It was the only sign they had that he was still fighting.

Ivan was in the hands of the doctors, though Oswald doubted they had any knowledge or ability to accurately aid the king. Outside, the gathering people began to join in cheers and songs as the celebration of victory started. But within the castle, sorrow and uneasiness filled the air.

Ulrich and Oswald found themselves alone as they walked down the castle's main hall. Silence followed them as they walked together, neither one so much as glanced at the other. The pair passed a few of Valkos' castle guards before rounding a corner. Once out of sight, Oswald turned fast and slammed Ulrich against the wall with his forearm against his throat.

Ulrich pressed back in defense but was taken too much by surprise to fight back. "What," he hissed between gasps for breath. "What are you…"

Oswald pressed harder, cutting off the rest of the question. "One," Ulrich grunts silently. "Just one more word whispered in that boy's ear, and it's over." Ulrich stiffened slightly in defense, but Oswald pressed harder, the fire and intensity in his eyes speaking all the words he couldn't.

Oswald finally loosened his hold, and Ulrich took a few soft breaths, "I don't know what you're…" Oswald pressed forward again in anger, crushing Ulrich's throat harder than the first time.

"Yes. You. Do!" Ulrich's face turned red as he began to claw desperately to get away from Oswald's firm grip. "I will reunite you with your brothers without regret." Ulrich gasped for breath when he suddenly fell to the floor as Oswald released him. "I see how you whisper poison into his ears, clouding his judgment. He is young and moldable yet, and you want to secure your place by his side."

Ulrich smiled between breaths, then getting up to his knees, he drew one deep breath, "You're a fool, Oswald. You can't threaten me. There are rules among our ranks, and threats are a serious matter. Your hands are tied, and I'm not afraid of you."

Oswald remained unfazed as Ulrich rose to his feet. "Oh Ulrich," he said, stepping in close, "Rules only matter if you care." Ulrich's stern expression softened at these words. "My duty is to my king and country," Oswald continued. "Your duty is to yourself. If I kill you, it will be for my king and country, and I will do so regardless of the consequences."

Oswald pressed forward slightly, forcing Ulrich to take a step back. He stopped when he felt the cool dampness of the stone wall behind him. "You wouldn't dare." He stated firmly as he found his strength.

"My duty is to my king and country, and I will protect it from any threats from afar and within…till death takes me," Oswald repeated.

Silence. For what felt like several minutes, neither one moved nor spoke. Each one was afraid to take their eyes off the other. Both suddenly break their stare when footsteps echo through the hallway. Ulrich quickly stepped away and headed out toward the celebration outside. "You are a coward, Ulrich," Oswald muttered to himself. "You try to hide behind a power you couldn't ever possess." A few castle guards rounded the corner of the hall, and Oswald followed Ulrich outside.

As the evening continued, everyone joined in the celebration. Merrek had just given a fine victory speech that honored those who made it home and bolstered the hearts of those who lost someone. As the music, food, and festivities grew, the armies of the visiting kingdoms intermingled with the locals as some greeted long-lost friends and others made new ones. Several of King Leoxtra's soldiers cheered as they reunited with their wives and families, sharing tales of the strange events in the recent war. King Ivan's name came up several times in the conversations across the courtyard as the tales of his current power grew with each retelling.

Oswald casually made his way through the crowd. He had been keeping an eye on Ulrich but had lost him after Merrek's speech as the mob of people thickened around the area. After a moment, he decided to relax and deal with that issue later. Besides, he still had not seen Aldrich, Rollins, or Thomas since he left the Field of Denesious with Haldair and Ivan.

Oswald wasn't too concerned about the other two but thought he should check on Thomas. He never got a chance to adequately explain the pain and discomfort that Thomas would feel after his injuries and was slightly concerned for his friend and his mental state under the circumstances. As the general moved through the crowd, casually greeting and congratulating some of the men that stopped him along the way, he directed his attention to the barrels of mead on the far end.

As unlikely as it would be, Oswald hoped he could get to Thomas before he was "Already drunk," he said, shaking his head. Thomas sat awkwardly at the table next to the mead stash, filling his pint directly from the barrel closest to him.

"Oswald!" Thomas greeted. He held his pint aloft and laughed. "Cheers to another victory and cheating death once more!" Without hesitation, he quickly downed the pint and began to refill it as Oswald stepped up.

The general grabbed the newly filled pint from Thomas, "How's the arm?"

Thomas awkwardly looked at his hand as if he wasn't sure what had happened to the pint he was carrying. Then, he filled another mug from the table before him. "Gets hard to swing a sword after a while," he raised his pint in cheers, and Oswald gently tapped it with the mug he took. Thomas nodded, "But it holds a mug just fine."

Oswald grabbed that mug as well before Thomas could finish it. However, Thomas was ready this time and quickly shoved Oswald, causing the general to lose his balance, stumble back, and fall into another soldier before hitting the ground with a soft thump.

"Now, now, general. This is no way to act in front of your men," said a familiar voice.

"Damn it, Thomas," Oswald muttered as he wiped off the spilled beer from his tunic. "I'm so sorry," he said aloud as he stood and turned to see who he had bumped into. Thomas laughed again, and Oswald's features softened when he realized it was "Merrek!" The baron held up his own mug, and Thomas and Oswald saluted with what remained of their own. "How's it going, my friend?"

Merrek shrugged, "No complaints worth complaining about." Then he glanced across the courtyard, "Except maybe one." Oswald followed Merrek's gaze and saw Aldrich conversing with several others.

On the far side of the courtyard, Ulrich made his way to the young prince. As he approached, Aldrich smiled, but the concern was still written on his face. "You did well today, Aldrich," he said. The prince nodded but said nothing as his gaze drifted up to the tower where Ivan had been taken. Sensing the tension and anger in the young prince, Ulrich leaned in and said, "Don't worry. Your men support you. You are the heir of Althalos, the head of all these so-called kings." Pride swept through the prince as Ulrich continued, "It would be unfortunate if your father met his end here. But," Ulrich lowered his tone. "It wouldn't be such a bad thing."

As he finished, Ulrich glanced up and noticed that Oswald and Merrek were watching from afar. He had no fear that they knew what was said, only concern for what they might do to disrupt his plans. As the crowds pressed around him, Ulrich shook those thoughts and brightened his mood, "But, enough of that talk. Tonight, we celebrate!"

Cheers and chorus could be heard all around; Merrek nudged Oswald, who was still staring at the place where Ulrich and Aldrich were. "That bastard," he muttered, wishing he could hear the exchange between the two.

"What was that?" Merrek asked.

Oswald snapped out of his thought, not realizing that he had spoken audibly, "Oh, it's nothing, Merrek." He smiled and returned to the group, "Just enjoying myself, as you should be. It was a strong victory for us."

Merrek nodded in agreement though his features became sullen as he glanced back in Aldrich's direction, "But at what cost? And for whose gain?"

Thomas slammed his empty mug on the table, "Well, gentleman, shall we get another?"

"You literally just got that drink a few moments ago," Oswald said.

"Well, yes," Thomas replied. He shook his cup upside down, squinted one eye, and stared into the pint. "But as you can see, it's as dry as the Dead Lands here." Oswald rolled his eyes, "And I still thirst, got to get that taste of battle out of my mouth."

Merrek chuckled, "One more wouldn't hurt anyone."

Thomas agreed and got up to get a different drink from the servers nearby.

While Thomas was gone, Oswald and Merrek got comfortable at the table and talked about recent events before Merrek finally asked, "How is Ivan?"

"I don't know," Oswald said. "Haldair is keeping watch on him constantly. He hasn't left him alone for a moment as of now."

Merrek nodded. "King Ivan is a strong man."

"You saw the same thing I did out there, Merrek. There isn't even the faintest idea about what happened among anyone."

Merrek agreed, "But Haldair knows more about that situation than he lets on, I'm sure of it."

"Oh, I know he does," Oswald stated. "But he hasn't said anything, from what I've heard anyway."

"Haldair is a conservative man. In my experience, he usually keeps things on a need-to-know basis."

Oswald stared at the table momentarily, "I think now would be a good time for people to start knowing about that sword if it's powerful enough to almost kill the wielder."

Just then, Thomas returned and set the mugs in front of them. "Men, you are in for a treat."

"Oh, no. What did you do?" Oswald asked.

"Drink up, my friends," Thomas said, ignoring him. "For the night is young, and we are only getting older."

The three raise their mugs together and drink. "Ugh!" Oswald coughed. "Ungelded? Thomas, you idiot. I don't like your unfiltered mead. You know this."

Thomas chuckled, "It's so good, though! It's a treat. I rarely come across it, so when I do, drinks all around!"

Merrek smiled as Oswald slid his mug across the table before Thomas, "Well then, you can drink two of these."

At first, Thomas shot a look of disappointment at Oswald, which was quickly exchanged for delight as he realized he now had double the drink. Merrek and Oswald watched as Thomas finished the first one of the two drinks before grabbing the second.

"Shouldn't you pace yourself?" Merrek asked.

"If I still feel anything by the night's end, I haven't done a good enough job."

Oswald just shook his head and let his eyes wander around the crowd. Everyone who is anyone seems to have made it. Anyone of rank or nobility, except for Ivan and Haldair. After a moment, Merrek set the rest of his drink on the table. "Alright, I have business I must attend to."

Oswald looked puzzled, "What business?"

"I have a certain brother-in-law I must continue to humiliate," he said as he stood.

"Are you ever going to give that a rest?"

Merrek paused, "I'm not sure. How long does a marriage last again?"

Oswald sighed, "Till death do them part."

Merrek laughed, "Sounds easy enough."

Oswald and Thomas had resumed their conversation when a firm hand grabbed the general's shoulder. He turned quickly to see King Haldair behind him. "Oswald," the king said solemnly.

"My lord, Haldair," Oswald greeted in surprise. Haldair's face said more than his, and Oswald knew nothing good was coming.

"Come with me," the king said urgently.

Chapter 35
Secrets and Surprises

Ulrich watched as Haldair and Oswald proceeded across the grounds back into the castle. The celebration around him did little as a distraction from the thoughts of what could be happening. Oswald's previous words resonated within and created a sense of urgency in Ulrich's plans.

Just then, Aldrich returned. He had been pulled away as others wanted to converse with the young prince. Ulrich observed Aldrich's slight stupor and helped the prince get stable in the chair next to his. "You okay?"

Aldrich nodded, "I'm fine."

The pair observe the party for a few minutes. Music and excitement filled the air around them. Ulrich casually glanced at Aldrich and then back to the party. "So," he began cautiously. "I saw Haldair retrieve Oswald and take him away. The first time anyone has seen the man leave your father's side." The general observed Aldrich's response. But Aldrich said nothing. "Your father would ask to see a simple general in his army before his only son and heir to his throne?" he asked. "Seems rather…degrading, if you ask me."

Aldrich's face began to show visible disappointment, but he still did not respond.

"He may be making last-minute plans that he doesn't want you to know about." Ulrich continued. "Plans for his succession. Or his sword."

"He can't!" Aldrich snapped. "No one has any claim to his throne but myself. And that damn sword belongs to me!" Aldrich immediately stopped as he realized he was almost shouting his words. The two men looked around quickly; the party continued around them as it had. Aldrich took a deep breath and leaned close to Ulrich so they could speak without anyone listening.

"I think your father conspires against you with Oswald and your uncle," Ulrich said.

"Why would he?"

"Just look at how he treats you," Ulrich urged. "Choosing his brother and his general, who is of no royal blood, I might add, over his son and heir? Does that not seem as if he has plans that may not align with your plans as future King of Kralavia?"

Aldrich raised an eyebrow, "King of Althalos, you mean."

"Oh," Ulrich stammered. "Of course, Sire. My apologies."

Aldrich nodded and sat silent as he mulled over these thoughts.

Captain Frendrell was walking across the courtyard through the party. After Oswald had left the conversation so abruptly, thanks to King Haldair, Merrek had left to scrounge up something to eat, and Thomas had been looking for someone who would still serve him a drink in his drunken state. Sure enough, the captain found a spare keg in the corner and decided he could simply help himself.

"Ah, ungelded," he said to himself. "As it should be." As he went to pull the cork on the keg, Thomas flinched hard when his recently injured hand gripped the pin. "Damn it all," he muttered, massaging his right hand. "Stop hurting already; I need my sword hand."

After a moment and some mustered resolve, he tried again to open the barrel, "Alright, cork, you cheeky bastard."

Switching to his left hand, Thomas finally freed the sweet ale from within. "See, either way, I'll accomplish my mission," he said to himself. He then tipped the barrel enough to pour himself a drink and downed the mug in a matter of moments before running another one to go back and enjoy with Merrek, who was sure to have returned by now to the table they had previously been at.

As he made his way along the far side of the courtyard, Thomas stumbled slightly and decided to sit behind a wagon before continuing. "I suppose Merrek can wait. I'll finish this drink to regain my composure." As he finished his drink, he heard familiar voices on the other side of the wagon. *Aldrich?* He thought, though too drunk to get up to verify.

General Ulrich and the prince were still seated at their table, which sat adjoined to the wagon that Thomas had just made himself comfortable. "I know I'll never wield that sword while my father lives. I'll have to wait it out," Aldrich's voice came through clearly.

"Why wait?" Ulrich asked plainly.

Aldrich tensed and straightened up, "Because my father will live, I'm sure. He will be weaker, yes, but he'll live."

"That doesn't have to be so," said Ulrich slyly. To which Aldrich shot him a stern look. "I was only saying that it may not be such a bad thing if he were to pass," Ulrich explained. "Your rule would go unchallenged, and you would have his weapon. And any plans he may be trying to make behind your back would never come to pass as you would be king, and none could challenge your authority." Ulrich guided Aldrich's gaze across the party to the table where Merrek was seated. Aldrich tensed and was about to respond when a sudden roar in the crowd caught the two men's attention.

Thomas froze. He couldn't believe what he heard and slowly looked around to see if his presence was noticed. Thankfully, it hadn't, as the commotion had the immediate attention of all around. Carefully, the captain got up and returned to where Merrek sat. *I need to find Oswald*, he thought as he staggered along.

As he went, he saw what had the sudden draw of the crowd. Several Halikian men were bare-knuckle boxing Vasalian soldiers and winning every round. Queen Vetrina smiled each time from her seat next to Leoxtra, and she watched with pride at the strength and constitution of her people.

"Come on now, lads!" Leoxtra bellowed. "These heathens can't beat you!"

"If we are so heathen, then why don't you fight Leoxtra?" Vetrina asked jokingly. "Show your men how it's done."

Leoxtra scoffed. "I haven't boxed in years; my time for tavern fights and petty squabbles is far over."

Vetrina smiled, "Then just fight me, hand to hand, tooth to tooth. No weapons and no games. Earn your honor here."

The crowd began to gather around as Leoxtra shifted uneasily in his seat. He didn't want to fight, even if it was only for fun. But he could not back down from a challenge in front of all his men and the people of Halika and Valkos, much less to a woman. Quickly the king bowed his head slightly, "Your Highness," he began. "I am flattered, I assure you. But I do not wish to harm a defenseless woman."

"Then this fight will be quicker than I thought," Vetrina replied.

She then proceeded through the crowd toward the open circle where the others had been brawling a moment ago. The crowd parted as she moved and then glanced back at Leoxtra, waiting for his response. "This isn't necessary," he said as he stepped through the crowd.

Queen Vetrina removed her outer garments, revealing a fitted and light leather apparel, and took her stance, "But it is," she taunted. "Come, show your men what a king can do in a fight." Leoxtra cautiously stepped across from the queen. Vetrina smiled and relaxed her stance to a more feminine pose as she teased, "Or will you still not fight a helpless woman?"

Leoxtra scowled and unfastened his sword belt, letting it fall to the ground, followed by his cloak. One of his men stepped up to remove the items as the king took his stance in front of the queen. The crowd began to shift as the citizens of Halika were behind their queen and Vasalia's people behind their king. The people of Valkos and Althalos were intermingled, not caring which side won, only cheering for the sake of the entertainment of it all.

"You'll soon find, Vetrina," Leoxtra said. "That I used to be undefeated in my boxing years."

Vetrina smiled, "Your reputation does not proceed with you. Perhaps you could show me?"

The crowd cheered as the two squared up; Vetrina wasted no time and lunged in quickly. Leoxtra dodged the first several strikes and blocked a few others. She stepped back, taunting the king to make his move, but he held his ground. Vetrina smiled and shrugged as he moved in again. This time she used her hands and feet, taking the king off guard. A quick front kick to the solar plexus sent Leoxtra stumbling backward.

Queen Vetrina smiled again and waited as Leoxtra caught his breath. However, this strike was just what Leoxtra needed to shake off his reluctance. And as soon as he stood up, he pounced forward. The two exchanged several blows, and, for a moment, it looked like neither one would be the winner. Finally, Leoxtra found his opening, and his fist made a firm connection to the queen's jaw, which sent her staggering back.

Vetrina quickly recovered and pressed her offensive again. She again found her mark and knocked Leoxtra to the ground. "My horses possess more skill than you do, King Leoxtra."

As the queen gloated, Leoxtra reached over faster than she could see and grabbed her ankle. His strength, mixed with her petite figure, allowed him to throw her off her feet and onto the ground beside him. The two stared at each other sternly until a soft smile crept over Vetrina's face. The crowd began to settle down as Leoxtra gave a smile of his own, followed by bellowing laughter. Both Leoxtra and Vetrina laughed, and the crowd cheered again.

Leoxtra got up and offered a hand to the queen, who took it with gratitude. Once, Leoxtra got back to his seat; he raised his drink. "I see why your men don't fight on foot, milady," he teased, still laughing.

Vetrina laughed as she raised her glass and met his, "And I see why they say to never turn your back on a Vasalian."

The two took a long drink, and as they set their mugs down, more cheers echoed from the men and women around them. As the people began to go about their previous fun, Leoxtra leaned close to Vetrina, "Perhaps a little taste of humility once in a while is good for me." Vetrina nodded and chuckled as the two resumed conversing with the others around them.

Thomas had made his way back to Merrek and hastily sat down. "Hey, Captain. Welcome back."

Thomas didn't acknowledge him at first and finished the last of his drink. "Where's Oswald?"

Meanwhile

Haldair and Oswald walked swiftly down the corridors of the palace. Terrowin Keep is the largest known keep in Kralavia. It was constructed of sheer stone, like the walls protecting the city. While the keep held a larger footprint than the castle in Althalos, it had second place for design and architecture. The keep was so large that several sections would often go on for weeks without human presence, as most of Haldair's dealings kept them within only certain parts of the structure.

Haldair moved quickly, enough so that Oswald had to pick up his walking pace to keep up with him. He had never seen the stout man move fast like this, but the circumstances were different this time. Oswald could tell the brotherly bond between Ivan and Haldair was strong, but he doubted anyone knew its extent.

Haldair ducked into the next hallway, heading down to his brother's room. He hadn't left his side since the battle ended until now, but Ivan asked to see Oswald, so he left him with the doctor but was in a hurry to get back. Haldair had known for years that being kings and with all the wars they fought, one of them would eventually see the end. But even with that, he never considered a world without his older brother…he never wanted to consider life without him. For Haldair, Ivan was always a solid rock to fall back on if he ever needed anything; for Ivan, the same was true of Haldair.

They stopped just outside the quarters that Ivan was in. Haldair motioned for Oswald to stop as he peered inside. The doctor was still inside Ivan's bedside, where Haldair had left them only a few minutes before. Seeing the pair at the doorway, the doctor turned to Ivan and said something inaudible before walking toward the door to greet them. He gave a quick bow to Haldair and a respectful nod of acknowledgment to Oswald.

"Any change?" Haldair asked.

The doctor shook his head, "It's hard to say, my lord; he's been in and out of sleep for hours now. What happened to him today cannot truly be examined or explained by the tools or medicines of mortal men. He is in the hands of Athalon and Athalon alone."

Haldair nodded, "I will continue to stay with him until I am sure he is okay."

"Let us hope he will be," the doctor reassured.

"Let us be for now; come back in an hour or so to check on him again, please."

The doctor bowed again, "Yes, my lord." As he left the room, he closed the door behind him, leaving Haldair and Oswald alone with the sleeping king. Haldair motioned for Oswald to wait and stepped up to the bed alone.

Haldair stood silently momentarily, waiting for his brother to wake and notice him. He didn't know what to do or say. He looked at the golden sword, propped up against the wall near the window. He approached it slowly, staring into the reflection cast by the blade. He remembered the moment he and Ivan gripped the hilt of the weapon. Though it was only for a moment, Haldair, for once, felt the raw power that his brother had had to wield for so many years, and he felt only a fraction of its burden. Haldair continued to stare intently at the sword for a moment.

"Why did you do this? Why take my brother from me?"

Oswald said nothing and remained where he was; he was not unaware of the suspicions nor the rumors about what that sword was. The powers seemed unending, and the likelihood that it had a mind of its own was more and more plausible the longer the general had been around it.

Haldair didn't take his eyes off the sword; to Oswald, it looked as though he was waiting for some response. Haldair's eyes were wet from tears he won't let fall. His face has become noticeably distraught by the recent events, but he is also angry at his brother for using the sword again and mad at the blade. Silence for what felt like to Oswald several minutes until a soft cough from Ivan broke them both from their thoughts.

Haldair rushed back to Ivan's bedside. "Ivan, I'm here."

Ivan's eyes finally opened, looking at Haldair's face. "I'm sorry, brother," his voice was so soft and weak that Oswald struggled to hear. "My dear brother."

A tear finally rolled down Haldair's face. He couldn't hold it back any longer and grabbed his brother's hand, "I thought I lost you out there."

Ivan blinked and deeply breathed, "For a moment, I swore I lost myself."

Haldair gestured to Oswald to come closer, "Oswald is here, Ivan."

Oswald moved up to the end of the bed and stood so Ivan could see him. Ivan turned his head toward him. "Ah…my dear boy… Oswald."

Oswald paused momentarily; he had never been referred to as a dear boy. But Oswald quickly shook this off and bowed, "My king."

Ivan smiled softly, "Oh, come now, Oswald. There is no need for those kinds of pleasantries. There has never been. Come…sit."

Oswald went around the bed, sat on the other side opposite Haldair, and took Ivan's outstretched hand. As he did, he saw noticeable burn marks on it from what he could only imagine was from gripping the Golden Sword. Ivan pulled Oswald's hand in and kissed it. Puzzled, Oswald and Haldair exchanged glances, unsure what to think of Ivan's attitude.

"It brings many warm feelings to my heart to see you both alive," Ivan said.

Haldair nodded, "We're just glad to see that you are alright, brother."

"Is Aldrich?"

"He's safe, Ivan," Oswald answered.

"He fought bravely today," Haldair said, chuckling. "Reminded me of you and me in our youth."

Ivan clenched his eyes shut, and a tear was squeezed through one of them. It rolled down his cheek and disappeared. "I had a dream."

"Of what?" Haldair asked.

"I saw myself standing at a crossroads," Ivan began. "Not in the center but rather at the mouth of one of the roads…and the other three roads, there were three men. They all looked just like me, but each had a few differences. Some were subtle, such as a scar I never received or a cloak I never wore, perhaps even an expression I have never managed to make. But some were obvious, a missing limb or an eye gouged out." He paused and coughed softly before continuing. "They all stood at the entrance to each road, staring at me. I couldn't speak to them. I couldn't reach out to them. I couldn't move toward any of them. But I could move away, only away…not forward."

Haldair glanced at Oswald but said nothing.

"Every path presented before me in my life, whether I took it or not, has led to war," Ivan continued. "And I can do nothing to change what choices my past holds. But I can change the path I am on now. The path that all of us are on now." Ivan pushed himself up in bed, and Haldair handed him a glass of water from the nightstand. "Thank you." He took a few large gulps and set the cup back down. Then he turned his head toward the Golden Sword and paused for a moment, almost lost in a trance.

Haldair and Oswald exchange a brief puzzled look, "Ivan?" Haldair asked.

Ivan continued as though he never paused, "That sword must never again be wielded." His voice was much firmer this time. "By anyone. Do you understand?"

Haldair eagerly nodded in understanding. He's waited for the day his brother would say these words. He's wanted nothing to do with that sword from the first time he laid eyes upon it. It was never meant to be used by them.

"We shall lock it away," Haldair said. "Where no one will find it."

"No." Ivan declared. "I don't want it anywhere near me, my family, the Five Crowns, or the whole of Kralavia. Take it out to sea and bury it beneath the depths. Where it can never see the light of day again."

Haldair bowed his head, "It will be done, brother."

Ivan smiled faintly, "Life has a way of balancing things. To wield a power so great an equal toll is taken."

"How can you put a value on years of life?"

Ivan sighed, "How indeed…I want what few prisoners remain of Stelmond to be released. Same with the Carnhellers. The war is over; let them return to their people peacefully."

"I am not sure Leoxtra will agree with that," Oswald said.

"Then I will speak with Leoxtra myself," Ivan said. "Peace is our best option going forward. It is the only option I am willing to abide with going forward. Send them home; I'm done fighting. You will need to let your men know. Will you see to it that this is completed?"

Oswald accepted his task without question, "Of course."

Haldair nodded hesitantly, "Yes," he said, looking at Oswald. "I can help see to that." Oswald nodded in return.

"Good," Ivan said. "Now, Oswald, I can hear the men enjoying their celebration. I do not wish to take you away from it but be sure to pass on the message that we will return to Stalbak in the morning."

"Are you sure you are strong enough to travel?"

"Of course, I am. I want to go home, my boy. I wish to recover in my own bed."

Oswald let out a small chuckle, "Understood."

"I will travel with you, brother," Haldair commented.

"No, Haldair. You have your own people to tend to. Let this old man worry about himself."

Haldair sighed, "Ivan, my people will understand. My place right now is at my brother's side."

Ivan chuckled lightly. As the chuckle turned to a cough, Haldair quickly poured him another cup of water and held it out for him. Ivan removed his hand from his face to reach for the glass; his hand was covered in blood.

"Oswald, fetch the doctor!"

Oswald quickly rose from his seat.

"No," Ivan said. He strained as he spoke. "I'm okay."

Haldair ignored him and repeated his command to Oswald, who began to leave the room again.

"I said no, Haldair." Ivan and Haldair lock eyes for a moment. Oswald awkwardly stood where he was, waiting for a decision between the two brothers. After a moment, Ivan said, "Oswald, could you leave us?"

Oswald hesitated, "Of course, my lord." He bowed his head but didn't move until Haldair gave a reassuring nod.

"And Oswald," Ivan said as the general approached the door. He paused and turned his head slightly, and Ivan smiled. "Enjoy the celebration and speak with your friends. Don't worry about me."

"As you wish." His words echoed inside him as he left the room and closed the door.

"Why didn't you let me have the doctor fetched?" Haldair asked once they were alone. "You're not doing well, Ivan."

Ivan smiled, "I am keenly aware of that, brother." Haldair said nothing as Ivan slowly pushed himself more upright. Ivan took a deep breath, "There are things we need to discuss now that Oswald has his orders."

"Anything, brother, just name it."

"Oh, stop with all that. I'm not going to die here, Haldair."

Haldair's eyes teared up again, "How do you know?"

Ivan sighed, "I just do, I am weak, and if I was to use the sword again, I probably would die, but I will live for now. Now let us move on to more important topics."

Haldair didn't say anything at first; he didn't want to argue. But who was to say if Ivan would die or not? Too many unknown questions and variables to accurately say anything was certain. He knew that Ivan knew better than anyone the state in which that sword put him. But with everything going on around the world, Haldair needed Ivan to be careful. He knew, as well as most, that this victory would be short-lived unless they got more answers.

Furthermore, Haldair knew that in order to keep the other kingdoms from total disbandment, Ivan needed to hold his seat in Althalos. And though Haldair agreed with Ivan that he could not use the sword any longer, he almost wondered if Ivan would have to before the end.

"What happened out there, Ivan?" he asked. "I've never seen it make you do that before. You were unstoppable and damn near invincible!"

"I don't know, it was almost as if it was limiting my power while using it before…until then," Ivan replied. Haldair pondered this notion as Ivan continued, "He spoke to me, Haldair."

"Who did?" Haldair asked. Ivan had his full attention now.

Ivan looked at the sword, "He did."

Haldair followed Ivan's gaze. He knew it. There had been many rumors of Athalon's disappearance and what truly became of the old gods after their weapons were destroyed. The fact that Athalon's sword remained intact after his disappearance meant little to most at the time. However, After the sudden and mysterious deaths of both the brother's father and grandfather, speculation had begun to build within them about the real reason Athalon left it and what he would do with whoever possessed it. "What did he say?"

"I don't know," Ivan replied. "I can't explain it."

"Try, Ivan."

Ivan relaxed his head against the wall behind the bed. "I understood it at the time before I flew into the air. But now I couldn't even begin to tell you what he said. But I could see so much. Across the span of time and…" he paused as he remembered. "Where is the woman that was with King Ordain?"

Haldair shrugged, "There was no woman there. What do mean? Who was she?"

Ivan winced as he tried to remember, "I don't know," he finally said. "But I know I saw someone there. Like she was whispering to Ordain. I…I can't explain it." Ivan glanced at the sword as his thoughts faded.

Haldair looked at the sword and glared in anger at it. "Some things in the world were never meant to be touched by man…nor should they ever be." He wasn't sure if the sword had a steady connection to the god or if he was even listening, but Haldair would have his opinion known.

"Haldair," Ivan choked. "Tears began to fall hard as he stared into the sword."

"Yes?"

"Aldrich, my son," Ivan swallowed hard. "He must never touch that sword. He can never wield it or feel its power…or its burden."

Haldair nodded. "I already promised you, brother, I will take the sword out to sea so it can never be found again."

Ivan ignored his brother's statement. "I know he wants it; he longs for the power that I held. But he can't ever have it; it will kill him, Haldair. Either by the burden of the sword alone or by the acts he may try to use it for, he will die either way."

"I understand; I will personally take the sword after you are home and safe."

"Thank you," Ivan said as he finally broke his gaze away from the weapon and grabbed his brother's hand. "Thank you." The two brothers sat silently for some time, enjoying the peace and the sound of the festivities coming through the window from the courtyard below. "Could you do just one last thing for me before you return to the festivities?"

"Anything."

"Could you fetch my son for me? It's time he and I talked."

Chapter 36
Decisions in the Dark

Aldrich had made his way through the crowd as the sprawl between King Leoxtra and Queen Vetrina ended. He suddenly became ill and needed to find a quiet spot away from the group. Thankfully, most of the crowd had moved closer to the center, giving the prince plenty of options.

A chorus of cheers echoed behind him as he went to the far wall; Aldrich grabbed his head to help stabilize himself. His whole body ached; he couldn't tell if he had too much to drink or if something else was bugging him. A little of both, he supposed, and even though he knew it would only make things worse, drinking away the feelings seemed like a possible solution.

Flashes of the recent battle, the screaming, and the pain entered his mind. When his father unleashed the full might of the Golden Sword and laid waste to the remaining troops. Envy? A possible explanation. Post-war victory jitters? Another possibility. Then he remembered what his father did to his authority in Vasalia, and Ulrich's words echoed back to the young prince. Aldrich suddenly got weak in the knees and knelt in the grass, hoping to ease the pain in his stomach. This thought fleeted away as fast he pondered it, for as soon as his knees hit the ground, the contents of his stomach rolled up in a fury.

"I don't know why you keep touching that stuff; you've proven you can't handle it," said a familiar yet despised voice behind him.

Aldrich wiped his mouth and turned to verify the name of the voice. He rolled his eyes as his ears proved true, *Merrek.* "What the hell do you want?"

Merrek's face held a cheeky smile, "Just to see what color your face changes to this time."

Just then, a stray bottle whizzed past Aldrich's head, missing his ear by a mere hair before connecting with the wall behind him. The prince moved to avoid the bottle so fast that he forced whatever little bit was left in his stomach out on the ground between him and Merrek. The baron laughed harder as he traced the bottle's path back to the crowd behind him.

Aldrich wiped his mouth off with his arm again and carefully stood. "Just what the hell is your problem with me anyway? You don't even know me, Merrek."

Merrek stepped in close, "Oh, I know you. I know you and every man like you, though…most of them were on the other end of my sword." His hand grazed across the ornately studded hilt of his falcon blade.

"You are just the same as me!" Aldrich snapped as he poked his finger into Merrek's chest. "Both men of noble birth, but I'm sorry the fate of our wealth and worth took different paths. Don't be bitter toward me just because your father lost your house's fortune on his own poor life choices. It's not my fault you had to sell off your sister to save your skin."

Merrek grabbed Aldrich by the chest of his tunic and gripped it tight. Though he spoke softly, Aldrich felt the world's weight in his words, "Don't ever speak of my sister," he began. "You have no right to judge my actions as a brother when I have already witnessed your qualities as a husband. You had no right to take her. You have no right to call her your wife. You are not worthy of her, nor shall you ever be. I see it in your eyes…she's nothing to you."

"I…she is…"

"Did you even say goodbye to her before you departed for Alkeroth?" Merrek interrupted. "Did you miss her while you were away? I will notice nothing but her absence for the rest of my life, and that is because of you. And I'll never forget that."

Aldrich said nothing.

"Keep in line. Or else all of Kralavia will tell the tale of the shortest royal marriage in existence." Merrek chuckled as he let go of Aldrich's shirt. "And the heir who never got to be king." Merrek paused, but Aldrich still said nothing.

The baron smiled, "Good talk Aldrich; I like when we do this." The prince tensed, and Merrek turned back to his table, "Don't forget to wipe that piss off your leg, prince," he called back. "Might flood the city."

Merrek's laughter echoed inside Aldrich as the baron walked away. He had now seen battle and earned the respect of many of his troops by their own mouths. Were they all lies? How is he still treated this way? Did Merrek only express what they all thought? What must he finally do to gain the kind of respect that makes a man fear stepping out of line in front of him? Aldrich rubbed his temples as his head began to hurt again.

"Are you alright?" Asked Ulrich as he approached. By now, the duel between Leoxtra and Vetrina had ended, and the crowd had begun to disperse across the courtyard again.

"I don't know what to do," Aldrich sighed. "I'm so lost Ulrich, no matter what I do… I'm still myself."

Ulrich places his arm around the prince's shoulders. "Perhaps that's exactly who you need to be," he said. "You need to stop fighting that. Stop trying to change it, stop letting others try to change you, and just embrace who you are." Ulrich slipped a small vial into Aldrich's tunic as he finished speaking.

"What was that?"

"You'll thank me later," Ulrich said, leading them back to the festivities. "Just…try to realize what potential lies within you. You are destined for great things, Aldrich Ventril, but not if you allow others to dictate how you should rule as a king. I saw you out there on the field today; I saw you fight. That was a man I would follow into any conflict without question. That was a man that I would be honored to call my king."

As the pair returned to their table, Ulrich noticed that Haldair was fast approaching with Oswald on his heels. Ulrich subconsciously touched his neck as he remembered his last encounter with the general since the war. Ulrich quickly leaned in and whispered to Aldrich, "Remember my words when the time comes…" he stepped back and bowed his head, "My king."

Ulrich walked away into the darkness and the cheers of the surrounding party. Oswald and Haldair reach Aldrich shortly after. Oswald's gaze focused on Ulrich as he slipped away. "What did he want?"

Aldrich started to shake his head before quickly remembering it would be a bad idea. "Nothing," he muttered as he gently massaged his temples.

Oswald eyed him carefully but said nothing.

"Your father is awake, Aldrich," Haldair said earnestly, oblivious to Oswald's notion. "He wishes to speak with you." Aldrich nodded and followed Haldair back to the castle. Haldair paused when he realized that Oswald had not followed, "Oswald?"

The general waved them off, "You two go ahead. I need to have a word with someone." Without waiting for a response, Oswald walked off after Ulrich.

Aldrich then turned to his uncle, "How is he?"

"Better than I expected," Haldair replied. "Your father is a strong man."

"Why does he want to speak to me? Another lecture, no doubt."

Haldair stopped in his tracks, "No, Aldrich. Your father has many plans for the future. The future of Althalos, the future of Kralavia…your future. He means to discuss them with you to better prepare you for what is to come."

Aldrich scoffed, "He's done a splendid job of that."

Haldair shook his head as they resumed their walk, "Whatever your thoughts, please know that your father is a sagacious man and has seen and done more in his life than anyone I know. He loves you and wants what's best for you and your people."

"I do question his methods then."

"Never forget who he is, Aldrich. He has more things to worry about than you even understand."

Aldrich remained silent as they entered the keep; *he wouldn't need to worry if he wasn't so weak.*

The rest of the walk to Ivan's chamber was silent and awkward. Discontentment rested on the prince's face, and although Haldair was unaware of the direct thoughts harbored within the young man's mind, he was no fool. A few times, Haldair tried to think of something to say to help ease the tension and break the silence, but each time he hesitated when he realized that it would only worsen things at the moment.

"Ah, Aldrich," Ivan said weakly as they entered his room. Ivan slowly climbed out of bed, and Haldair quickly attempted to help him up to his feet, but Ivan merely batted his hands away, expressing that he could do it himself. As he tried to straighten himself, the wounded king paused, the pain in his body made clear on his face.

"Can I get you anything?" Haldair asked.

"No, Brother. Thank you." Ivan began to take a few steps, and even though he was wincing, with every step, strength seemed to be returning to his legs. "Haldair, will you excuse us for a moment; allow a father and son to talk privately?"

"Of course, brother. Let me know if you need anything."

"I shall. Thank you, Haldair."

Haldair left the room and closed the door behind him. There was an awkward silence for a moment as Aldrich didn't want to look his father in the eye. He knew he had been drinking heavily, and his father would disapprove.

Ivan walked up to Aldrich, face to face. Even with Ivan being weakened and slightly hunched over, he still easily stood over Aldrich, who was much shorter. "Let me see your hands," Ivan said, breaking the silence.

Aldrich looked puzzled but reluctantly revealed his hands, palms up. Ivan took them immediately and turned them over on his own. The cuts and minor bruising remained evident from the war they had just endured. "Now you know the horrors of battle, my son, and I pray you never have to see another one in your lifetime."

Aldrich stared at his hands as his father held them. Then, for the first time in weeks, Aldrich looked at his father eye to eye. Ivan's eyes were slightly bloodshot and moist from the tears he had shed moments earlier with Haldair. Aldrich's eyes were also bloodshot, but for a different reason; Ivan realized this.

"How much have you been drinking?" Ivan's voice was calm but firm.

Aldrich gulped, though he couldn't be sure if it was nerves or his stomach trying to heave again. *Here it comes,* he thought. "A little bit, I guess," he replied.

"You look green, Aldrich."

"Maybe a little more than a bit. My apologies if the festivities outside disturbed your rest," Aldrich said, trying to change the subject.

The king shrugged, "They didn't." Ivan glanced out the window and recalled his days as a young man, partying after gloriously won battles. Just another habit he didn't want Aldrich to get sucked into. He walked over to the bed.

Aldrich grew annoyed and impatient, he wasn't sure if it was just the buildup of what had happened so far or the alcohol, but he wouldn't stand for it any longer. "So, what now?" he blurted out. Ivan stopped, but before he could respond, Aldrich pressed further. "What—what is it? Because I was drinking? Is that the new issue now? Is that the new problem I have to work on? No, we are done! I'm never good enough; there's always something!"

Ivan sighed. He had things he wanted to say, but with his son in his current state, it was best to let him finish.

"I am a man, Father!" Aldrich continued. "I'm not a child anymore, and yet you and everyone else treat me like I am one, sometimes like I'm less than one. I know that they say, 'Aldrich did this wrong', or 'Aldrich did that wrong', or 'Aldrich isn't ready', and 'Aldrich screwed up once again'. Everyone, especially you, sees nothing but my flaws! All my life, I have sought your approval, and the way I strived to do that was to be you! And only in the passing weeks have you decided to change yourself. After years, the way of thinking that I thought was the only way was suddenly outdated. It changed. And I'm in the dark. You always speak to me like I'm such a disappointment. Am I a father?" tears began to form in the young prince's eyes.

"Aldrich," Ivan whispered.

"What do I have to do? Must I slay a thousand men? Must I bed a million women? Must I sail to the ends of the world and bring back the heads of the nine gods? Tell me…TELL ME! Am I a disappointment for trying to simply be like you? I looked up to you, I worshipped the ground you walked on, and not even now do you give me your approval—not even now, after I have experienced the hell of battle alongside you…" Ivan took a step toward his son as his voice began to quiet. "Not even now?" Aldrich started to feel choked up as he finished. All the things he'd felt over the years now suddenly poured out.

Ivan slowly walked to Aldrich and stood in front of him. His expression was still emotionless as Aldrich started to cry. After a moment, Ivan grabbed his son and firmly and lovingly embraced him. Aldrich was shocked. "I am proud of you, Aldrich." Confusion was the only emotion the prince could feel. After a moment, Aldrich accepted it and embraced it. "All your life, I have been proud of you. But simply put, I was scared."

The two separate, "Scared of what?"

Ivan glanced at the sword, "I've seen what power can do. What it can do to a king…to a kingdom…to the world." He looked at his son, "I don't want that for you. I never wanted my past to become your future." Aldrich wiped his face as his father returned to the window, "Some powers are too strong for us…beyond our understanding. You need to understand this, Aldrich."

Aldrich scoffed to himself. Whatever heartfelt emotion they shared was lost again as Aldrich felt his father's lack of desire was his weakness. *He just doesn't want me to be as powerful as he is.*

"We are going to plan a more peaceful future, you and I," Ivan said. "With the help of your uncle and Oswald."

Aldrich's anger began to boil again as he connected Ulrich's words to his father's, "Why Oswald? He's just a general."

Ivan glanced over his shoulder, "Don't speak of your friends so poorly, Aldrich." His gaze returned to the window. "Oswald is a leader and probably one of the most capable leaders I know." Ivan's voice fell soft, "If fate had dealt us a different hand, I believe Oswald would have made a great king."

The prince's anger continued to grow as his father spoke. More and more, Aldrich felt that any genuine respect was just words. But now, he knew it to be fact. Ulrich was right.

"You and I will be spending more time together going forward. I need to prepare you for what is to…" Ivan's words are cut short by a sudden cough. More blood. As he finished, the king sat on the bed and grabbed the already bloodied rag from the nightstand to wipe his face. Afterward, he went for a drink before realizing it was empty. "Would you mind filling my cup for me? There is a pitcher on the dresser behind you."

Aldrich said nothing but began to fulfill his father's request and took the cup to the dresser.

"Aldrich. I know I haven't always been the father that…that you deserved," Ivan said weakly as he lay down. "You've been given a great burden to hold on your shoulders. It is something I never would've wished upon myself, and it is unfair of me to place it on my son, but it is for the better of our people…and our future."

Aldrich kept his back to his father and started to fill the cup with water. More thoughts rushed through his mind as Ulrich's voice echoed inside him. *Your men support you. You are the heir of Althalos.* He pulled out the small bottle Ulrich had given him and stared at it momentarily. *It would be unfortunate if your father met his end here.* A tear began to fall down his face as he remembered more. *It wouldn't be such a bad thing…* Aldrich's fist tightened around the vial as a cough from his father broke his thoughts.

"Going forward," Ivan said. "When we return home, I want things to be different. I want us to be closer. No more pawning you off on my generals; I want to start personally overseeing your leadership progress. You fought well today. And I love you, my heir, my son."

Aldrich casually glanced over his shoulder before returning his gaze to the vial in his hand. *Embrace who you are,* more of Ulrich's words whispered in his head. The prince tensed and finished pouring the water. *I think it's too late for that now, Father,* he thought. The cup in one hand, the vial in the other. A slight hesitation as another tear fell from his face and hit the dresser.

Could he finally be all that he knew he could be?

Chapter 37
What No One Saw Coming

Ulrich nervously passed the grounds. Occasionally, he would glance up at the tower where Ivan was and quickly turn away to avoid staring. Whether or not Aldrich would follow through with it was on the prince, but Ulrich knew that if Aldrich failed, he would also be in danger. Ideally, he would've wanted to have more time with Aldrich before having him make such a profound decision. However, circumstances had set this choice up very differently. Only time would tell if it was the right one.

As he moved through the crowd, Ulrich paused sparingly to avoid any long-term confrontation with Oswald. After Haldair took the young prince inside, it was all Ulrich could do to keep away from any chance of another…conversation. The general thought as he walked; having Aldrich take the throne was only one part of his plan, but Oswald was getting too close now and would ruin the further steps he needed. He may have to get rid of him as well. But how?

"Hello, general," the voice cut deep as Ulrich spun to see.

Ulrich groaned, so much so avoidance, "General Cromwell."

"Walk with me," Oswald said. Ulrich tried to resist initially, but any attempt at his excuses eventually became irrelevant. Oswald wouldn't budge. "Walk."

Oswald guided the two as they walked to the outer edge of the crowd. He didn't fully know what Ulrich was trying to do or put in motion, but he intended to find out. He would not let Aldrich be corrupted. Oswald had fought for too long and tried to guide Aldrich as best he could for as long as possible. He'd be damned if all his efforts to help mold Aldrich into even a decent king were ruined by someone just itching for power.

"Oswald, I don't think this is exactly necessary."

Oswald stopped short, "I wish it wasn't."

"Ulrich crossed his arms defiantly; what're you going to do? Kill me? Kill me here with all of our allies watching?"

Oswald glanced around at the crowd, "The option is not off the table yet."

The two stopped near the corner of the main entrance, and Oswald tucked them around the pillar, out of sight of the rest of the party. Ulrich sighed, "So what do you have in mind? Murder? A robbery gone wrong?" He smiled, "Suicide?"

"I haven't quite decided yet," Oswald snapped. "I figured it might just be a detail I could save for later. Or perhaps ambiguity is the easiest route."

"You really think the people, our men, or the KING will accept that?"

Oswald shrugged, "Would they believe it? Perhaps…perhaps not. Will they care enough to figure out the truth? No. You're nothing more than a snake disguised as a man Ulrich. And I have met many men like you, but unfortunately, you have chosen to take up a very threatening position, and that is something I cannot allow anymore." He had no objective evidence of any actual foul play, nor did he know any specifics of anything Ulrich and Aldrich were planning. Nevertheless, he needed some answers. Ulrich had been too elusive to be completely innocent.

"Threatening?" Ulrich scoffed. "Threatening to what, Oswald? You're too scared that you won't be his right hand when Aldrich comes to power anymore." Oswald twitched when they heard the words. He tried not to take it personally, but Ulrich had a minor point. "You already screwed yourself on that; you didn't need me to intervene. That boy is an attention-seeking little bastard, so riddled with father issues that he was so easy to win over, and yet you and all your compatriots tried your hardest to make an enemy out of him. Cause you're scared of him. You know what he can become. You know what he will become."

"I do know," Oswald stated. "And whatever he becomes, he will not become it because of you."

"No," Ulrich confirmed. "He'll become it because that's what he was meant to become. We all have a destiny, Oswald; you can have as little of an effect on him as I can. You must wake up and realize you cannot stop what will happen. No one can! And no one should. Aldrich will be a powerful king, and I will be at his side the whole time."

Oswald had his arm tensed and readied to connect with Ulrich's face when, "Oswald!" The general stepped back to see who called him, and Ulrich attempted to slip away before Oswald stopped him. "Oswald!"

Soon, Thomas' figure staggered through the crowd toward them. How he managed to stay upright, Oswald could only guess. "What is it?" he asked as Thomas reached them.

"Oswald," Thomas paused as he leaned on his friend for support. Oswald winced as the smell of booze perforated his nostrils.

"Well," Oswald urged. "Spit it out, man."

"Ulrich and Aldrich are," Thomas fumbled over his words. "Planning something." Whether he didn't notice or didn't care that Ulrich was standing a mere few feet away was anyone's guess.

Oswald rolled his eyes and glared at Ulrich, who merely raised a brow at the drunk captain. "Explain."

Thomas continued, "I couldn't hear that much, but it was something about Ivan dying sooner rather than later."

A muscle twitched in Ulrich's face, but the others hadn't noticed.

"You're drunk, Thomas," Oswald said. "Go to bed."

"No!"

"Thomas."

The captain grabbed Oswald's tunic, "Yes, I know I'm drunk, but I also know what I heard. Something bad may happen, Oswald."

Oswald helped his friend sit down on a nearby bench. He couldn't rule out what Thomas said in light of the events he witnessed. But in this drunken state, he knew Thomas was far from reliable. That said, even drunk, Thomas was no fool. "I will speak with Aldrich and find out what was said, in the meantime…"

"You can speak with him shortly," Haldair's gruff voice interrupted. The group saw Haldair standing nearby with his two remaining barons, Leon and Merrek, behind him. "We are going to have a meeting. I've already sent people to collect the others to attend. Aldrich will be there, and the two of you must also be there." Haldair was about to turn and walk away when he noticed Ulrich sulking in the shadow. "You too, Ulrich. We have urgent matters to discuss and all must be present."

They met in King Haldair's war room when all the others were assembled. Each stood around his large center table with the map of the nine kingdoms of Kralavia within. "I know this meeting is taking you away from the celebration…and the heartache." Haldair began. They had lost many good men today. Among those were three of his own barons, Clayton, Jacob and Ivor had all been lost in the battle. Bronwyn, the captain of Ivan's personal guard was also lost. However, Haldair knew that some talks must be done before things got out of hand. "I felt that we needed to discuss certain matters under the circumstances before we part ways tomorrow."

Queen Vetrina agreed, "We must send word to the other kingdoms to let them know what happened here and what we've seen."

"What of Carnheller?" asked Leoxtra. "Has any word come from them yet?"

Haldair shook his head, "Nothing that I have here. But I'm more concerned about the power vacuum that King Ordain's death has created." Murmurs of agreement and concern echoed across the room.

As the talk continued, speculations and fear rose through the group about the sudden appearance of the creatures of legend and what purpose they had with Stelmond. Haldair and Leoxtra agreed that, somehow, both Stelmond's attack and the raid at Stelbeck Keep were connected. Vetrina was not as easily convinced at first, but conceded her point as Leoxtra shared more details and the few words that Admiral Mortenson had said.

Merrek and Leon mentioned that they might work with Stelmond's people to transition power appropriately since they were the neighboring country. Oswald agreed and suggested that they also seek to investigate the temperament of the people. "The nation of Stelmond has always been elusive," Oswald said. "We should not assume we know how they will greet us based on Ordain's actions."

Leoxtra concurred. "Do you have enough force to defend yourself properly during this time, Haldair?"

Haldair nodded, "With Ordain gone and his army destroyed, we should have no problems should they decide to push back a bit."

"We still have several of Stelmond's troops held prisoner here," Vetrina began. "We should try to see what they know before we make any final decisions." A chorus of agreement came from the group.

"How is Ivan?" Leon asked.

Haldair and Oswald exchanged glances. Both knew that Ivan's health was failing, but when it would do him in completely was another issue. "He is regaining his strength," Haldair answered. Satisfaction echoed across the room.

"Well, then," Vetrina said. "I think we've missed enough of the celebration, and I, for one…"

A firm knock on the door interrupted the queen mid-thought. The group looked toward the door to see Aldrich slowly entering. His steps were strong, but there was a leeriness in his face. Haldair was the first to speak, "What is the meaning of this, Aldrich?"

The others quickly picked up on what Haldair was referring to; the Golden Sword was around the waist of the young prince. Ulrich did all he could to hold back his smile. Oswald glanced in his direction but didn't say anything. Merrek placed his hand on the hilt of his sword, and murmurs grew around the others.

"My father is dead."

Chapter 38
Suspicions

Oswald wandered the halls of Terrowin Keep alone. He was looking for Haldair, though he already knew where he'd be. King Haldair had not left his brother's side since the announcement from Aldrich the evening prior. No one could blame him, though. The news came as a shock to all of them. Oswald, like the others, wanted to say something, but with Aldrich's tone and the Golden Sword in his possession, for better or worse, all held their tongues.

Haldair was the first to move after the prince's statement as he raced to Ivan's chamber to check for himself. After the initial shock, Leoxtra had Leon and Merrek spread the word and close the celebration outside. General Rollins had sent riders to Althalos and the other kingdoms to share the news.

The events of last night played over and over in Oswald's head as he ascended the final set of stairs. Something didn't sit right with him. Thomas' rant on hearing about some plot seemed more and more likely since the king had appeared to be on the mend when he had last spoken to Haldair and the general. However, Oswald could not overlook the idea that Ivan's injuries were beyond their understanding. Who would say that Ivan took a turn for the worse in those moments after he and Haldair had left him?

The door to Ivan's chamber creaked open as it always had. Oswald sighed; indeed, Haldair had not moved since yesterday evening. The servants had redressed the deceased king, allowing him to rest with regal dignity. But Haldair remained on his knees at the bedside, clutching Ivan's cold and lifeless hand. "Your majesty. You must rest," Oswald said softly. His throat choked a bit.

Haldair raised his head, his eyes bloodshot and still tearing, "Why, Oswald?" He paused to take a deep breath and calm himself, "Why would he be taken from me?"

Oswald knelt beside Haldair and tried to comfort him. "Every one of us has a time, Haldair," he looked at Ivan. "Some sooner than others."

Haldair sniffled, "But he was fine when I left him! He walked across this very room without assistance."

Oswald pondered this statement momentarily. He always struggled with sentiment when talking to Thomas, so here with kings made it more challenging.

"Come, Haldair," he said finally. "We shouldn't stay here."

Oswald awkwardly tried to pull Haldair up to no avail. "I belong with my brother, Oswald."

"You've done everything you can, Haldair. Let me take you back to your chambers; you need some rest and peace…and let your brother have the same." Haldair said nothing and didn't move. "You must come to bed, Haldair; we will travel to Stalbak in the morning."

Haldair sighed as he stood; Oswald was right; they needed to start to move on. Too many things were happening already, and this was only part of the mess they had to deal with. "The Golden Sword is supposed to be at the bottom of the sea, Oswald." The general said nothing. "I'm not going to just sit around the let Aldrich do whatever he wants, especially with that weapon."

"I agree. But there's no telling what Ivan told his son while we were away."

"Ivan would never have backed on his word!" Haldair snapped.

Oswald conceded this point. Despite the prince's words the other night, Ivan would not tell Haldair one thing and then tell his son another. "I'm sure Merrek would love the chance to pry that sword away from him."

Haldair managed a small chuckle at Oswald's comment. "Indeed. Out of everyone there last night, Merrek seemed ready to fight on the spot."

Oswald nodded as he remembered.

The two walked to the door, and Oswald offered to assist the king to his chambers, but Haldair refused. "Do you need anything?"

Haldair shook his head, "No, but thank you for everything." Oswald watched as Haldair's plump figure made its way down the hall. The king had gotten no further than five steps when he stopped suddenly and turned around. "Ivan believed in you more than anyone else on this earth; I know he never would have told you that himself. He had often told me that if he could have chosen his heir, it would have been you."

Oswald humbly dropped his head. "I live to serve, my king."

Haldair nodded, "Which is why you have always been a man to follow, Oswald, a true leader. Ivan saw it, and so did I. You are destined for great things, general."

"Thank you, Haldair."

Haldair smiled and turned away. "Aldrich will need you before the end, Oswald. Whether he sees it now or not. And Your name will be remembered, Oswald Cromwell, that I know for certain."

The king's voice echoed down the hall as he walked away, which left Oswald alone to ponder his word. But he wasn't the only one to hear Haldair's words. Ulrich, who had been following Oswald in hopes of finding out what he knew about Ivan's death had been sulking around the corner. After hearing Haldair's final comment, Ulrich left to report this news to Aldrich. *We'll see how long you last when I tell the king this news, General Cromwell.*

Oswald glanced back into Ivan's room. Memories played in his head as he approached the bed; Ivan had been like a father to Oswald since he began to rise up the ranks of the king's army. Although Oswald didn't show, Ivan's death affected him as much as Haldair.

He admired the lavianite and gold inlays on Ivan's armor, the crown of Althalos etched on the center of the breastplate. It was similar in style to the rest of the army's armor; however, Ivan's was more heavily decorated as king. With a final sigh and brief goodbye, Oswald turned to leave. He stopped suddenly as his foot struck something under the bed.

Curious, he knelt to inspect the object, only to find it was the empty mug. Oswald recalled his conversation with Ivan as he held that very same mug in his hand. So many things he should've said, some things he didn't need to.

So many years ago, he and Thomas were eager to fight, and Ivan took them in. Tears began forming as he sat there. His feelings finally getting the better of him. "We didn't want to serve; we just wanted a fight." He looked at the dead king, "Oh, how things have changed." The general took a deep breath to try and stop the tears, "Thank you, Ivan Ventril. Thank you for who you made me to become."

After a moment, Oswald looked down at the cup in his hands. He rotated the mug gently as he tried to relax and compose himself. He paused when he looked inside; a white, partially dissolved substance was resting at the bottom. The pitcher was only used for water. *Medicine perhaps?* He thought as he brushed it with his finger. Then Thomas' words echoed again in his mind:

Or something more sinister?

Chapter 39
The Funeral

Stalbak, Althalos

Solemn hearts and grim expressions greeted the procession entering the city. King Haldair led the way with Aldrich at his side. Behind them were Althalos's generals, along with Thomas and several others. Further back, surrounded by his personal guard, was King Ivan. Though the carriage was enclosed, it was intricately carved, and the black stained wood contrasted nicely against the gold trim. The sun shone brightly over the area, glistening off the lavianite within the structures and on the troops' armor; still, no cheerful smile nor victory cries were uttered.

Flags of Althalos were draped along the way. The blue and white colors could be seen everywhere as the people showed their love for their fallen king. Haldair and Aldrich didn't speak on the way in. But Aldrich didn't mind, the less conversation, the better. The Golden Sword hung at his side, which more than caught the eyes of the people as he passed them.

When they arrived at the castle, Laura, Wully, and Alfred stood on the steps to greet them. Aldrich and Laura exchanged glances, but her eyes were fixed on her brother, who rode in behind Ivan's carriage. Merrek set his eyes on the group as he rode up and greeted them. After the initial exchange, Haldair escorted Ivan to the Great Hall to prepare the ceremony while the others entered.

Despite being gone for several weeks, only a little conversation occurred between the group. Laura and Aldrich exchanged a few words, and though she tried to find words to express some news to him, she couldn't bring herself to share it—not yet, anyway. This silence was just as well since the officials quickly gathered the prince as they needed to question him about the events of the war and Ivan's fate in the aftermath. Laura stood nearby as Aldrich conversed with the others. More thoughts raced through her mind as she watched her husband's hand never let go of the sword at his side.

Wully, Merrek, and Oswald awkwardly stood off to one side of the main hall within the castle. Wully shared a bit about the brothers, Alfred and Douglas. But after that, his topics of conversation quickly ran out. The visions began to race through his mind again as he recalled Ivan standing proud on a battlefield, immediately followed by Aldrich being crowned king. Fear crept into him as he stood there, realizing that the events were coming true, and gave Wully pause as he processed the rest of the events and how they would fit together. He was hesitant to share this information with Oswald and Merrek just yet, which only exacerbated the silence surrounding them.

Merrek felt no particular way about the lack of conversation. After he greeted Laura upon his arrival, he was dismissed by the others as Aldrich and Laura took precedence from the gathering crowd. So, he stood with Oswald and Wully but focused on the prince and his sister.

The following morning, everyone gathered in the Great Hall. Two months ago, it held a joyous and exciting event as the prince and his new bride married. Now, the mood was sullen and dreary as the funeral for their king commenced. The nine old gods stood as they always had between the windows on the far end of the hall. Though their golden hue was not enough to brighten the room or the feeling of those within this time.

Gathar stood under the gods at the end of the room overlooking the crowd gathered within. The public, which had spilled out into the courtyard, was still difficult to contain as members from the other kingdoms had shown up to pay their respects to the fallen king.

"Ladies and gentlemen, esteemed guests and royal court members," he began. "Today, we gather here in solemn remembrance and heartfelt tribute to honor the passing of our beloved king, Ivan Ventril. We stand together, unified in our grief, to bid farewell to a monarch who guided our nation with wisdom, strength, and unwavering dedication."

Gathar's words were solid and accurate, but nothing would bring the cheer back to the people there that day. The sun shone brightly, reflecting beautifully off the woven lavianite within the dark-colored clothing of the Althalothians in attendance. The other nations stood intermingled with the locals as they also paid their respects to the fallen king. A cool breeze swept over the area as the autumn air moved in; the windows were open, allowing his voice to carry to the crowd outside in the courtyard. "Ivan Ventril was not merely a ruler; he was a beacon of hope. A symbol of unity and a custodian of justice. His reign marked an era of progress, prosperity, and profound compassion after the Great War of our forefathers. We are here today to reflect upon the immense contributions and indelible legacy a truly exceptional leader left behind…"

Gathar continued, "Throughout his reign, Ivan Ventril governed with the utmost integrity and a deep-rooted sense of responsibility toward his people. His unwavering commitment to justice and fairness instilled a sense of trust and security within our society. Under his benevolent rule, the welfare of the citizens was always at the forefront, and no voice was left unheard. King Ivan embodied the noblest qualities of a true leader, fostering an environment where every individual was valued, and their aspirations cherished."

Oswald looked to his left, studying each column of people in turn. While the people stood where they could outside the walls of the Great Hall, within, the Five Crown Alliance was columned to allow each kingdom to take their spot. Valkos was in the far-left column, Haldair at the front, along with his barons and the rest of the nobility. The general looked at Haldair for a moment, and he could read the emotions on his face immediately. Haldair had not only lost a brother, but he lost a brother when he wasn't looking. When he wasn't there by his side when he assumed that his brother would be alright. Oswald knew that, in some way, Haldair felt responsible.

Directly behind King Haldair was Merrek. His face was neutral; he couldn't honestly care less about Ivan's death. Oswald knew he never cared for the royalty in Kralavia. Merrek respected Ivan, of course, but whatever emotion he held today was a mix of fear and hatred. Fear because the Althalothian king was dead and hatred for who he knew would take his place.

"…Beyond his remarkable governance," Gathar said. "Ivan Ventril was a visionary whose foresight shaped our nation's destiny. He championed education, recognizing that knowledge is the cornerstone of progress. His unwavering support for the arts and sciences fostered creativity and innovation, making our kingdom a hub of intellectual advancement. Ivan Ventril's dedication to the pursuit of knowledge and his passion for learning will forever remain an inspiration for generations to come…"

Oswald continued to scan the crowd. Althalos was the column to the left of the main walkway from the doors leading up to the podium beneath the gods. At the front of it were Aldrich and Laura, followed by anyone else of nobility, title, and wealth. He watched Aldrich standing in the row before him. The prince only had a little expression as he stared at his father's stone coffin. It's as though the night before drained all emotion from him. Aldrich's face looked stern and blank; his eyes looked as though they were not staring at Ivan but rather through him, lost in thought. Next to him, Laura looked sad, not on her behalf, but mainly for the others. She didn't know Ivan personally but always respected his name and what he had done.

Ivan was a good and honest king and an excellent brother to Haldair, whom she did know very well. She was sad for her husband, sorry for

Haldair, and sad for the people of Althalos, for which she would now be responsible. Personally, Laura's vision of marriage was a more traditional one, and she now would never get the chance to have any sort of relationship with her father-in-law. Oswald noticed that Laura looked uneasy; even through the sadness. She stood firm but held her lower stomach as if in pain.

"Moreover, our king was a unifying force," Gathar stated as his speech continued. "He bridged divides, healed wounds, and brought together people from all walks of life. It was under his rule that the Five Crown Alliance came to be formed, the greatest unified force Kralavia has ever seen. His diplomatic prowess and tireless efforts to build bridges of understanding forged lasting alliances with neighboring realms and fostered peaceful coexistence. Ivan Ventril's commitment to fostering unity and cooperation serves as a shining example in an often-tumultuous world…"

To his right across the aisle, Oswald saw Vasalia. King Leoxtra at the head, followed by his own group of nobility. Leoxtra had a look, not of sadness, but rather, respect, on his face. Though he and Ivan were not what one would call 'friends' and had very different ways of thinking, Leoxtra always respected Ivan as a man and as a king. He felt as though Ivan understood him well, which was rare as Leoxtra's over-the-top personality could sometimes throw people off or cause them to cast an unfair judgment on his quality as a leader—as Oswald himself knew well. But King Ivan had always respected Leoxtra and was always more than fair. Leoxtra was truly sad to see him go.

"…As we bid farewell to our beloved king, let us not dwell solely on the sadness of his passing. Instead, let us celebrate a life well-lived, an extraordinary reign that has left an indelible mark on our nation's history. Let us honor his memory by carrying forward the values he held dear— compassion, justice, strength, and a relentless pursuit of excellence…"

As Gathar continued, Oswald brought his attention to the column on the far right. Halika, and Queen Vetrina Dogas at the front. Beside her was King Rolland Gallant from Taureau. None from his court came with him, and Oswald couldn't blame them. The same could be said of the absence of King Joshua from Alnirya and King Forest from Ornion. In all honesty, King Gallant was present as emotional support for Vetrina more than he was to show respect to Ivan.

Oswald observed that the queen's face was stern, showing no sadness or emotion. Ivan was an ally, it's true. But his death strikes her more as an inconvenience. She was a part of the Five Crown Alliance because Ivan had been the man he was after the reforming of the kingdoms took place. King Rolland disagreed with this, but Vetrina didn't care. She always respected Ivan as he respected her, but that was as far as their relationship ever went. Still, she knew now that Ivan was dead, the politics would change for her in the north, especially against the Dun-mar.

"…To our departed king, we offer our deepest gratitude for his selfless service and unwavering dedication. Your memory will forever be etched in our hearts, and your wisdom will guide us through the trials that lie ahead. As we navigate the path forward, we shall draw strength from the legacy you have left behind—a legacy of progress, unity, and the unyielding spirit of our great nation of Althalos."

The historian's voice rang through the Great Hall, and the crowd was silent as he spoke. The respect Ivan had gained from his people as well as the people from his allies, was immense and could still be felt here. Sorrow was also an overwhelming emotion, so much so that Oswald felt as if the statues of the gods themselves were also sharing in the grief.

"…May you find eternal peace, dear Ivan Ventril. May your soul rest in tranquility, knowing that your people will continue to honor your vision, uphold your values, and strive for a better world, guided by your exemplified principles."

The general continued to look around, mainly to keep himself from breaking down. Ivan was the only real father figure Oswald has had in his life, and his death hurt him very deeply, though he didn't show it like most did. He has never been the type to openly display emotions, for better or worse.

"…Farewell, our noble king. Your reign may have ended, but your legacy shall forever endure," Gathar closed his speech, and the crowd took a moment of silence and bowed their heads. "We will now hear words from Haldair Ventril, King of Valkos and its people, and brother to our late King, Ivan Ventril."

Gathar stepped aside as King Haldair approached the podium. Haldair looked across the crowd, "Ivan…" he began. His voice wavered, and he cleared his throat to start again. "Ivan was a good man, a man I always looked up to and a man I always aspired to be like. He was a man we all respected regardless of our feelings toward him. He was…" he paused. "He was a good man."

There was a moment of silence as Haldair looked down at his paper. He took a few deep breaths and slowly regained his composure. After a moment, he looked up at the people watching him; his eyes were moist from the tears he had been fighting to keep at bay.

"Ivan was a good king; he had the respect and the support of his people," Haldair said. "And he had such an impact during his reign that he also had the respect and support of our allies, the members of the Five Crown Alliance, and the people in those kingdoms. He was a man that led this country from the pain the Great War had caused into an age of peace and prosperity for all of us. He established new forms of trade and policies that improved the country of Althalos and the countries of our allies." He glanced down again, "Ivan was a great king."

Tears fell as Haldair could no longer hold back, "But before these things, Ivan was a son, a father." He exchanged a brief nod with Aldrich. "And…and a brother," he sobbed. "He was my brother, my first friend and companion, my guardian through my childhood, and a person I held nothing but love and respect for."

Oswald watched as Haldair fidgeted with the papers on the podium. Tears were dropping hard as the broken king continued. "I wrote this on the journey here from Terrowin. I don't think it does justice to the man he was, but I will read it for you now."

Haldair began:

On fields of battles, we bravely fought,
A bond of blood so profoundly wrought.
My fallen brother, now at rest,
These words I speak with heaviness pressed.

Through childhood's days, we roamed as one,
Our laughter echoed beneath the sun.
Side by side, in mischief and glee,
Together we were forever free.

As time flew by, we faced life's tests,
Shoulder to shoulder, we met the best.
Through joys and sorrows, hand in hand,
Our brotherhood, an unbreakable band.

I remember your smile, bright as the stars,
Your courage blazed like fiery mars.
Your gentle soul, compassionate and kind,
Forever is etched within my mind.

Oh, fallen brother, my heart will weep,
For the memories held, so close, so deep.
In dreams, you'll visit a beacon light,
Guiding me through this eternal night.

Though you are gone, I'll carry your flame,
Honor your name and etch it in fame.
Your spirit lives on forever more,
In every beat of my heart's core.

So rest, dear brother, in peaceful slumber,
Know that your sacrifice shan't be a blunder.
For I'll cherish your love, your valor, your worth,
And keep your spirit alive on earth.

Though my tears may fall, my spirit won't break,
In brotherhood's bond, forever I'll make,
A promise to you, my fallen kin,
To honor your memory through thick and thin.

So, goodbye for now, until again we shall meet,
In Athalon's arms, where eternity greets.
Know that I love you, my brother; so true,
And in my heart, forever, I will always hold you.

Haldair made it through his poem before he began to break at the end. Gathar approached the sobbing king and gestured for him to return to his seat.

"Thank you, King Haldair Ventril." He raised his hands, "Athalon, father and creator, we ask that our great King Ivan Ventril be passed easily from your world into your arms forevermore."

"Forevermore," the crowd echoed.

Chapter 40
Absolute Power…

"Aldrich!" Oswald called. He was speaking to Gathar and Neilith among the crowd gathered in the garden. After Ivan's body was placed in the tomb beneath the Great Hall alongside his father, most of the patrons in attendance remained within the castle grounds to mingle and express their condolences to the royal family.

The prince turned around. "Oswald."

"Why didn't you speak for your father?"

"I spoke with Gathar and requested that I not speak during the ceremony." Gathar nodded in acknowledgment behind the prince.

"Why?"

"I didn't feel I needed to," Aldrich responded coldly. "I'm his son; everyone should know how I feel right now." He turned back to the other two. "Now I have other things to attend to, Oswald. Thank you."

Oswald was about to protest when he spotted Ulrich heading his way. As more people gathered around the prince, General Cromwell retreated slowly. He didn't like the prince's sudden change in attitude since the king's death. The lack of remorse and Ulrich's whispering in his ear gave him reason to be suspicious. But he tried to shake the thought. *This is proof of nothing,* he thought as he wandered back to the Great Hall. As he entered, he noticed Haldair standing near the statue of Denesious and made his way through the crowd to the stout king.

Meanwhile, in the courtyard, the prince felt a soft hand on his shoulder, "Aldrich?" came a familiar voice.

The prince turned and greeted his wife, "Yes, Laura."

"I need to talk to you about something, Aldrich." She glanced around the gardens, "Privately?"

Aldrich scoffed, "Can it wait? I have some important things to attend to right away."

"Please, Aldrich," Laura insisted as she grabbed his arm. "This is important."

"Enough!" Aldrich snapped. He yanked his arm away and brought his hand up striking his wife across the face. Without hesitation, Aldrich immediately turned and walked away with Ulrich.

As the people bustled around her, a silent tear fell from her eyes as she gently placed her hands on her stomach. Her face throbbed, but she managed to hold her composure. No one seemed to notice, and those that may have said nothing.

After a moment, Laura looked around and through the crowd, she locked eyes with Wully. Her throat began to choke up as she wondered if he had seen what happened. Furthermore, with the news she needed to share with the prince, Laura was unsure how to share that with Wully. Before Wully could blink, she quickly shuffled off to the far edge of the gardens. There it was more secluded and, in the company of the decorative flowers of Stalbak, Laura broke down.

She didn't get more than a few minutes when her brother called out to her. Laura wiped the tears away quickly, "Merrek!"

The two greeted each other and embraced in a warm hug. "I'm here, Laura."

"Merrek, there's something I need to tell you."

Earnestness showed on Merrek's face, "What is it?" Before Laura could answer, he knew. Her head had dropped, and his eyes followed as Laura's hands still caressed her torso. "Are you sure?"

Laura nodded, "Yes, Merrek." If he hadn't seen the altercation, she wasn't going to bring it up. She knew that her brother would already be upset enough as it was.

Merrek's expression was pure joy for his sister but immediately turned to anger as he thought, "That rat bastard…"

Oswald and Haldair stood in silence for some time as the broken king stared up at the face of the god of his country. "Do you think they are still out there?" Oswald said, breaking the silence. "Or if they even care about the happenings of this world?"

"I know they do."

Haldair never broke his gaze, and his swift response surprised Oswald. "I wonder what it was like when they lived among us?"

"It was a better time, Oswald," the king sighed. "Before the Great War, that is." There was another moment of silence between the two as Haldair continued to look upon the statue of Denesious. Oswald's eyes danced across the others as well. "I would give anything to get your words of wisdom right now."

Oswald looked over, not knowing how to answer the question and also wondering why it was asked in the first place. He was not known for his wisdom in sorrow-filled times, especially with Thomas. But after seeing Haldair's expression next to him, he realized the question wasn't for him, but for Denesious.

As Ulrich led Aldrich away from the crowd, he pulled the prince close, "My king, I need to speak with you about something."

"I'm not king yet, Ulrich," Aldrich replied. "What do you need?"

Ulrich bowed his head, "My apologies, my lord." He realized that Aldrich had not yet embraced his new role, and so he continued with his questions. "When is the coronation?"

"Eight days from now, I'm told. There is a seven-day mourning period for the death of a king, you know that."

Ulrich leaned in close, "Would it not make more sense to have the coronation tomorrow? It would be before the nobles leave, and I think your coronation may be better received by the other rulers if they were here to see it themselves."

The prince pondered momentarily before raising his eyebrow, "Can that be done?"

"You're going to be king, Aldrich," Ulrich smiled as he placed his hand on the prince's shoulder. "You can do anything."

Aldrich agreed and immediately looked around for Gathar, who he found across the garden near the Cradinlings main display, speaking to members of Leoxtra's court. "Sir, I need a word."

Gathar excused himself from his conversation and turned to the prince, "Of course, milord."

Aldrich glanced at Ulrich, who had followed, and nodded in assurance to the young prince. He then turned his attention back to Gathar, "We will have the coronation tomorrow. Have people come through to take down the funeral decor and replace it with only the colors of Althalos."

"But, but…" Gathar stammered in shock. "But my lord, that cannot be done."

Aldrich caressed the hilt of the Golden Sword in its sheath. "It can and it will. Make it happen, or you won't be any more fortunate than your predecessor." Gathar nodded, and Ulrich took his cue to speak to him about the coronation details as Aldrich excused himself and sought out the closest personal guard he saw. "I need you to carry a message to the members of the Five Crowns for me."

Chapter 41
Tensions Rising

Oswald quickened his pace down the long hall. He had only just heard about Aldrich's plan with the coronation and was heading to find Haldair. But from the shouting and wailing that echoed through the castle—it seemed the news had already reached the king.

Leon passed the general as he got closer to the source of the noise. "Haldair?" he asked as he gestured further.

"Yes," he nodded in agreement. "Merrek is with him."

Oswald rolled his eyes and continued, "Oh, this will be fun."

"The nerve of that…!" Haldair's voice bellowed loudly as Oswald reached the door. Carefully, he opened the door and peered inside but quickly pulled back as the vase came hurling at the wall next to him with a crash. "…that pompous little…pup!"

Oswald stepped through and paused in astonishment. The room was utterly destroyed. Merrek stood across from Haldair against the outer wall while the king paced within the chamber. "I take it you've heard then," Oswald said as he entered.

Haldair's face boiled, and he kicked a small chair across the room into the wall, "Indeed I have!"

"We found out as the guests were leaving earlier this evening," Merrek said.

Haldair scoffed, "By Athalon, that boy will face the wrath of me."

"Easy now," Oswald said. He grabbed the chair that had been kicked against the wall and set it upright, gesturing to Haldair to sit. Then he turned to Merrek, "What all do you know?"

"Aldrich ordered the Temple of the Gods be redecorated overnight for his coronation tomorrow morning."

Oswald dropped his jaw. He knew it was happening tomorrow, but to what extent and how it would be done were details he did not have.

Merrek nodded, "Yes, Oswald, it's happening as we speak."

Oswald looked at Haldair, who had finally calmed down a bit. They meet eyes for a moment, but Oswald could feel the anger of the stout king, more so than Oswald has ever felt from Haldair in all his years of knowing the man.

"So, what of the mourning period?" Oswald asked. "Will the people not have but a night to grieve for their king?"

"The people of Althalos will grieve for many years to come, Oswald," said Haldair. "Regardless of the mourning period. But this is disgraceful! He shows no compassion or respect for my brother…his father!"

"Perhaps I could speak with Aldrich," Oswald suggested. "Maybe I can persuade him to change his mind."

"Good luck Oswald," Haldair scoffed. "He has been sealed away for the night and will not be taking guests, per order of Aldrich Ventril, Crowned Prince of Althalos," he finished sarcastically.

Merrek smiled, then turned to the general, "Something needs to be done, Oswald."

"I agree, but if I can't get to him tonight, I don't know what can be done."

"Nothing can be done now," Haldair said as he shifted in his seat. "The damage is already done, and the disgrace is already bestowed. I've had my rant; let's just retire for the night; it will be another long day tomorrow." Neither man said anything momentarily before continuing, "Merrek, we leave tomorrow for Terrowin right after the coronation. I can't stand to be here any longer and watch this spiral."

"Um, yes, milord," Merrek replied skeptically.

"Leave me."

Oswald made his way to the door with Merrek. As they left, the baron turned around, "My lord, is there nothing we can do about…"

"I have just lost my brother!" Haldair exploded out of his seat. "I don't need any more bickering, plotting, or questioning! I need silence now! I need peace and silence! Now leave me!" Merrek bowed and said nothing as he and Oswald left the room. Haldair slumped into his chair again and muttered, "Let me grieve my brother in peace, though this place no longer has any." Before Oswald shut the door, Haldair raised his head, "Thank you both for being here with me; I apologize for my anger; it wasn't meant to be directed at either of you."

"No apologies needed, your majesty," Oswald said. "Your anger is warranted."

Oswald closed the door and met Merrek, who was waiting for him further down the hall, "Something needs to be done, Oswald," the baron said as he matched Oswald's stride. "If this is how Aldrich is going to start his rule, then his rule shouldn't start at all."

"What do you suggest we do then, Merrek? Kill the prince? He grew up under me; he's almost a brother."

"No," Merrek sighed. "I don't know what we can do; I just know we can't sit idly by and let it all happen!"

Oswald tried to reassure him, "Aldrich is harmless, Merrek…"

"Harmless?" Merrek exclaimed. "If he is so harmless, why did you even threaten Ulrich?"

Oswald shot him a questioning glance, "How did you?"

"Yes, Oswald, I saw you hit him, and I know why because I see it too. His words are poison."

Oswald stopped walking as they reached the junction to another hall, "Ulrich is the threat, not Aldrich. That said, there's no telling how much Ulrich's words have already sunk their teeth into the lad." He shrugged, "Regardless, there isn't anything we can do; threats only go so far, and Ulrich is protected. Aldrich will be king tomorrow, and that's it."

Merrek conceded his point and was about to call it a night when his face lit up, "Call in a witan, pass a vote of no confidence, and you take the throne."

"What?" Oswald could barely process what he just heard. Ivan had in the past mentioned that he thought that Oswald would make a great king. But the general never took it as more than that, a compliment of his character. He never dreamed that he would ever actually sit on the throne.

Merrek excitedly stepped closer, "Ivan always favored you; everyone knows this. And besides, you're more worthy of it than anyone I know in this country."

"I don't know how to rule."

"Of course you do; you're one of the finest generals I've ever seen."

"Yes, I can lead an army," Oswald protested. "But doing that and leading an entire kingdom are two very different things, Merrek."

Merrek nodded, "Well, either way, Oswald, your kingdom is about to be ruled under the thumb of a man who can do neither. Are you prepared to see that?"

The general shook his head, "Regardless, Merrek, a vote of no confidence is not a law in Althalos; that's Valkos' thing. So either way, Ivan's successor would be the one on the throne. Now, shall we move on with our evening or stand in the hall whispering intensely?"

Merrek looked back and forth down the hall; he'd almost forgotten where they were. "This isn't even my country; I still pity your people. If I were in your power position, I would do more in this situation."

Before Oswald could respond, Merrek stormed off down the hall. Oswald stood silently and alone for some time, processing the recent events and what Merrek had just shared. He couldn't deny the pieces of truth in Merrek's words, but he couldn't bring himself to abandon the prince and cast him away so quickly. In war, things always seemed so black and white to Oswald, but now…it was all shades of gray.

Meanwhile…

Laura had remained at the far end of the garden through the remainder of the gathering after the service. As the crowd slowly withdrew, she felt more and more at peace. It was dusk, and the Cradinlings were beginning to glow around her. They were woven in their intricate designs as the colors lit up the courtyard. Though the light brightened the area around Laura, she found little comfort in tonight's display. So many things to process, so many feelings. She still needed to speak to Aldrich, but now, she was afraid. Fearful of what he would do or want in light of the news she bore. He'll need to know at some point; she won't be able to hide it for long.

"Laura?" a soft voice said behind her.

Laura turned, and a gentle smile grew, "Wully." She stood to greet him and hugged him tightly.

"Is everything alright?" he asked. "No one has seen you since the ceremony. What happened?"

Laura glanced down and returned to the bench she had been seated on; Wully sat beside her and took her hand in his. She smiled, but as her eyes met his, tears began to trickle down her face.

"Oh, Wully," she started. "I'm sorry."

"Sorry for what?" he asked.

Laura recounted her conversation with her husband earlier and mentioned how angry he got and struck her before she could tell him the news. Wully asked what she was trying to say to him; she placed her hand on her abdomen and looked down, "I'm pregnant."

Wully's heart dropped. The child wasn't his, but he knew that once Aldrich had heirs to his throne, any chance of them staying close or being together significantly dropped. Though no tears fell, his eyes began to water. *"Wully,"* the voice in his head called out to him again. *"Remember."* Wully glanced around and then back at Laura, who still had her head down. Then he saw it; in his mind, the visions came again, but this time they were less intense and moved quickly until he reached the one of him and Laura.

Wully remembered the vision of the two together:

Laura began to cry. Take care of him, Wully, please. The older version of himself responded. I will, my love. He is yours; he will be everything to me. He will be all I have left of you... Wully began to cry. Laura lethargically put her finger to Wully's lips. He is ours, Wully. That's what I want for him; I want him to know...

As the vision faded, Wully blinked away the tears, gently placed his hand under Laura's chin, and raised her head. "I will always be with you," he said softly. "I have loved you a long time, and I can't imagine my life without you."

Laura smiled, pulled his hand to her cheek, and drew close. She ran her finger through Wully's hair and kissed him. The surprise in Wully only lasted a second as he embraced Laura. "I will always love you, Wulfred Siggard," she said as she pulled away. "I will do my duties to Aldrich and the Althalothian people. But I will ensure that you are with me."

Chapter 42
Corrupts Absolutely

Despite the murmurs of dissatisfaction with the ceremony, the coronation went very smoothly. The visiting crowd was significantly less than it was for Ivan's funeral; most of the extended courts that came to show their respects to the deceased king had already left for home. Apart from the leading members of the Five Crown Alliance and the local court of Althalos, very few were there to show support for the new king.

The Great Hall held the ceremony—despite the protests of some. Laura stood next to Wully and Merrek, and though they didn't show it, she could feel the tension radiating off them. Merrek's thoughts were still running through various scenarios about to displace the newly crowned king.

Wully, on the other hand, glanced up at Denesious' statue overlooking the stage; his vision of Aldrich being crowned king played again in his mind. He wasn't there to see Ivan fight with Stelmond, but he knew what had happened if his visions were true. Now, Aldrich being crowned king means two of his visions have come true. The more he thought about this, the more it worried him. Were the visions shown to him so he could stop them? Or was there something else he was supposed to do with the information? When will the others come to pass? Wully glanced at Laura out of the corner of his eye. What would mean of the visions of the two of them?

After the ceremony, Aldrich gathered the alliance's leaders in his father's study. The center table is made of a long, solid dark wood. In the center was a carving of five crowns intertwined with each other. Ivan had identical tables made for each of the others so that no matter which kingdom hosted, they always had the same table to meet and plan around.

A disgruntled Haldair was in attendance with Leon and Merrek. Aldrich had his three generals, Oswald, Rollins, and Ulrich. King Leoxtra had one general and a few nobles, and Vetrina was accompanied by a few of her commanders. Each person gathered around the table with Aldrich at the head. The king wore similar clothes to what his father wore, and the crown of Althalos sat on his head.

"Leaders of the Five Crowns, friends, allies," Aldrich began. "Thank you for meeting with me today, and my deepest apologies that it is under such unfortunate and unforeseen circumstances." The guests at the table sat quietly and seemed more as if they were humoring the new king rather than actually listening as Aldrich continued. "The passing of my father is most troubling. Kralavia has lost a legendary leader, but rest assured that in his place, I intend to bring forth a new expansive, prosperous era. You shall see the growth of power by hand and the destruction of our enemies."

"Our enemies have already been vanquished. You know this," Vetrina interjected. "Or have you forgotten the reason for which so much blood was shed the past several weeks?"

"I have forgotten nothing," Aldrich snapped. "I have not forgotten the blood, nor the sacrifice, nor the fact that though we have won a battle or two in the past few weeks, the war is far from over."

Leoxtra smiled, "What are your intentions, Prince Aldrich? Our enemies are all but wiped out, we have no reason to assume the war will continue apart from some light skirmishes here and there, but we're all used to that and can handle each one in our own way."

Murmurs of agreement moved across the table. Aldrich clenched his fists but relaxed as he met Ulrich's reassuring gaze, "Prince?" he asked. "My dear King Leoxtra, have I not yet earned the respect that is required for you to call me by my rightful title?"

Leoxtra's nostrils flared. "There has been a coronation, yes. But you have done nothing in my eyes to have earned the title you say you possess; until then, nothing has changed."

Aldrich gently gripped the Golden Sword that hung at his waist, "Everything is about to change, my friends. Our enemies will retreat; they will crawl back to their lands, lick their wounds, and regroup. In short order, Kralavia will be facing yet another siege by hostile forces intent on our collective destruction, only this time, it will not be so easy to drive them back. They will gather others to their cause, numbers unlike any we've seen before."

Leoxtra sat dumbfounded, "What proof do you have of this?"

"What more proof do you require, Lord Leoxtra?"

"There has been no indication of any sort of retaliation!"

"I would have to agree with Leoxtra on this one, Aldrich," Haldair said. "Stelmond has relinquished the Valkon land they took, and not only that, but they also set free the prisoners of war so they could come home, and they have asked that we do the same with the prisoners we took. That doesn't sound like a country about to attack again."

Leoxtra nodded in agreement, "So I ask again, what proof is there?"

"Isn't the very nature of our enemies not proof enough?" Aldrich asked, ignoring Haldair's comments.

"No, boy. It is not," Leoxtra fumed. "Many lives have already been lost. I'm not interested in getting involved in yet another conflict so soon. Especially one that isn't warranted."

"Nor am I," Vetrina chimed in.

The young king ignored them as he made his way around the table, fingering the sword's hilt gently from his belt. "I am proposing a counterattack. Against Carnheller and against Stelmond, and lastly, against those rats from the Dead Lands that slaughtered innocent Althalothian villagers. The demise of their allies will follow suit. We must gather our full strength, raise the taxes and put it all into the production of siege weapons and the growth of our armies and fleet. Every able-bodied lad able to carry a weapon will be recruited for this to be done. When this is over, the number of resources that could be pulled from newly conquered lands will open up new possibilities for trade, manufacturing, wealth…"

Leoxtra slammed his fists into the table and stood. "We are NOT interested, Aldrich! What is this?"

Haldair also rose, "This alliance was made to defend these lands and our people! To protect and provide! We are not warmongers, Aldrich!"

Queen Vetrina agreed, "Ivan would never have suggested this."

Aldrich smiled with annoyance, "Right you are, my friends. That is why the alliance was formed. My family formed it; my father was a noble warrior in his time, but in the end, he lost something; His backbone."

Haldair and Leoxtra glanced at each other and back at the new king. Aldrich stopped at his chair and continued, "My father became weak; he forgot what is needed to be a king, the ability to take the fight to your enemy, the understanding that sometimes to reach peace, one must start a war. I have this ability that he lacked, and I have this understanding. I am ready to do what needs to be done, and it appears that the first thing to be done is disbanding this now pointless alliance."

Shock and gasps filled the room. Whispers soon became apparent as concern and anxiety flooded the scene. Aldrich watched as he proceeded to walk around the table once more. More of the members rose from their seats as the conversations began to intensify. Haldair was the first to address Aldrich directly after his statement. "Aldrich?"

"Calm yourself, Uncle," Aldrich said. "This is not a declaration of war by any means. Well…" he paused and glanced up. "I guess that depends on how reasonable you are willing to be. You will not ride to war with me; fair enough. But I intend to go through with this, and in the end, there is no army greater than my own."

"Then take your army and fight your own wars," Vetrina stated. "If this alliance is over, then I do not wish to have any part of this any longer." She locked eyes with Aldrich as she began to leave. "I will leave then if I no longer hold business here in Althalos."

"I require your assistance nonetheless, Vetrina. If not by manpower than by financial power." Aldrich then turned to address the rest of the room, "Your kingdoms will pay a handsome tribute once a month. This will show good faith and will exclude your lands from my conquest. An Althalothian outpost will also be established in your kingdoms, ensuring that you are under my protection as long as you stay in line."

"Who exactly do you think you're talking to, boy?" Leoxtra barked.

"I am talking to my loyal subjects, Leoxtra!" Aldrich snapped back. "Unless this is not the case. I would be happy to rediscuss it."

"All you've proven to be capable of discussing is how much horse dung comes from your mouth!" Leoxtra turned to Haldair, "And you willingly stand by and let this…this boy carry our weapon?"

Aldrich gripped the hilt of the Golden Sword tightly. His eyes were a blaze of fury, but Leoxtra wouldn't back down. "You can't do this, Aldrich," a voice said firmly. The tension broke as Aldrich and the others turned to see Rollins as he stepped up the table. Oswald's face remained in shock while Ulrich gave Aldrich a look of approval.

"Care to speak up, General?" Aldrich asked.

Oswald recovered from his initial shock and grabbed Rollins' arm, "Don't, it's not worth it."

"How about you stay out of this, Oswald," Aldrich said, gazing at Rollins. "General Rollins has something to say."

Oswald was taken aback, shocked by the young king's newfound attitude. He glanced down and noticed that Aldrich was still white knuckling the hilt of the Golden Sword. Rollins took a breath and stepped forward. "Your father had so many plans for the future, Aldrich," he began. "He wanted peace and prosperity, not just for Althalos, Terrowin, or the Five Crowns but for all of Kralavia. This…what you're suggesting is not peace, and it will never lead to peace. This will only lead to destruction. You will destroy everything. What you're suggesting, Lord Aldrich is a conquest, not peace. And I don't think that is in the best interest of the future of Kralavia."

Silence.

No one moved or spoke while waiting for Aldrich to respond to Rollins' statement. After what seemed like an eternity, Aldrich smiled and chuckled as he returned to his spot at the head of the table. The king stared intently for several seconds at the symbol embedded in the tabletop, and for a moment, everyone thought they could relax.

Suddenly, Aldrich threw his chair to the side and quickly drew his sword. His eyes turned white, and the air intensified around the blade, "I am the future of Kralavia!"

He swung the blade at Rollins in one swift motion, and in that instant, Rollins' body blew apart. Oswald and Haldair were closest and felt the pressure of the impact as the blood and parts flew around the room. Everything was covered.

As Aldrich sheathed the sword, his eyes returned to normal. Oswald looked down at what remained of his comrade. Where did he go wrong? What brought Aldrich to this place? The boy that he had helped raise and teach was now a monster. In that instant, more thoughts flew through Oswald's head—he could hardly believe what had just happened. Then, he remembered what Thomas had said, that he overheard Aldrich and Ulrich plotting something. That, along with the suspicious residue within Ivan's cup combined with the most recent shocking event, forced Oswald to question if he should do something.

Ulrich, however, crossed his arms and had a look of total satisfaction on his face. His plan had worked better than he initially thought. Aldrich would do all the work, but Ulrich would reap the reward.

Aldrich grabbed a rag from his pocket and wiped his face, "There are only two ways this meeting ends. You accept what I have proposed and walk out those doors with your lives." He paused as he stepped over to General Rollins' remains, picked up his head from the blood-soaked hair, and held it up for all to see. "Or, you deny me, and you will share the same fate as our departed General Rollins," he tossed the head on the table. "But do not think of me as ignorant or weak as you thought. I know what I'm doing…" He drew the Golden Sword once more as he walked back to the head of the table. The unstained golden hue cast brilliantly off the lavianite within the room.

Aldrich looked at the sword briefly before turning his attention back to the council, "…And I have the power to do it."

Merrek wiped the blood from his face and stared at Aldrich with the same shock and anger everyone else had at what had just happened. Never before has anyone openly murdered anyone in the manner Aldrich just did. The baron directed his gaze at Oswald, I told you so written all over his face. Oswald dropped his head at the truth of the matter before he turned his attention back to the new king.

Aldrich produced a parchment from the desk behind him. "Here are my terms and conditions for us going forward; you don't need to give me an answer today, but I will be expecting one within the week." As the sheet is passed around, Aldrich has the servant at the door start to attend to Rollins' remains. Sadness, silence, and fear filled the room as they all read the details of what the new king desired to instate. Each knew they needed to do something, but each knew that so long as Aldrich held the sword, nothing could be done.

After the final member read the terms and passed the parchment back to Aldrich, Merrek was the first to speak, "The house of Frosbike…" he said as he rose from his seat. Haldair eyes met Merrek's briefly. He could've ordered Merrek to yield, but he restrained himself. Whether by fear of further arguments or excitement for what may happen if Merrek is allowed to pursue this course of action, he couldn't say.

Aldrich looked over as Merrek stood tall, with a commanding posture. But Merrek held no fear over him anymore, "Yes?" he asked.

Merrek gripped the scabbard with his left hand just below the hilt. Ready to draw if needed. "Refuses your terms."

Noise filled the room as the others murmured to themselves. Disbelief and horror filled those in attendance. Oswald subtly tried to urge Merrek to withdraw and keep quiet.

Aldrich and Merrek never broke eye contact as chaos ensued around the room. "Does it?" he asked.

"Yes," Merrek replied firmly, cutting the king off.

Aldrich held his hands in silence before continuing, "I suppose I should have expected this from you. So, Merrek, what do you propose as an alternative?"

Merrek unsheathed his sword.

Aldrich smiled, "You truly are a naive fellow."

"Your father's shiny toy doesn't frighten me, Aldrich. You're still just a child."

Aldrich clenched his jaw, swung the Golden Sword in front of him, and slammed down on the table they sat at, instantly shattering it. Everyone jumped back and covered their faces as the table splintered and broke apart.

Merrek didn't move as the shards flew past him, "Spoiled child," he muttered.

Aldrich boiled as he marched toward Merrek in confused anger; *why is he not afraid of me?* He swung his sword at the baron's face but stopped short. Merrek didn't flinch. Aldrich held the blade for several seconds. He didn't want to kill Merrek like this; he needed him to be humiliated. Merrek casually raised his falcon blade and gently connected it with Aldrich's, pushing it away.

"Why don't we settle this outside, king?" Merrek asked smugly, "You up for a rematch?"

Aldrich laughed, "You would fight me again?" he gestured to the sword he held. "Even now?"

Merrek stepped forward, "Always."

Chapter 43
Rematch

Stalbak Castle Courtyard, Althalos

The gathering crowd was much smaller than the last time they faced off. But Aldrich didn't mind. The important people were there to see it, and that's all that mattered to him. He gazed around the area to see who all had come to witness. Within the courtyard was the castle staff, word had spread quickly after Aldrich made his challenge known. On the balcony, Laura stood next to Wully, Oswald, and Haldair. Around them were the others from the meeting.

The sun was setting. The gentle rays glistened off the upper portion of the castle. In the distance to the east, the tops of Purple Mountains could still be seen reflecting the sun's light. The new king looked around. Only one day prior, this place had been filled with mournful conversations as the nation and parts of the world came to grieve Ivan. Today, they would mourn again as Aldrich would finally show them his mettle and rid himself of a lifelong annoyance.

Merrek stepped up to the same spot he had before and glanced over Aldrich's shoulder at the balcony behind him. Laura dropped her head; she could hardly stand to watch this again. Haldair gave an approving yet cautionary look before Merrek glanced to his right at the setting sun.

"Take a good look," Aldrich scoffed as he dropped his outer cloak. "It'll be the last time to see it."

Merrek smiled and removed his cloak, "So sure, are you?"

Aldrich drew his sword. Immediately his eyes whitened, and the golden glow radiated off the blade. He could feel the power building within. The air grew dense around the pair until, suddenly, it receded. Aldrich's eyes returned to normal, and the sword's glow dimmed to a faint shimmer. Fear crept into Aldrich as he realized that what control he thought he had over the weapon quickly proved him wrong. He shifted to his ready stance to make it seem like the shift in the weapon wasn't intentional.

Merrek paid little mind to what Aldrich or sword was doing. He drew his blade, stabbed it into the ground before him, and knelt before it. The falcon hilt still had some shine in the dimming light of the evening. He grabbed a handful of the soft earth and stone on the edge of the walkway where he stood and rubbed it in his hands. "So, Aldrich," he said, standing up and taking his sword. "What exactly is your angle in all of this? Where is all of this going?"

"Talk and fight, Merrek," Aldrich sneered. "I've got a schedule to keep here, and you're merely delaying me."

Merrek shrugged, and Aldrich lunged forward. As the swords clash, the onlookers express a series of mixed emotions. Ulrich observed the fight from the ground level beneath the balcony with confidence in his king. He knew what he would lose should Aldrich lose, but his fears were behind him after seeing what he could do with the sword.

As the others on the balcony observed the fight, King Leoxtra pointed out that Merrek's sword hadn't shattered when coming into proximity with the Golden Sword as others had done, "It appears Aldrich is playing with his food."

"Then he's a fool," Vetrina said. "He should know Merrek is more skilled. The longer this duel continues, the more chances Merrek has to devise a solution."

"Merrek made his bed," Haldair cut in. "Whether he wins or loses, he must lie in it." Oswald glanced at Haldair, who never took his eyes off the fighting below. He knew Haldair had to hold himself firm, but those words felt hollow inside.

Aldrich pressed his attack against Merrek. He noticed that either Merrek was easing into it, or Aldrich had improved. Perhaps he wouldn't need the power of the sword after all.

"So, you want to know where this is all going?" He asked as the two connected. "I was certain that I was quite transparent about it earlier."

Merrek pushed him back and reset his stance, "Just what is the end goal, though, Aldrich? Build the army, build an empire, siege other kingdoms, decimate your enemies, but in the end, you will still have nothing."

"I will have everything, Merrek," Aldrich said, gritting his teeth. "And when I'm gone, my children will have everything. I will not see them grow up as I did. I will not raise them with a purpose only to take it away from them when it is time for them to claim it!"

Merrek continued to circle; he needed to keep some distance between himself and the king. He knew that Aldrich had the upper hand with the sword, but if he could find a way into the young man's mind, Merrek hoped that it would bring out a mistake that he could prey upon. He thought about Aldrich's recent statement as he continued to casually stride around, waiting for Aldrich to make his move.

Merrek smiled; he found it.

The baron paused and faced the king directly, "That's a pretty impassioned statement. Am I sensing some lasting resentment toward our dearly departed king?"

Aldrich gritted his teeth, "Ivan was weak; his time on my throne was far from over!" Angered, he slashed the sword against the ground; the sword glowed and opened up the ground without resistance.

With jest, Merrek raised his sword and shook the tip in Aldrich's direction, "Now, now, my child. Didn't like that?" Aldrich yelled and slashed the earth again as he stepped closer. He couldn't get the sword to unleash itself fully but was happy he could demonstrate some power now. He hoped that fear would drive Merrek away and others to respect him. "Tell me," Merrek said, unfazed by the king's antics. "How long did it take you to set up your little display. It looked so sweet, such a heartbreaking and perfect little picture. It's amazing how gullible people can be, don't you think?"

Aldrich realized he may have said too much. If the truth of his father's death got out, Golden Sword or not, he would be in for a turbulent reign. "I'm afraid I don't get your meaning, Merrek."

"Oh, I'm certain I was 'very transparent', Aldrich."

The king hesitated, and Merrek made his move; the two clashed again, but though he pressed every angle, Merrek was slightly surprised that none of his attacks had found its mark. It was evident that the pair were more evenly matched during this encounter.

As the fighting continued, Oswald looked across the crowd below. From what little he could tell, no one had sided with either of the men dueling. This opinion became more evident as the general remembered his feelings and conversations. They don't like their new king, but they dare not—at least for now, speak or side against him. It was getting dark, and the bright colors of the flowers around the edge of the courtyard that further into the garden began to get brighter, softly illuminating the area. Some of the servants had already started to light the torches around the outside of the castle.

Despite the dimming visibility, Oswald could still see Ulrich. The general remained where he stood at the base of the wide stone stairs that wrapped around the part of the courtyard leading to the balcony above. Ulrich's smirk grew with each successful block or clever offensive strike from Aldrich.

Merrek backed off and began pacing back and forth, studying Aldrich up and down. "I understand, Aldrich, more than you know." Aldrich lunged again, but Merrek held his ground. There was no time for flair or fancy tricks this time. He was holding his own, but Merrek had begun to wonder if he would ever find his opening. "I understand being resentful of your kin and what legacy they've left for you to deal with, good or bad, hell just look at my family and see where it's gotten me."

"We are not the same!" Aldrich stepped back to catch his breath. He realized he had been too rash early on and now needed a way to get that same reaction out of Merrek. Then, he had an idea, "I have taken a long look at your family, and it is quite comical."

Merrek remained neutral, "I missed the joke."

"Oh, the joke is coming, Merrek; just be patient. This duel is matched, it seems, your learned skill and my gained power. it can go on forever." He moved and sent a few testing strikes. Merrek easily deflected them while pacing in a circle waiting for the attack. "You may bicker with me about what my end goal is, but I ask you, what is yours? You're not going to kill me here, Baron of Frosbike. And if you do, then there is a lot more shit heading your way, so you tell me, how does this end?"

"Well, at the moment, I've chosen to focus on killing you," Merrek said. "And frankly, whatever happens after that, I haven't put much thought or care into."

Aldrich scoffed, "Well, that means there's some space opened up in your big imaginative brain." He lunged and tested Merrek's blade once more. "So, think about this," the blades locked, and Aldrich stepped in close. "Tonight, after this is over, I'm going to go up to my chamber where I can clean your blood off my clothes and get into my bed where my gorgeous and very, very submissive wife will be waiting for me. Did you know that about her, Merrek? Did you know about the much more wild side of your sister?"

Merrek's eyes widened as he shoved Aldrich back, and while Aldrich attempted to catch himself, the baron was already on him. Blow after blow came in raining hard. Aldrich struggled to keep from tripping over his feet as he was driven back. As the two held fast against the last blow, Merrek grabbed the hilt of the Golden Sword in an effort to rip it from Aldrich's hand. But no sooner had he touched it, when both the fighter's eyes turned white. Power surged through them as the air around the pair began to build until suddenly Aldrich tensed and used the sword's power to blast Merrek back.

Still holding to the strength, the sword gave him, Merrek recovered quickly and charged again. The rage attack continued for several minutes, and the Golden Sword returned to normal again. It took some time, but

Aldrich became more in control as he struck and continued his taunt, "She will bear me a son." Merrek hesitated, and Aldrich's heel found his chest and sent the baron stumbling back.

Merrek quickly regained his composure, "Then I'll kill him too."

"Then she shall bear me another and another," the king teased. "She will give me everything I want, and in return, I will give her everything you never could. Wealth, stability, a home that can be filled with life rather than be gutted for anything of worth."

Merrek charged at Aldrich, unleashing a desperate battle cry. He hit hard, wielding his sword in both hands, and delivered a series of unrelented and devastating strikes against his opponent. Aldrich smiled; his counter plan was working. He summoned more power from his weapon, giving him strength and speed to match Merrek's ferocity. "Yes, yes! That's it, come on, Merrek!"

The excitement in Aldrich at the prospect of victory was very short-lived. Despite the added power from his sword, Aldrich realized that Merrek had been holding back. So instead of a rage-drunk opponent that swung aimlessly, he was met with a war-hardened fighter who no longer thought but reacted.

Merrek began to gain the upper hand, swinging and striking without thought or care. Each move from Aldrich was deflected and countered. Finally, Merrek's fury found its mark as his blade connected with the king's hand. "Come on, Aldrich! Is that all you've got?"

"Ah!" Aldrich cried out as he dropped the sword. The cut was deep, and Aldrich ducked away in pain, but Merrek wasn't finished. A firm fist connected with the king's jaw and sent him crumpling to the ground. The time is now; he must use the sword. He would not face such humiliation a second time. He had the power; he was king.

Merrek stepped up and raised his sword above his head. Aldrich quickly grabbed the sword with his uninjured hand and held it out to block Merrek's blow. His eyes became white, and the sword glowed brightly. Before Merrek's blade made contact, Aldrich let out a wild yell. In an instant, Merrek's sword shattered, and the concussion sent him sprawling back.

Aldrich's eyes returned to normal as he found himself struggling to stand. Merrek lay several paces away, also attempting to rise. "Give it up, Merrek!"

The baron ignored him. The pain was incredible, and the blow had shredded the tough leather overlay on his tunic. Once on his knees, Merrek observed his sword—what was left of it. The beautiful falcon hilt was all that remained still firmly held his hand. Nearby he noticed the blade pieces scattered around the smooth stone surface covering most of the courtyard.

He drew a deep breath and gripped his stomach, breathing hurt. But he would not give up yet; he couldn't. It may be difficult to breathe, but he could still manage, so the fight would continue. Merrek glanced up at his family and friends on the balcony and the crowd around him. As he drew up to one knee, he began to chuckle. His life flashed before him. The victories, failures, and everything in-between…comes down to this moment.

"What happened to beating me with your own skill Aldrich?" Merrek's chuckling turned to frustration. "You hide behind a power you're not strong enough to wield!"

Aldrich moved closer. "I am strong enough, and I always was. I just needed to realize it."

Merrek finally stood and held his arms open. "Kill me then…there's nothing you can take from me."

"Oh, you're right, Merrek," Aldrich sneered. "There is nothing I can take from you because you never had anything to begin with. Your life is all you have left." He raised his sword, "You were always meant to lose, to fail, to fall. Every victory, Merrek of Frosbike, it was all leading to your inevitable defeat."

He paused.

Everyone watched eagerly as the veteran fighter stood defenseless and weak, accepting his final defeat. Aldrich held his sword, ready to strike. He wanted to kill Merrek, but, at the same time, he didn't. He could be free of this thorn in his side. But at what cost? Merrek no longer fought back and had no weapon; his death now would be scoffed at by those watching. He clenched his teeth, "Give up, Merrek, concede to me."

Merrek smiled, "That's always been my problem, boy. I never could figure out how to give up. I'm a relentless bastard, that's for sure. You'll have to kill me. You might as well, maybe then you'll finally win at something."

Aldrich began to bring the sword down on his opponent, and Merrek closed his eyes and embraced his coming death. But no sooner had he shut his eyes when a loud crash was heard. Merrek opened his eyes, and instead of Aldrich before him, Haldair stood in his place. Aldrich lay on the ground recovering from the hit to his head.

Haldair placed a hand on Merrek's shoulder, "This is over now."

Aldrich gripped his jaw and scrambled to his feet, "You can't do this! That's treason!"

"And an unfair advantage in a fight is breaking the law of the challenge, Aldrich," Haldair said sternly. "This is over."

"But…" Aldrich stammered. "But you can't strike me and interfere!"

"I just did." Haldair's voice deepened, "This is over, Aldrich!" He then turned his attention to the crowd, "Disperse! I suggest the members of the now disbanded Five Crowns all follow my example and take this time to take their leave from this place."

"I know Vikram," Haldair said. "But there's nothing we can do but

Chapter 44
Regret

The evening was late, but there would be no peaceful nor quiet rest in Althalos tonight. Instead of the usual soft sounds of the night, hoof beats on the hard stone and the bustle of men and wagons filled the city. King Haldair and King Leoxtra ordered their men to return home immediately after the duel in the courtyard. The kings remained at the castle gate with Queen Vetrina, who would return to her home country through Althalos's northern entrance.

"So?" Vetrina asked as she mounted her horse. "Is this the end of our Alliance? What are we to do should the need arise? The Dun-mar are always looking for a fight, and with so much of our continent untraveled, it seems unwise to leave any nation alone. Especially after what we witnessed on the field with Stelmond."

Haldair nodded, "There is a truth in those words."

"The alliance may be officially disbanded," Leoxtra said. "But should aid be required, you need only call."

Vetrina bowed her head, and with a nod to her commander, they rode off.

"Speaking of Stelmond," Leoxtra said as the echo of the horses from Vetrina's group grew silent in the distance. "What are we going to do about the leadership there? Tomwick doesn't have any heirs to take his now vacant throne."

"We could have Clayton and his people oversee the power exchange until a new king can be found to lead Stelmond," Merrek said.

Both kings turned to see the baron leading his horse with one hand clung softly to his torso. His shirt was open, exposing the wrapped bandages covering most of his chest and stomach.

"Not a bad idea, Merrek," Haldair said. "But I doubt that under the current circumstances, Stelmond nor Aldrich will let a baron from Valkos step into that role. Besides, I heard Aldrich is already speaking to Stelmond and will appoint a new king for them himself."

Merrek's grip tightened on the reigns.

Leoxtra huffed, "That boy knows nothing of what it takes to be king! He is foolish and selfish!"

"I know Vikram," Haldair said. "But there's nothing we can do but hope that Athalon may yet control the sword, and the boy comes to his senses."

"Let us pray that happens soon before he turns the sword against us," Merrek said. "I fear what may occur if we deny his demands." He glanced down at his bandaged torso.

"If we unite, we can fight back!" Leoxtra said as he climbed into his carriage.

"Leoxtra, we've all seen what that sword can do," Haldair explained. "Just days ago, we saw Ivan take on an army almost single-handedly, not to mention the creatures he fought as well."

"Even united, I wouldn't want to risk the loss of life," Leoxtra conceded. "I know Vetrina will accept his offer and pay him his monthly sum. But I cannot."

Haldair's eyes widened.

"That boy won't get a single shilling from me, Ventril."

Haldair took a long breath, "The choice is yours to make, Leoxtra; just be cautious, my friend." The two kings grabbed the others forearm, and Leoxtra climbed into his carriage. As the door was shut, Haldair stepped up to the window, "What of Carnheller?"

Leoxtra leaned closer, "It is as we already agreed. My fleet will pound Carnheller until King Valtor finally bids me an audience to answer for the death and destruction of my lands."

Haldair nodded, "I will funnel some resources to you for this excursion," he paused and glanced over his shoulder. Merrek was talking to the carriage driver of Haldair's carriage some distance away. He turned to Leoxtra, "There is more at work than we know, and I think whatever pressure is behind Carnheller will reveal what we need."

Leoxtra nodded, "If this means war, Haldair, just know Vasalia fights for justice and for Kralavia, neither of which reside in Althalos anymore." Before Haldair could respond further, Leoxtra tapped the inside of his carriage, and with a quick crack of the whip, he was off with his small company behind him.

"Shall we then?" Haldair asked as he gestured to his carriage. "Our people have all already left."

"Wully told me to wait here," Merrek answered. "He was going to try to arrange for me to say goodbye to Laura."

Haldair nodded in understanding. He didn't want to be anywhere near Althalos right now, but he knew that Merrek would not see his sister again for some time; the least he could do was suffer a few extra moments now for that.

Thankfully, they wouldn't be waiting long. The sound of horses approaching hit their ears, and Haldair's company perked up as the oncoming party got closer, Haldair could see Aldrich's face a scowl in the torchlight.

Aldrich and his company stopped a few paces from the waiting group. Wully dismounted and began to walk toward Merrek, but Aldrich remained on his horse. "Uncle," he greeted firmly.

Haldair crossed his arms, "Aldrich."

"I'm going to skip the pleasantries and just get down to business since I know you are so eager to leave," Aldrich said. "You and Merrek are hereby banished from Althalos on account of your behavior today. After you leave, you will not be permitted to enter my land under penalty of death unless I call you here myself."

Haldair was unfazed, "I figured that."

While Aldrich was talking, Wully moved close to Merrek, and they walked around Haldair's carriage. Wully grabbed a few bags from the ground and offered to help Merrek by taking them so they could talk.

"This is for you, my friend." Wully produced a small wrapping from his satchel. Merrek carefully opened it. Within were the broken shards of his once beautiful falcon blade and an ingot of pure lavianite. "Here in Althalos, lavianite can be used as both the core metal and to repair the metal; perhaps you can do the same with your sword."

Merrek closed the wrap and stood speechless momentarily as he tried to find words to express his gratitude. But before he could speak, Aldrich's voice called out.

"Wully!"

Wully stepped back into view of the main group. "Yes, milord?"

"Will you be venturing back with your kin?" Aldrich asked.

Wully looked at Haldair and then at Merrek, who gently shook his head and mouthed, *"Protect her."* Wully paused momentarily and remembered the visions that showed him and Laura together.

"My duty is to protect Lady Frosbike," he bowed. "Milord."

Aldrich smiled, "Queen now, Wully. But thank you." He looked at Merrek, hoping to get one more metaphorical dagger in him. Merrek's face was stone; he knew he needed Wully to stay and protect Laura since he could not.

Aldrich looked at Wully and continued, "If you choose to stay, you must swear to me here and relinquish all ties to Valkos and its people."

"Now see here," Haldair interjected. "You're asking the man to give up his birthright and turn his back on who he is, Aldrich. Can he not serve her and remain loyal to both kingdoms?"

"No, Uncle, he cannot. I don't want such ties from my palace to yours."

Wully remembered the visions again—him and Laura together. He knew what he needed to do despite the painful decision. "I will swear, milord."

Aldrich smiled again, thinking he'd won but unaware of Merrek's plan, "Then swear it, here and now." He raised his hand and gestured to those behind him. Ulrich, who was behind Aldrich with the others, now prompted his horse forward to be a witness.

Wully knelt before the mounted king and swore his oath before standing again. Aldrich nodded to Ulrich, who nodded in return. Aldrich drew his sword and held it out, "I name you now Wulfred Siggard, Captain of the palace guard. You shall take Bronwyn's recently vacated position. May he rest in peace."

Wully stood and then bowed, "Thank you, milord. I will do my best to be worthy enough to follow in his footsteps."

"I know you will." Aldrich sheathed his blade, "Now, mount your horse, and I shall meet you at the palace."

Wully bowed his head, turned to Merrek, and mouthed, "I'm sorry," before mounting his horse and riding off with one final salute to King Haldair.

As Wully rode off, Merrek stepped forward to Aldrich. "I wish to say goodbye to my sister."

"I'm sorry, Merrek, she didn't wish to come with me to send you off."

"What?"

"You see, your actions and attitude of late have offended her greatly, and your insolence this morning was the final straw for my poor wife."

"What are you talking about?"

"Check yourself, Merrek!" Aldrich's tone deepened. "You're a failure! I'm surprised she tolerated you this long."

"Sire," Ulrich inquired. "Should we not get going? We have things to attend to before the evening ends; the army must march soon."

Haldair perked up, "What army?"

"None of Valkon's concern, Uncle," Aldrich snapped. Then he turned to Ulrich, "But I think you're right." The king gestured his men, and the group shifted as Aldrich left. "Have a good journey, King of Valkos."

Haldair exhaled heavily before he shrugged and moved his plump figure into the carriage. Any hope he had in his brother's son is now gone.

Merrek carefully climbed onto his horse and looked on, watching Aldrich ride away. "What have we done?" His gaze climbed the smooth sides of the castle until he reached the windows of Laura's room. "What have I done?"

Chapter 45
The King's Command

As the king and Wully reached the castle, Aldrich said, "Go to the library, Gathar will be there, and I already instructed him to show you your new chambers and explain what your duties will be."

Wully bowed and left. He didn't like what he had to do, but he knew in his heart that it was the right decision. As he stepped inside the castle, pieces of his visions flashed in his mind. The future events would yet unfold before him, though why Wully felt the need to observe and partake, he wasn't quite sure. Something deeper was pulling at him, and though he couldn't tell what it was, he could not ignore it either.

"How did you know that he would stay?" Ulrich asked Aldrich as he approached.

Aldrich smiled, "I didn't know for sure," he admitted. "But with the banishment of Merrek, I knew that Wully would feel the need to step up in his absence."

Ulrich grinned and nodded. "The army will be ready to move by morning."

"Whose garrison will be leading the attack?"

"General Cromwell's, milord," Ulrich stated. "I thought he could use the time away for a little while, given his recent attitude toward you."

Aldrich thought on this for a moment, "Has Oswald been informed? I have heard nothing from him."

Ulrich hesitated. He had already gone behind Oswald's back to assemble his men, hoping his assumption would pay off. He needed Oswald away so that he could work with the king and secure himself and his plans for what he hoped Aldrich would follow. "Well, Sire," he said rather shyly. He tried to sound humble and suggestive to persuade Aldrich to agree on his own terms.

"I figured it best if you, as king, were to give your general the command. It would sound better coming from you than me, giving you more experience in exercising your authority."

Aldrich nodded, and the two men began to walk inside, "Ulrich, my friend, I think you may be right. Have Oswald meet me in my study so I can give the order."

Ulrich bowed his head, "Of course, milord." The two walked in silence through the main hall for some time. The general was about to break off and leave the king to continue to his study when he remembered, "There is another thing, milord."

Aldrich paused and turned, "What's that?"

"It's about this Alfred Trench," the general began. "He's been staying here for a while after his village was raided by the people of the Dead Lands. He had requested an audience with you, but I thought it best to have him wait until all the formalities were attended to."

The king looked puzzled, "Who is he?"

"His father served in your father's army years ago; he seems to have a good head on his shoulders. When he heard about the plans to move your army to clear his village, he asked me again today if he could speak with you. I apologize; I had almost forgotten after everything else that happened."

Aldrich nodded, "Of course, have him meet me in my study and then have Oswald meet me after."

"At once, my king."

"I may have an idea for this Alfred Trench, depending on how he is when I speak with him."

"How so?" Ulrich asked before he departed.

"Well, after we purge the territory and Fort Elias, it will require a new governor, will it not?" Ulrich agreed. "I will speak with Trench, and if he seems worthy, he may make a good leader there since he is familiar with the area and the people already; there may be no opposition to the newly appointed governor."

"Well said, milord, well said."

"Have Oswald sent for as well. I wish to give him my new orders," Aldrich turned to leave, "All must follow the plan as it has been, and the world will soon run smoothly."

Ulrich bowed and turned on his heels to execute Aldrich's orders. As the king entered his study, a slight breeze moved the tapestry on the wall in the hall, Aldrich quickly turned, but there was nothing to see. He sat at the desk and began to prepare several forms needed for his generals tomorrow.

Through the study doorway, a pair of purple eyes watched the king closely. He could not see them even if he wanted to. The figure watched as a few servants walked past, never noticing the feminine figure leaning against the tapestry on the wall outside the study. The bright eyes glowed through the hood's darkness as she turned and watched Ulrich walk down the hall. An evil smile grew across her face as she proceeded to follow him.

Meanwhile, Aldrich finished the last decree signing and fixed his seal at the bottom of the page. After folding the documents, he set them on the main table, ready for tomorrow. The fire crackled in the fireplace and startled Aldrich slightly, he turned to look, and after a moment, he noticed the empty mantle where the Golden Sword once sat. The king subconsciously gripped the sword in his belt.

Memories flashed in Aldrich's mind, and he suddenly saw his father standing by the fire, eyes glowing brightly. Aldrich turned and saw himself from that day in the doorway when his sword was shattered. He quickly shut his eyes to block out the painful flashback. A knock at the door promptly brought Aldrich out of his daze, and he blinked quickly to force away the tears.

In the doorway stood Alfred Trench, "Come in," Aldrich said as he cleared his throat. "Mr. Trench, I presume. I've heard much about you and your family."

Alfred bowed slightly, "Good things, I hope, milord."

Aldrich nodded, "I heard your father served well under mine."

"That he did, Sire; he died for king and country, as I am willing to do."

Aldrich smiled at this; his plan might be easier than he thought. "So, why did you want to speak with me, Alfred Trench?"

Alfred stiffened, "As you know, lord, my village was attacked, my people hacked and slain in the homes they built, my family was killed except for my brother…who died here not long after I arrived. I heard you were planning to launch an attack on the people that raided the land where my village is from. I served as the town guard in Greebold's Trench and had fighting experience. I wish to join the army, moving to purge our land of them. I know vengeance is seldom the answer, and I know what was done cannot be undone, but I do believe that justice is required and that I can help. I wish to avenge my family, my lord."

Aldrich sat silently momentarily, thinking about what he had just said. He didn't want to seem too eager to gain this man's ability and willingness to serve. "Do you know who currently sits on the governor's seat in Fort Elias?"

"Serrek, of the Dead Lands, Sire."

"Correct," the king confirmed. "Now, if Serrek is to be removed from that position, which he is, I have been considering a replacement for that very seat. Someone I can trust and have my best intentions at heart, someone willing to die for king and country." Alfred said nothing but continued to listen. "I will allow you to go with my army, but I'll also offer you more than that if you'd be inclined to take it."

A smile crept across Alfred's face, "I will, my lord. What do you need me to do?"

"That's just what I wanted to hear, Mr. Trench," Aldrich said. "I will have you lead the attacking army alongside Oswald Cromwell, my best-attacking general. If the attack goes well and you and Oswald can overtake the area and purge it of them, I will appoint you Governor of Fort Elias and its territory."

Alfred looked stunned, his mouth half open for a moment before his smile grew more prominent, and a soft chuckle emerged. "Sire, I…"

Aldrich held up his hand to silence him, "Excuse me? What's funny?"

"Not you, lord, I assure you," Alfred apologized. "It's just that I know Oswald. He grew up in the same village as me; we were childhood friends…for a time. Oswald was closer to Thomas as a young boy, but Douglas and I never felt excluded when we played together."

Aldrich internalized this information quickly. He really didn't have any knowledge of what Oswald did before the army because Oswald was never one to talk about his past much at all. He was aware that Oswald had come from that region of the country but nothing beyond that. "Then, this military venture will start with a reunion of old friends. Oswald will be here shortly to go over this plan with us," he finally said. "Mr. Trench, do you accept my offer?"

"Yes, of course, milord," Alfred bowed his head. "For king and country."

"Good man." The two got further acquainted, and Aldrich shared his plans for Greebold's Trench when another knock came from the doorway. "Ah, here is your friend now," Aldrich said. "Come in, general."

Alfred stepped aside as General Oswald Cromwell stepped in and greeted the king. "You sent for me?"

"Yes, Oswald. I need you to prepare to move out."

Oswald's face went white. "Why? Is something wrong?"

Aldrich grabbed the document he had signed and sealed earlier and handed them to the general, "Yes, Oswald. The people of the Dead Lands are inhabiting our land after mercilessly killing our people. We need to eradicate them and repopulate that area with Althalothians."

"What?" Oswald exclaimed. "I understand what happened, but Aldrich, what about the deal made with them? They answer to you as king!"

"A deal that was made by a king that is dead!" Aldrich snapped. "It holds no weight over my shoulders, and if I were in my father's shoes at that time, the deal never would have been made in the first place!"

Oswald cooled off before responding; he knew he would get nowhere in a shouting match with a king. Not to mention a king that blew up another for simply talking out of turn. "With all due respect, you're going to begin your rule by undoing what your father put in place in the name of peace?"

"My father only wanted peace because he doubted my strength as a ruler; my father was a weak man who couldn't even stand up straight after wielding my weapon!"

Oswald stood silent, shocked at what the young king had just said. After a brief moment, the silence was broken by another voice. "Oswald?" Alfred asked.

Oswald turned to finally address the other man in the room. He raised an eyebrow, "I don't believe we've met."

Alfred stepped forward, "We have, Oswald, back in Greebold's Trench."

"I don't follow."

"It's Alfred, Oswald. We grew up together as friends all those years ago."

It took only a moment for Oswald's tone and complexion to lighten from his dark expression from his conversation with Aldrich. The confusion turned to joy as he approached Alfred, and the two grasped each other's forearms. The general patted him on the shoulder, "It's been so long, my friend. Alfred Trench, right? That's indeed a name I have not heard in a long time."

Alfred smiled back, "And look at you, went and made yourself a general with a fierce reputation, I hear."

Oswald laughed, "Stories and songs always tend to make the heroics out to be much more than they are."

"How is Thomas? Is he still with you?"

"Oh yes," Oswald chuckled. "He hasn't left my side since before I can remember," Oswald recalled Thomas' rapidly declining mental state and other circumstances. But he kept silent on that part. Best to let Thomas speak for himself when he can. "Thomas is doing fine, just fine. And what about Douglas?"

The room's tone changed fast at the mention of Alfred's brother. Alfred looked down at his feet and then back up, his eyes moist with tears, but he fought them back as soon as they came. "He uh…he…" He stammered. "That's why I'm here, Oswald. Douglas was killed."

"What?" Oswald could barely believe it. "How?"

"He was wounded badly in the raid on our village and died of those wounds here shortly after."

"I'm sorry, Alfred, I didn't know."

Alfred nodded, "It's okay, Oswald."

Aldrich cleared his throat, "I hate to break it up, gentlemen, but we have things to do. The army has to move at first light to make it there by nightfall, so make a surprise attack. Oswald, you and Mr. Trench will lead your garrison and make the attack under the cover of darkness. No one lives; man, woman, or child. They all need to die."

Oswald dropped his jaw, "But…"

"No buts! No excuses!" Aldrich said. "This will be done, and my orders will be carried out. Are we clear?"

After a moment, Oswald realized he couldn't fight it, and the general and Alfred did a half-bow in acknowledgment.

Aldrich smiled, "Good, now leave me. The army is ready and waiting for you to ride out. Get with them, and I expect you to leave at daybreak."

Oswald said nothing but turned and left the room. Alfred stopped before following, "Yes, milord."

Once the two men were in the hallway and the door was shut, Oswald moved quickly down the corridor; Alfred struggled to keep up. "What's wrong, Oswald? This needs to be done."

"You don't know the half of it, Alfred, so don't try." Oswald was in no mood to reconsider his thoughts. It had been a happy reunion for him to see Alfred again, but the idea of trying to convince him that Aldrich's plan shouldn't be done was too much at the moment.

"They raided our village!" Alfred pleaded; he wanted Oswald to understand and struggled to know why he didn't. "They killed our people!"

Oswald stopped suddenly and turned around. "They attacked because it was that or die! They had no other choice! Ivan understood this, and he gave them a chance to make it right and start a better life, and they willingly took it! They aren't bad people…" he calmed himself. "They were just broken people."

Plans started to form in his mind as Oswald continued down the corridor. Alfred followed in silence. He would need to talk to Thomas first, but Oswald had already begun to make up his mind. *I can't do this,* Oswald thought to himself; *I need to leave.*

Chapter 46
The Choices We Make

Stalbak Castle, Althalos

The sun had barely broken the horizon when General Cromwell made his way to the castle gates. Thomas was waiting for him, seated on his horse. The captain noticed the solemn expression that Oswald carried. "I take it you didn't know about it either?" Thomas asked as the general approached.

"What gave it away?"

Thomas shrugged as he handed his friend the reigns to his horse, "Just a hunch."

Oswald mounted his steed, "We should probably make sure that our men are getting ready." He looked at the rising sun, "We need to be on the move if we are to be there by sundown."

Thomas looked puzzled, "The men are already assembled."

"Are they?"

"Yes," Thomas answered. "The 2nd Battalion is outside in the city's staging area by the eastern gate."

Now Oswald was puzzled, "I only just received the order late last night. Who assembled our men without telling us?"

"I did!"

Oswald and Thomas whirled around at the source of the voice. Oswald already knew it, the voice he had grown to hate over the years, "Ulrich."

"I was instructed by King Aldrich to assemble your attacking force yesterday," Ulrich said. "Your army is ready and waiting for you outside the city walls."

Oswald moved so fast that neither Ulrich nor Thomas had time to think. He leaped off his horse and, in two strides, reached Ulrich. His fist connected with Ulrich's face hard, knocking him to the ground. The fallen general quickly tried to get up and shrug off the embarrassing fall. But as fast as he stood, he dropped to a knee and clutched his face in pain.

"You can't do that!" Ulrich hissed through his teeth.

Oswald raised his fist again, and Ulrich covered his face in reflex. "I swear to Athalon, Ulrich, if I survive this coming battle, I will kill you, regardless of the consequences." Oswald then turned on his heels and mounted his horse. "You will never change, Ulrich. Forked tongues seldom speak true words." He nodded to Thomas, and the two proceeded out of the keep into the city.

One of the guards near the gate walked over to Ulrich, who was finally standing. "Are you ok, sir?"

"I'm fine," Ulrich muttered.

"That was quite a blow he laid."

Ulrich spat out some blood and wiped his nose, "Yes, if Oswald should return from this, he is to be arrested for treason by order of King Aldrich of Althalos."

"But sir," the guard began. "Even under the circumstances, Cromwell is a general; we can't just arrest him without a king's document…"

"By order of King Aldrich of Althalos!" Ulrich interjected. "Oswald Cromwell is to be arrested for treason upon return to the city! Have I made myself clear yet?"

"Uh…yes, yes, sir." The guard saluted Ulrich and then turned to walk back into the keep.

Ulrich looked at the closed gate Oswald just left. "You better hope you die with what's left of your honor out there, Oswald."

Frosbike Manor, Valkos

Merrek entered his hometown to cheers and applause as news of his victory at the Field of Denesious still pressed upon the people's minds. But the weight of the loss within his heart kept him from enjoying the praise. He glanced around at the exterior of his manor; it was his now. Haldair no longer had any hold over the baron. Still, as he entered his home, a silent, cold chill hung in the air. Though none of the people knew it, darkness hung in the air around Frosbike Manor.

Aldrich was now king, and his sister was loyal to him. For a moment, he wished that the king had killed him. If Haldair had not intervened, then Merrek could at least have been spared the pain of the loss. Not only of his duel with Aldrich but of his sister. No doubt Aldrich had fed her full of his lies. Whether she genuinely believed them or not, Merrek would never know now. He was banished, and Laura had agreed to it. Still, something in Merrek's heart told him there was more than initially revealed.

He lit a fire in the main hall and sat alone in the dark. Whispers of his failures and his fears moved through his mind. For several hours, Merrek stared at the broken shards of his falcon blade on the table before him. The firelight danced in his eyes—reflecting the same fire that grew in his soul.

Without warning, Merrek gathered up the pieces of his blade and took them to his blacksmith. "Can you repair it?" he asked, dropping the pieces on the craftsman's workbench.

The smith shook his head, "The only way to fix this would be to melt it down entirely and reforge another from the scrap it is." Merrek dropped his head. "I'm sorry, my friend, but metal doesn't snap back together like that."

The baron knew this, of course, but he had hoped there may have been some way to repair the blade without losing the whole sword altogether. The falcon blade was the last thing he had from his parents. Then, he remembered what Wully had told him back in Stalbak before he left. "Hold that thought."

Merrek ran back to the manor and rushed to his things brought in by the coachman. There, where he had hidden them, was a brick of raw lavianite and a small parchment that Wully mentioned would aid whoever was reforging the sword.

Upon his return, he handed the smith these items and asked again if the sword could be reforged. The smith looked questionably at the parchment at first, but a smile grew across his face. "Where did you get this?"

Merrek only smiled in return.

The smith nodded in understanding. "Yes," he said. "With these instructions and this particular metal. I believe we can repair your sword. But…" he cautioned. "It will not be the exact blade you had before."

Merrek raised an eyebrow, "What do you mean?"

The smith laid the parchment on the table and explained. "Lavianite has very unique properties, as you're aware. Able to be molded into the fabric and be flexible, while also be used to reinforce other metals to make them more durable." The baron nodded. "That unique ability will allow me to fix your sword now that I have the means by which the Althalothians do that. In the process of repairing your sword, the lavianite can be liquefied and used to connect the broken shards, but the lines where the pieces meet will be blue. Creating a unique pattern in the blade."

"But will it be as strong as before?"

"Stronger," the smith assured. "This is a metal forging secret that is well guarded in Althalos. Though it may not look it, your sword, with the lavianite within, will be one of the strongest in the kingdoms."

Merrek was pleased by this news, and a plan began to unfold in his mind. As the smith started his work, the baron watched eagerly. Patience would have to be his ally if anything was to succeed. It would take time, but Merrek hoped his plan would work. Only time will tell. Thankfully, time was all Merrek had.

Chapter 47
Calm Before the Storm

The Eastern Fields of Althalos,

His horse's hooves on the soft earth echoed across the open fields. Oswald had been riding ahead of the rest of the army for some time now. He had told the others that he needed to scout ahead and insisted he go alone. In all reality, this was only partially true, as the realization of what was coming weighed heavy on his mind.

The sun was sitting high in the sky now. The men were making good time, and at their current pace, they would be at their planned encampment by nightfall. Tomorrow, a very different sun would rise in the wake of what was going to happen. He knew this wouldn't be a fair fight; the people of the Dead Lands, though victorious in their takeover of Greebold's Trench, would not stand against the army of Althalos.

The general paused and glanced around at the landscape; he remembered several moments of his childhood and the adventures of his time in the army under Ivan—so many memories. The sounds of the men and horses of his military caught his ears; he glanced around one final time. He figured this may be the last time he would get to see his country.

The timing was good, and Oswald's men had reached their camp point as the sun fell below the horizon. As he made his way through the encampment, Oswald noticed Alfred kneeling near a small fire, sharpening his sword. "You should get some sleep, Alfred," Oswald said as he dismounted.

Alfred paid him no mind and continued to work on his blade. Oswald sat beside him and touched his shoulder, "Alfred. Are you ok?"

Alfred stopped and looked up at Oswald; his eyes were moist, "There are a lot of memories here, Oswald." A tear fell down his cheek. "So many good memories that only hurt now."

Oswald drew a silent deep breath. He was never very good at emotional conversations. Despite all the thoughts shared with Thomas and his rantings, Oswald always felt he had little to contribute. He always reserved himself, which made it hard to relate to others. After a moment, he remembered something Ivan had shared with him long ago when he was first promoted to general.

Oswald smiled, "A wise man once told me, oftentimes you'll find that it's the happiest memories that hurt the most, my friend. There is no pain truly as great as the memory of something that once brought you the greatest amount of joy."

Tears began to become steadier in Alfred's eyes. "I should've left with you and Thomas when you left to join the military. I was just too weak back then to do it…" He drew a deep breath to compose himself and resumed the work on his weapon.

"You were never a weak man, Alfred," Oswald said. "You loved your family and home; we never blamed you for that."

Alfred chuckled with annoyance, "Who would've figured that joining the military would have spared the most horrifying sight in my life? I wouldn't have had to watch my family be slaughtered… My mother, children, wife, and brother would never have died in my arms."

With a final stroke of the stone across the blade, Alfred stopped and gazed upward. Oswald followed, and the two sat silently for some time. "My home and my family are all gone, burned to the ground," Alfred finally said. "And I know vengeance isn't a good answer, but as for their murderers." He held up his newly sharpened blade in the firelight. "The dawn will bring forth their reckoning."

A soft sigh came from the general. There wasn't much else to say at this point. Oswald stood and walked toward his horse. "Make sure you get some rest, Alfred," he said as he pulled himself into his saddle. Alfred didn't take his eyes off his work. After a brief pause, Oswald guided his horse around and left.

When he reached his tent, Oswald walked up to the front and pulled the flap back. He needed to leave, and soon. A plan was already forming in his mind. Hopefully, it would work.

Oswald quickly rummaged through his things and packed only what he needed. He needed to move carefully; death would be the only thing waiting for him if he got caught. But then, he knew death would call him even if he stayed. He glanced around the tent as he finished giving it one last look over. His armor was displayed on the armor stand in the corner; his eyes froze as the sight caught their gaze. The light of the candles danced across the crest of Althalos, the intricately woven lavianite, and the blue and white cape.

The general shook off the feelings and thoughts of doubt that suddenly plagued him. He grabbed his sword and turned to leave, only to find, "Thomas…" The captain had a drink in his hand, and he looked concerned. Oswald regained his composure right away and stepped back.

"What're you doing, Oswald?"

The general stared at Thomas briefly before he could put the words together. "I'm leaving Thomas," he finally said. "If I stay, then I'll be forced to do something that…something that I cannot do."

Thomas nodded. His lips scrunched together as his nostrils flared. To push back the tears, Thomas glanced around and blinked several times. He knew this was coming, but it didn't make the hurt any less. "Where will you go?"

"I'll need to leave Althalos. Alnirya isn't far, maybe a two-day ride."

"Then what? You just live out the rest of your life? Alone?"

"I can't stay here, Thomas," Oswald said. "All my life, I have sat back and done what I've been told. I've simply followed in the shadow of fate, thinking it would lead me to a satisfactory place in my life. Quite the opposite. I will do what you got me to do all those years ago, Thomas. I will get up and leave here to find something better."

Thomas sighed and dropped his eyes. He couldn't bear to look his friend in the face right now. "I understand, Oswald. I won't stop you."

"Thomas." Oswald stepped forward and offered his hand. Thomas puzzled, looked at his hand and then back at Oswald. The general smiled, "Come with me."

Thomas could barely contain his excitement. He grabbed his friend's hand and nodded vigorously.

"How does that one song of yours go again?" Oswald said softly. "We know that brothers can't be parted. But if it's our fate this day to die…"

"Just know I'll always walk beside you. Till death, but no goodbye," Thomas finished.

The two men smiled and embraced warmly. Their friendship, they both knew, would always last, despite how different they were as people. They pulled away, and Oswald patted Thomas on the shoulder as he wiped a tear off his cheek. "Let's get out of here, my friend. Grab your things, and I'll meet you by the horses."

Both men exit the tent and go in opposite directions. Oswald made his way back over to where the horses were but took a detour to stop and grab them some food. He tiptoed through the darkness around the pavilion tent to the front of it. A lone guard was standing at the door. Oswald knew he couldn't get anything out of there without this guard noticing.

"You there," Oswald said firmly as he stepped out of the shadows.

The guard became startled, "Who goes there?" Oswald stepped further into view. "General, sir! My apologies. I didn't recognize you in the darkness."

"It's ok; you did nothing wrong."

"What can I do for you, general?"

"I was just coming to let you know I've arranged for someone to take your place on this watch," Oswald explained. "We will be breaking camp in two hours, so I figured you could use a couple of hours of sleep before the battle."

Relief swept over the guard's face. "Oh, thank you, sir. When will they be coming?"

"I'll watch until they show up; they're on their way now. Go on now; get some sleep before we need to move."

"Thank you, sir. You are very kind."

Oswald smiled as the young guard walked down the row of tents and then out of sight. He quickly moved into the tent and made his way to the back where the food was stored and filled a sack before exiting the tent and creeping back into the shadows as he approached the horses.

As he got there, Thomas was already waiting. After helping Oswald secure his things, the two men quietly led their horses to the edge of camp. Oswald looked ahead quickly and noticed the fire that Alfred was sitting by up ahead was put out, and all was dark. *Alfred must have gone to sleep,* he thought. They move past the smoldering coals of the fire. Almost there.

"Oswald?" The voice pierced the silence causing Oswald and Thomas to jump and draw their swords.

The two turn around to face the person who called out to them. "Alfred," the general said.

The young soldier stood casually with his sword still in his hand, "Thomas?"

The men exchanged glances, and neither knew what to say, "Alfred, I know this looks strange," Oswald said as he sheathed his blade.

"What're you two doing?" Alfred asked, ignoring Oswald's statement.

"We're going out," Thomas said quickly. He was desperate for any reasonable explanation to come to him. "…For a walk." Alfred showed little sign of conviction. The captain glanced at Oswald. Oswald knew that he was passing the responsibility to him just by his look.

"Really?" Alfred asked. "What are the horses for?"

Thomas took a quick swig from his flask and responded with the first thing his alcoholic brain could think of, "We get lonely." Oswald dropped his head. Even in the face of death and trouble, Thomas still held his humor.

Alfred wasn't amused.

"We can't stay here anymore, Alfred," Oswald finally said.

"All these long years you've been gone," Alfred said. "Off fighting the good fight with King Ivan; what's changed, Oswald? What is so different now that you will betray everything you've fought for?"

"I'm betraying it if I stay," Oswald explained. "This isn't the same Althalos anymore, Alfred. At least not the one I knew, not the one I fought so hard to defend. That Althalos is just a ghost now…soon it won't be more than a memory. I'm afraid the heart of what we stood for died with King Ivan. Ivan's reign brought peace and prosperity, not wars without provocation."

Alfred tensed, "What did the reign of King Ivan ever bring me, Oswald? I'm here because he failed to stop an attack by an enemy he chose to seek peace with rather than justice. Aldrich is giving me a chance to claim that justice."

"You can't trust Aldrich," the general pleaded. "I suspect that Ivan is dead because of him, Alfred. And we all saw what happened to General Rollins. He has no feeling of empathy for your plight or anyone else's. He acts in whatever way suits his interests. Right now, it just so happens destroying these people meets his self-interests. Tomorrow wiping out his own people could be what he wants, and unquestioning loyalty is the only way he'll get it."

"You think I'm blind, Oswald?"

"You are if you can't see what we're saying, you're blinded by what has happened," Thomas said. "If a raging Dun-mar would have offered you what Aldrich did, you still would have taken it."

Alfred scoffed, "Thomas, you're so drunk you're probably seeing triple of everything."

Thomas crossed his arms, "At least I'm not blind."

"I am not blind!"

"Shut up!" Oswald interjected. He knew this bickering would go nowhere. "Shut up, both of you!" Alfred and Thomas both brought their gaze to Oswald. He sighed, "I'm not going to force you to believe us, Alfred. You haven't seen everything we have. Just be weary."

Alfred shook his head, "If you feel so strongly about who sits on the throne or what laws they've introduced or actions they've pressed into motion, then do something about it, Oswald. Instead, you're just running; you're just cowards, the both of you."

Thomas could feel his face growing red as he stepped toward the young soldier, "I am *not* a coward!"

"You're every name for a nuisance under the sun, Thomas," Alfred said, holding his ground. "Puffing up your chest and getting in my face doesn't change that; it doesn't change who you are. You're cowards, the same as you were all those years ago. This isn't the first time I've seen you two run."

"In times like this, well, sometimes you have to run," Oswald admitted.

"You always run, though! You have no idea what it was like after you left. Your mother died only a few weeks after you stepped out the door. Did you know that, Oswald? Did you know Douglas and I had to bury her because you weren't there? Too busy chasing after your father, who would never return. Chasing after a long-lost hero that no one has ever heard the name of. Have you found him, by the way?"

Silence.

"You left the village; you left me," Alfred said. "I thought I'd never see my friends again. Here we are reunited; all it took was for me to lose everyone else." He chuckled in frustration, "And now you're leaving again."

"Listen to me, Alfred," said Oswald calmly. "We will see each other again. I know we will. But what is about to happen is something we cannot do, but I understand if it's something you need to do."

"How? Where will I see you?"

The general shrugged, "I don't know, so much has happened in the past few weeks, so much change. I know we will see each other again. I only hope that circumstances are not at the end of a sword…" he paused. "Speaking of which." Oswald undid his belt and handed the sheathed weapon to Alfred. "Take this."

"What?" Alfred asked.

Oswald gestured to Thomas. "Your sword."

"My, what now?"

"Your sword, Thomas."

Thomas gripped his belt tightly. "What about it?"

"Give it to me," Oswald said.

"Why?"

"Alfred will be needing it," he replied.

"Give him yours."

Oswald rolled his eyes, "I just did."

Thomas looked at his sword sheepishly, "Fine." He slowly removed his belt and handed the sheathed blade to Alfred.

Alfred held both swords curiously, "What will I be needing these for?"

"Well, tomorrow, when the fight is said and done, whether Althalos wins or loses, we will be dead. And these are…" he gestured to the weapons, "Your proof of that."

"Then tomorrow will truly be a depressing day," Alfred said. "For it will be long remembered as the day the great General, Oswald Cromwell, was defeated in battle."

Oswald smiled sadly, "I'm just a man, Alfred. People will forget quickly."

"I never will," he replied. Alfred then bowed his head to Oswald and Thomas.

The men bowed their heads in response and turned around to grab their horses and lead them away. They got no further than a few steps before Oswald stopped, returned to Alfred, and embraced him. "You were, and always will be, a dear friend. If you are ever in need and come for me, I will answer, and my door will always be open to you."

Thomas mounted his horse, "Yeah, I'm dying out there tomorrow too, Alfred, don't forget that. Thomas Frendrell. Don't let the people forget it either, Thomas Frendrell, Captain Fendrell… Or General. I once was that too…"

Alfred smiled. "In the end, my friends, all we will be is stories told. And if the story is good enough, it will never truly be forgotten."

Oswald mounted his horse and nodded in reply. Then he turned to Thomas, "Come on, Thomas. We have to hurry."

"Wait!" Alfred's face lit up. "You'll be needing these, though." He dashed to a weapon rack nearby and carefully set the swords he had been carrying on the ground. Then grabbing two generic blades, he returned to the waiting pair, "They aren't as nice as yours, but I'm sure the two of you can make do. I wouldn't want my friends to be alone and unarmed."

Oswald smiled as he accepted the sword, "Thank you."

Thomas grabbed the other one, saluted Alfred, and led his horse away to join Oswald, who was already walking away from the camp.

Alfred was left alone. He retrieved the swords they had given him and stared at the hilts in the dark. Their names and titles were engraved on the base of the blade, as was the custom for their positions of authority. "Farewell, my friends," he muttered. "Althalos will feel the loss of your absence. And it may need you once again."

Chapter 48
Last Chance

The air was crisp as they rode, harder and harder. They were desperate to clear the area before dawn came—before death came. The two traveled through the fields and farms that surrounded the small village before Oswald brought his horse to a halt atop a miniature mound that overlooked the area.

"Why are we stopping?" Thomas asked. "We should put more distance between us and them as soon as possible."

Oswald nodded, "Indeed. But there is something I have to do before we leave." He gave Thomas a sincere look. "And then something that we both need to do right after."

Before Thomas could retort, Oswald put a heel to his horse and rode on toward the village. Thomas let out a soft sigh and followed suit. The pair rode on until they reached the foothills. There, Thomas saw the lights of Fort Elias in the distance, "Oswald!" he cried out. "We can't go there!"

"We have to, Thomas!" Oswald called back without stopping.

"Why? They'll just kill us!"

"We have to try!" Oswald said as he brought his horse to a stop nearby. He looked up at the dark outline of the fort against the sky, "Ivan would have wanted me to try."

Thomas nodded. As much as he didn't like wasting more time on their only chance of escape, he understood Oswald's need to try. Truthfully, Thomas admired Oswald for that quality. But Thomas would never let him know that.

Each dismounted as they approached the gate and stepped into the light on foot. Oswald banged on the large wooden gate and called out several times. Moments later, more lights appeared across the top of the wall, and a guard leaned over the edge to observe who would come bothering the quiet peace of the countryside this time of night. "State your business!" he called down to the visitors.

"I am General Oswald Cromwell of Althalos, and I am here on behalf of King Ivan Ventril."

"Do you think me a fool, man? King Ivan is dead!"

"That is why I am here," Oswald said. "There is something your lord needs to know about the death of our king."

After a moment of silence from the guards above, the gate opened, allowing Thomas and Oswald to enter. "You'll need to leave your weapons on your horse, gentlemen," another guard said as they stepped through the keep. "Then you may follow me to our lord Serrek."

Oswald and Thomas exchanged a brief glance before handing over their swords and horses to the guards. The guard looked the two men up and down before he gave them an approving grunt and turned around to walk to the keep. They both follow him closely. Oswald looked around and remembered being here as a child, running around without a care. His father would take him and Thomas here and show them the fancy weapons and all the horses. That was the purest form of fun for the young boys at the time.

As they made their way through the courtyard and then up the stairs to the main hall, they could hear loud voices from inside, happy voices. Oswald's stomach turned as he listened; the joy here would make his news all the more difficult to present.

The main doors opened to a room full of people feasting and celebrating in the joyous festivities of songs, drinking, and laughter. Oswald stopped short as he entered as three young kids ran past his feet, nearly tripping him as they chased each other. On the far side of the room, sat a large man in dark armor. His helmet was removed, showing a heavily scarred face. Beside him sat another man, he had worn, weathered features but dressed well. Based on where he was seated, Oswald assumed that might be Serrek. On his right sat an elderly man, with long gray, thinning hair. As the guard approached the trio, Oswald was surprised that was the elderly man that he spoke to and not the week dressed, younger man in the middle.

The frail man eyed the pair suspiciously as the guard talked to him. Thomas shifted uncomfortably, looking for a means to make a quick getaway if needed. All of Oswald's thoughts told him to run, and though he considered it, he couldn't turn from them.

The frail man got up and followed the guard as they returned to the waiting pair. "What?" the man hissed through his teeth. "Is your purpose here?"

"Are you Serrek?" Oswald asked firmly. He wasn't about to let some petty feelings and procedure keep him from giving the warning he had. "My message is for him."

"Serrek is busy. If you can't deal with me," the old man said. "Then you can leave."

Thomas and Oswald exchanged a brief glance before they looked over the guard's shoulder at the others in the room. The old man followed their gaze to the head of the far table where he had just been sitting. "He doesn't look that busy." Oswald remarked. Without warning, Oswald shoved the guard and stepped around the old man.

"Hey!" the old man hissed as he moved to block the general. Oswald rolled his eyes and shoved the man to the floor. The guard quickly collected himself and drew his sword. But Thomas was already there, he grabbed the guard and held his dagger against his neck.

The sudden commotion had drawn the attention of several in the vicinity which spread throughout the room. The man in dark armor stood along with several others ready to fight. The old man spryer than he appeared sprang up at Oswald, eager to even the score.

"Easy Whistler," came a firm voice above the rest. Oswald watched the room following the source of the voice. The well-dressed man from the far table had made his way over in the commotion. "That's no way to treat our guests," he said as he helped the old man up.

Whistler hissed between his teeth and stormed off. "Are you Serrek?" Oswald asked.

The man nodded. Then he addressed Thomas. "If you could be so kind and release him. I don't have very many and we still have duties that need to be completed." Thomas glared at the guard he still had pinned before slowly releasing him. Serrek nodded and the guard sheathed his blade and walked toward the back of the room. "Come with me." Serrek said, as he led them to a door at the back of the main hall.

Most of the crowd had resumed their meals and conversation. However, Thomas noticed the dark-armored man had yet to remove his eyes from the group. Whistler, on the other hand, to shamed to be bothered, kept his eyes on the party and ignored the guests further.

As Serrek led them into the room, the guard stopped them. "Only one may enter with Lord Serrek."

Thomas and Oswald exchanged a brief glance. Without a word, Thomas positioned himself outside the door across from the guard.

Oswald was then led inside. The room was in good condition though it appeared several pieces of furniture and décor had been removed. But that didn't matter to Oswald; he had more pressing matters than the use of the space within the newly reclaimed fort. Toward the back of the study was a young lad. *Curious,* he thought.

The general stopped a few paces before the desk and noticed as Serrek sat next to the boy he wore a large gold medallion. The etching within the necklace bore a sigil he knew well, a stag in the center with a flowered wreath around the outer edge. This symbol had been the crest of the Elias family, the family that had ruled this region under the Ventrils almost since the beginning.

"Do I know you?" Serrek asked bluntly.

Oswald bowed, "I am General Oswald Cromwell of Althalos. I've come here…"

"What business does a general of Althalos have in a small fort like mine?" Serrek snapped. Whatever courteous composure he had earlier, was gone now. Oswald figured that without his audience, Serrek could show his true feelings. For better or worse. "All the necessary agreements have been made, and all the documents have been signed. We have every legal right to be here now, and this fortress is mine."

Oswald swallowed hard. Serrek was right, of course. Ivan had already drawn up the paperwork and sealed the order before coming to Fort Elias to speak to them. Why he thought leading with authority he technically didn't have any more would be a good idea had passed his mind. "Lord Serrek, I agree that you are within the law now, but that is why I am here with the news I bring for you. I will speak plainly so my words are not misinterpreted."

Serrek leaned forward and rested his elbows on the desk, "I'm listening."

"With all due respect to you and your people. You need to take your people and leave right now."

Serrek bolted out of his chair, knocking it over. "Why? What is the meaning of this?"

Oswald's hands came up in defense, "I know, this is sudden, but I assure you…"

"Sudden?" Serrek repeated. He walked around the table and stopped in front of Oswald. "What are you trying to do here, *general?*" he asked mockingly. "As I recall from the documents of King Ivan, you as a general have no authority over me as governor unless you bring a document confirming your orders with the king's personal seal."

"It's not like that, Serrek," Oswald explained. "There is an army coming!"

Serrek's complexion softened briefly before it turned hard again, "Why? What business would they have over here? These lands are now peacefully controlled by the crown of Althalos."

"That isn't stopping the army from marching to your doors, Serrek. I did what I could; my last resort was to warn you and your people. I'm sorry."

"Ivan gave me his word!"

"King Ivan is dead, Serrek." Even as he said it, it was still hard to believe. Ivan was the king, but Oswald, after spending so much time under direct authority to him, felt like Ivan was more than just another figure in his life. Ivan had been a mentor and a friend to Oswald. Titles that were hard to earn in Oswald's experience.

"I know this, Oswald," Serrek said. "But his contracts and his word didn't die with him."

Oswald agreed. "I wish that was the case, but I'm afraid they did, Serrek. His son wears the crown now and has already begun undoing everything Ivan had in place. Allowing you to keep this land under his rule is one of the first things King Aldrich wishes to undo."

Serrek's head dropped as he leaned back against the table. He had no options. Every attempt to cross the Dead Lands failed, and the idea of trying to get another nation like Alnirya or Ornion to take them now would be pointless. They had tried that before, only to be met with hate and war. "So, you would have me run?"

"I don't know what else you could do…"

"But…my people." Serrek's tone had softened, and Oswald knew all too well the weight of the decision before him. "We have nowhere else to go, Oswald. Would you have us go back to the Dead Lands?"

"You have lived there before," Oswald said hesitantly.

"We survived there, Oswald," Serrek said. "We never lived there."

Oswald glanced at the map on the wall, "Can you not settle elsewhere?"

"Where would you have us go?" Serrek asked as he stood and gestured at the map. "Ornion? Taureau? They never wanted us. Or maybe we can cross the Great Mountain Ridge to the north and see what may or may not lie there for us? We are not two vagabonds as you and your friend are. We are a people." He glanced at the doorway, "No one will look twice at us before shutting us out. And I cannot take them all to such treacherous places."

"Lord, your people need time to prepare to leave. The army will be here at dawn. And they have no intention of taking prisoners."

"What were the orders given to the army?"

Oswald sighed again, "Leave no one alive, women and children included." A chill went down his spine. He suddenly remembered the young boy sitting in the corner behind the table as he finished. But he couldn't dwell on such things; he had delivered his message. All he could hope now was that Serrek would understand and do what was best for his people.

"You're right, Oswald," Serrek said with renewed resolve. "My people will need time to prepare." He marched to the door and flung it open before storming out.

"What are you doing?" Oswald called after him.

Serrek ignored him and pushed his way through to the center of the room. "My people! I know this week of celebration has been well-deserved and even more well-earned. But we need to get ready now! King Aldrich has turned his sword against us!"

Shouts of anger echo across the room. Thomas stopped Oswald by the door. "Is this how it was supposed to go?"

Oswald shrugged, "We're about to find out." His words were uncertain. He didn't know Serrek very well, but based on this moment, he felt the man was uncontrollable.

"But now, my friends," Serrek continued. "We have tonight before the army reaches us." Shrieks and more shouting resonated from the crowd, and he raised his hand to silence them. "What say you?" The cry grew louder and more inaudible. Serrek raised his hand again. "Well, here's what I say. I say we kill the bastards! Every single one of them!"

The crowd roared with excitement. Oswald and Thomas could only watch as the fear of the people was masked by their pride. Oswald and Serrek locked eyes for a moment through the crowd. Oswald shook his head, which only hardened Serrek's more.

"We beat them before on their own land! And now we have their weapons, their armor, and their fortress! We can beat them again!" Oswald's heart sank as Serrek finished his speech. The crowd continued to cheer and applaud.

Thomas leaned closer to Oswald, "I'm going to assume this is not how it was supposed to go."

Oswald said nothing. He turned to leave, and Thomas followed. As they stepped outside, though Oswald didn't say it, Thomas could tell he was hurting. The cheers of the crowd still resonated behind them in the main hall. Oswald sighed as he untied his horse.

"Oswald? Are you ok?" Thomas asked.

Oswald shook his head, "Just more death, Thomas. Why can't they see it?"

Thomas grabbed his horse, "They made their choice, Oswald. You can lead a horse to water but can't make them drink it. Their deaths aren't on our hands." The two begin to head toward the main gate. Oswald knew Thomas was right, for seldom though he was.

"Would you like to see me be a coward, Oswald?" Serrek's voice echoed across the courtyard. Oswald turned, walking toward him, Serrek with his people gathering behind him.

"I simply don't wish to see you die," Oswald replied.

"We have never crossed paths before, Oswald. This is far too little interaction for your heart to be broken over my fate."

The general stopped and turned fully to face the people of the Dead Lands and spoke loud enough for all to hear. "If my heart breaks, it does not break for your death, for I don't know you, and you hold no emotional attachment. It breaks for the death of what you and your people stand for. This was supposed to be a new beginning…you…you are all a new beginning. We were supposed to have peace above all else despite any blood, innocent or guilty, you may have shed. Peace. That was what Ivan wanted. And in life or death, I stand with my king's wishes."

Murmurs moved through the gathered audience. Serrek stood as he had, though his expression softened more as Oswald's words sank in. "You are an honorable man, Oswald Cromwell."

"I've always tried to be, but I'm afraid some things in life can…" he paused as the weight of the words pressed in on him. The general turned deserter. Honor will not be how the kings will remember him. "…They can get in the way of that."

Serrek nodded, "They always do."

"I didn't wish to see you have to sacrifice any more than you have already."

"When you awaken every morning in a house that's been caving in for decades when you have to walk three miles for water that's not even clean. But it's all you have when you manage to survive daily as your stomach is eating itself and all your kin drop dead around you from starvation. Then we can talk about what sacrifice truly is," Serrek sighed. "What about you, Oswald? What have you sacrificed? Your men? Or the horses that you ride into battle? But you see, the difference is that you'll always be promised a warm fire and a home, a purpose at the end of the day. I respect you, General; I do. But I can't expect you to understand."

Oswald mounted his horse, "You can live with dignity, Serrek. But no one dies with it. No matter how noble the cause or honorable the death. There is no dignity in death and sacrifice. Only how you live."

"You best run along now, General." Serrek gestured.

"Not general anymore, Serrek. Just Oswald will do fine."

Serrek smiled, "Then we have both been revoked of our titles today, for better or worse."

"For better or worse," Oswald said. After a quick nod, Thomas mounted his horse, and the two shifted to leave. "You won't be seeing us on the battlefield, Serrek. I won't fight against you."

"Good, because I'd hate to have to kill you."

Oswald chuckled as he put a heel to his horse and rode out the front gates of the fort with Thomas on his tail.

Chapter 49
To Fight Another Day

It was after midnight when they arrived at a small field outside the village. "We shouldn't linger long," Thomas suggested. "The sun will rise quickly." Oswald nodded and dismounted. The town had been cleaned and repairs made to the damaged structures, yet the taste of death still hung in the air.

His pace slowed as he looked around. Memories flooded Oswald's mind as the two stepped through the outskirts of the place they had once called home. Oswald led the way through the streets, and more memories flashed in his mind as the reality of what they were about to do set in. He never really cared if he ever came back, but perhaps that was only because, up until now, he could've.

They paused when they reached the village's northern edge, near Bolger's Stead. The large pig farm was a primary source of meat for the village and a place both Oswald and Thomas had worked at while they were young boys. A little further out was another farmhouse. The dark silhouette stood alone on the horizon, and Thomas knew why Oswald needed to be there.

The house was weather-beaten and falling apart in several places. Weeds and tall grass had taken over the fields. Whatever farming this place had done in the past, it was clear that no one had maintained it for years.

As the two approached the house, Oswald noticed a stone protruding from the ground to the side of the house. Thomas followed. He already knew what they would find; it wasn't any surprise to them. Neither man had been back home since they left. They were always too busy. At least, that's what they told themselves. So, when letters came that Oswald's mother had died, neither one responded.

Thomas stood silently while Oswald knelt before the gravestone. "Goodbye, Mother," he said. "I'm sorry I couldn't find Father, even though I know that was more my wish than yours."

The silence for Oswald was broken when Thomas suddenly stirred his horse as he mounted. Oswald stood and followed his gaze. "Oswald! Look!" There to the southwest, past the village and Fort Elias, light on the horizon. Faint sounds of metal and horses began to be carried by the breeze. "We should go."

Oswald faced the grave one final time, "Goodbye." In one swift motion, he climbed up and sent his horse into a hard gallop.

The two men rode hard for some time in silence. Whether Oswald needed to say goodbye to his mother or if it was to his old life, Thomas couldn't tell. Perhaps it was both. Perhaps the goodbye was more of an apology. Though Thomas didn't feel it, he knew that Oswald had. The weight of failure for what Aldrich had become and the tyranny Althalos would now be under.

Once Greebold's Trench and the surrounding area were out of sight, the two slowed. They had a long way to go, and they didn't need to kill their horses. A familiar cork pop reached his ears shortly after, and Oswald realized Thomas had used this opportunity to take a swig of liquor from his flask. "At least some things never change, though change they probably should." He chuckled.

"Why would I change? I'm perfect just the way I am."

Oswald rolled his eyes.

No sooner had Thomas replaced his flask when he began to hum a tune. Oswald smiled but said nothing. He recognized the tune as one often sung in the taverns across Kralavia. The hummed theme grew louder before Thomas broke out in a soft song:

Even if our way is shut,
And the door ahead is barred.
We're the ones to break it down,
We are the Vanguard.

If the battle gets too hard for you
Know you'll never be alone,
I'll hold my ground, and we'll make our stand,
We'll make our strength known.
I know that all of us,
May not win this fight.
So I'll see you all with Athalon,
If we don't make it through the night.

We know that brothers can't be parted,
But if it's our fate this day to die,
Just know I'll walk beside you,
Till death, but no goodbye.

By the end, Oswald had joined in, and the two followed the road ahead. Two men of Althalos, now dead to the world. The morning sun was breaking in the east, to the north before them, the Great Mountain Ridge began to take shape in the distance, giving testament to the grander they held.

Alnirya was no threat to any neighboring country. However, the kingdom was no friend to Althalos and had never been. The chances of the two refugees being spotted or coming home were near the same as Athalon himself returning. Oswald loved his country, but he didn't regret his decision. All his life he had followed orders. All his life he had accepted his charge and the direction of those above him. Perhaps there's more he should've done? Perhaps not. No one saw this coming.

As the duo got further from the familiar landscapes of Althalos, a bittersweet mixture of anticipation and melancholy filled their hearts. Oswald couldn't help but steal one last glance at the rolling hills and trees of the country he knew, fading into a hazy silhouette against the early morning sky. Both knew that this new land could bring them new and promising adventures in a part of the world that neither had been before. Still, a lingering for home would always be with them.

As the two friends disappeared onto the horizon, their steeds trotted toward the unknown. A glimmer of possibility lingered, a silent reminder that the end of one chapter is merely heralded by the beginning of another. And although neither man knew for certain, something deep within them told them that their story with Althalos may yet be far from over.

Epilogue

Heaven's Peak, Northern edge of the Great Ridge Mountains

The walk upward was perilous, to say the least. The mirky forest that wrapped the mountain's base was full of dark and mysterious creatures, most of which were only mentioned in legends. The old man carefully guided himself through the woods to the hidden doorway in the foothills of the great peak. There, he entered the dark and musty tunnel that emerged some distance up the side of the mountain.

The man took a deep breath as he exited the mountain pass onto the edge of the steep slope that would be the second half of his journey. He paused as he gazed over the landscape. From here, one could already see the edge of the nine kingdoms nestled safely within the northern Great Mountain Ridge borders—to which this peak connected. He glanced up at the road he would travel next, he could skip it if he so wished, but it was not in his nature to do so.

The wind blew hard as he climbed, making it more difficult as he fought for a secure footing. The path was treacherous, with no clear step or foothold across the rocky surface of the edge of this mountain; any human would be foolish to attempt it—thankfully, he was no human.

"Denesious," a deep voice greeted him as he made the final step on the summit.

"Obar," Denesious acknowledged. "Still here?" he chuckled. "I know we decided to go into hiding and wait, but this might be excessive."

Obar smiled but remained silently seated cross-legged on a flat and smooth part of the mountain that protruded around the rim. There were nine of these seats in total, one for each of the gods when they would sit in the pleasant company of each other with Athalon. Denesious glanced around at the long forgotten and rugged area. "Those days are behind us."

"Yes," Obar agreed. "But we should wait for Athalon to reveal his plan before we get too involved."

Denesious leaned on his staff and chuckled, "I would agree with you, and I did for many years." He stepped closer. "But some others have deemed it right to get involved, and so in response, we must also."

Obar stood and walked to the southern edge that overlooked the nine kingdoms. "I am aware," he said, stroking his long dark beard. Denesious stepped up. He and Obar were similar in height, though Obar looked taller because of his girth.

"Then you know why we must do more."

Obar shook his head, "Dolos can only go so far," he paused as he looked up, "Athalon will only allow so much."

Denesious scoffed, "We don't know what Athalon will do, but nor can we wait to see." He pulled Obar close, "There is something more going on than just the petty jealousy of our brother."

Obar raised his brows, "What do you know?"

Denesious shook his head, "Nothing definitive, only visions. Visions that I have passed to whom they belong. But in truth, they revealed nothing that we aren't already aware of…" his voice trailed off as he stepped back to think.

"Well?" Obar asked impatiently as he stepped closer to Denesious, "What do you plan to do?"

Denesious turned and looked to the north, "Our world, though focused on the nine kingdoms of ours, is so much bigger than the humans realize. And there are secrets here that are as old as we are." He looked at Obar, "Kralavia will not give in to Dolos' fear tactics for long. Based on the events of the kings and the visions that are to come yet. I think that more of us survived than we originally knew and that together, they seek to use the humans to reveal and kill Athalon."

Denesious knew that Obar would be hesitant to join the fight unless more assurance of victory was guaranteed. It would be a long fight, but the visions of the future would come to pass if he had to personally ensure it. Obar stroked his beard again and looked out in the distance. From this peak, they could all watch the whole continent of Kralavia, observing everything at once.

"I'm inclined to agree with you," he finally conceded. "But what do we do?"

"What indeed?" a sharp feminine voice said behind them.

Denesious was the first to turn and see "Valenear." The goddess smiled coyly and bowed her head slightly. Standing straight, she removed her hood, revealing her face and long black hair. Her skin had a faint hue of purple as it always had, and she wore her usual fitted robe that was split on each side the length of her legs, revealing the daggers strapped to each thigh.

"I thought I saw your secretive handiwork. King Ordain would not have marched into Valkos without some suggestive help." Valenear's smile remained as she walked toward them, with each step she almost glided across the ground. "And I give you credit for your use of General

Ulrich," he continued. "But why not just whisper to Aldrich directly? Why go through another?"

Valenear chuckled, "Now, brother, where's the fun in that?"

"You won't win," Denesious replied. "No matter what plan Dolos has made."

"And what of my plan?" a hollow voice echoed across the summit.

Denesious and Obar turned to see Dolos' dark, overshadowing figure on the edge of the mountain peak. His body was clad in black armor with a tattered, dark cloak. Obar stood defensively, "What do you want here?"

"What do I want?" Dolos repeated. "I want the same as you. You come here, to the place where Athalon first touched the ground. You come here to see if he still will?"

"Do not pretend to seek Athalon out of some pitiful state," Denesious snapped. "Always in the shadows. You think you can manipulate them from afar or that your armor will protect you."

"Hiding?" Dolos exclaimed. He raised his hand, and his large Guan Dao blade appeared in his grasp. "You're one to talk! Old man!" In a flash, Obar had his battle-ax ready, Denesious tensed, and the massive blade came crashing down on him.

A wave of pressure exploded as Denesious blocked Dolos' attack with his staff. Despite the gridlock of force, Dolos pressed harder. Denesious held firm, but his appearance began to change as he did. His long beard vanished, and his long white hair turned thick and brown. The youth returned to his face and his clothing the same. Dolos pulled away from him, "Secrets indeed."

Denesious' staff returned to his original form of a spear, and he stabbed it into the ground. "We can fight until we've destroyed the whole world, and we would be fighting still."

Dolos slammed his weapon into the ground, "My plan will unfold whether you like it or not."

"Your puppet has failed."

"That was but one piece of a much larger puzzle," Valenear said as she stepped closer. "But. I think we need to be careful." Dolos expressionless form stood still. "He saw me," she continued. "He spoke through the blade wielder."

Denesious and Obar glanced at each other. Excitement shone in their eyes. How or why Athalon used King Ivan was unknown to them. But if the god felt the need to personally interject at that time must mean something.

Valenear stood next to Dolos, her slim petite figure was small next to the Dolos' broad size. The armor-clad god looked up briefly, "It matters not. King Valtor's army may have failed at Stelbeck Keep," Dolos admitted. "But Stelmond's fall was planned, and our next move is still in play. Carnheller will not go down easily. Leoxtra's a fool if he thinks he will break us."

"What do you have left? Even your control of the weather and trying to intercept their calls for aid around Vasalia and Valkos didn't work." Denesious stated. "Aldrich may be able to be used by you, but he is too weak to sustain Athalon's weapon. Besides, the people will turn on him before long."

Laughter bellowed from Dolos' helmet. The only way to know of any emotion behind the mask. "The would-be king is only but another pawn. I am waiting for someone stronger."

"To what end then?" Obar asked, finally breaking his silence.

"Athalon's, of course," Valenear said.

Denesious cringed, Valenear's words had become poison. She was always the elusive enchantress, but since Athalon left, he watched as she was pulled into Dolos' lies more and more. He should've known that she'd survive the onslaught of the humans' war against them. She was cunning and smart; he'd give her that. But he knew that she would not see the victory she hoped for. "You can't win. But if you insist on starting this fire, it will not only be us, but the world that is turned to ashes."

"What?" Valenear asked playfully. "You think you can stop us? Your overwhelming love of the humans has only made you weak. You saw how they were so quick to betray you. Yet here you stand. Still trying to be the hero, Denesious?"

Denesious said nothing.

Dolos laughed, "Hero? Please..." his tone grew dark. "Some of us were born to be something greater."

"I do not wish to fight you," Denesious sighed. Even if he could it would not do any good. Athalon had grid locked them since the beginning, no god can defeat another. Why in the hands of the human, their own weapons could be used against them—he never knew. And where they go after death? Was something none of them knew. They had always trusted Athalon without question. Still, Denesious couldn't help but feel a tinge of doubt in his mind as the events of the world unfolded.

"Athalon knows what he is doing. But I pity you, Dolos. And you, Valenear. We were made for so much, and you've done nothing but bring dissension and death to both the humans and us."

Dolos' slammed the Guan Dao into the ground again, "Do not pity me, Denesious! I was with you in the light once…but I chose to reject it."

Valenear smiled playfully as she walked to the summit's edge, "Until next time, brothers." Her figure vanished as quickly as she spoke.

Dolos also turned to leave when Denesious called to him, "You may hide your face behind that armored mask now, but we all know what you were."

The armored god walked to the edge before facing the other two, "What you thought you knew, you must forget. This war is not over." He vanished as Valenear had, leaving Denesious and Obar to sit in silence for a moment. Dolos's voice suddenly came across the wind, "This has only been…*The Reckoning*."

END

Prologue
Kralavia Book 2: The Spark of Rebellion

The Third Age—6090 A.C.

For twenty years, Aldrich ruled with an iron fist. Over that time, the jeweled beacon of hope and prosperity Althalos gave the other nations began to fade. The oppression laid on his people, and those of the neighboring countries grew as the king sought to secure his foothold across the continent. At first, many tried to stand against Aldrich and his tightening fist. But any rebellion was instantly crushed, and all resistance removed from thought.

Aldrich sought loyalty above all else and used the fear of his weapon to get it. At Ulrich's suggestion, he appointed Henry Raden as King of Stelmond, and because of the friendship the two shared in their days growing up, Henry pledged his loyalty to Aldrich and Althalos. At first, the people of Stelmond resisted, hoping to keep their freedom and set a king for them from one of their own. But as quickly as the rumor reached Aldrich's ears, he quelled the notion in one swift stroke. Genocide, some called it, but history would record it as something else.

Still eager for answers from Carnheller for the assault on Stelbeck Keep, King Leoxtra launched a campaign against the island nation to get King Valtor to come to terms and talk. However, as much as he pummeled the tiny kingdom, he could never get them to yield.

The nations of Alnirya, Taureau, and Ornion maintained their neutrality as best they could. For several years, Aldrich allowed this, as his focus was securing his stronghold among the others.

Prince Johnathon grew under his father's tutelage, much to his mother's disdain. Laura could only do so much despite her best efforts as Aldrich raised their son. Wully held his charge, and among all the grief and heartache of the following years, he was a steady rock that Laura grew ever more grateful to have at her side. Thankfully, not more than a year after Jonathan was born, Laura had another son, Fredrick. Though Aldrich would be proud of both children, he always favored Jonathon.

Then, when all hope seemed lost, whispers grew of a weakness in the king. Soon, these rumors spread, and more and more began to confirm that the same sickness that took his father might take Aldrich too. Plans were made in the shadows, and hope began to sprout in the darkness.

To show his strength against spreading lies, Aldrich turned his military might against the nations around him. Skirmishes developed as Althalos continued to encroach on the other kingdoms. Not wanting to risk open war with the Golden Sword, the other countries would keep their defense to a minimum. Still, losses were heavy as renegade groups and minor factions terrorized the Althalothian army.

As the years went on, the chaos intensified. The elusive Dun-mar from the Great Mountain Ridge began to attack more openly and with more significant numbers against the people of Taureau and Halika. Vasalia had re-engaged with Carnheller, and Althalos pressed against Ornion and Alnirya. It seemed that nothing would extinguish… The Spark of Rebellion.

Index

A.C.—(After Creation) All time moves linear from the beginning and all records indicate the starting point when Athalon made humanity.

Aetos—Capital city of Ornion.

Athalon—Leader of the gods of old, Male. Commissioned the others to help make Kralavia and he himself started the human race. Large stature with a golden hue to his skin. Long white hair and white eyes as bright as starlight, and golden armor.

Althalos—Central kingdom in Kralavia and erected in homage to the god and creator, Athalon. The original banner under Athalon was a dark background with a golden sword pointed up and a golden crown around the blade. The current banner after King Ivan settled the lands was a blue and white checkered background with a golden crown in the center.

Althinian—The core of a star. Used by Athalon in the creation of the nine weapons that are wielded by the gods in Second Age before the Great War.

Alynia—one of the nine gods of old. Female, athletic stature, with long blonde hair that was often kept in intricate braids. Fitted leather outfit and wielded the bow and arrow weapon made of Althinian.

Alnirya—Northwest kingdom of Kralavia and erected in homage to the god Alynia. The original banner was a dark background with a golden bow and arrow in the center. The current banner is deep red and black checker pattern with a bright red dragon as its emblem.

Animas Ventril—Previous king of Althalos and ended the Great War. Son of King Ventril, and father to Ivan and Haldair.

Arkeanos—Capital city of Vasalia.

Basilisk—a reptile body the size of an average dog, short rear legs and winged arms. A long reptilian tail with the head of a serpent. Cannot fly but can glide short distances.

Broden—One of the nine gods of old. Male. Short and slender, with short black hair, and never wore armor and wielded the bo staff of Althinian.

Carnheller—Eastern Island nation erected in homage to the old god Dolos. The original banner was dark with a golden Guan Dao in the center. The current banner is a red and black checkered pattern with a black scorpion in the center.

Cradinlings—A luminescent flower species that grows wild throughout Kralavia. Comes in several different color patterns and styles. Some plants are long and veined with large leaves, others with large, beautiful flower heads on tall stalks.

Daymar—Capital city of Carnheller.

Denesious—One of the nine old gods. Male. Tall and slender in stature. Long brown hair and bright green eyes. Adorned with a long green cloak and wields the Althinian spear.

Dire Wolves—A large wolf. Overall size comparable to cattle, with the strength of a bear.

Dolos—One of the nine old gods. Male, average stature. Always wearing full black armor, his face is never seen. Wields the Guan Dao weapon of Althinian.

Dragons—Four legged winged beasts the size of a small house. Blows fire in a sticky liquid form that even water can't remove immediately.
Drakes—Small winged lizards about the size of a horse. They have no front legs, but rather arms that are part of the wings. Blows fire or intense heat from its mouth.

Eltalion—Capital city of Halika.

Eric Valtor—King of Carnheller.

First Age—Years 1 A.C. to 3000 A.C. Each Age lasts three thousand years.
Forest Ja-keel—King of Ornion.

The Great War—The sixty-year war near the end of the Second Age. The war was started by King Ventril of Althalos. In Athalon's absence King Ventril used the weapon of the god and raged war against the other gods. Ventril's son Animas, was the one that ended that war, thus bringing in the Third Age.

Gordost—Capital city of Stelmond.

Greebold's Trench—A small village on the western border of Althalos. Childhood home of Oswald Cromwell and Thomas Frendrell.

Haldair Ventril—King of Valkos and younger brother to King Ivan of Althalos.

Halika—Northeast kingdom of Kralavia. Erected in homage to the old god Kilith. Old banner was dark with two short swords with crossed blades. The new banner is green and gray with a brown horse as the center emblem.

Ivan Ventril—King of Althalos. Older brother to King Haldair of Valkos and son to King Animas.

Joshua Lyne—King of Alnirya.

Kilith—One of the nine old gods. Male. Tall and slender in stature, and wears leather fitted armor. Medium length blonde hair, fair skin, and wields the short sword of Althinian.
Lavianite—Precious metal of Althalos. Super strong and versatile. Used in reenforcing weapons and armor of the troops of Althalos and as decorative pieces within the clothing, jewelry, and architecture.

Lexon—Capital city of Taureau.

Renibaun—one of the nine old gods. Male. Short red hair with an average build and sturdy. Adorned with thick plated armor and wields a giant Althinian hammer.

Rolland Gallant—King of Taureau.

Roseust Tree—A large thick tree that has pale red, almost pink-colored leaves. It blooms small bright white flowers twice a year, in the early spring and late fall. While scattered around Kralavia, this tree species favors rocky soil, and densely grows along the mountain regions in Stelmond, and Vasalia.

Obar—One of the nine old gods. A tall but brawny, bearded figure. With short brown hair, and a heavy but flexible armor blend of various materials, wields a two headed battle-ax that is rough and simple in appearance but also made of Althinian.

Ornion—Southernmost kingdom at the mouth of the Great River. The old god Obar called this place home long ago. The sigil before the war was a black and silver pattern. Since the Great War, an eagle was added as the emblem.

Oswald Cromwell—General of the Althalothian army under King Ivan.

Scorpios—A scorpion that is as large as a larger breed of dog. Often found roaming the Dead Lands.

Serrek Logon-son—Leader of the people exiled to the Dead Lands.

Stalbak—Capital city of Althalos.

Stelbeck Keep—The coastal fort of Althalos is near the city of Alkeroth in Vasalia.

Stelmond—Heavily wooded country to the south. Established for the old goddess Valenear. The old banner was a simple black flag with twin daggers that crossed in the center. Since the Great War, their emblem became checkered with purple and black, with the silhouette of a bat, wings spread in the center.

Taureau—Northern kingdom of Kralavia set as homage to the old god Broden. Covering most of the grasslands in the north their sigil did not change from the old days, and still holds the silhouette of a charging bull on simple brown pattern.

Thomas Frendrell—Captain of the Althalothian army under King Ivan.

Terrowin—Capital city of Valkos.

Tomwick Ordain—King of Stelmond.

Unatari—(The Creators) The name of the nine gods as a collective.

Valkos—Central country of Kralavia. Established as a homage to the old god Denesious. The old banner was green and red with a single spear across the center. Since the Great War, the coat of arms has been red and gray with a falcon as the emblem.

Valenear—One of the nine old gods. Female. Slender and fierce. Purple tinted skin, dark hair and a long black fitted robe with slits up each side to reveal her legs to which is strapped her pair of Althinian daggers.

Var—Capital City of Alnirya.
Vasalia—Eastern kingdom covering most of the coastlands of Kralavia. Established for the old god Renibaun. The old banner was a golden lion on a field of green. Since the Great War, the lion was placed on a red and white background with gold trim.

Vetrina Dogas—Queen of Halika.

Vikram Leoxtra—King of Vasalia.